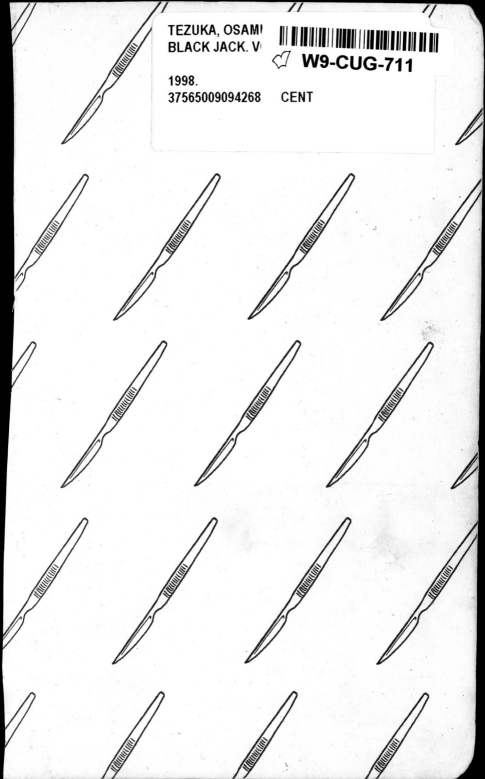

«**Black Jack** is primarily a fun, fast-moving read, but that aspect of it almost conceals the cartoo... explorations of ethical questions. Beneath its surface simplicity lie moral issues that elevate it fro... entertainment to art.»
Comics **Journal**

«In **Black Jack, Osamu Tezuka** has taken the tricky terrain of hospital stories and transferred ... to the comic page. It's a risk few others would take -- sure **ER** works well on television, but in co... Tezuka pulls it off with ease...Chock full of drama and perplexing ethical questions, **Black Jack** ... treat from Japan that's not to be missed.»
Sci-Fi Universe

«Of all his characters, **Black Jack** was perhaps closest to Dr. Tezuka's heart. The «manga god» p... his understanding of the human organism into these tales of a brilliant maverick who lives on th... ting edge in more ways than one.»
Manga Max

«It incorporates comedy, visual gags, pathos, tragedy, and adventure into a single series, but just ... it becomes a complete artistic hodgepodge, it is saved by Tezuka's underlying intellectual curiosit... his relentless pursuit of higher philosophical issues -- in a comic designed for children, he even explores the ethical dilemma of mercy killings.»
Frederick Schodt, manga writer

«Anyone who remembers the delirious pleasures of spending a weekend afternoon with disbelief ... pended by an imaginative and gripping comic-book series, and laments not having experienced ... again in the last, oh, 15 years or so, should seek out at once the **Black Jack** graphic novel.»
San Francisco Bay Guardian

VIZ GRAPHIC NOVEL

BLACK JACK™

VOL. 1

This volume contains the BLACK JACK
installments from MANGA VIZION
Vol. 3. No. 9 through Vol. 4, No. 3 in
their entirety.

STORY AND ART BY
OSAMU TEZUKA

ENGLISH ADAPTATION BY
YUJI ONIKI

Touch-Up Art & Lettering/Mary Kelleher
Cover Design/Hidemi Sahara
Layout & Graphics/Benjamin Wright
Editor/Annette Roman

Senior Editor/Trish Ledoux
Director of Sales & Marketing/Oliver Chin
Managing Editor/Hyoe Narita
Editor-in-Chief/Satoru Fujii
Publisher/Seiji Horibuchi

Published by Viz Communications, Inc.
P.O. Box 77010 • San Francisco, CA 94107

10 9 8 7 6 5 4 3 2
First printing, August 1998
Second Printing, September 1999

Vizit our web sites at www.viz.com, www.pulp-
mag.com, www.animerica-mag.com, and our Internet
magazine at www.j-pop.com!

Get your free Viz Shop-By-Mail catalog!
(800) 394-3042 or fax (415) 546-7086

BLACK JACK GRAPHIC NOVELS
BLACK JACK
TWO-FISTED SURGEON

VIZ GRAPHIC NOVEL

BLACK JACK™

VOL. 1

STORY AND ART BY
OSAMU TEZUKA

CONTENTS

OPERATION ONE

WHERE'S
THE DOCTOR!?

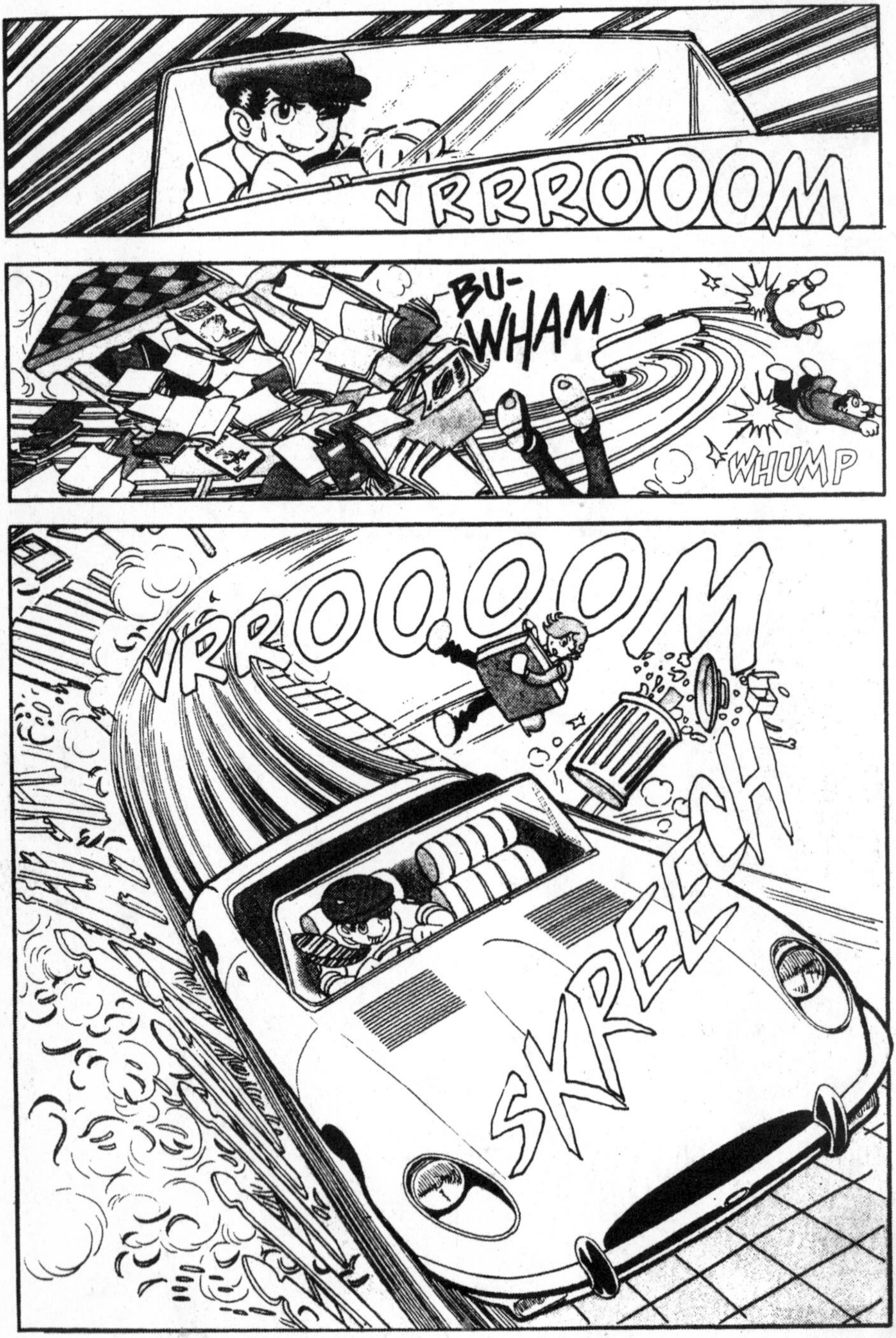
VRRROOOM
BU-WHAM
WHUMP
VRROOOOM
SKREECH

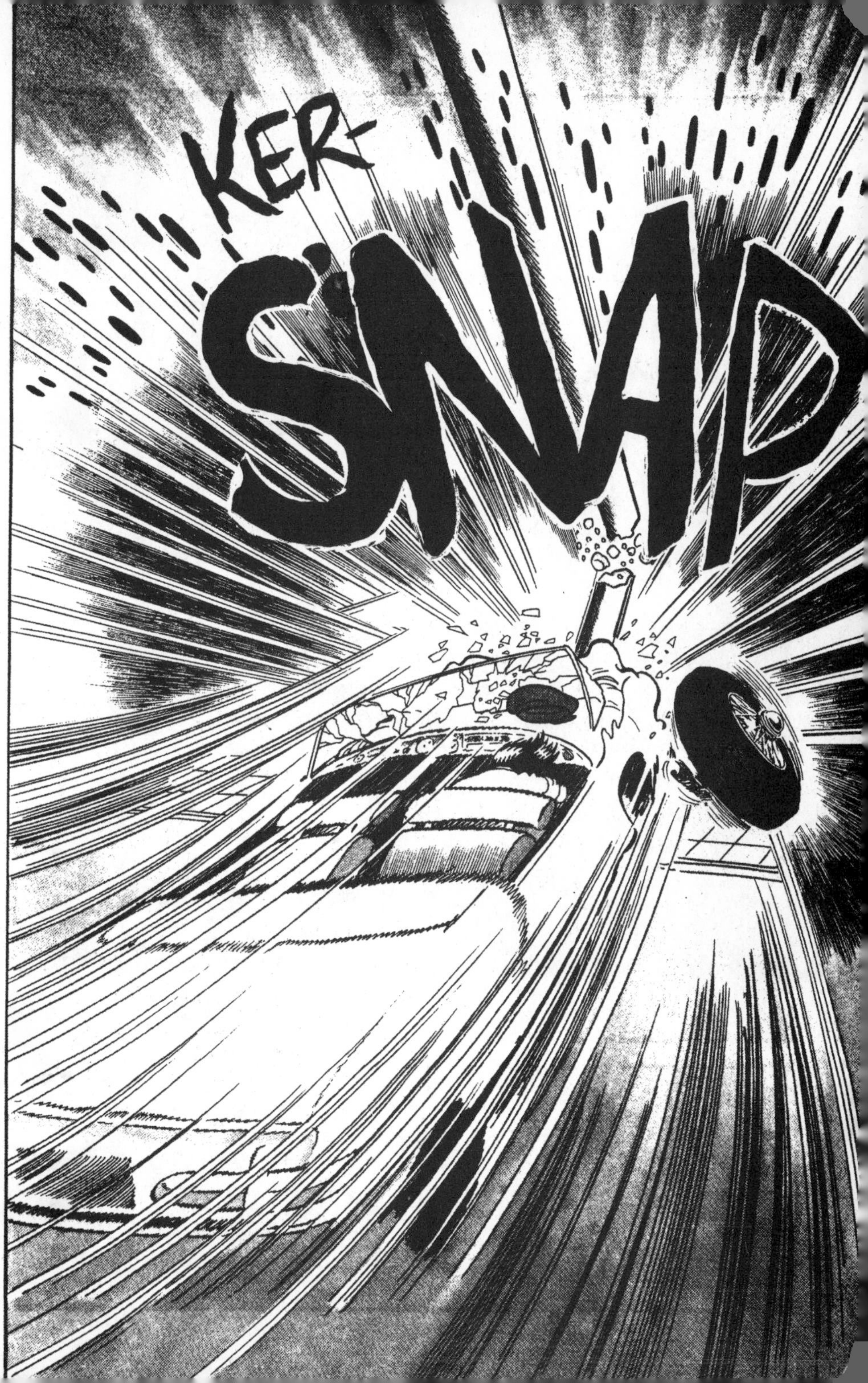
KER-
SNAP

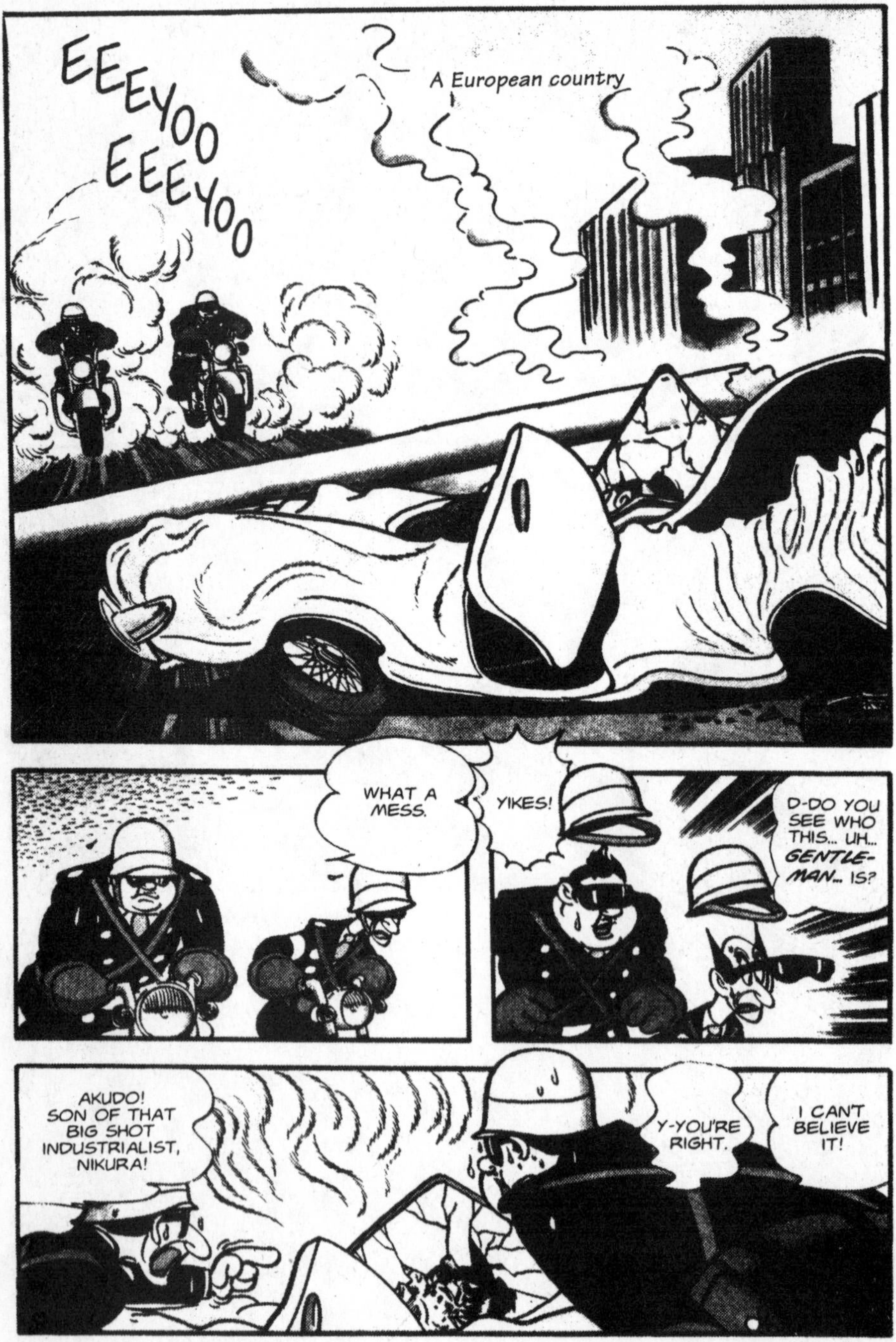
EEEYOO
EEEYOO
A European country
WHAT A MESS.
YIKES!
D-DO YOU SEE WHO THIS... UH... GENTLEMAN... IS?
AKUDO! SON OF THAT BIG SHOT INDUSTRIALIST, NIKURA!
Y-YOU'RE RIGHT.
I CAN'T BELIEVE IT!

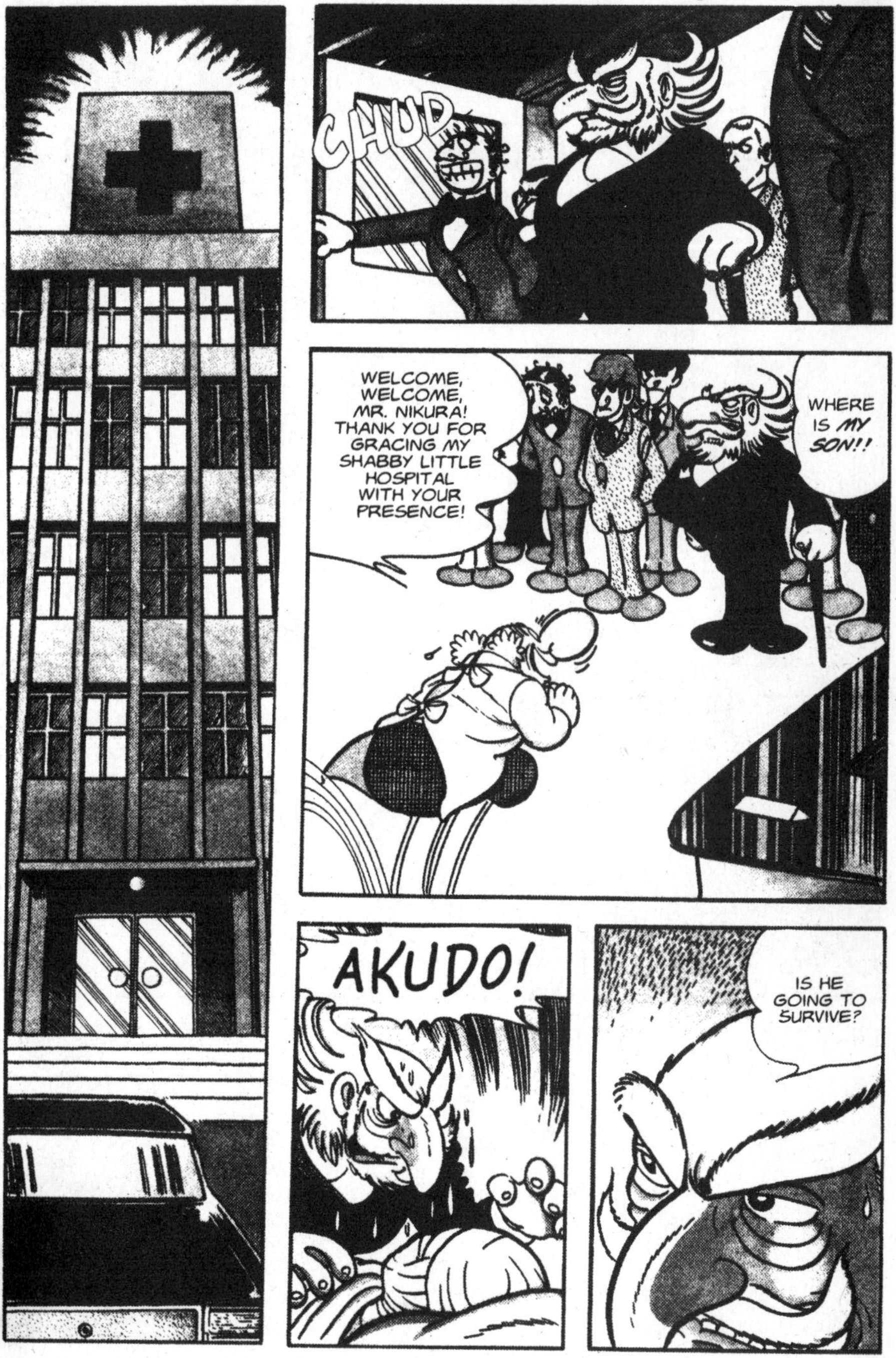
CHUD
WELCOME, WELCOME, MR. NIKURA! THANK YOU FOR GRACING MY SHABBY LITTLE HOSPITAL WITH YOUR PRESENCE!
WHERE IS *MY SON!!*
AKUDO!
IS HE GOING TO SURVIVE?

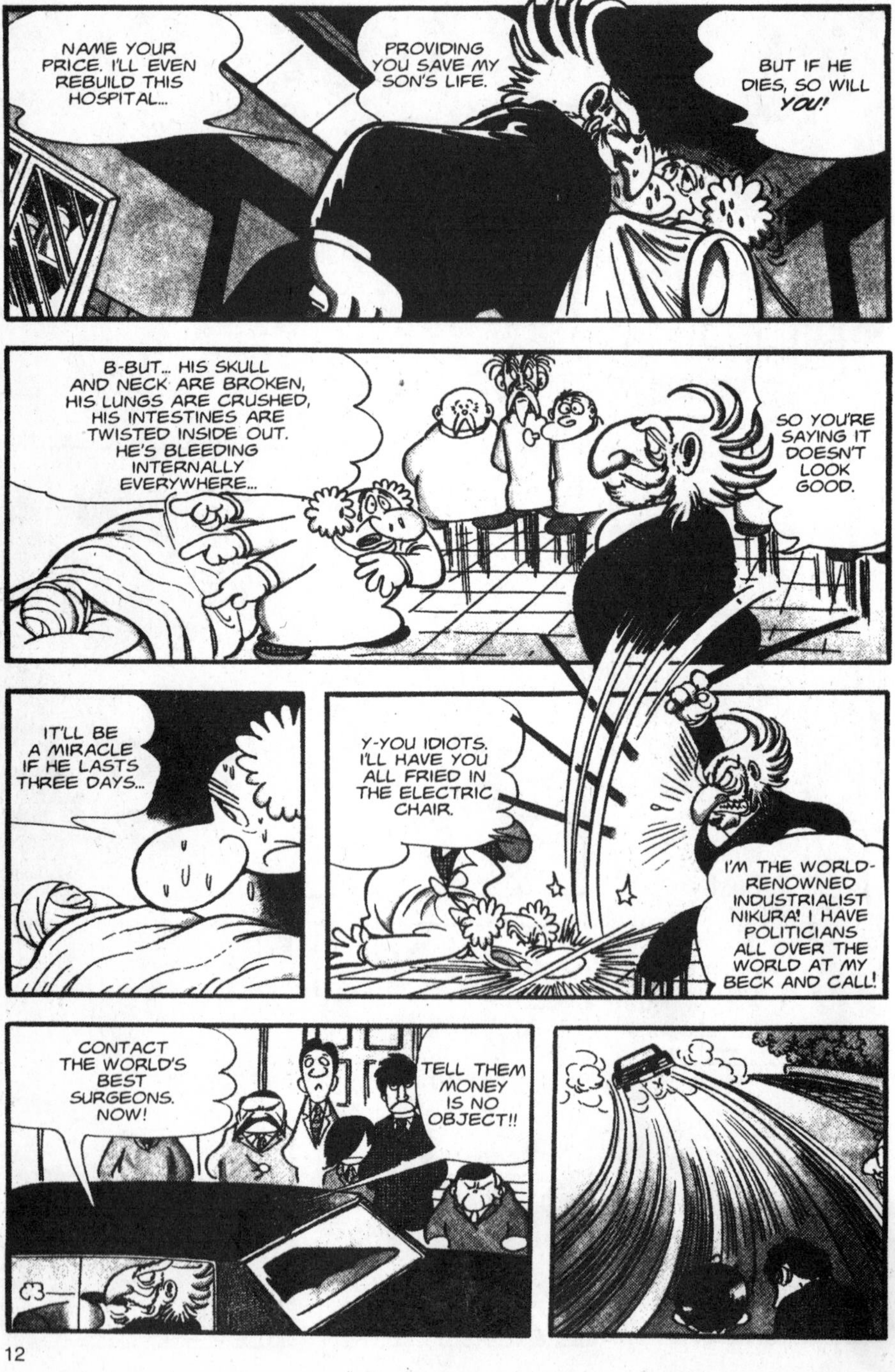
NAME YOUR PRICE. I'LL EVEN REBUILD THIS HOSPITAL...
PROVIDING YOU SAVE MY SON'S LIFE.
BUT IF HE DIES, SO WILL YOU!
B-BUT... HIS SKULL AND NECK ARE BROKEN, HIS LUNGS ARE CRUSHED, HIS INTESTINES ARE TWISTED INSIDE OUT. HE'S BLEEDING INTERNALLY EVERYWHERE...
SO YOU'RE SAYING IT DOESN'T LOOK GOOD.
IT'LL BE A MIRACLE IF HE LASTS THREE DAYS...
Y-YOU IDIOTS. I'LL HAVE YOU ALL FRIED IN THE ELECTRIC CHAIR.
I'M THE WORLD-RENOWNED INDUSTRIALIST NIKURA! I HAVE POLITICIANS ALL OVER THE WORLD AT MY BECK AND CALL!
CONTACT THE WORLD'S BEST SURGEONS. NOW!
TELL THEM MONEY IS NO OBJECT!!

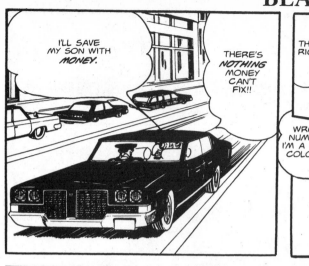

I'LL SAVE MY SON WITH *MONEY.*

THERE'S *NOTHING* MONEY CAN'T FIX!!

THAT'S RIGHT!!

WE NEED THE WORLD'S BEST SURGEON!!

WRONG NUMBER! I'M A GYNE-COLOGIST.

OPERATE ON SOMEONE WHO'S GUARANTEED TO DIE?

I REFUSE !!

HOW ABOUT *10 MILLION* DOLLARS?

WE'VE FOUND SOMEONE WILLING TO OPERATE...

...BUT HE SAYS HE CAN'T GUARANTEE ANYTHING...

THAT WON'T DO!!

CHAIRMAN NIKURA, WE FOUND A SURGEON WHO CAN SAVE YOUR SON.

HE'S JAPANESE. A GENIUS. HE HAS SAVED 300 LIVES SO FAR.

WHAT'S HIS NAME?

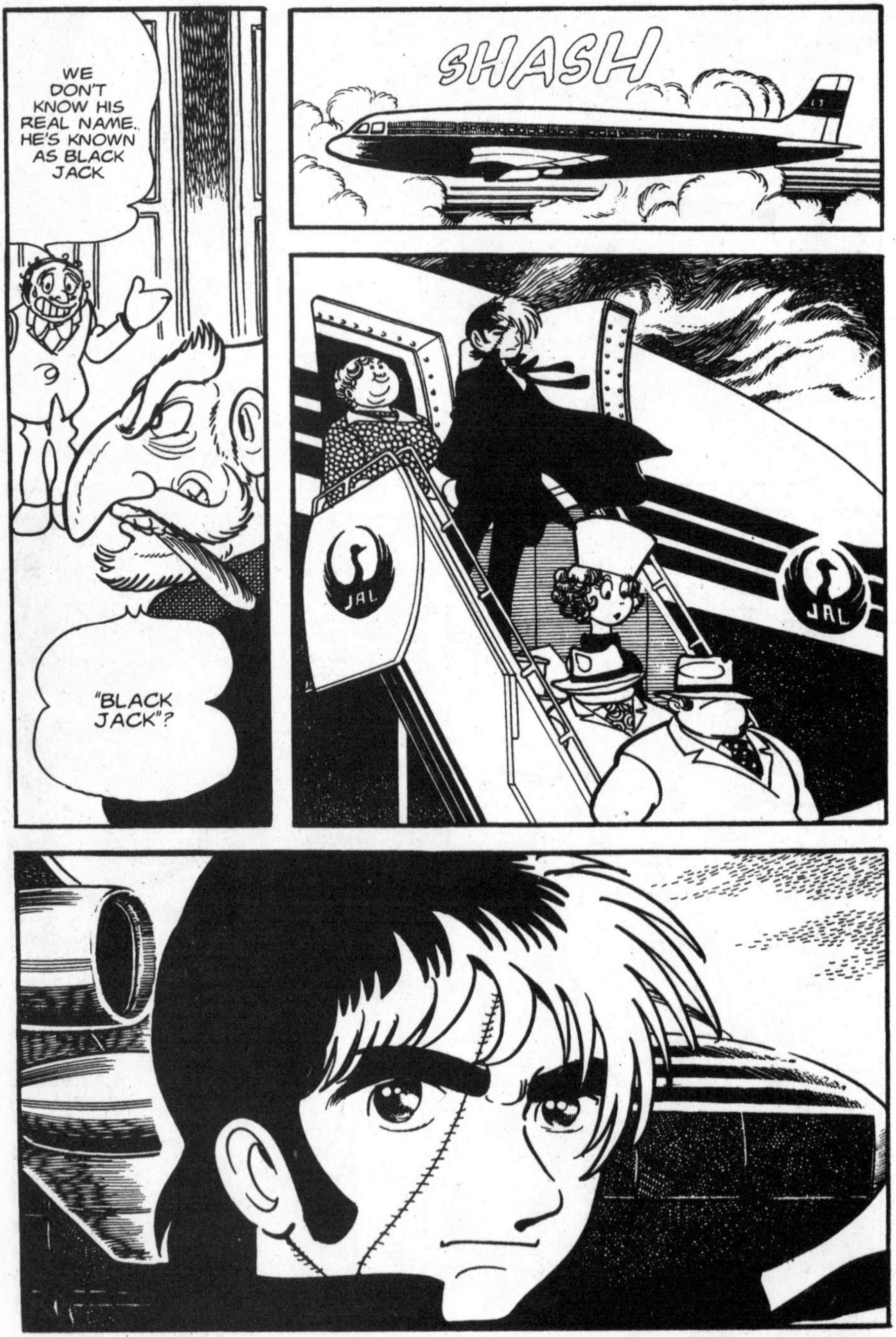
WE DON'T KNOW HIS REAL NAME.. HE'S KNOWN AS BLACK JACK
"BLACK JACK"?
SHASH

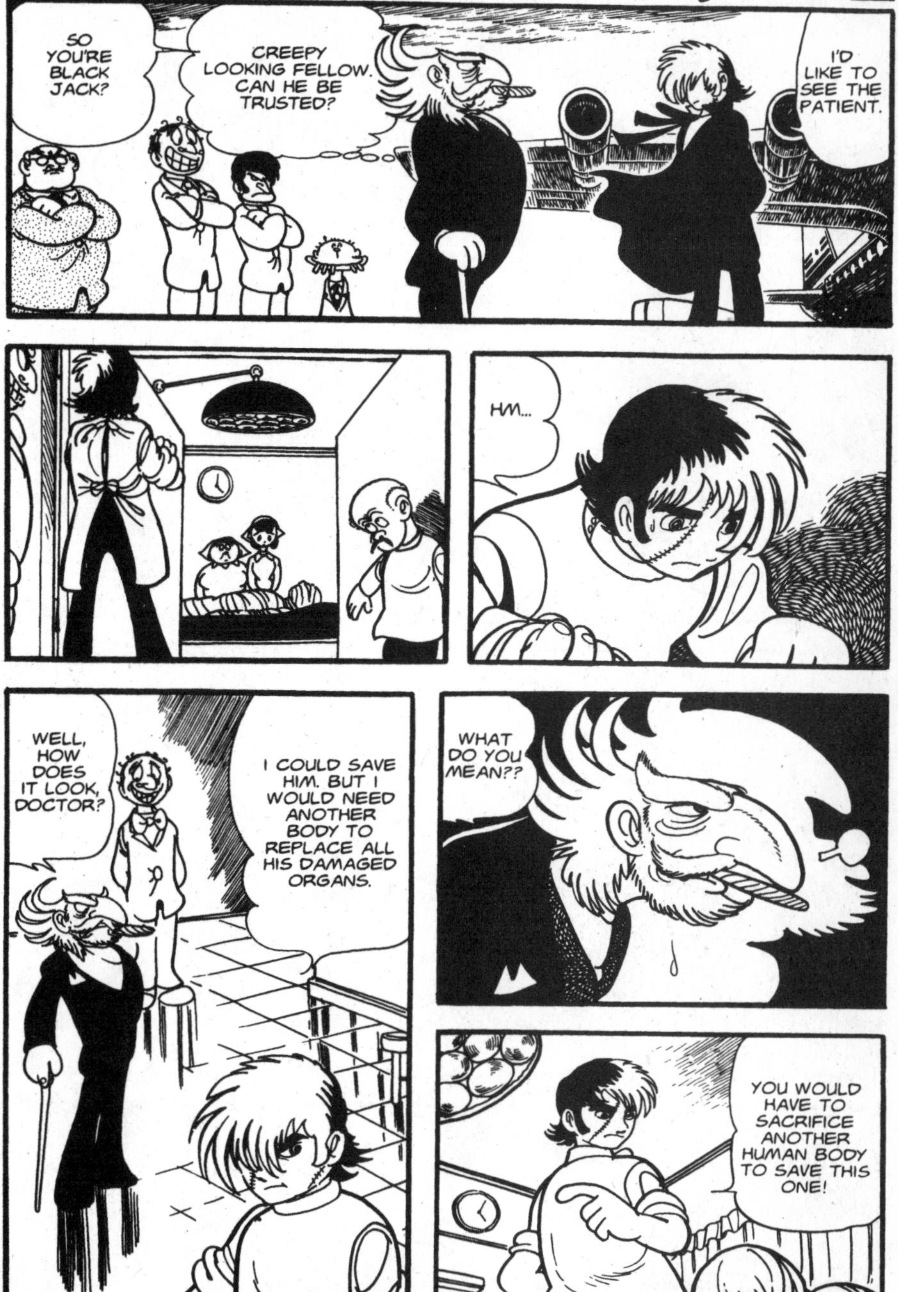
SO YOU'RE BLACK JACK?
CREEPY LOOKING FELLOW. CAN HE BE TRUSTED?
I'D LIKE TO SEE THE PATIENT.
HM...
WELL, HOW DOES IT LOOK, DOCTOR?
I COULD SAVE HIM. BUT I WOULD NEED ANOTHER BODY TO REPLACE ALL HIS DAMAGED ORGANS.
WHAT DO YOU MEAN??
YOU WOULD HAVE TO SACRIFICE ANOTHER HUMAN BODY TO SAVE THIS ONE!

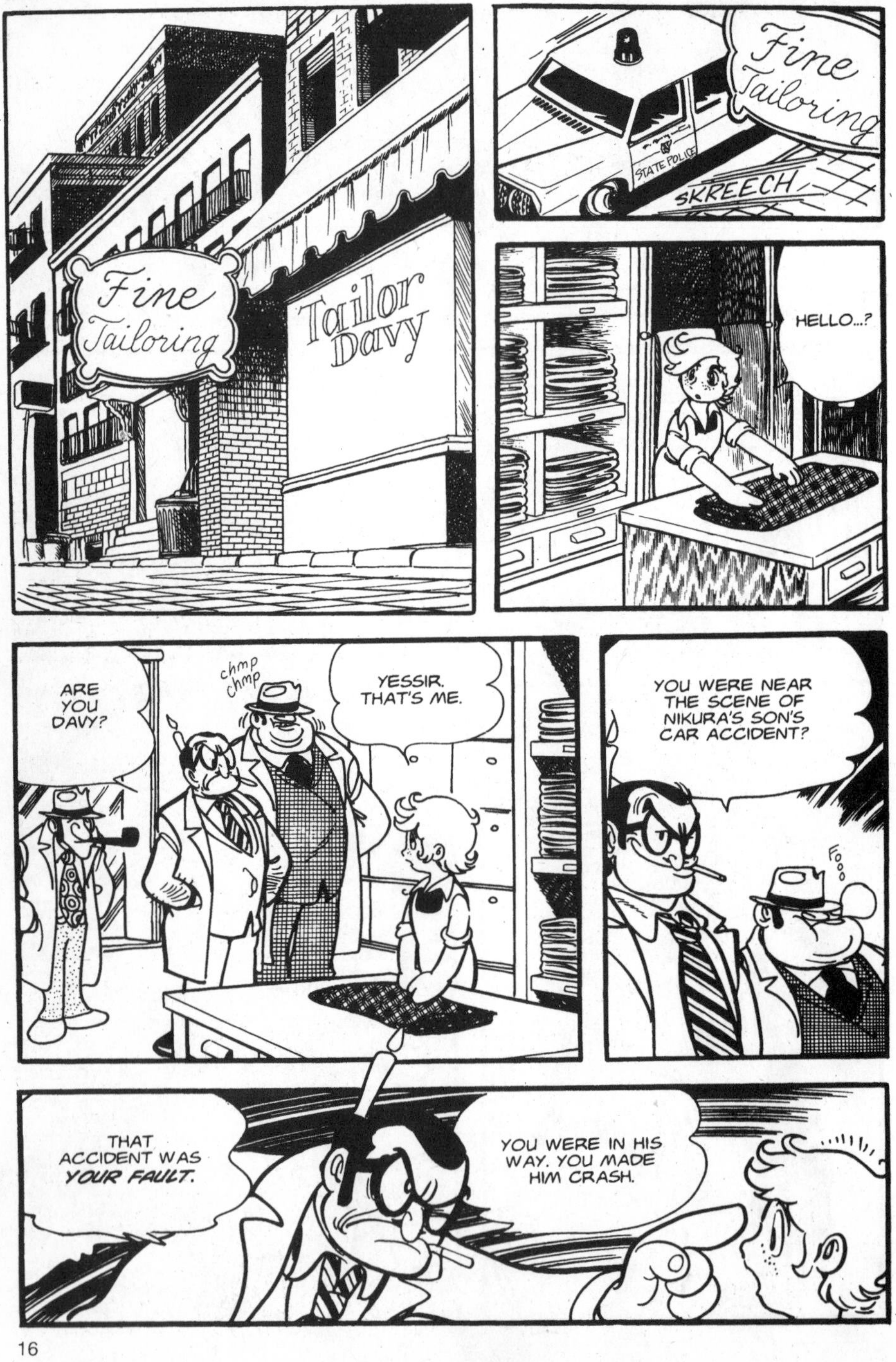
Fine Tailoring
Tailor Davy
Fine Tailoring
STATE POLICE
SKREECH
HELLO...?
ARE YOU DAVY?
chmp chmp
YESSIR. THAT'S ME.
YOU WERE NEAR THE SCENE OF NIKURA'S SON'S CAR ACCIDENT?
Fooo
THAT ACCIDENT WAS YOUR FAULT.
YOU WERE IN HIS WAY. YOU MADE HIM CRASH.

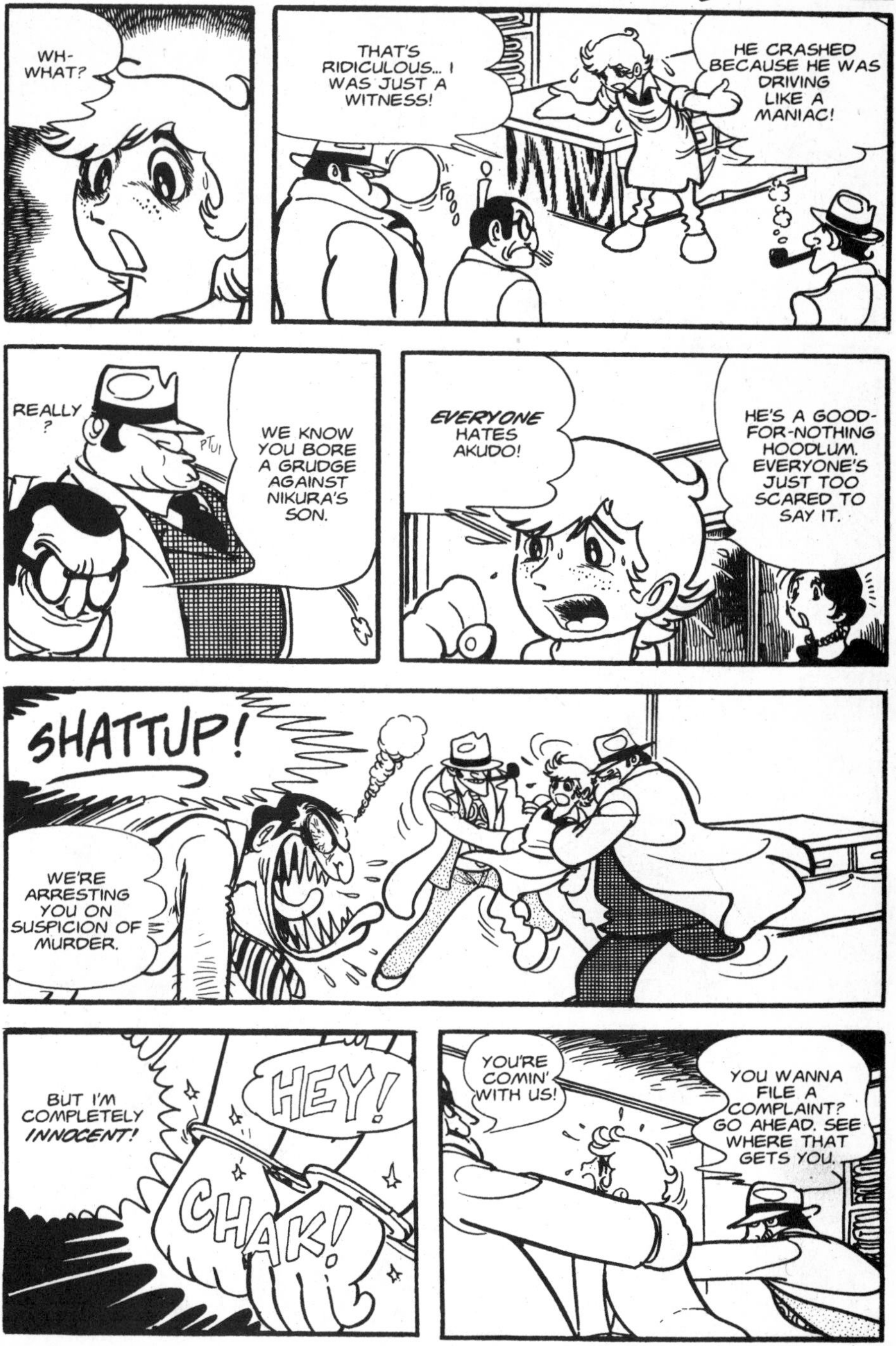
WH-WHAT?
THAT'S RIDICULOUS... I WAS JUST A WITNESS!
FOO
HE CRASHED BECAUSE HE WAS DRIVING LIKE A MANIAC!
REALLY?
PTUI
WE KNOW YOU BORE A GRUDGE AGAINST NIKURA'S SON.
EVERYONE HATES AKUDO!
HE'S A GOOD-FOR-NOTHING HOODLUM. EVERYONE'S JUST TOO SCARED TO SAY IT.
SHATTUP!
WE'RE ARRESTING YOU ON SUSPICION OF MURDER.
BUT I'M COMPLETELY *INNOCENT!*
HEY!
CHAK!
YOU'RE COMIN' WITH US!
YOU WANNA FILE A COMPLAINT? GO AHEAD. SEE WHERE THAT GETS YOU.

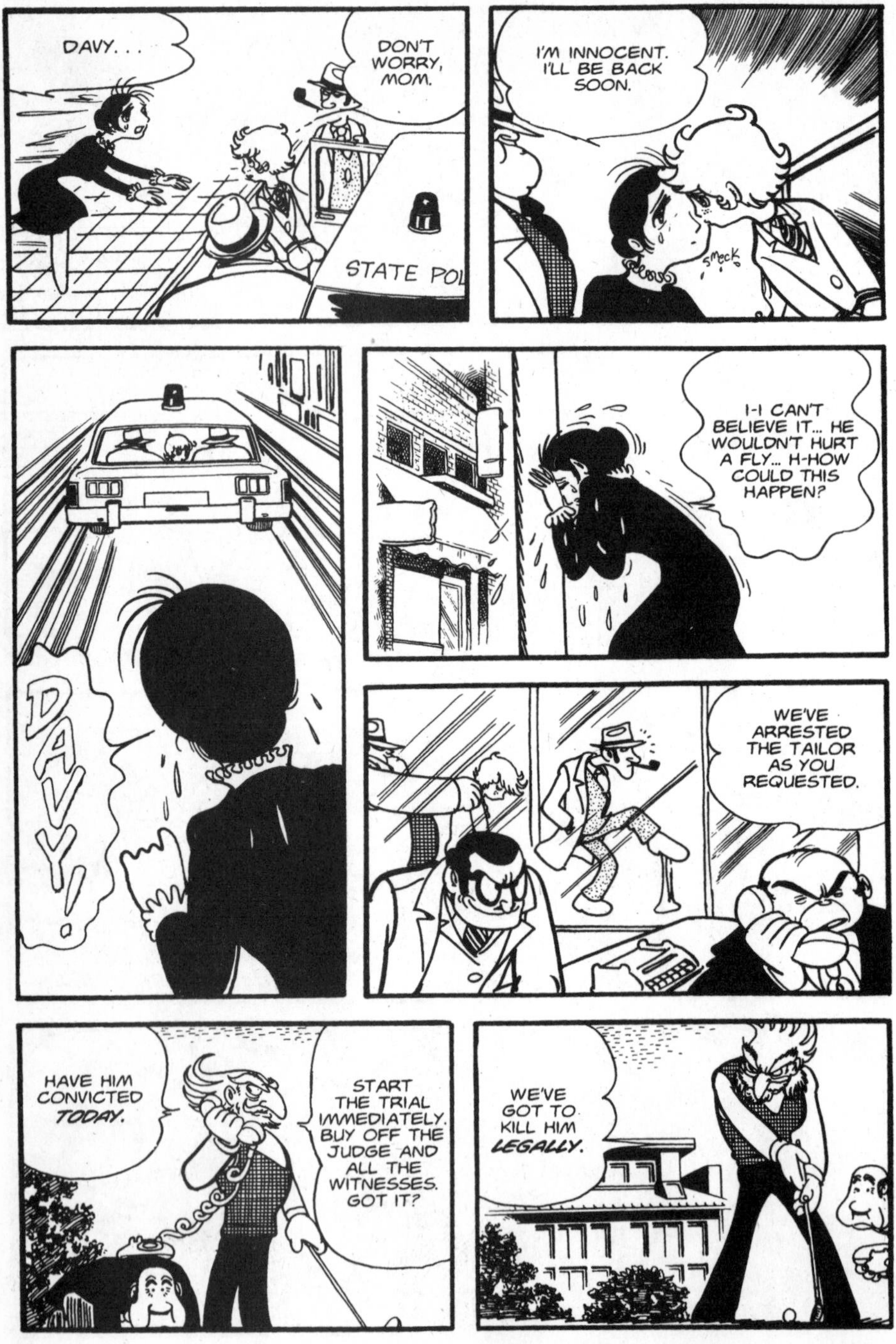
DAVY. . .
DON'T WORRY, MOM.
STATE POL
I'M INNOCENT. I'LL BE BACK SOON.
SMACK
DAVY!
I-I CAN'T BELIEVE IT... HE WOULDN'T HURT A FLY... H-HOW COULD THIS HAPPEN?
WE'VE ARRESTED THE TAILOR AS YOU REQUESTED.
HAVE HIM CONVICTED *TODAY*.
START THE TRIAL IMMEDIATELY. BUY OFF THE JUDGE AND ALL THE WITNESSES. GOT IT?
WE'VE GOT TO KILL HIM *LEGALLY*.

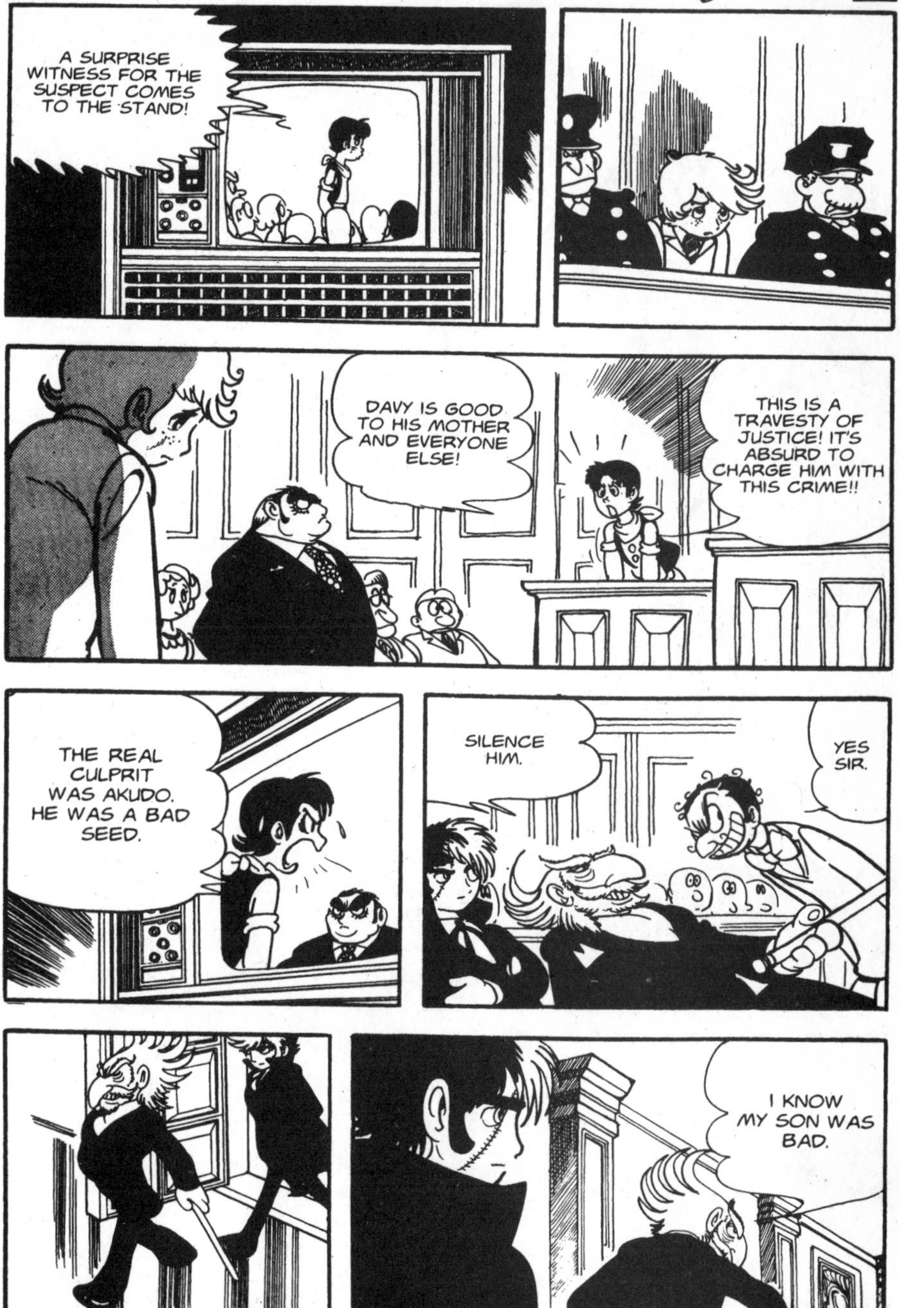
A SURPRISE WITNESS FOR THE SUSPECT COMES TO THE STAND!
DAVY IS GOOD TO HIS MOTHER AND EVERYONE ELSE!
THIS IS A TRAVESTY OF JUSTICE! IT'S ABSURD TO CHARGE HIM WITH THIS CRIME!!
THE REAL CULPRIT WAS AKUDO. HE WAS A BAD SEED.
SILENCE HIM.
YES SIR.
I KNOW MY SON WAS BAD.

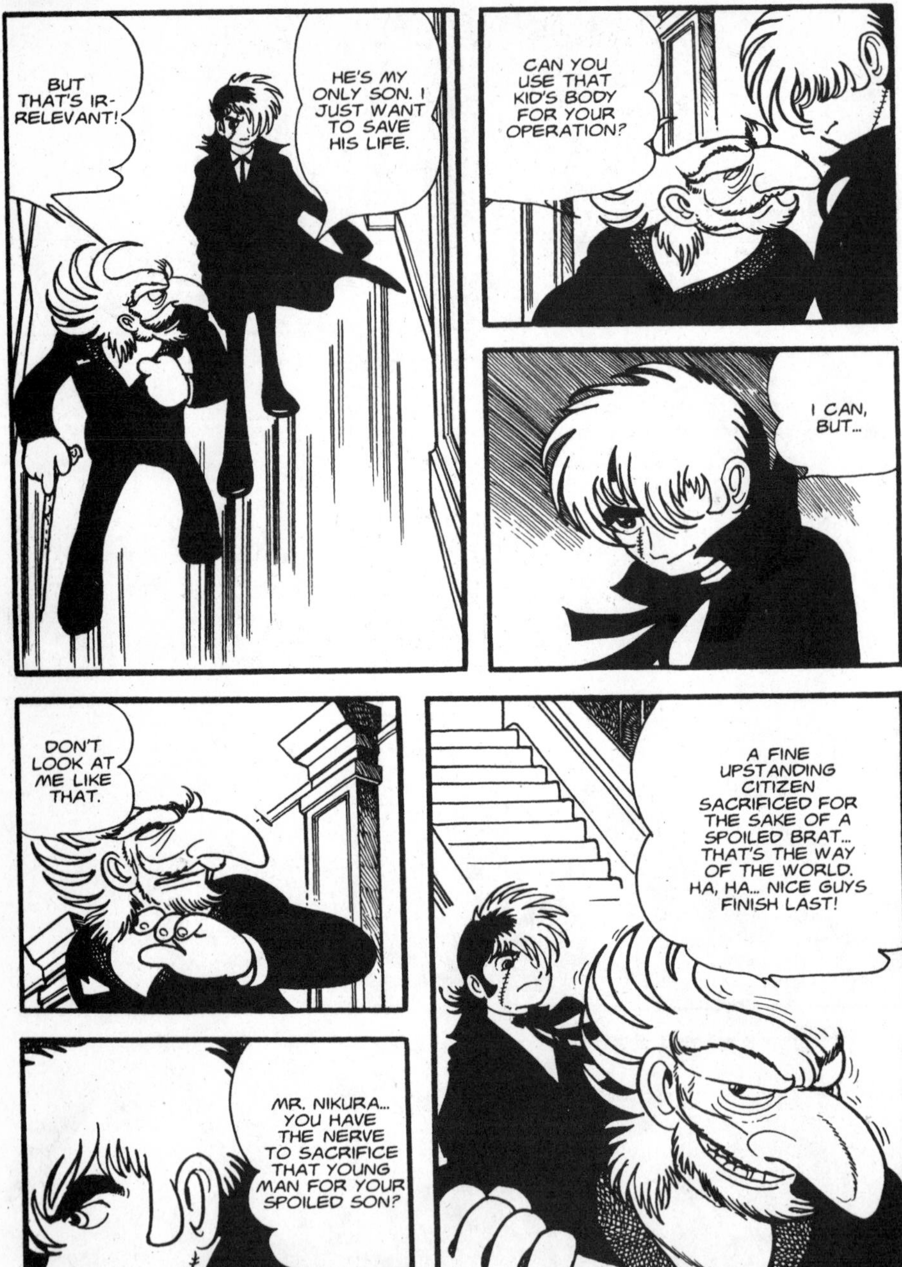
BUT THAT'S IR-RELEVANT!
HE'S MY ONLY SON. I JUST WANT TO SAVE HIS LIFE.
CAN YOU USE THAT KID'S BODY FOR YOUR OPERATION?
I CAN, BUT...
DON'T LOOK AT ME LIKE THAT.
MR. NIKURA... YOU HAVE THE NERVE TO SACRIFICE THAT YOUNG MAN FOR YOUR SPOILED SON?
A FINE UPSTANDING CITIZEN SACRIFICED FOR THE SAKE OF A SPOILED BRAT... THAT'S THE WAY OF THE WORLD. HA, HA... NICE GUYS FINISH LAST!

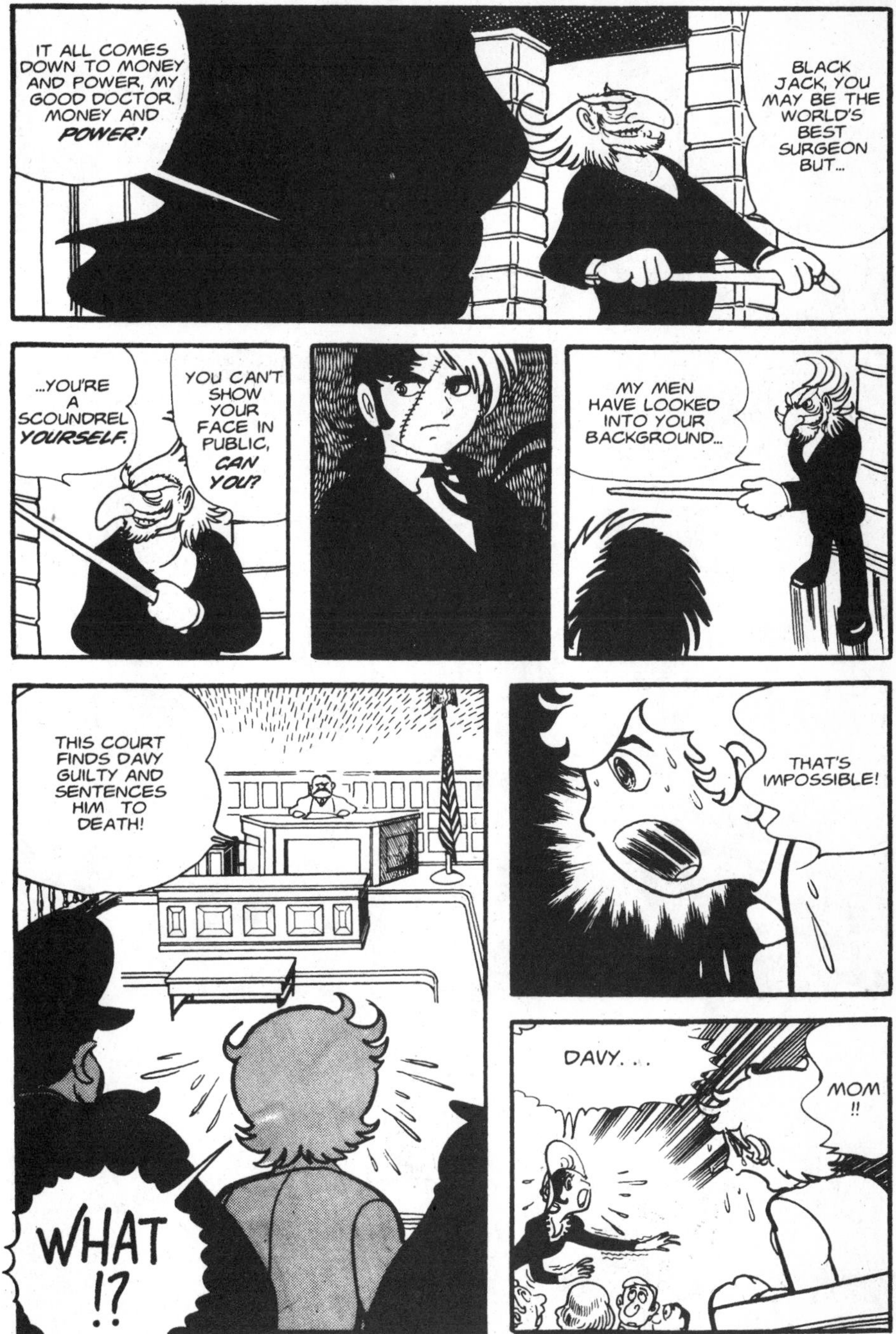
IT ALL COMES DOWN TO MONEY AND POWER, MY GOOD DOCTOR. MONEY AND POWER!
BLACK JACK, YOU MAY BE THE WORLD'S BEST SURGEON BUT...
...YOU'RE A SCOUNDREL YOURSELF.
YOU CAN'T SHOW YOUR FACE IN PUBLIC, CAN YOU?
MY MEN HAVE LOOKED INTO YOUR BACKGROUND...
THIS COURT FINDS DAVY GUILTY AND SENTENCES HIM TO DEATH!
WHAT !?
THAT'S IMPOSSIBLE!
DAVY. . . .
MOM !!

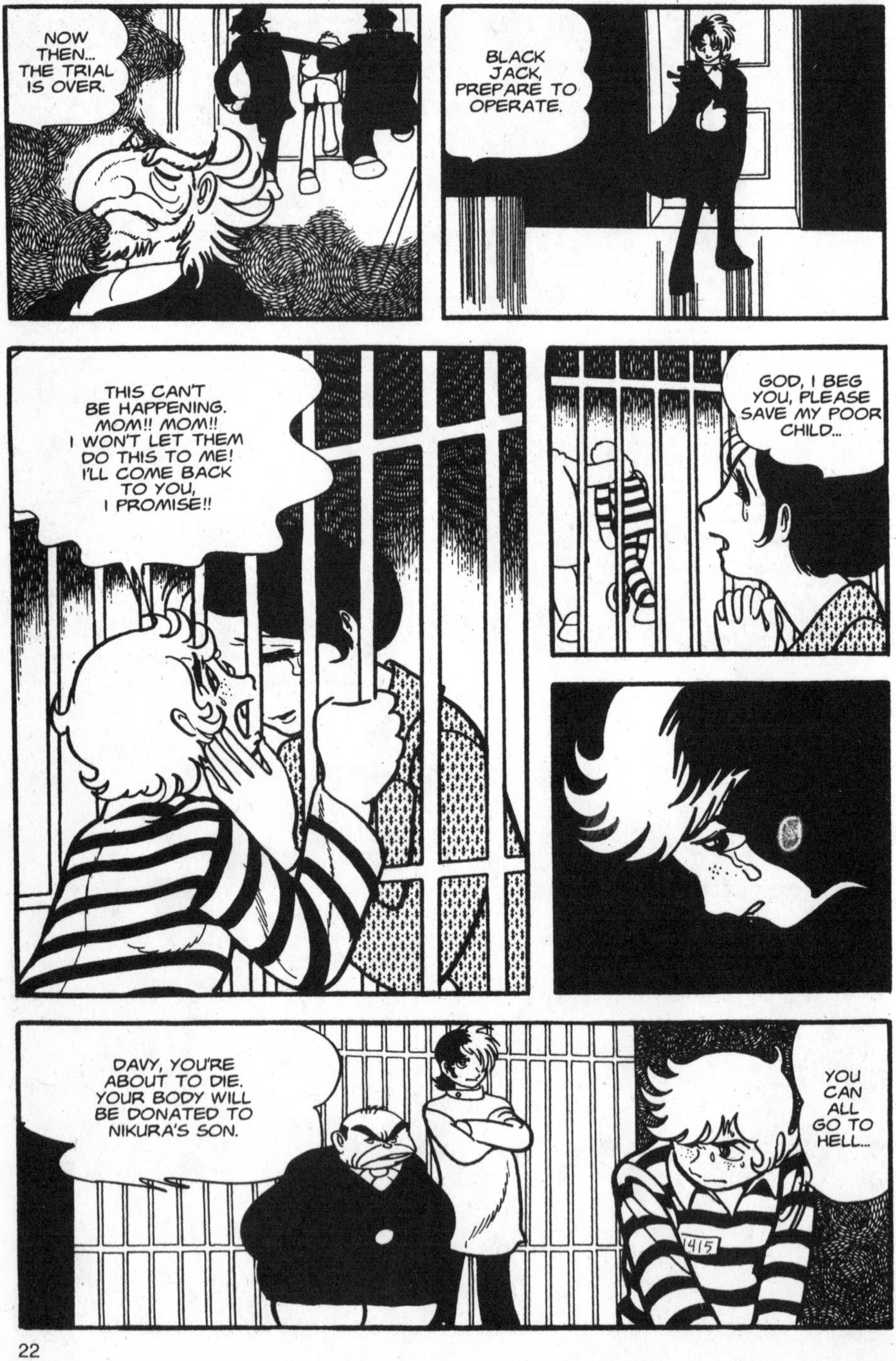
NOW THEN... THE TRIAL IS OVER.
BLACK JACK, PREPARE TO OPERATE.
THIS CAN'T BE HAPPENING. MOM!! MOM!! I WON'T LET THEM DO THIS TO ME! I'LL COME BACK TO YOU, I PROMISE!!
GOD, I BEG YOU, PLEASE SAVE MY POOR CHILD...
DAVY, YOU'RE ABOUT TO DIE. YOUR BODY WILL BE DONATED TO NIKURA'S SON.
YOU CAN ALL GO TO HELL...
1415

...WHERE YOU BELONG!!

DONE WITH YOUR PRAYERS?

PUT OUT YOUR ARM.

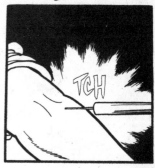

TCH

MOM...

DISINFECT HIM.

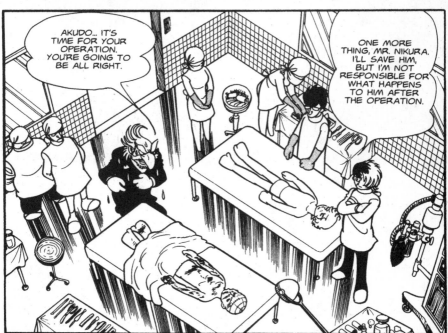

AKUDO... IT'S TIME FOR YOUR OPERATION. YOU'RE GOING TO BE ALL RIGHT.

ONE MORE THING, MR. NIKURA. I'LL SAVE HIM, BUT I'M NOT RESPONSIBLE FOR WHAT HAPPENS TO HIM AFTER THE OPERATION.

OF COURSE. AS LONG AS HE FULLY REGAINS HIS HEALTH!

YOU'LL HAVE TO LEAVE THE ROOM NOW.

I NEED TO WORK ALONE!

GWNCH

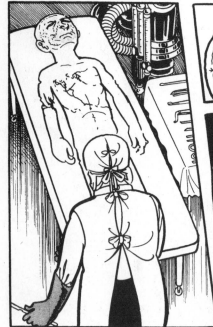

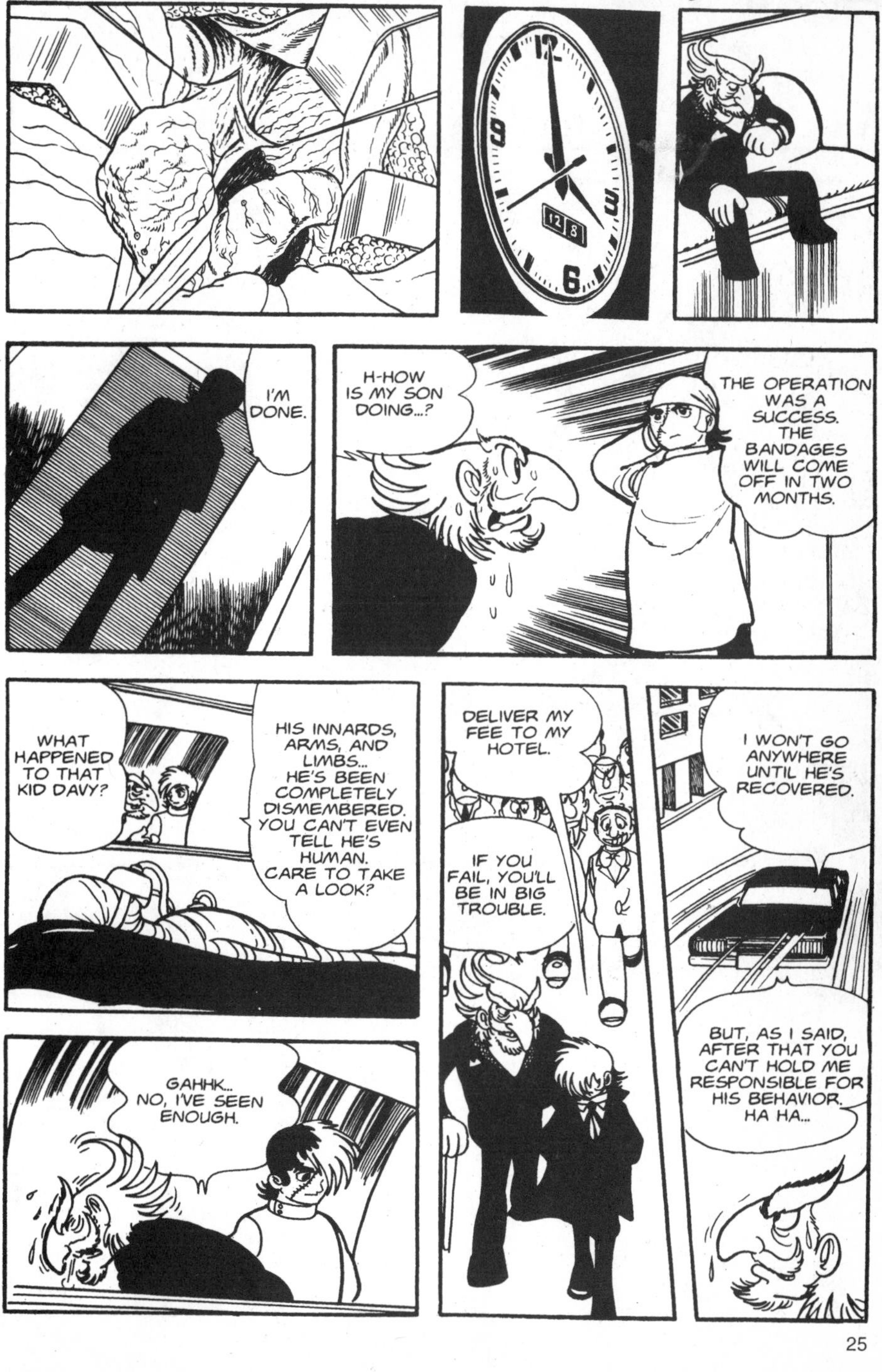
I'M DONE.
H-HOW IS MY SON DOING...?
THE OPERATION WAS A SUCCESS. THE BANDAGES WILL COME OFF IN TWO MONTHS.
WHAT HAPPENED TO THAT KID DAVY?
HIS INNARDS, ARMS, AND LIMBS... HE'S BEEN COMPLETELY DISMEMBERED. YOU CAN'T EVEN TELL HE'S HUMAN. CARE TO TAKE A LOOK?
GAHHK... NO, I'VE SEEN ENOUGH.
DELIVER MY FEE TO MY HOTEL.
IF YOU FAIL, YOU'LL BE IN BIG TROUBLE.
I WON'T GO ANYWHERE UNTIL HE'S RECOVERED.
BUT, AS I SAID, AFTER THAT YOU CAN'T HOLD ME RESPONSIBLE FOR HIS BEHAVIOR. HA HA...

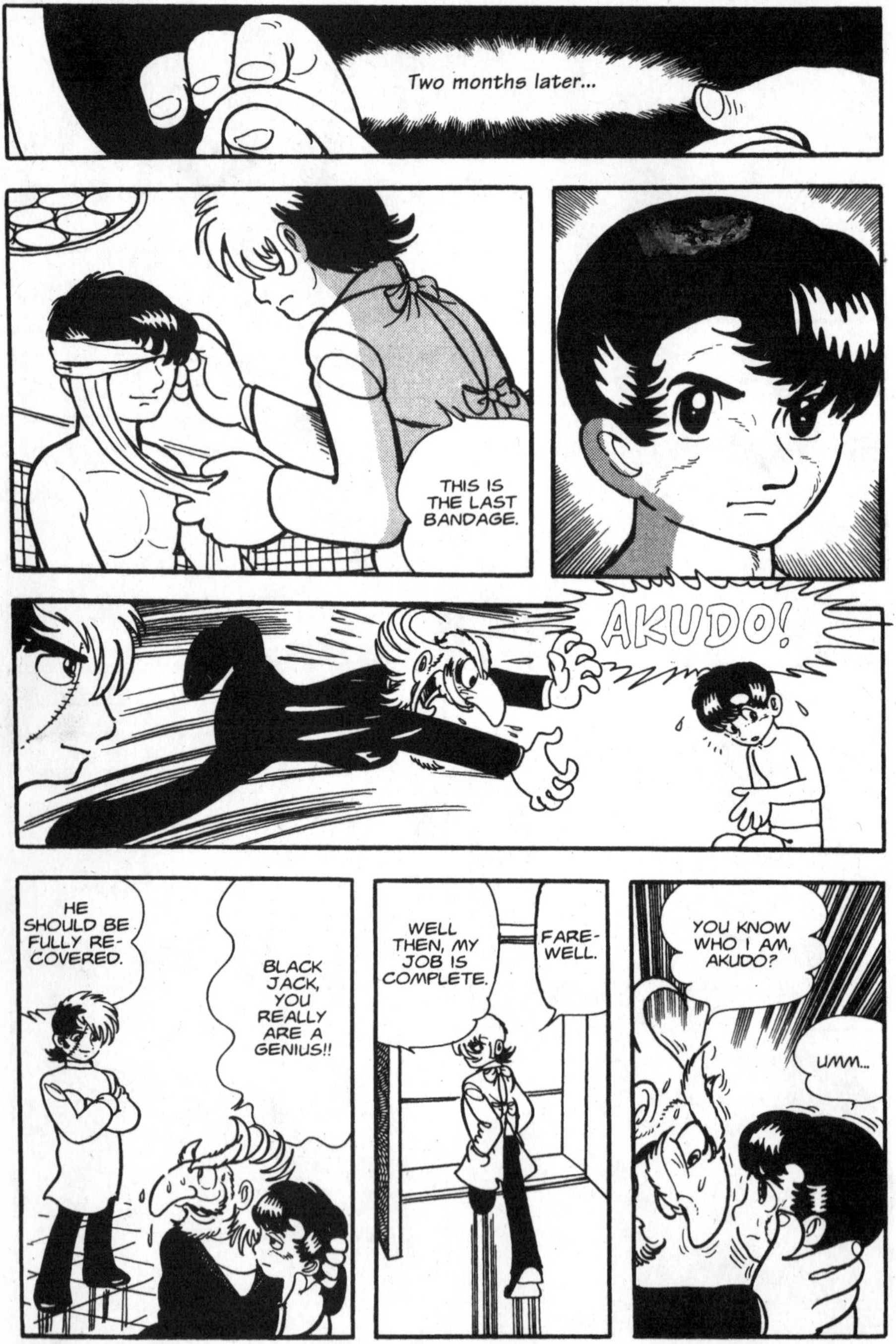

Two months later...
THIS IS THE LAST BANDAGE.
AKUDO!
HE SHOULD BE FULLY RE-COVERED.
BLACK JACK, YOU REALLY ARE A GENIUS!!
WELL THEN, MY JOB IS COMPLETE.
FARE-WELL.
YOU KNOW WHO I AM, AKUDO?
UMM...

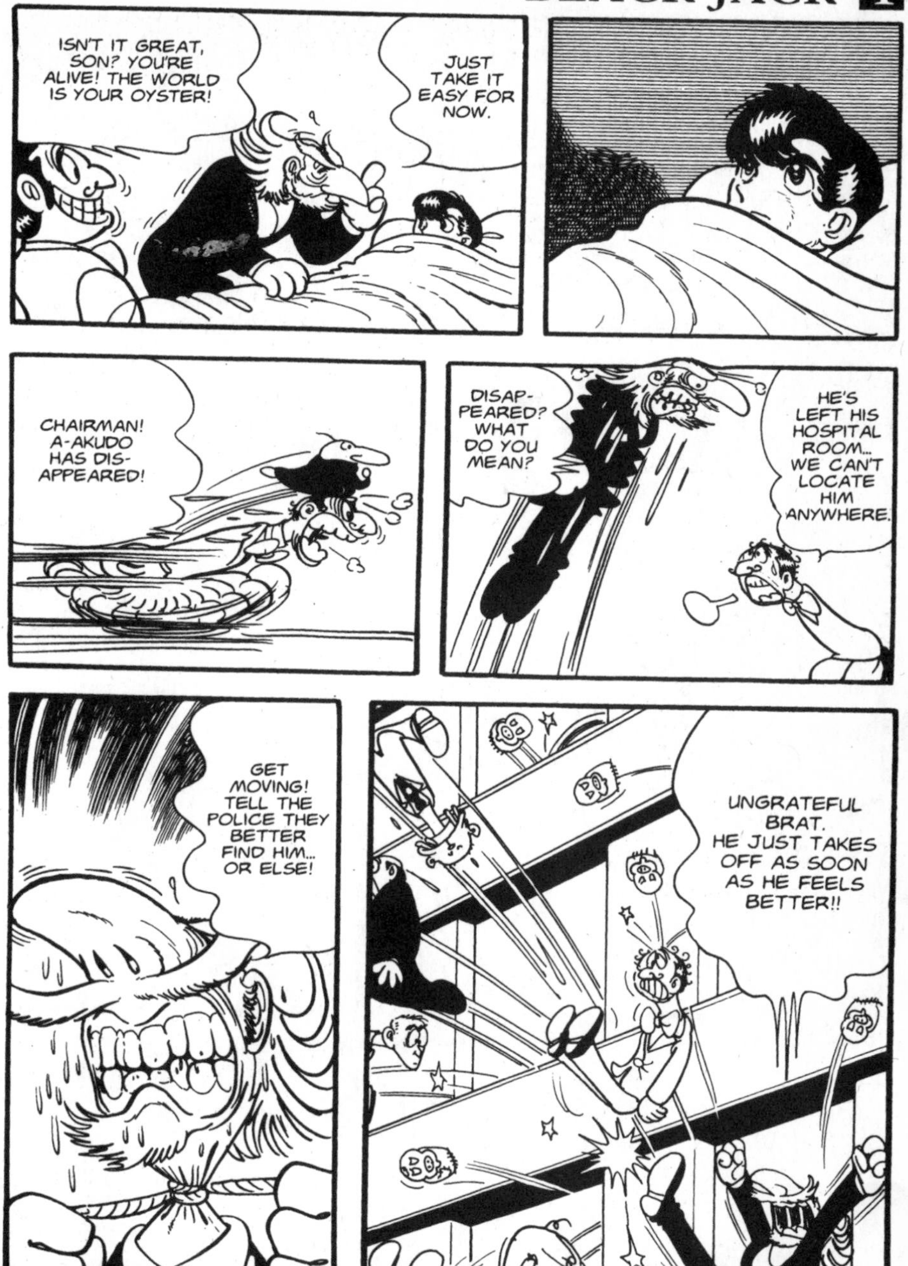
ISN'T IT GREAT, SON? YOU'RE ALIVE! THE WORLD IS YOUR OYSTER!
JUST TAKE IT EASY FOR NOW.
CHAIRMAN! A-AKUDO HAS DIS-APPEARED!
DISAP-PEARED? WHAT DO YOU MEAN?
HE'S LEFT HIS HOSPITAL ROOM... WE CAN'T LOCATE HIM ANYWHERE.
GET MOVING! TELL THE POLICE THEY BETTER FIND HIM... OR ELSE!
UNGRATEFUL BRAT. HE JUST TAKES OFF AS SOON AS HE FEELS BETTER!!

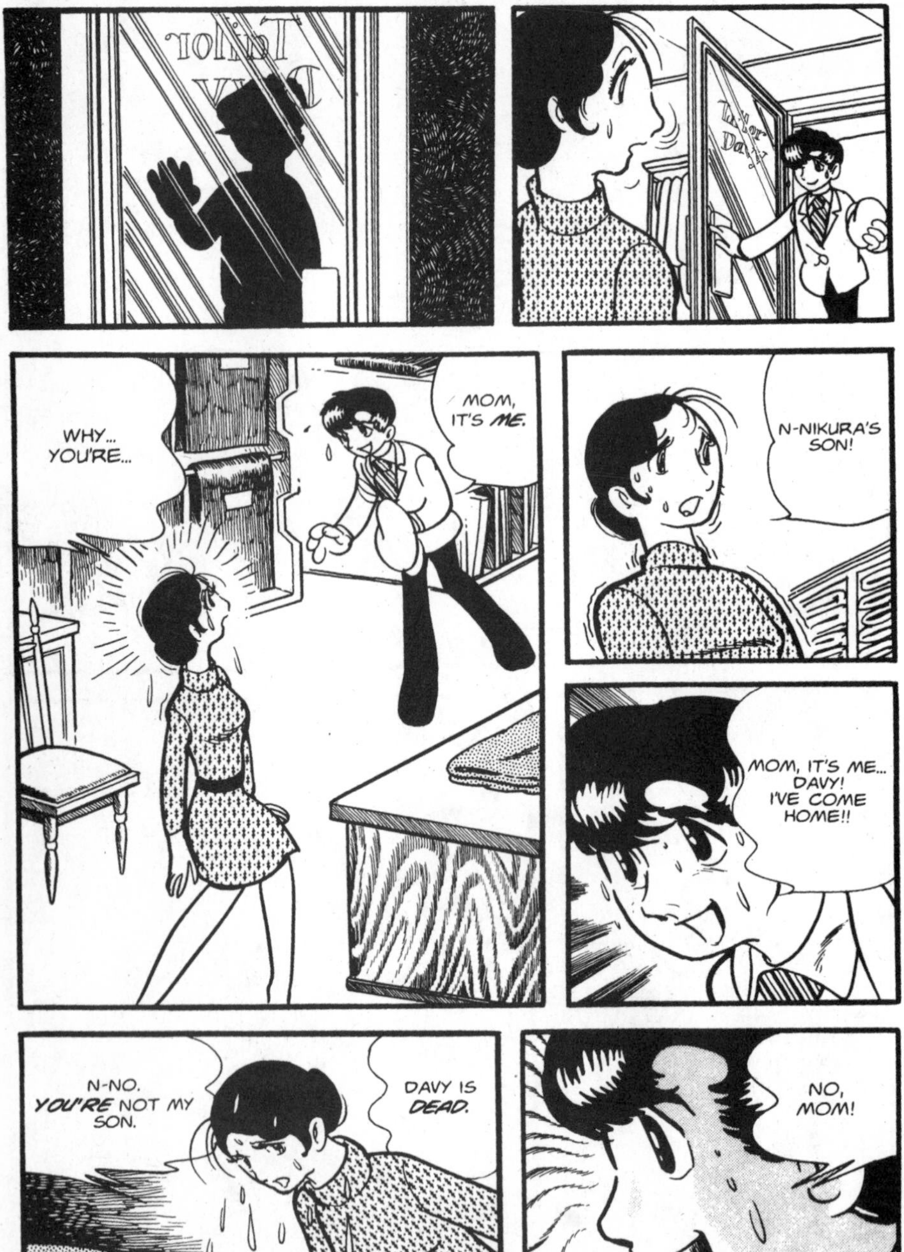
WHY... YOU'RE...
MOM, IT'S *ME*.
N-NIKURA'S SON!
MOM, IT'S ME... DAVY! I'VE COME HOME!!
N-NO. ***YOU'RE*** NOT MY SON.
DAVY IS ***DEAD***.
NO, MOM!

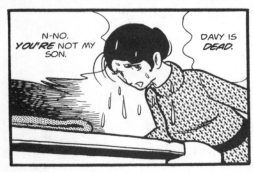

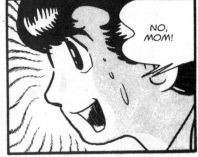

IF YOU DON'T BELIEVE ME, WATCH ME WITH THIS FABRIC.

YOU'LL RECOGNIZE THIS.

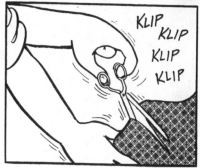

KLIP KLIP

KLIP

KLIP

...

KLIP

KLIP

KLIP

YOU'RE CUTTING...

...JUST LIKE DAVY...

KLIP

MOM, IT WAS AKUDO WHO DIED. DOCTOR BLACK JACK JUST DID PLASTIC SURGERY ON MY FACE SO I'D LOOK LIKE AKUDO.

HE TOLD ME THAT AKUDO'S BODY AND SOUL WERE BOTH ROTTEN TO THE CORE, SO IT WOULD HAVE BEEN POINTLESS TO OPERATE ON HIM!

D-DAVY...

I HAVE A DIFFERENT FACE, BUT I'M STILL YOUR SON. IS THAT ALL RIGHT, MOM?

NOW LET'S MOVE SOMEWHERE FAR AWAY. AKUDO'S FATHER IS LOOKING FOR ME...

WHERE DID YOU GET ALL THAT MONEY!?

BLACK JACK GAVE IT TO ME SO WE COULD FLEE THE COUNTRY.

THAT DOCTOR MUST BE AN ANGEL, MOM.

All we know about Black Jack is that he is Japanese. His background and real name remain unknown. Yet this mysterious surgeon performs miracles day after day. . .

OPERATION TWO

THE FACE
IN THE
AFFLICTION

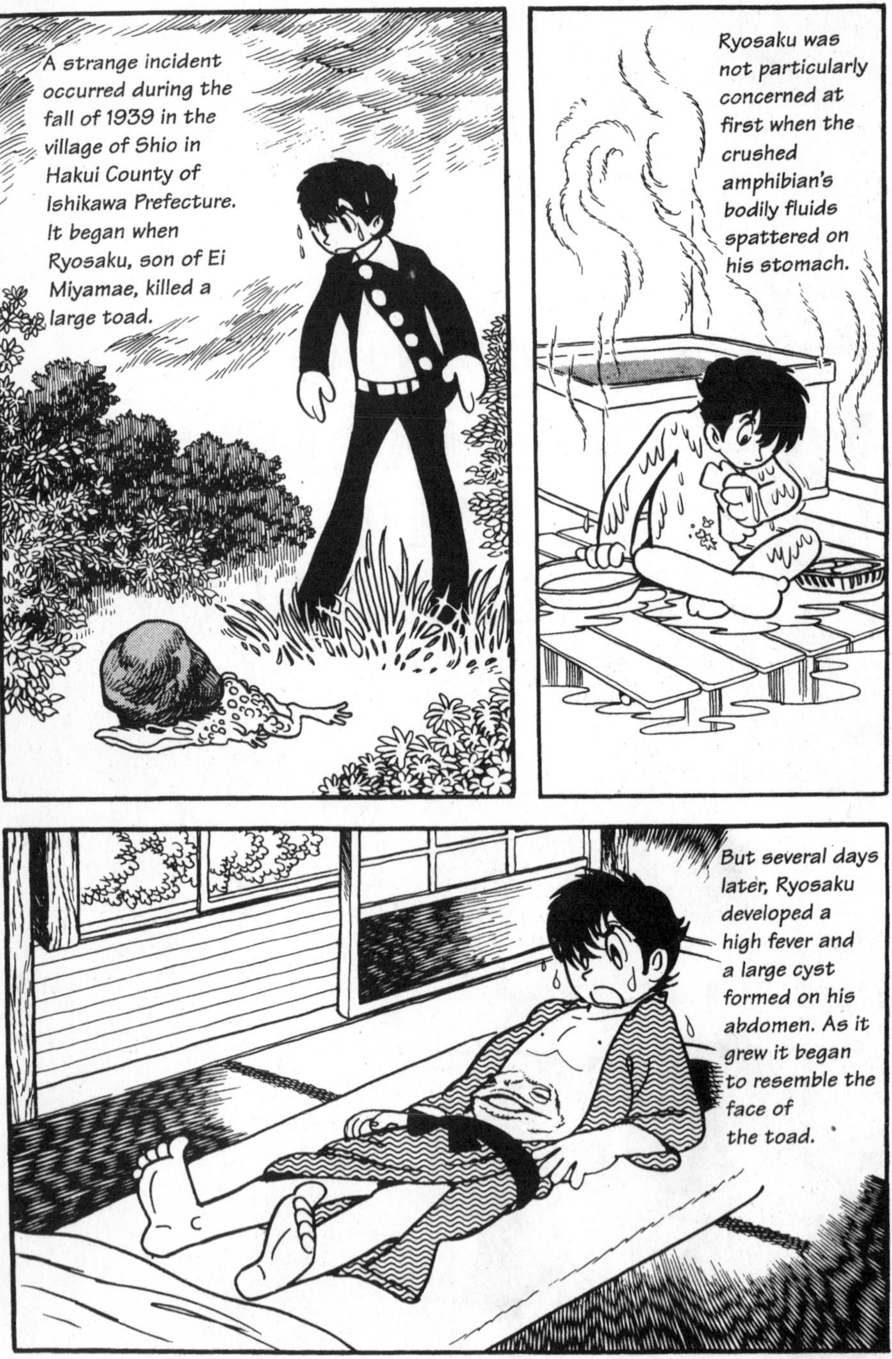
A strange incident occurred during the fall of 1939 in the village of Shio in Hakui County of Ishikawa Prefecture. It began when Ryosaku, son of Ei Miyamae, killed a large toad.
Ryosaku was not particularly concerned at first when the crushed amphibian's bodily fluids spattered on his stomach.
But several days later, Ryosaku developed a high fever and a large cyst formed on his abdomen. As it grew it began to resemble the face of the toad.

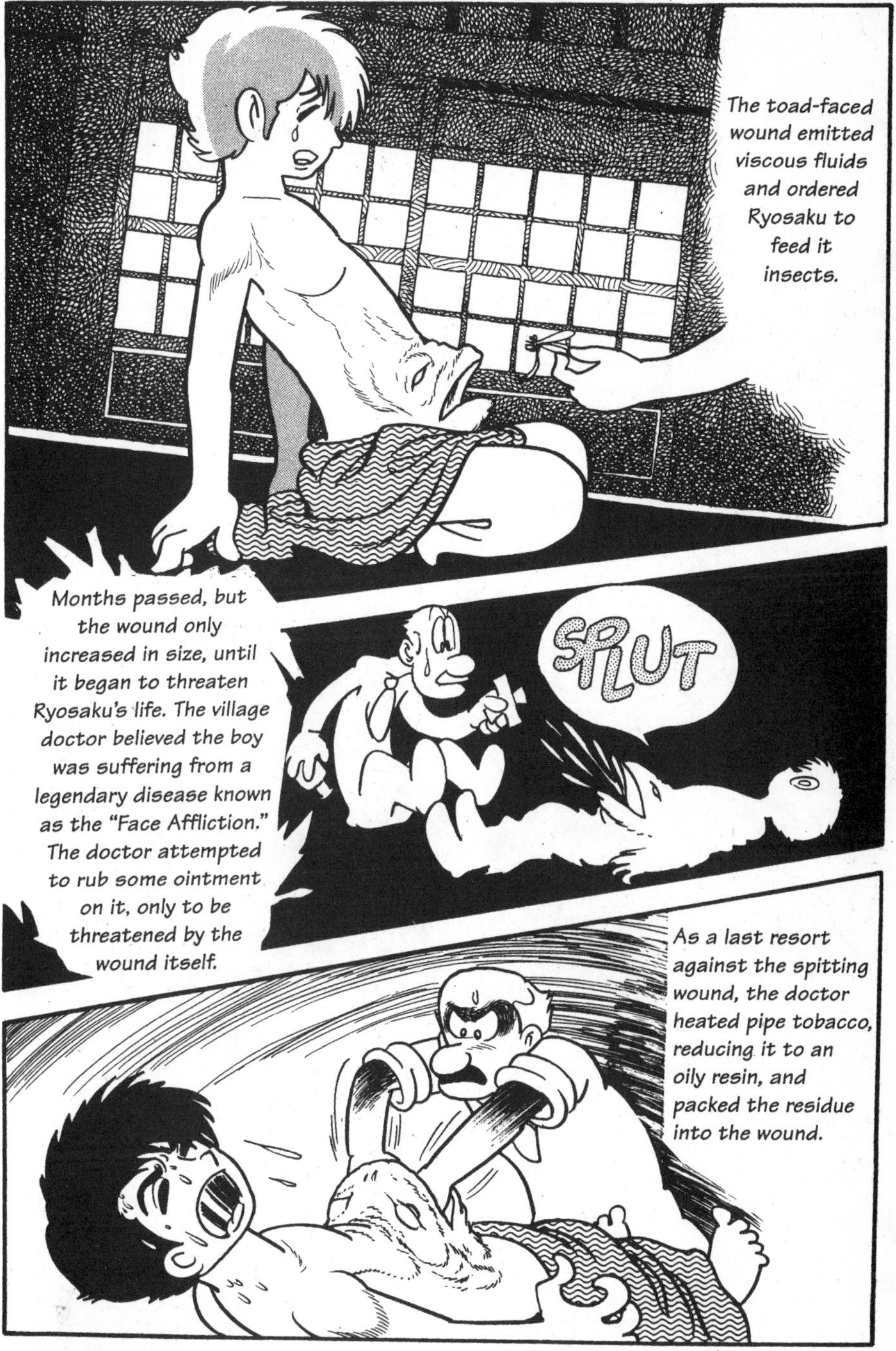
The toad-faced wound emitted viscous fluids and ordered Ryosaku to feed it insects.
Months passed, but the wound only increased in size, until it began to threaten Ryosaku's life. The village doctor believed the boy was suffering from a legendary disease known as the "Face Affliction." The doctor attempted to rub some ointment on it, only to be threatened by the wound itself.
SPLUT
As a last resort against the spitting wound, the doctor heated pipe tobacco, reducing it to an oily resin, and packed the residue into the wound.

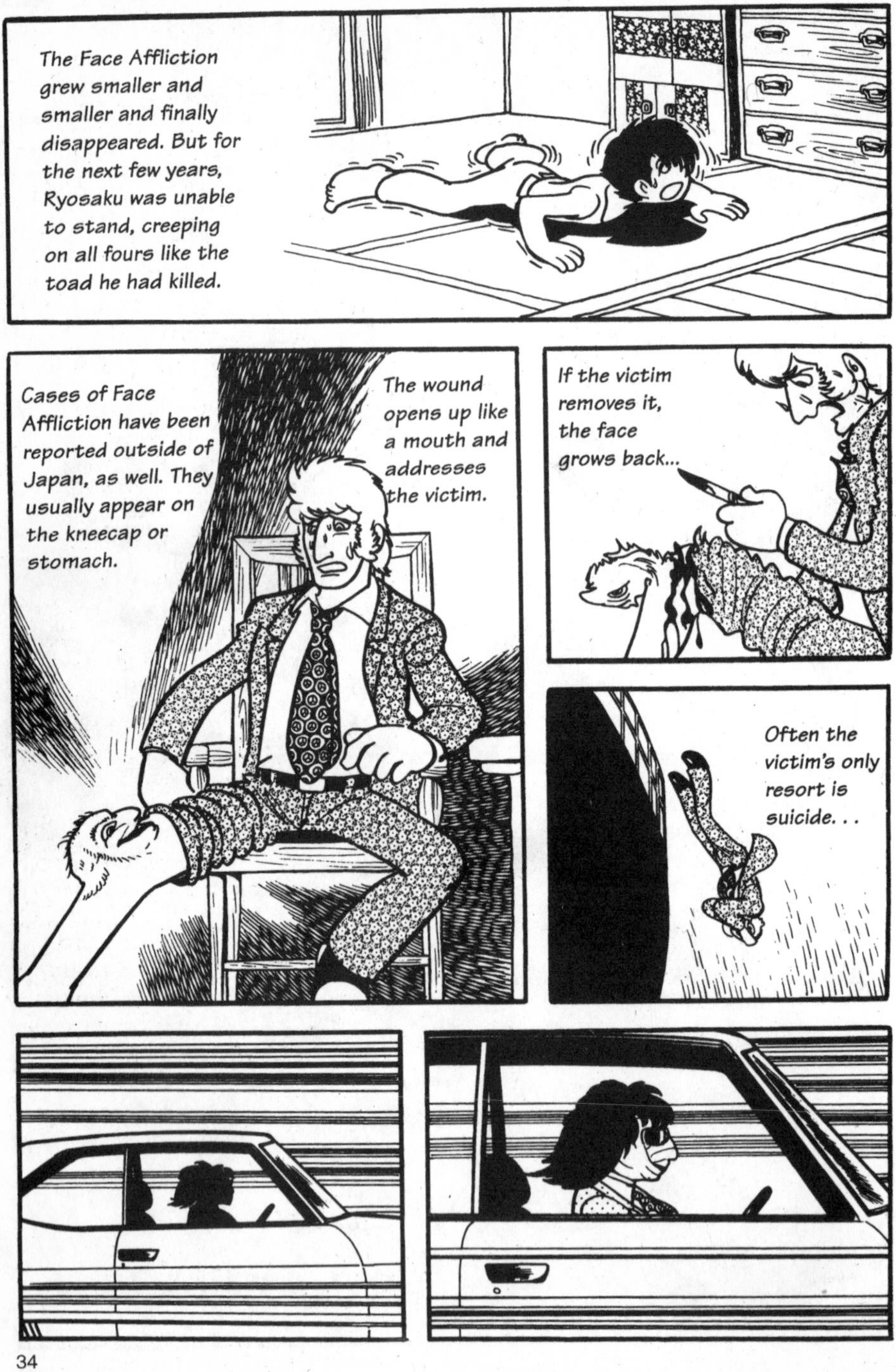
The Face Affliction grew smaller and smaller and finally disappeared. But for the next few years, Ryosaku was unable to stand, creeping on all fours like the toad he had killed.
Cases of Face Affliction have been reported outside of Japan, as well. They usually appear on the kneecap or stomach.
The wound opens up like a mouth and addresses the victim.
If the victim removes it, the face grows back...
Often the victim's only resort is suicide. . .

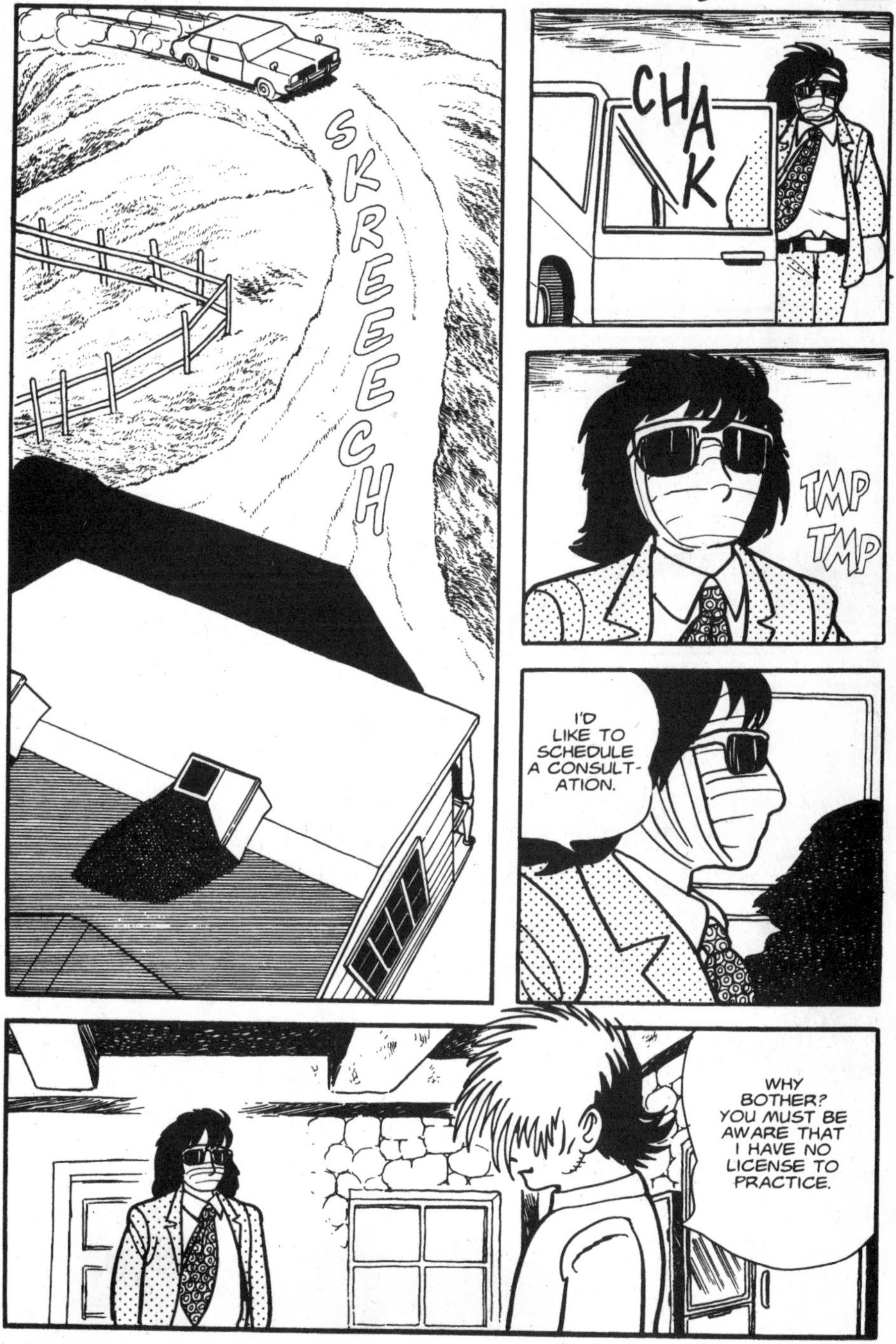
SKREEECH
CHAK
TMP TMP
I'D LIKE TO SCHEDULE A CONSULT-ATION.
WHY BOTHER? YOU MUST BE AWARE THAT I HAVE NO LICENSE TO PRACTICE.

YES, I KNOW THAT. I HAVE TO KEEP THIS VISIT A SECRET.

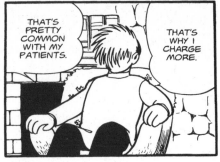

THAT'S PRETTY COMMON WITH MY PATIENTS.

THAT'S WHY I CHARGE MORE.

CALL IT A "MUM'S THE WORD" FEE.

THAT'S FINE. HOW MUCH WILL IT BE?

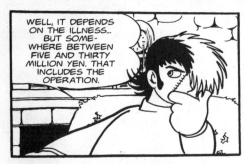

WELL, IT DEPENDS ON THE ILLNESS... BUT SOMEWHERE BETWEEN FIVE AND THIRTY MILLION YEN. THAT INCLUDES THE OPERATION.

ONCE I'M CURED, I'LL PAY YOU. I'M NOT SURE IF YOU CAN CURE ME, THOUGH.

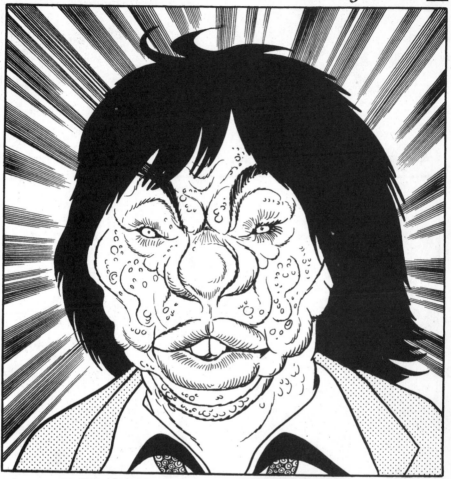

HOW HORRIBLE!

IS IT FROM EXTREME ECZEMA? OR SOME DRUG OVER-DOSE?

NEITHER.

DOCTOR, HAVEN'T YOU EVER HEARD OF THE FACE AFFLICTION?

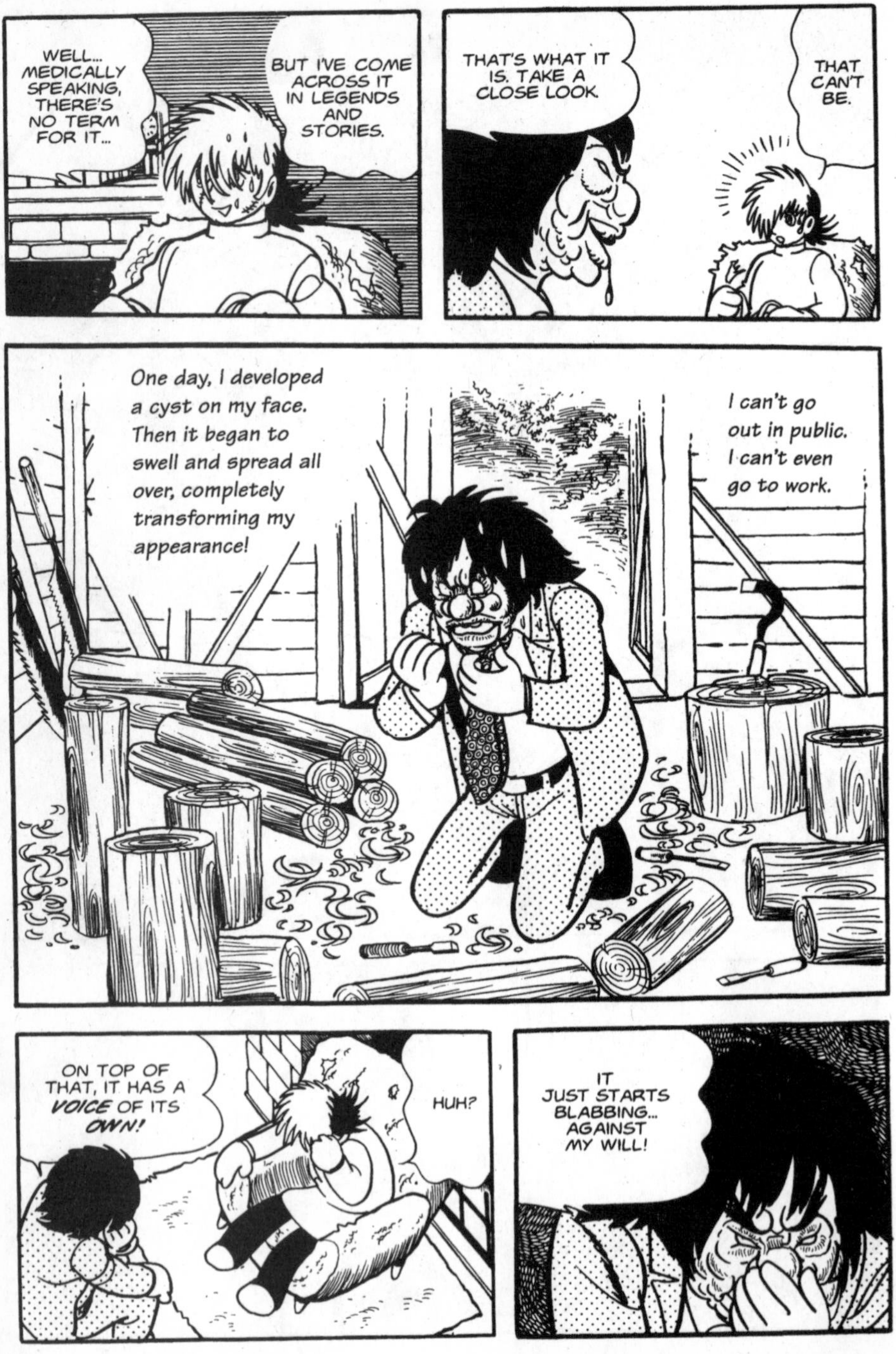
WELL... MEDICALLY SPEAKING, THERE'S NO TERM FOR IT...
BUT I'VE COME ACROSS IT IN LEGENDS AND STORIES.
THAT'S WHAT IT IS. TAKE A CLOSE LOOK.
THAT CAN'T BE.
One day, I developed a cyst on my face. Then it began to swell and spread all over, completely transforming my appearance!
I can't go out in public. I can't even go to work.
ON TOP OF THAT, IT HAS A *VOICE* OF ITS *OWN!*
HUH?
IT JUST STARTS BLABBING... AGAINST MY WILL!

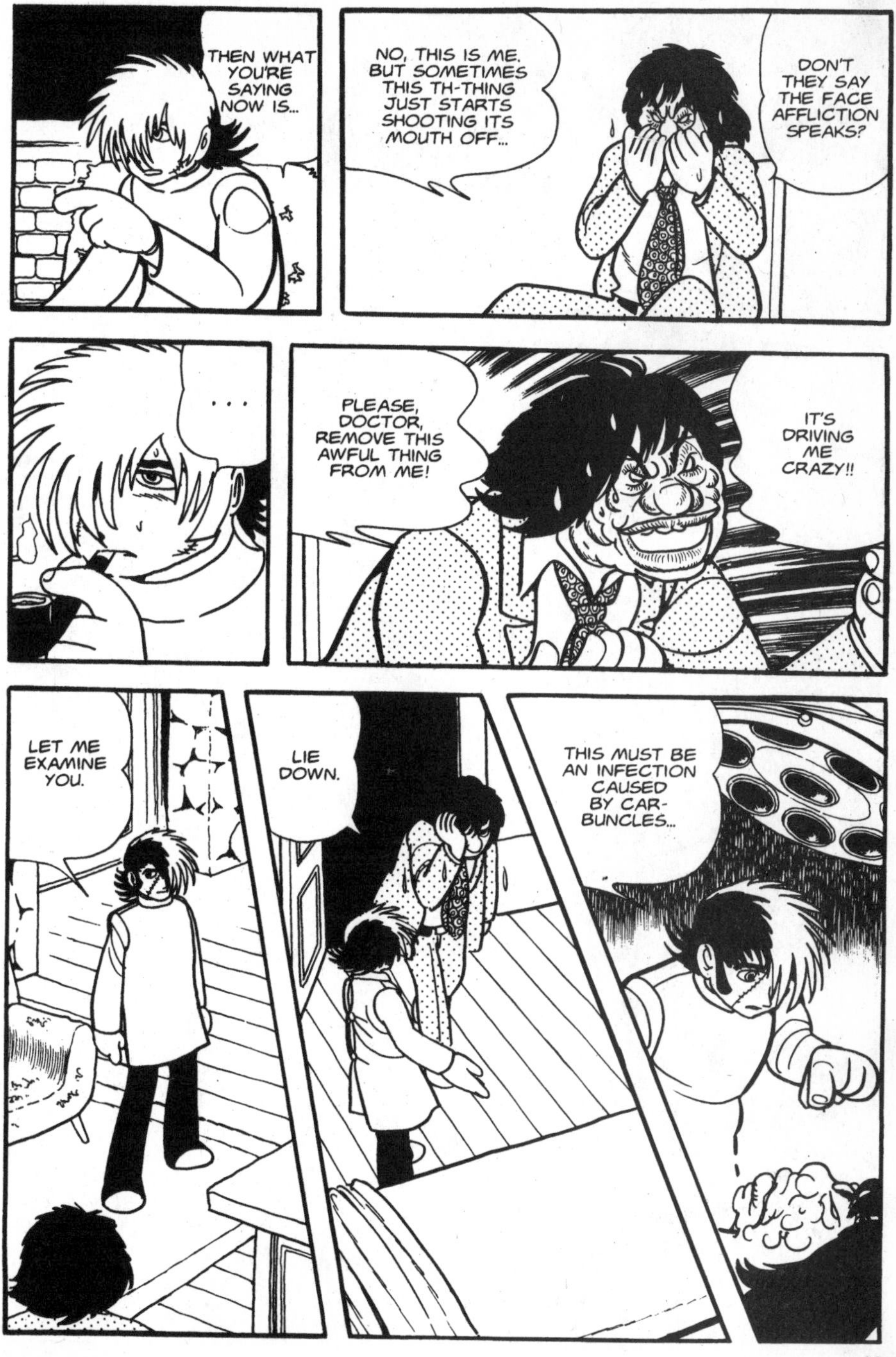
THEN WHAT YOU'RE SAYING NOW IS...
NO, THIS IS ME. BUT SOMETIMES THIS TH-THING JUST STARTS SHOOTING ITS MOUTH OFF...
DON'T THEY SAY THE FACE AFFLICTION SPEAKS?
...
PLEASE, DOCTOR, REMOVE THIS AWFUL THING FROM ME!
IT'S DRIVING ME CRAZY!!
LET ME EXAMINE YOU.
LIE DOWN.
THIS MUST BE AN INFECTION CAUSED BY CAR-BUNCLES...

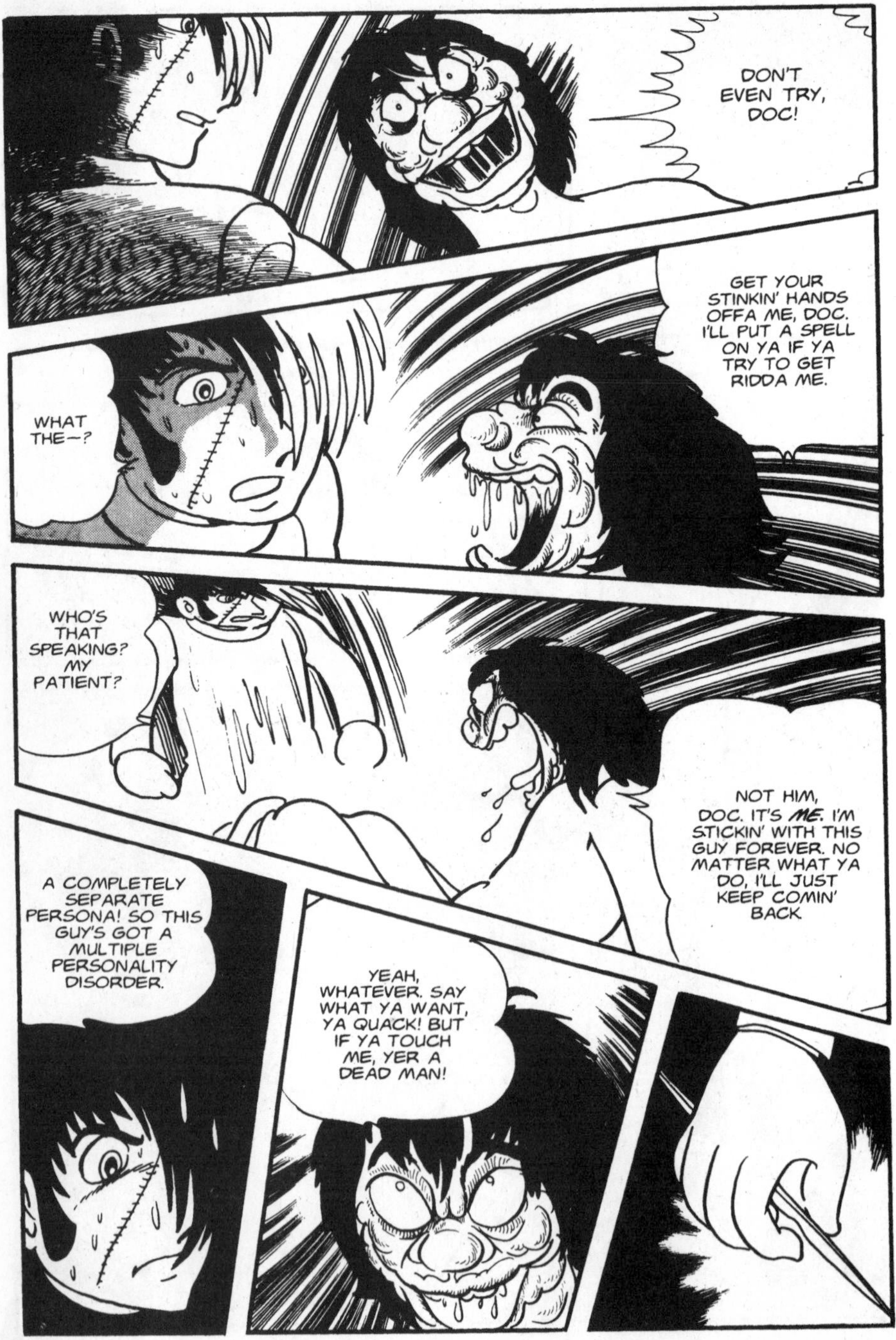
DON'T EVEN TRY, DOC!
WHAT THE—?
GET YOUR STINKIN' HANDS OFFA ME, DOC. I'LL PUT A SPELL ON YA IF YA TRY TO GET RIDDA ME.
WHO'S THAT SPEAKING? MY PATIENT?
NOT HIM, DOC. IT'S *ME*. I'M STICKIN' WITH THIS GUY FOREVER. NO MATTER WHAT YA DO, I'LL JUST KEEP COMIN' BACK.
A COMPLETELY SEPARATE PERSONA! SO THIS GUY'S GOT A MULTIPLE PERSONALITY DISORDER.
YEAH, WHATEVER. SAY WHAT YA WANT, YA QUACK! BUT IF YA TOUCH ME, YER A DEAD MAN!

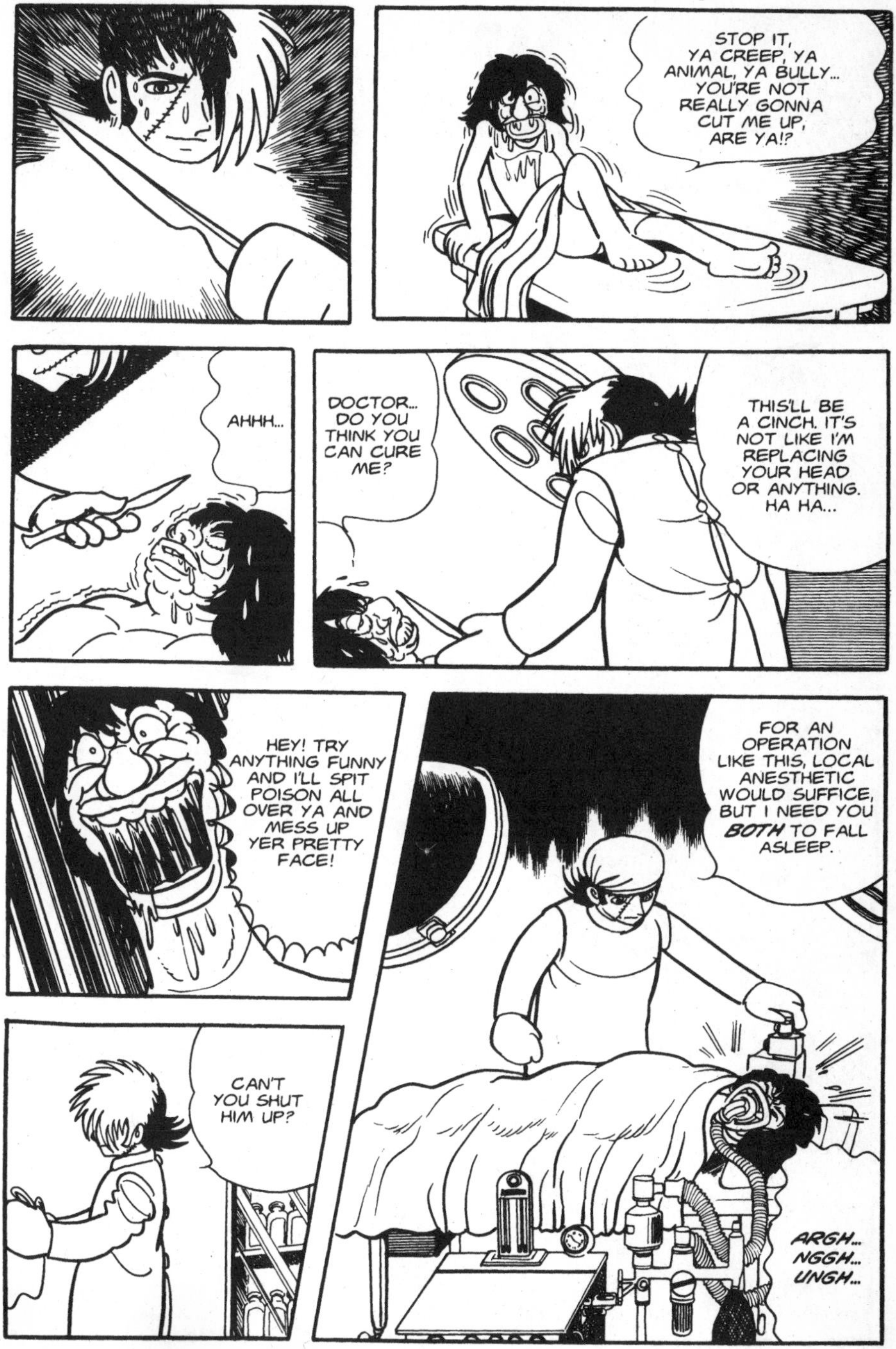
STOP IT, YA CREEP, YA ANIMAL, YA BULLY... YOU'RE NOT REALLY GONNA CUT ME UP, ARE YA!?
AHHH...
DOCTOR... DO YOU THINK YOU CAN CURE ME?
THIS'LL BE A CINCH. IT'S NOT LIKE I'M REPLACING YOUR HEAD OR ANYTHING. HA HA...
HEY! TRY ANYTHING FUNNY AND I'LL SPIT POISON ALL OVER YA AND MESS UP YER PRETTY FACE!
CAN'T YOU SHUT HIM UP?
FOR AN OPERATION LIKE THIS, LOCAL ANESTHETIC WOULD SUFFICE, BUT I NEED YOU *BOTH* TO FALL ASLEEP.
ARGH... NGGH... UNGH...

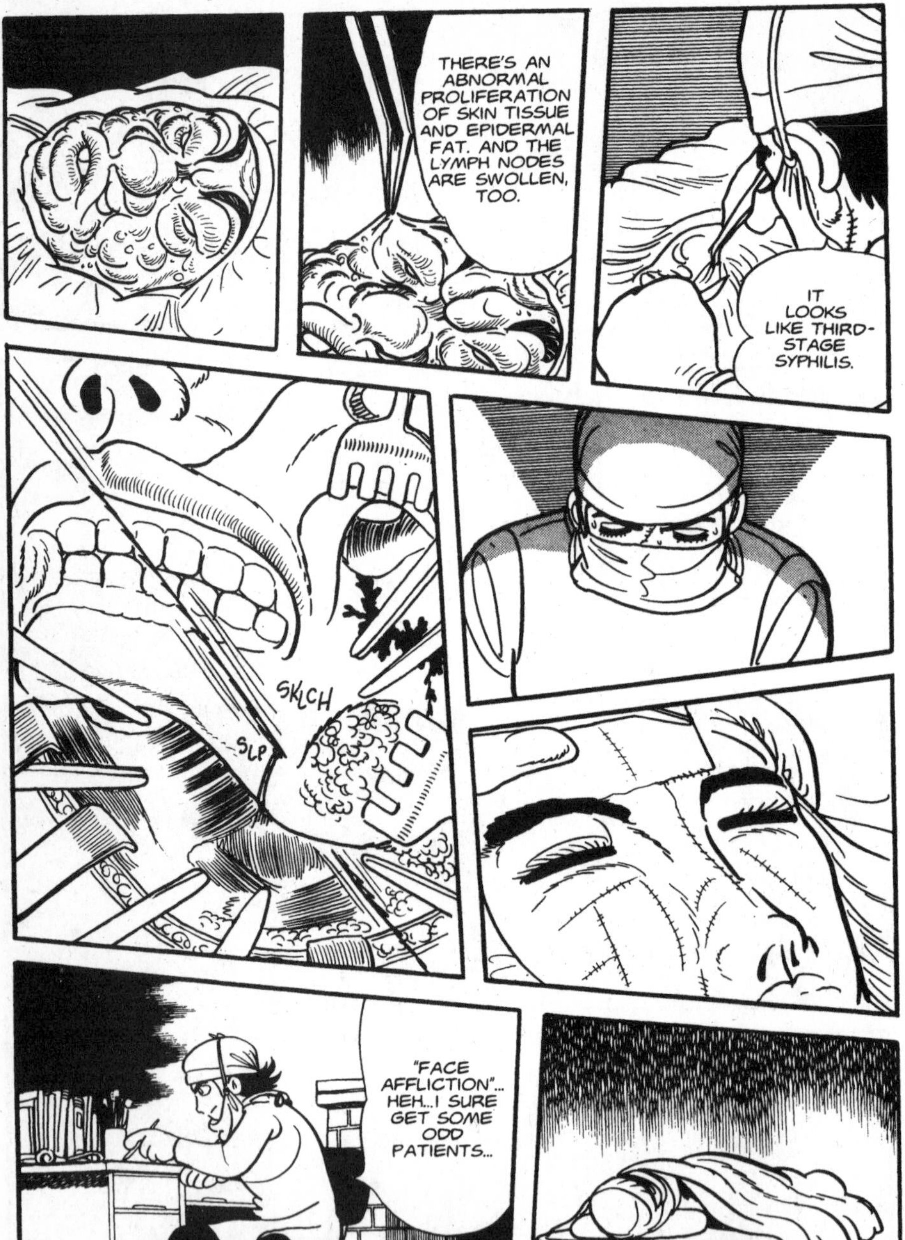
THERE'S AN ABNORMAL PROLIFERATION OF SKIN TISSUE AND EPIDERMAL FAT. AND THE LYMPH NODES ARE SWOLLEN, TOO.
IT LOOKS LIKE THIRD-STAGE SYPHILIS.
SKLCH
SLP
"FACE AFFLICTION"... HEH...I SURE GET SOME ODD PATIENTS...

DOCTOR, AM I CURED!?

YES, YOU SHOULD BE RECOVERING WELL.

MY FACE FEELS FUNNY.

THAT MEANS IT'S HEALING.

I TOLD YA IT'D BE USELESS, YA QUACK!

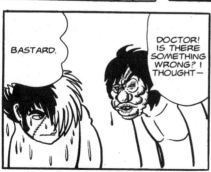

BASTARD.

DOCTOR! IS THERE SOMETHING WRONG? I THOUGHT—

HEY, DOC! I'LL BE HERE TILL HIS DYING DAY.

UNTIL HE CROAKS— THEN I'LL BE KAPUT TOO. HEE, HEE, HEE...

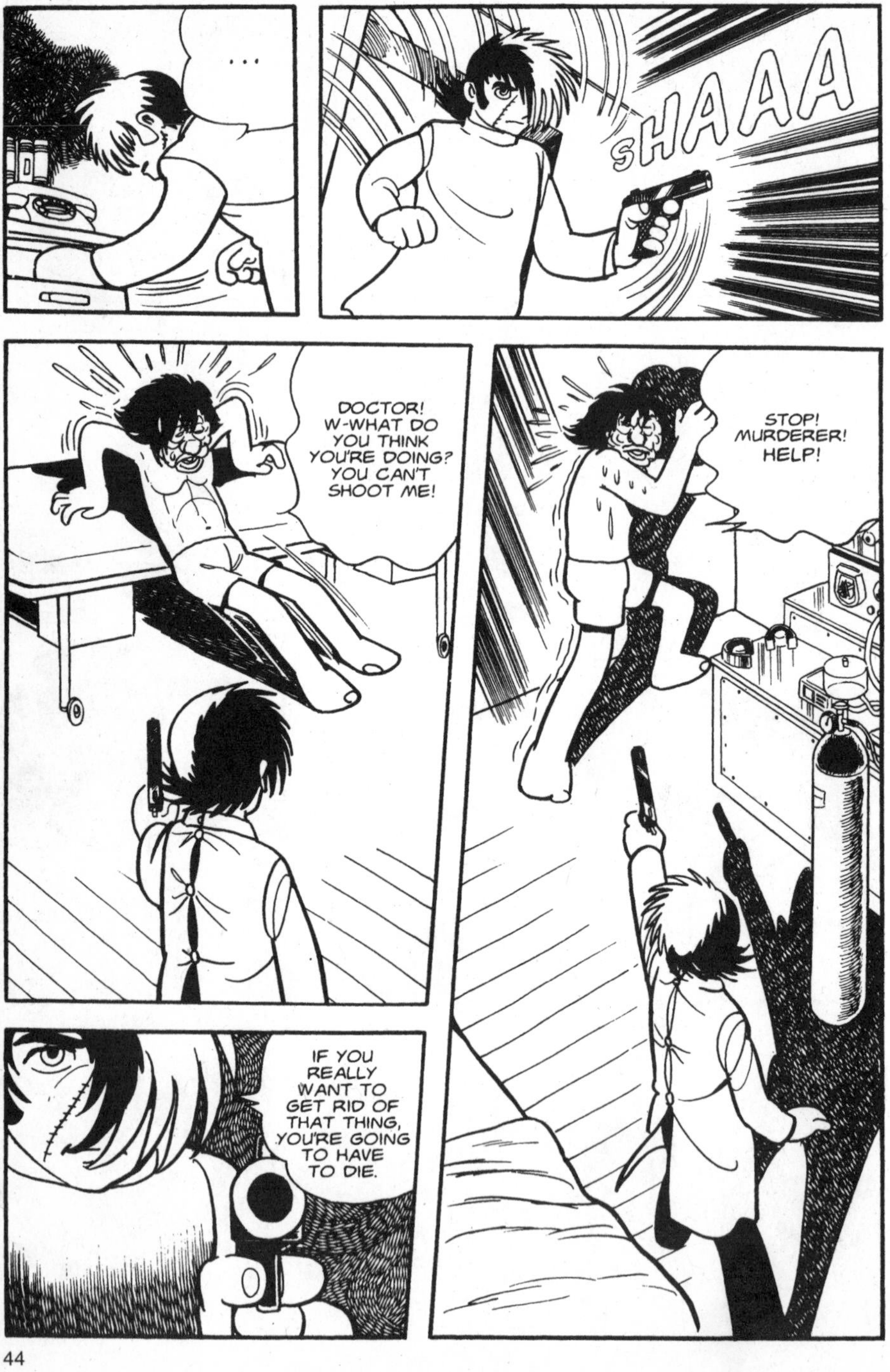
...
SHAAA
DOCTOR! W-WHAT DO YOU THINK YOU'RE DOING? YOU CAN'T SHOOT ME!
IF YOU REALLY WANT TO GET RID OF THAT THING, YOU'RE GOING TO HAVE TO DIE.
STOP! MURDERER! HELP!

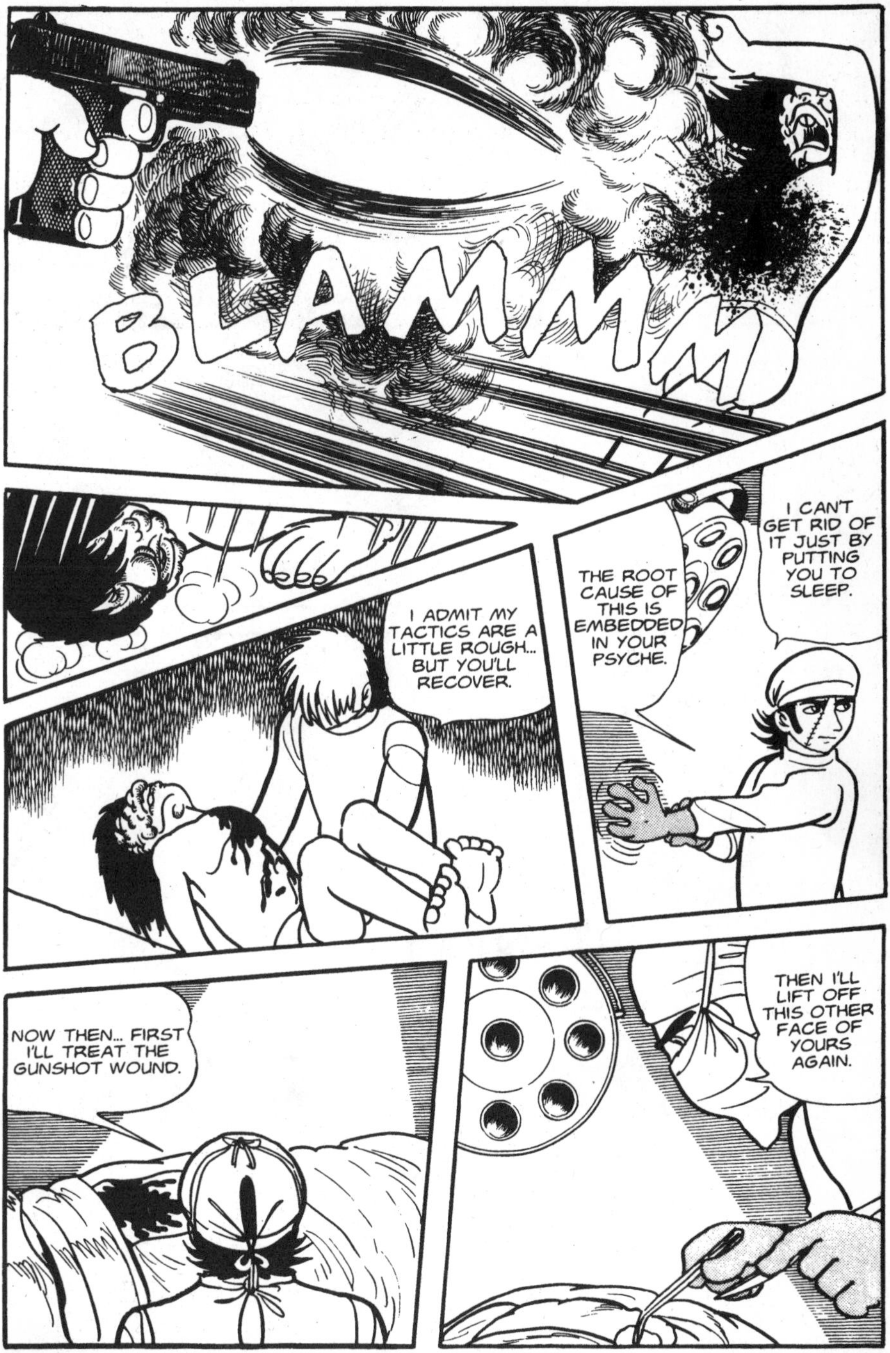
BLAMMM
I ADMIT MY TACTICS ARE A LITTLE ROUGH... BUT YOU'LL RECOVER.
THE ROOT CAUSE OF THIS IS EMBEDDED IN YOUR PSYCHE.
I CAN'T GET RID OF IT JUST BY PUTTING YOU TO SLEEP.
NOW THEN... FIRST I'LL TREAT THE GUNSHOT WOUND.
THEN I'LL LIFT OFF THIS OTHER FACE OF YOURS AGAIN.

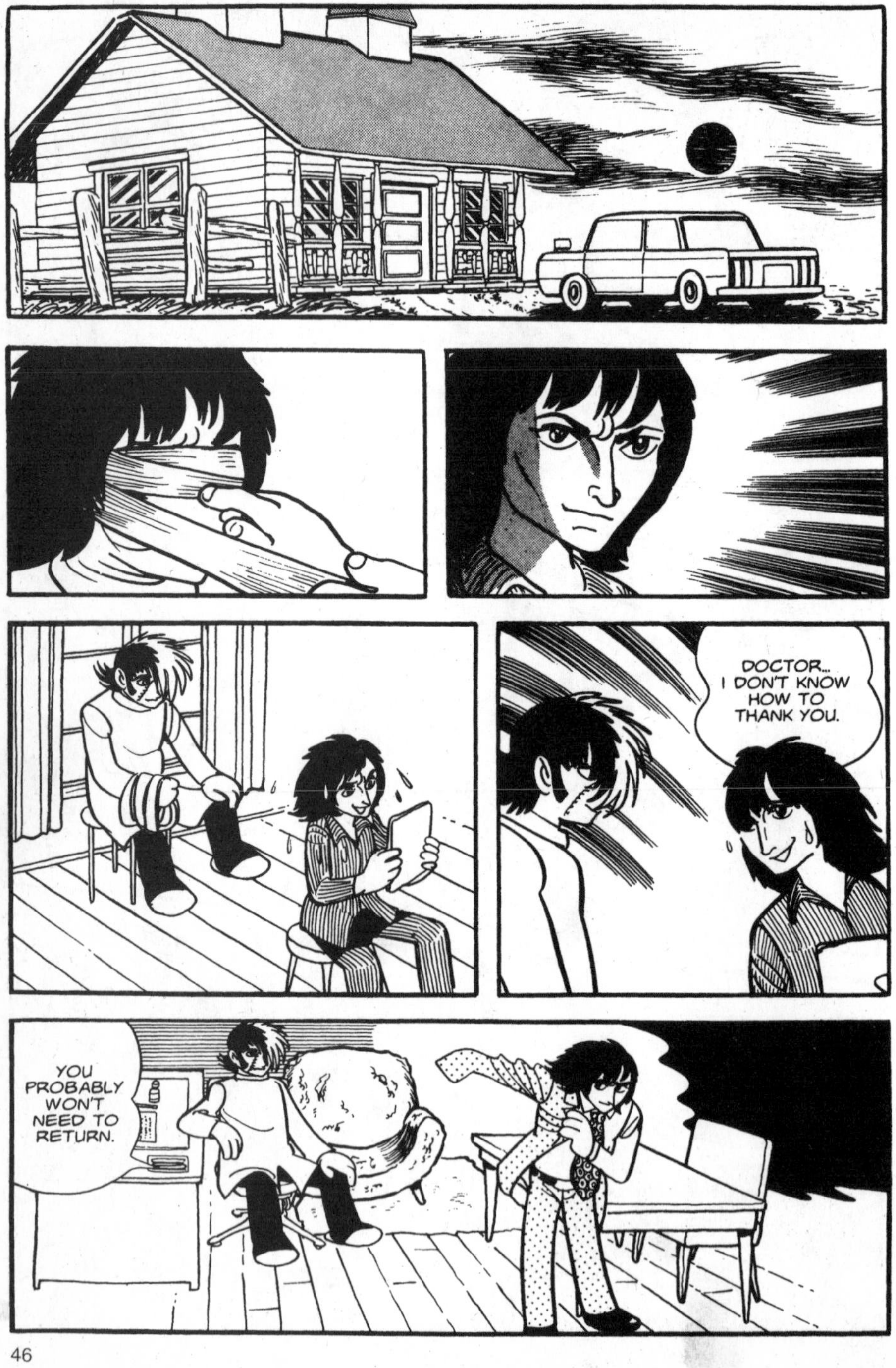
DOCTOR... I DON'T KNOW HOW TO THANK YOU.
YOU PROBABLY WON'T NEED TO RETURN.

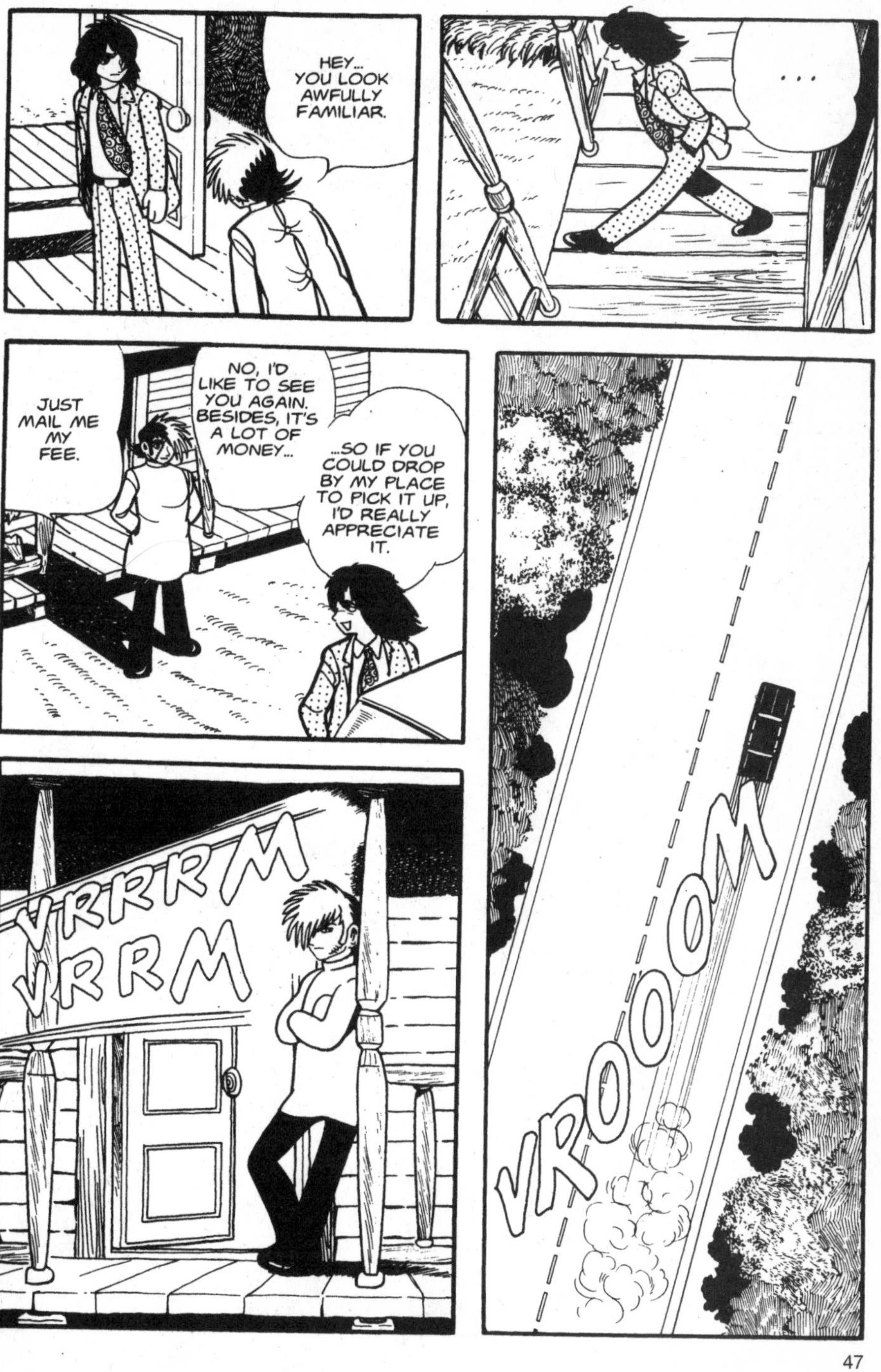
HEY... YOU LOOK AWFULLY FAMILIAR.
...
JUST MAIL ME MY FEE.
NO, I'D LIKE TO SEE YOU AGAIN. BESIDES, IT'S A LOT OF MONEY...
...SO IF YOU COULD DROP BY MY PLACE TO PICK IT UP, I'D REALLY APPRECIATE IT.
VRRRM VRRM
VROOOM

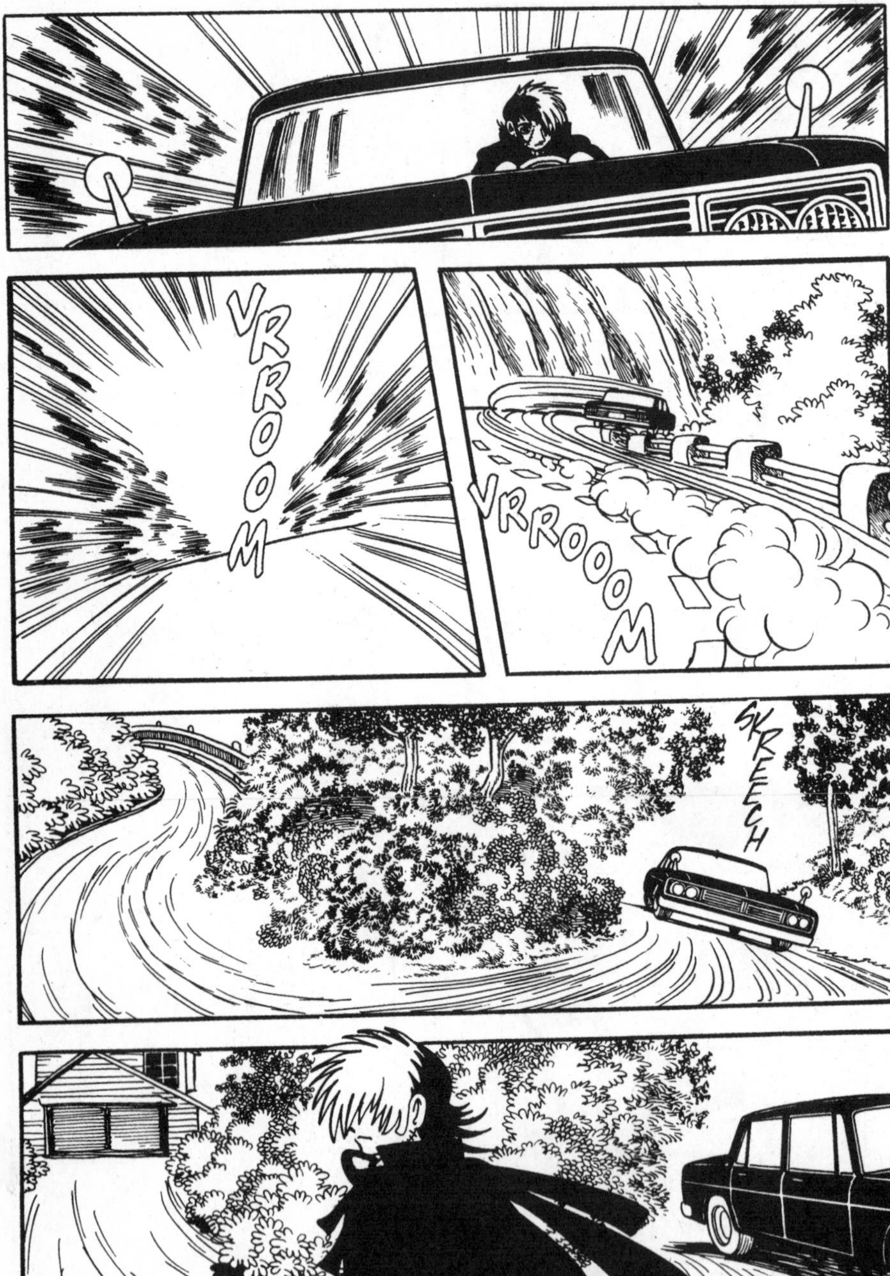
VRROOOM
VRROOM
SKREECH

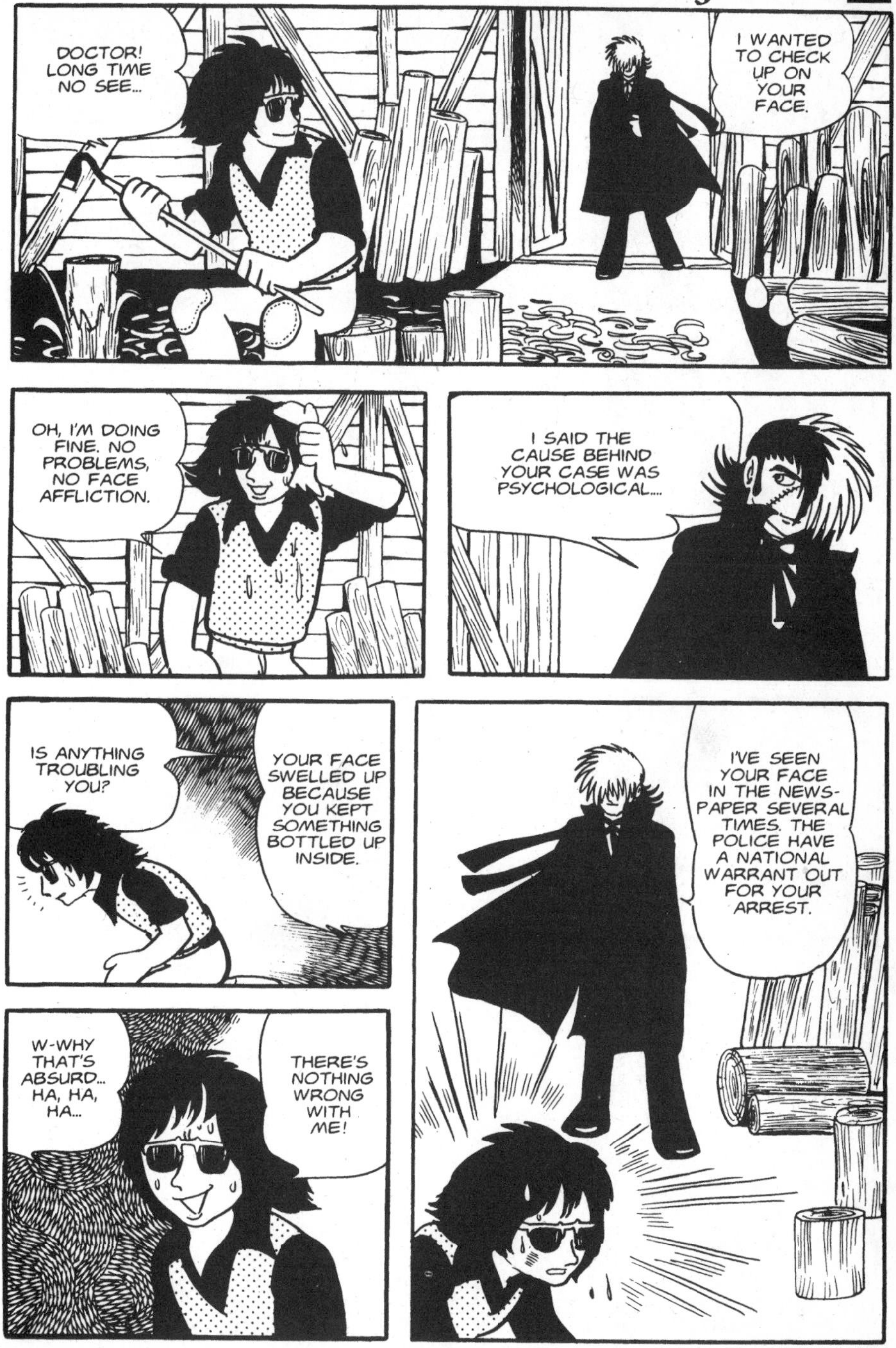
DOCTOR! LONG TIME NO SEE...
I WANTED TO CHECK UP ON YOUR FACE.
OH, I'M DOING FINE. NO PROBLEMS, NO FACE AFFLICTION.
I SAID THE CAUSE BEHIND YOUR CASE WAS PSYCHOLOGICAL....
IS ANYTHING TROUBLING YOU?
YOUR FACE SWELLED UP BECAUSE YOU KEPT SOMETHING BOTTLED UP INSIDE.
W-WHY THAT'S ABSURD... HA, HA, HA...
THERE'S NOTHING WRONG WITH ME!
I'VE SEEN YOUR FACE IN THE NEWS-PAPER SEVERAL TIMES. THE POLICE HAVE A NATIONAL WARRANT OUT FOR YOUR ARREST.

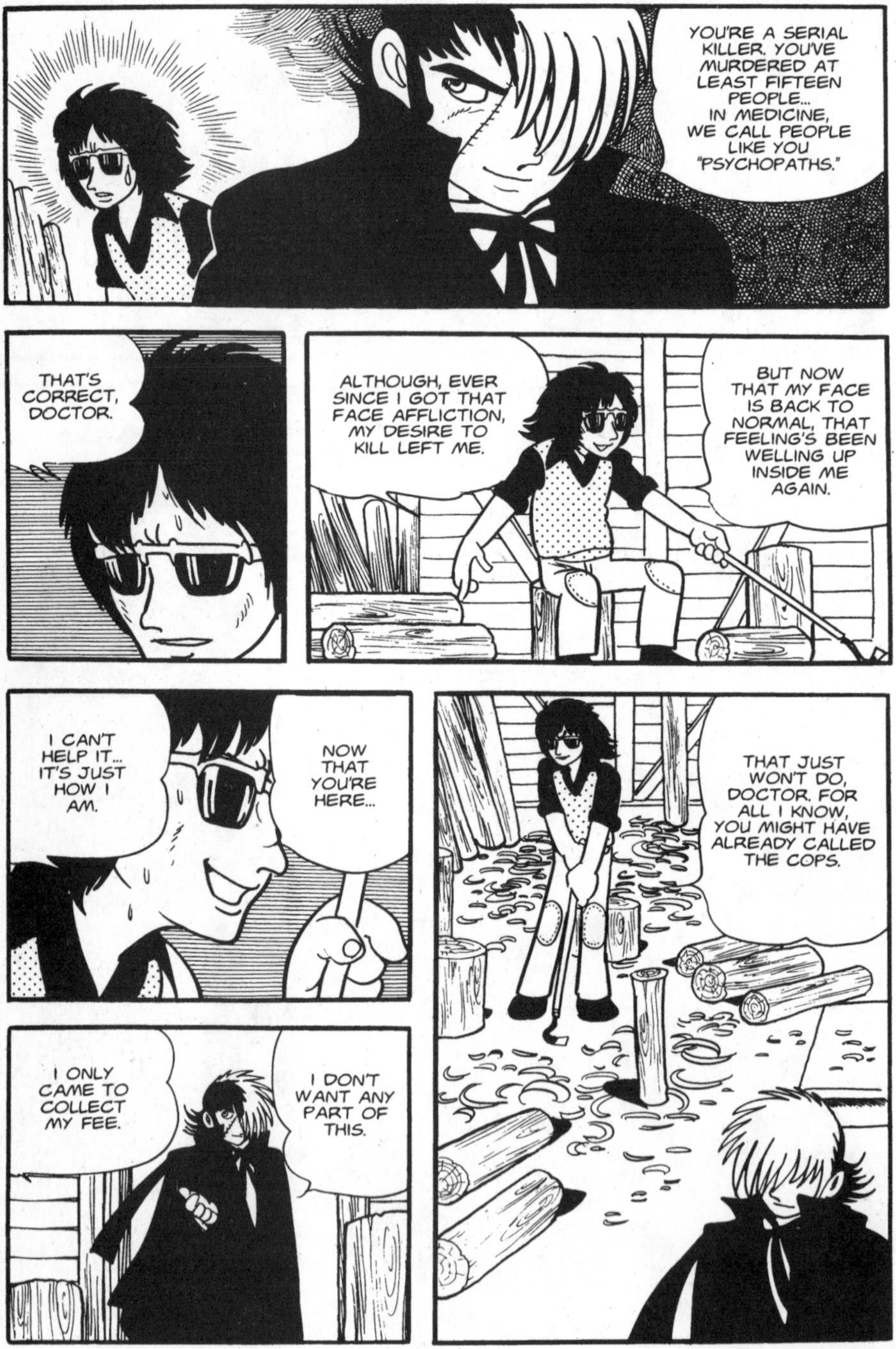
YOU'RE A SERIAL KILLER. YOU'VE MURDERED AT LEAST FIFTEEN PEOPLE... IN MEDICINE, WE CALL PEOPLE LIKE YOU "PSYCHOPATHS."
THAT'S CORRECT, DOCTOR.
ALTHOUGH, EVER SINCE I GOT THAT FACE AFFLICTION, MY DESIRE TO KILL LEFT ME.
BUT NOW THAT MY FACE IS BACK TO NORMAL, THAT FEELING'S BEEN WELLING UP INSIDE ME AGAIN.
I CAN'T HELP IT... IT'S JUST HOW I AM.
NOW THAT YOU'RE HERE...
I ONLY CAME TO COLLECT MY FEE.
I DON'T WANT ANY PART OF THIS.
THAT JUST WON'T DO, DOCTOR. FOR ALL I KNOW, YOU MIGHT HAVE ALREADY CALLED THE COPS.

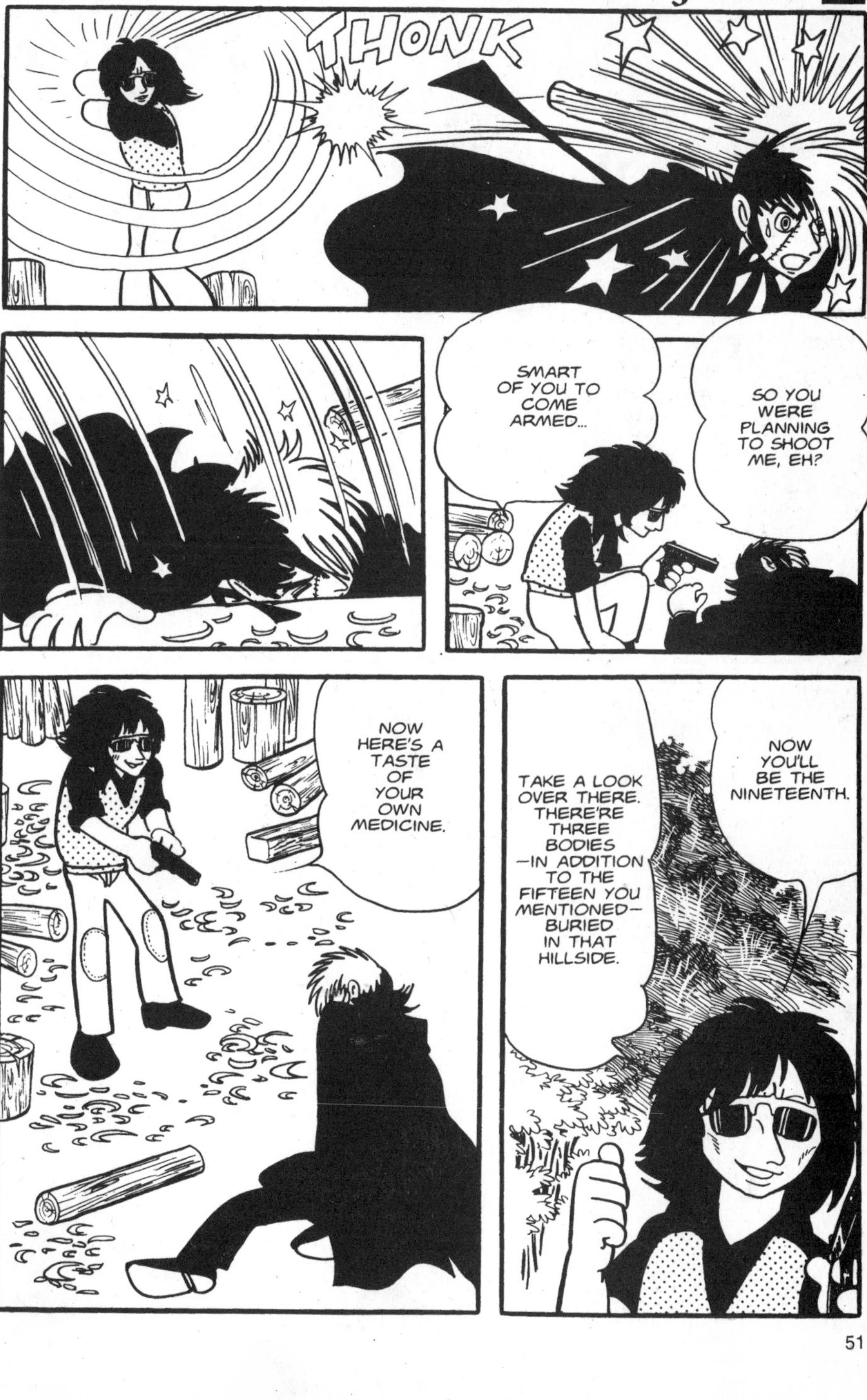
THONK
SMART OF YOU TO COME ARMED...
SO YOU WERE PLANNING TO SHOOT ME, EH?
NOW HERE'S A TASTE OF YOUR OWN MEDICINE.
TAKE A LOOK OVER THERE. THERE'RE THREE BODIES —IN ADDITION TO THE FIFTEEN YOU MENTIONED— BURIED IN THAT HILLSIDE.
NOW YOU'LL BE THE NINETEENTH.

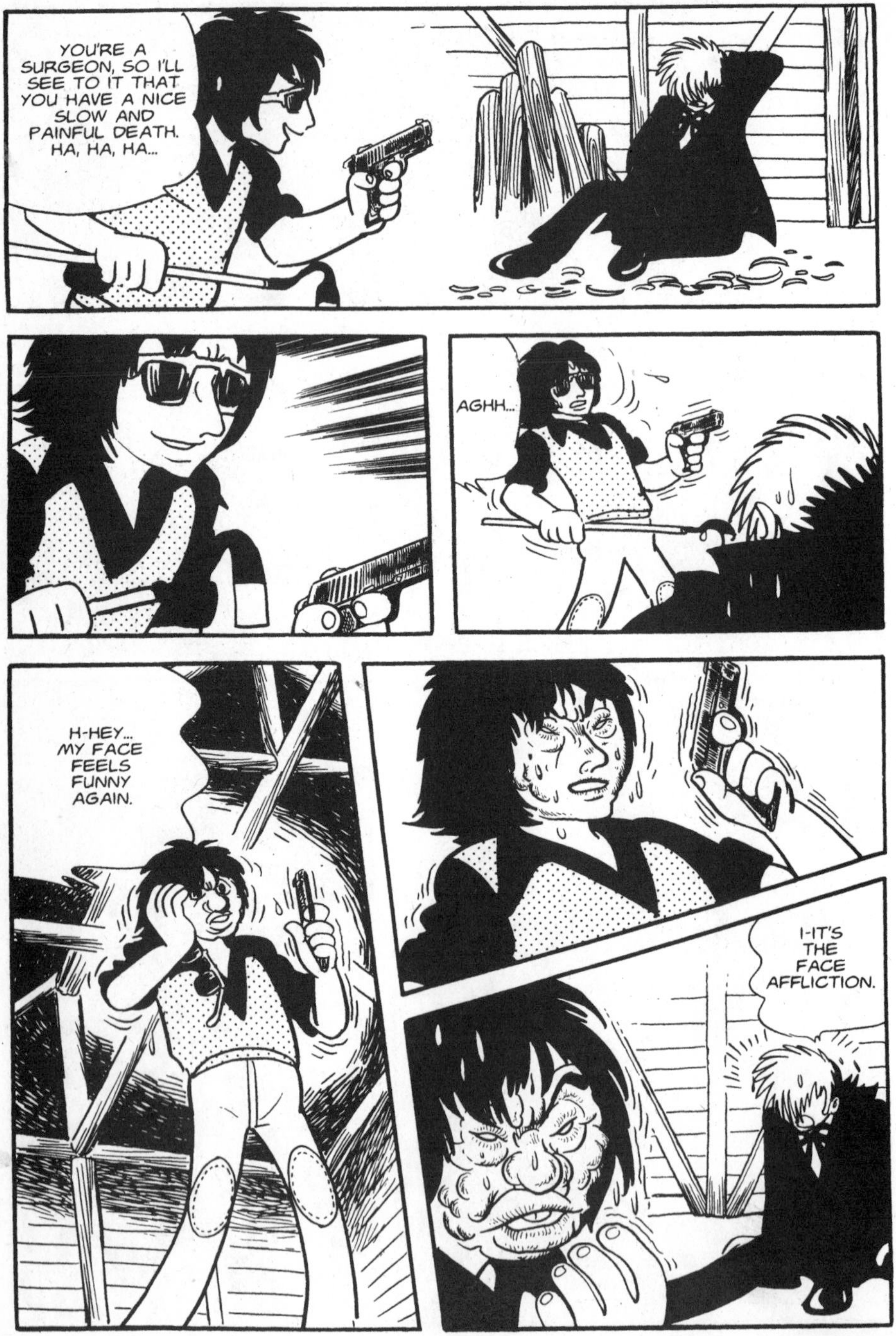
YOU'RE A SURGEON, SO I'LL SEE TO IT THAT YOU HAVE A NICE SLOW AND PAINFUL DEATH. HA, HA, HA...
AGHH...
H-HEY... MY FACE FEELS FUNNY AGAIN.
I-IT'S THE FACE AFFLICTION.

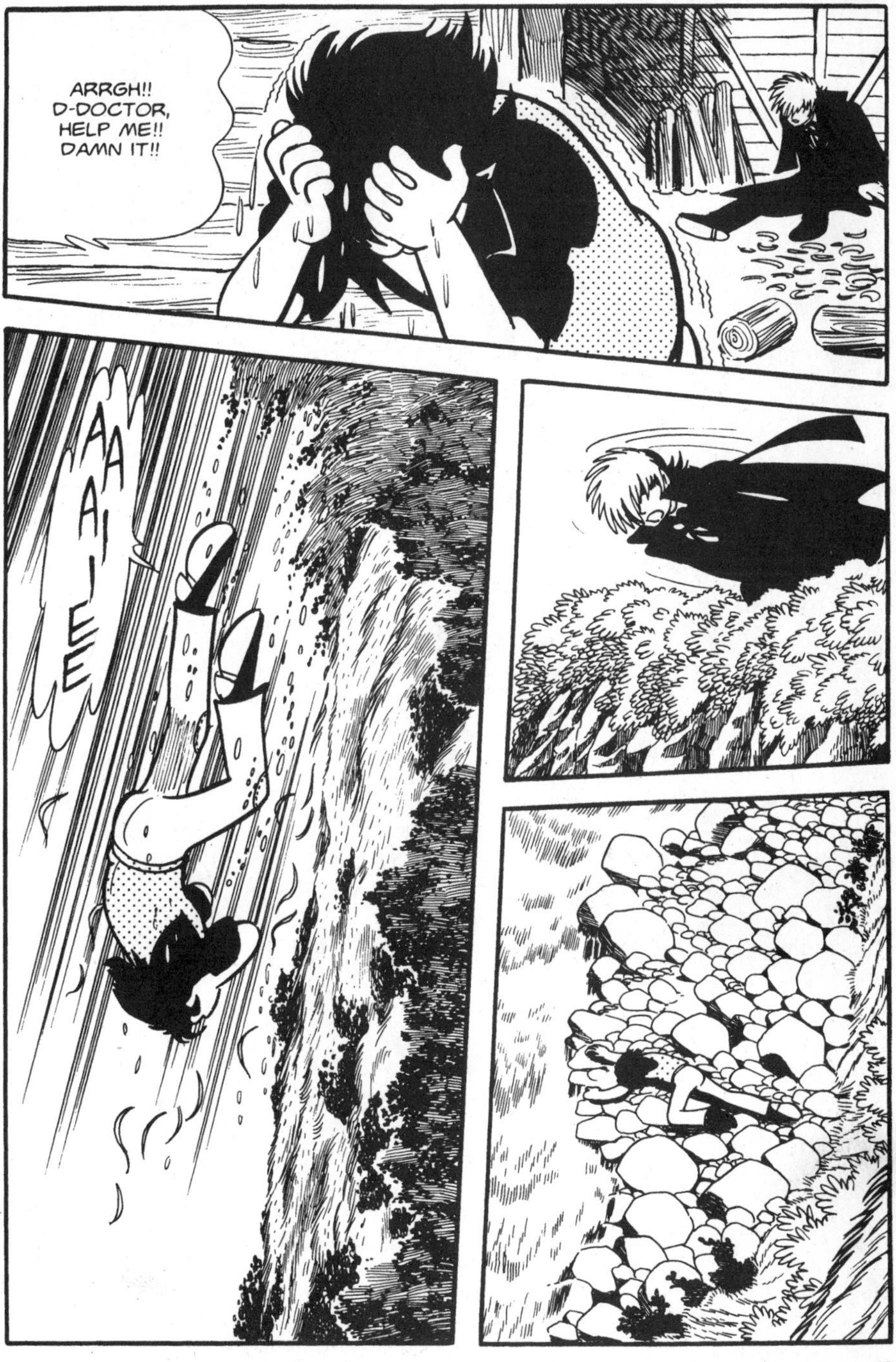
ARRGH!! D-DOCTOR, HELP ME!! DAMN IT!!
AAAIIEEE

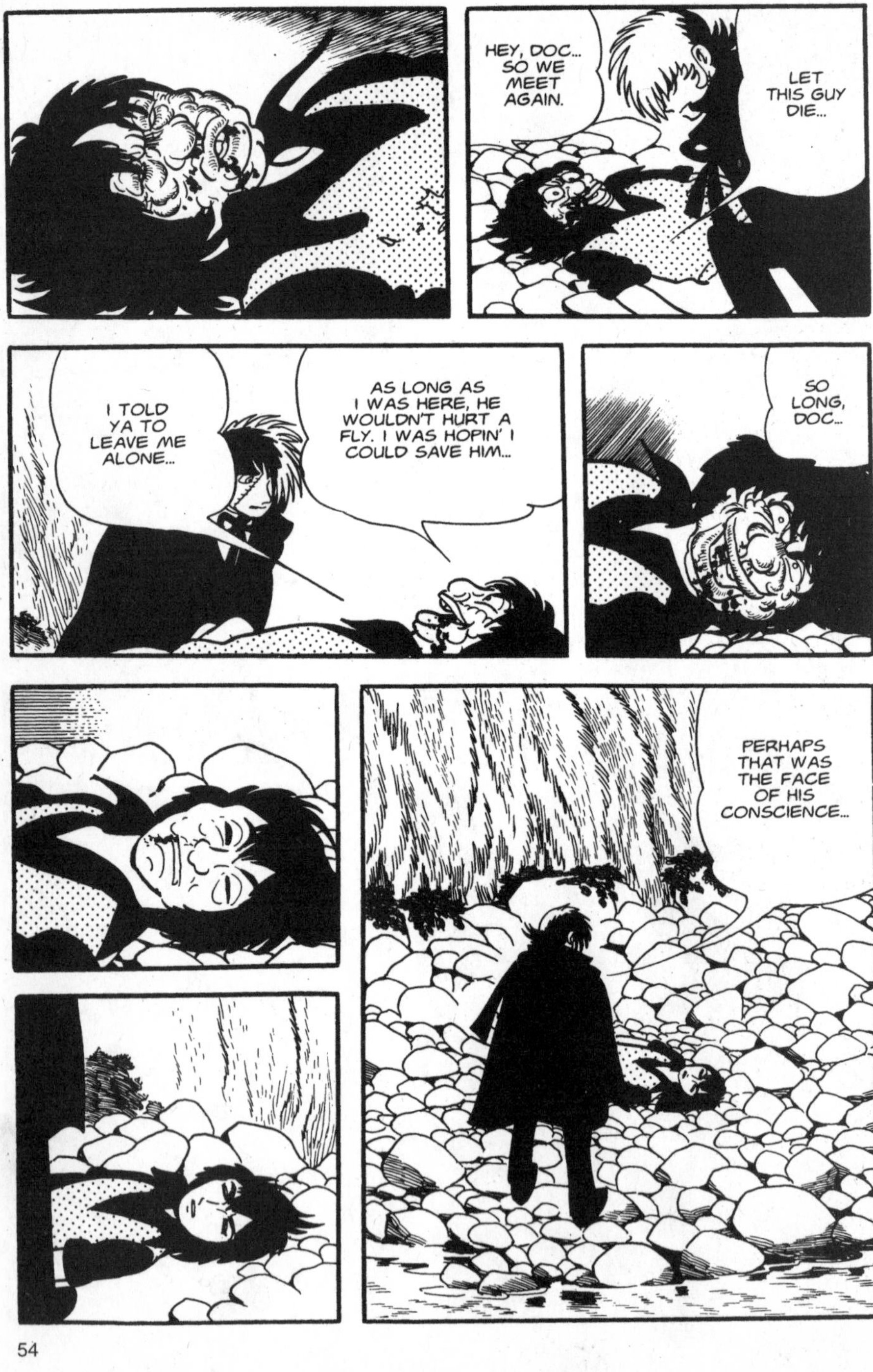
HEY, DOC... SO WE MEET AGAIN.
LET THIS GUY DIE...
I TOLD YA TO LEAVE ME ALONE...
AS LONG AS I WAS HERE, HE WOULDN'T HURT A FLY. I WAS HOPIN' I COULD SAVE HIM...
SO LONG, DOC...
PERHAPS THAT WAS THE FACE OF HIS CONSCIENCE...

OPERATION THREE

THE TERATOGENOUS CYSTOMA

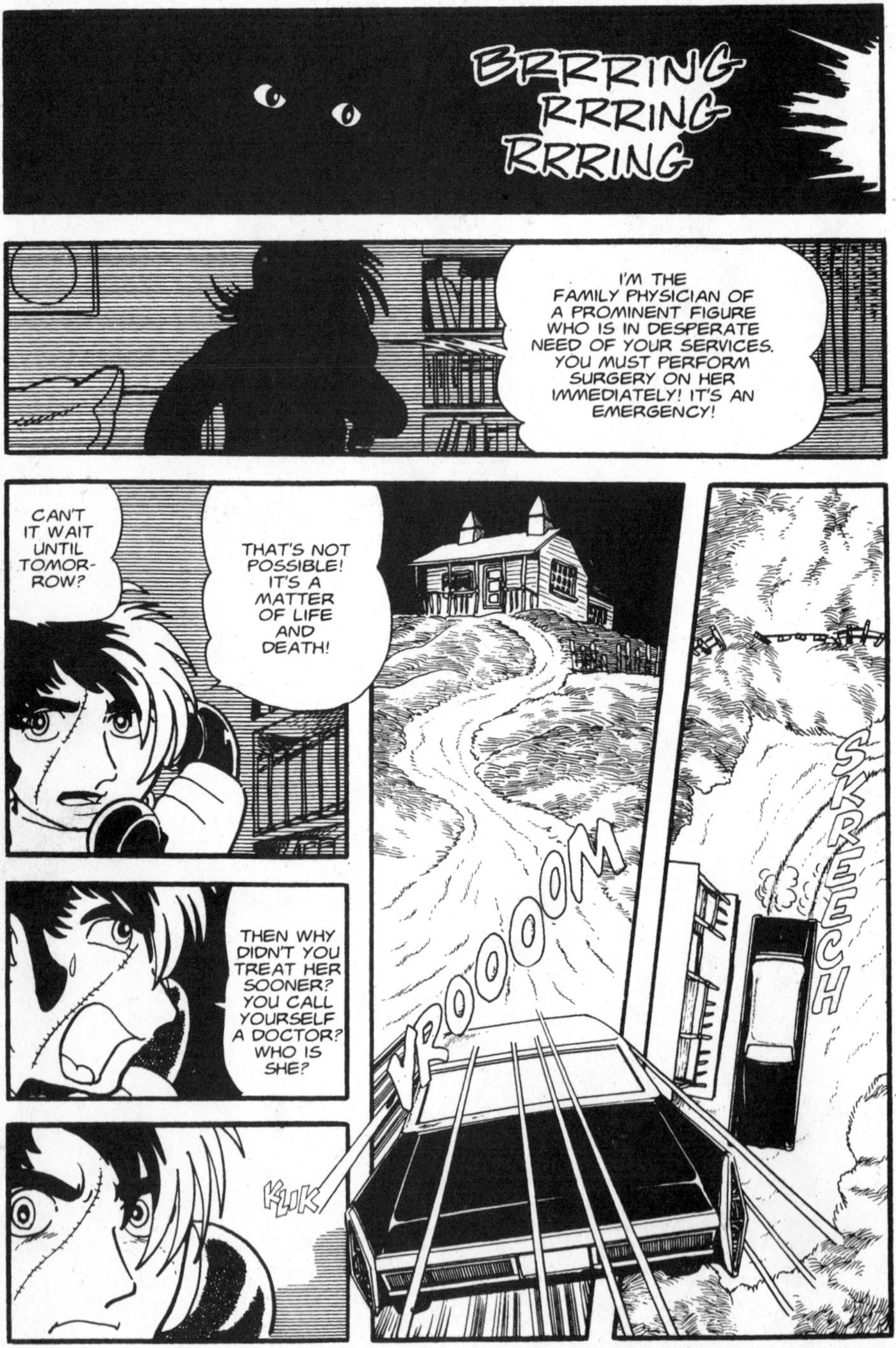
BRRRING RRRING RRRING
I'M THE FAMILY PHYSICIAN OF A PROMINENT FIGURE WHO IS IN DESPERATE NEED OF YOUR SERVICES. YOU MUST PERFORM SURGERY ON HER IMMEDIATELY! IT'S AN EMERGENCY!
CAN'T IT WAIT UNTIL TOMOR-ROW?
THAT'S NOT POSSIBLE! IT'S A MATTER OF LIFE AND DEATH!
THEN WHY DIDN'T YOU TREAT HER SOONER? YOU CALL YOURSELF A DOCTOR? WHO IS SHE?
KLIK
VROOOOM
SKREECH

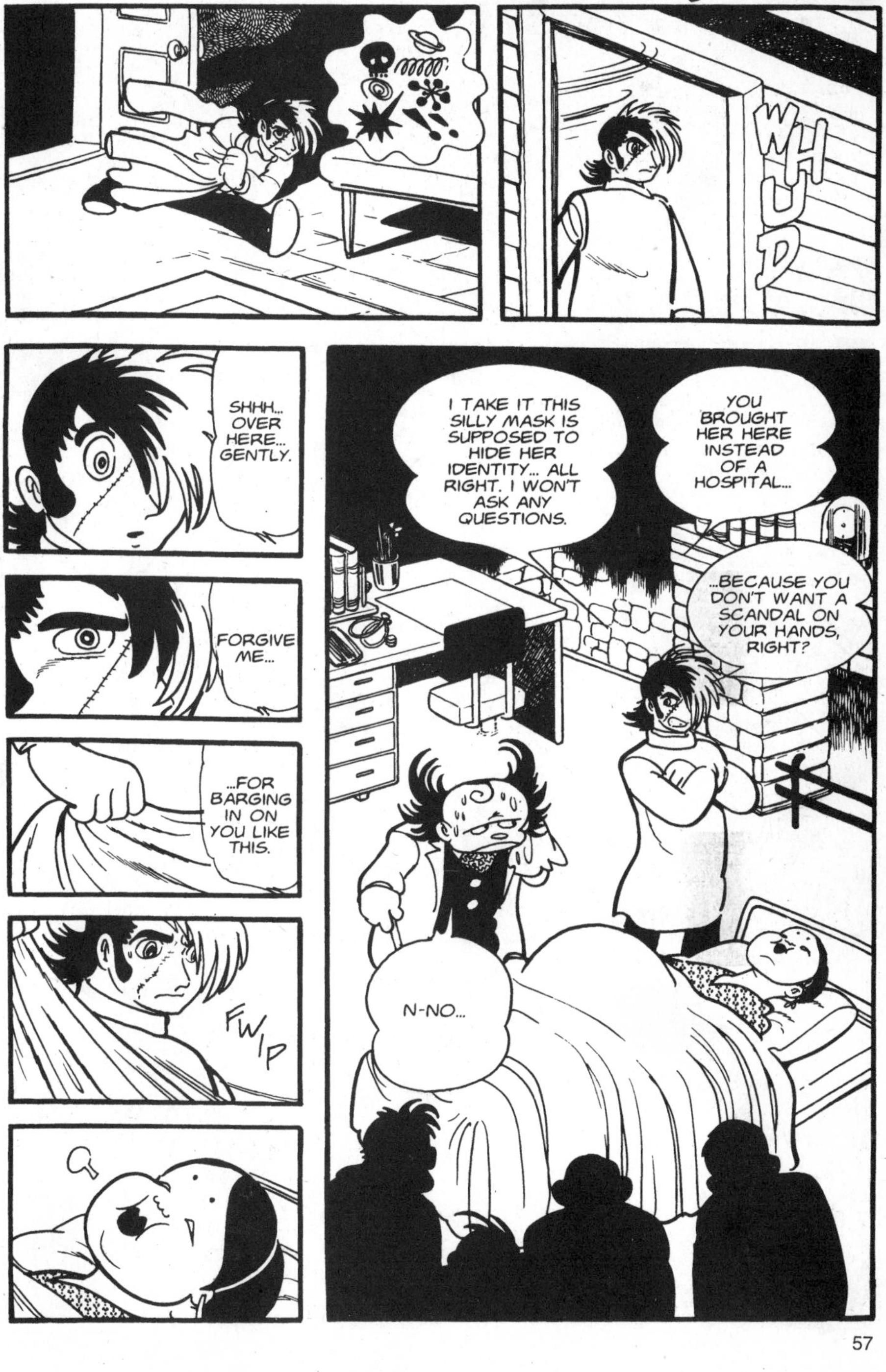
WHUD
SHHH... OVER HERE... GENTLY.
FORGIVE ME...
...FOR BARGING IN ON YOU LIKE THIS.
FWIP
I TAKE IT THIS SILLY MASK IS SUPPOSED TO HIDE HER IDENTITY... ALL RIGHT. I WON'T ASK ANY QUESTIONS.
YOU BROUGHT HER HERE INSTEAD OF A HOSPITAL...
...BECAUSE YOU DON'T WANT A SCANDAL ON YOUR HANDS, RIGHT?
N-NO...

I AM DOCTOR KANI FROM YOKOBAI HOSPITAL...

NO HOSPITAL IN THE WORLD IS CAPABLE OF PERFORMING THIS SURGERY!

YOU'RE OUR ONLY HOPE.

NICE TO KNOW YOU HAVE FAITH IN ME...

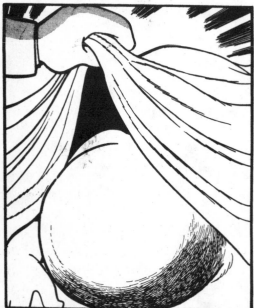

A GROWTH, EH? A *HUGE* ONE...

A CYSTOMA...

WHY DON'T YOU JUST REMOVE IT?

THIS CYSTOMA IS... *ABNORMAL.*

LET'S SEE NOW...

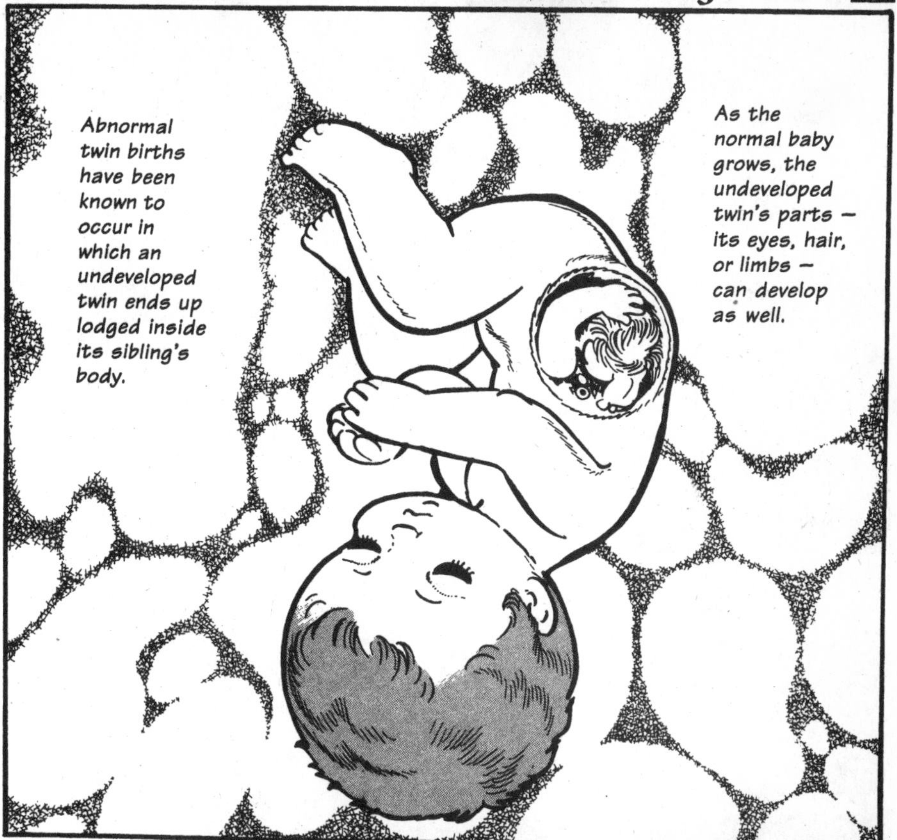
As the normal baby grows, the undeveloped twin's parts — its eyes, hair, or limbs — can develop as well.
Abnormal twin births have been known to occur in which an undeveloped twin ends up lodged inside its sibling's body.

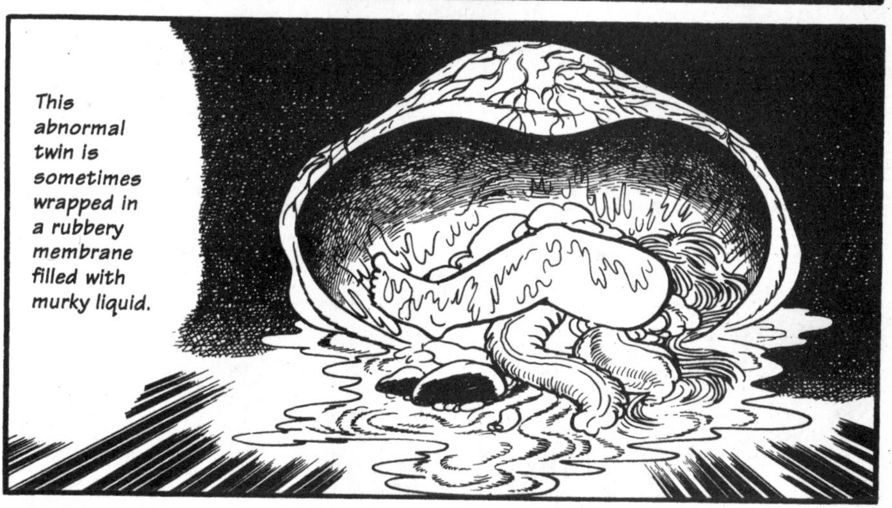
This abnormal twin is sometimes wrapped in a rubbery membrane filled with murky liquid.

The sack of membrane can grow to the point where it protrudes like a growth. It's called a TERATOGENOUS CYSTOMA.

HERE IS THE X-RAY.

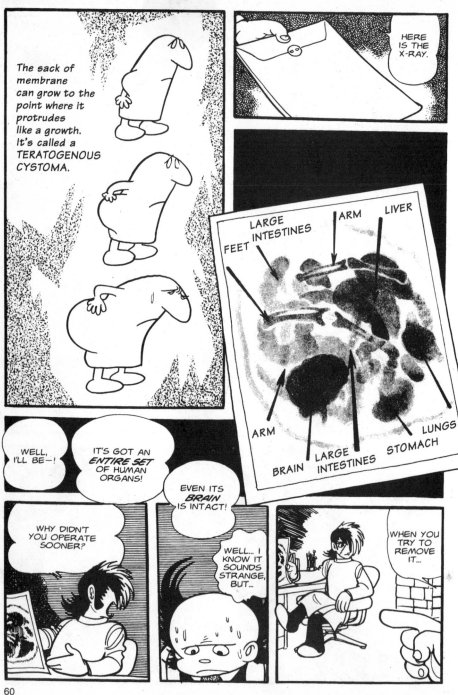

LARGE INTESTINES

FEET

ARM

LIVER

ARM

BRAIN

LARGE INTESTINES

STOMACH

LUNGS

WELL, I'LL BE—!

IT'S GOT AN *ENTIRE SET* OF HUMAN ORGANS!

EVEN ITS *BRAIN* IS INTACT!

WHY DIDN'T YOU OPERATE SOONER?

WELL... I KNOW IT SOUNDS STRANGE, BUT...

WHEN YOU TRY TO REMOVE IT...

60

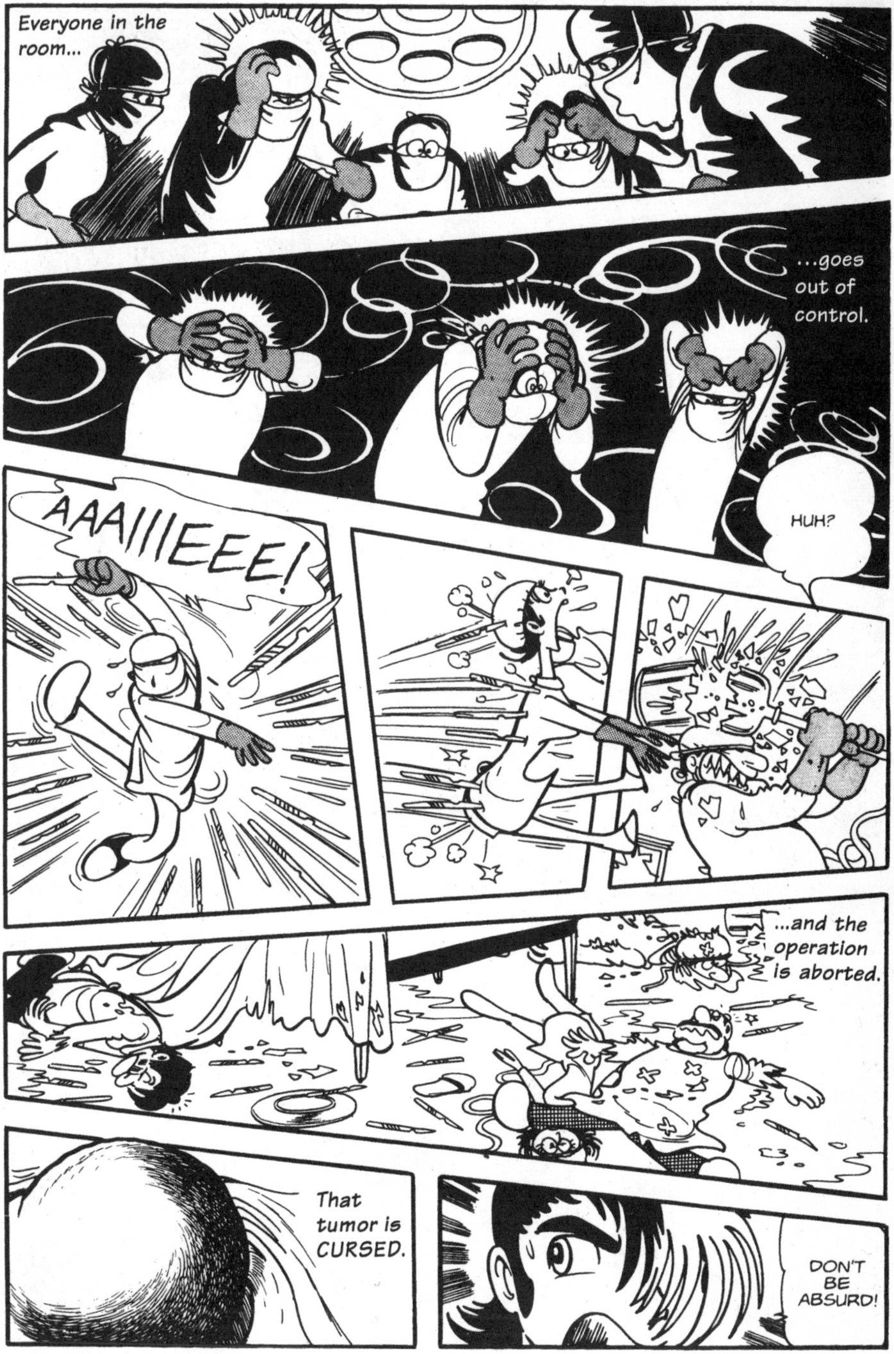
Everyone in the room...
...goes out of control.
AAAIIIEEEE!
HUH?
...and the operation is aborted.
That tumor is CURSED.
DON'T BE ABSURD!

I'VE HEARD OF A MUMMY'S CURSE, BUT...
A *TUMOR'S* CURSE? HA, HA, HA...
WELL...
SHALL I ASSIST YOU, THEN?
NO THANKS. YOU CAN ALL LEAVE THE ROOM.
NOW THEN... I'LL BEGIN...
THIS "CURSED" OPERATION...
AARRGH

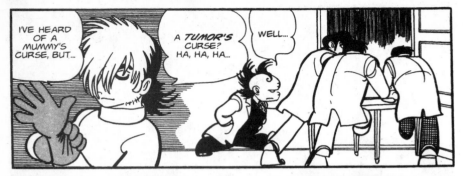

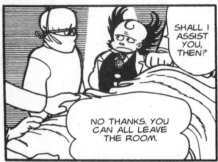

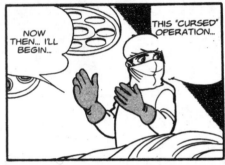

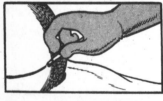

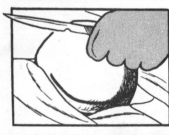

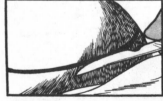

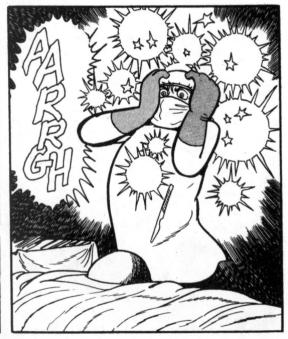

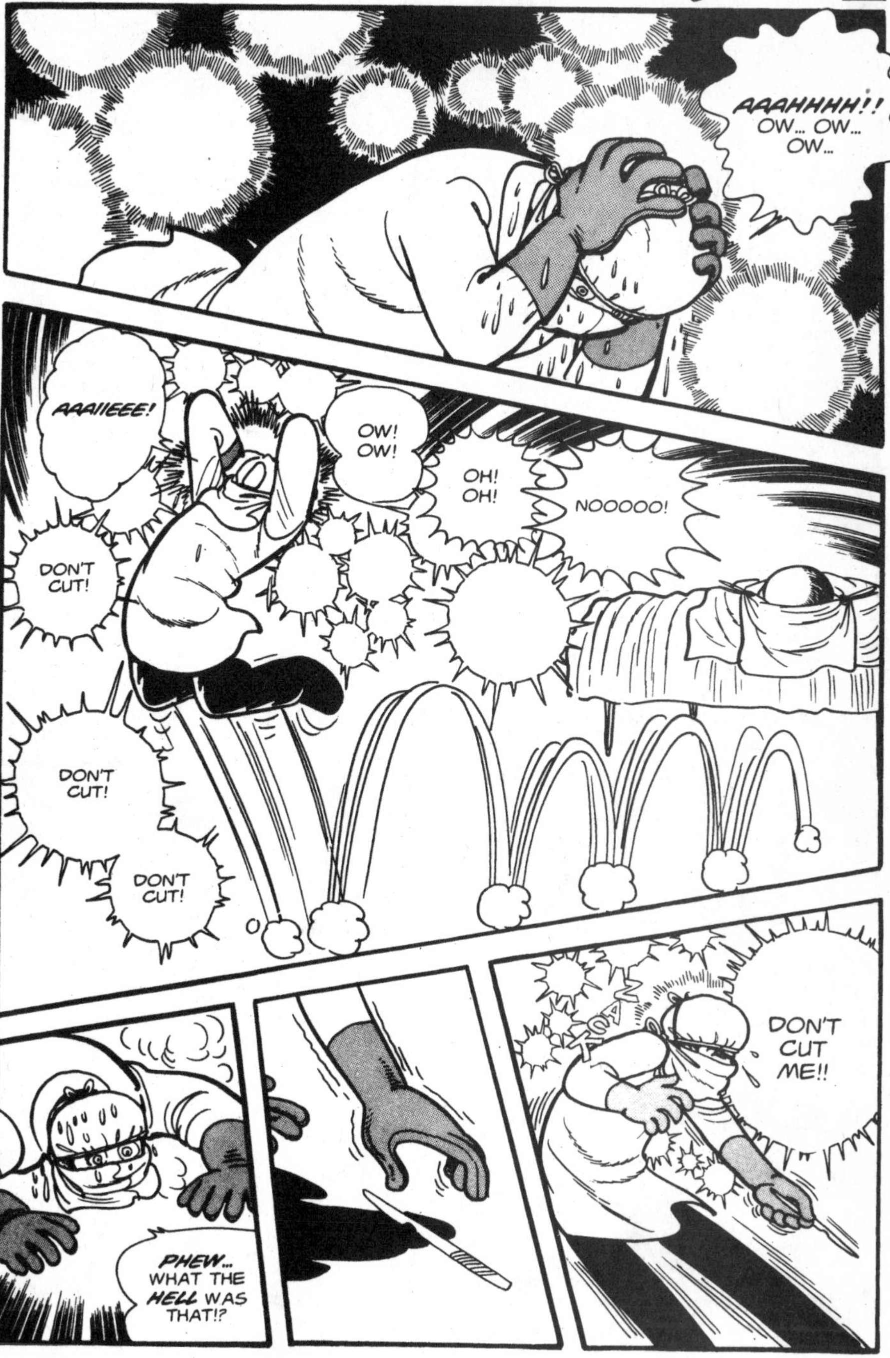
AAAHHHH!! OW... OW... OW...
NOOOOO!
OH! OH!
OW! OW!
AAAIIEEE!
DON'T CUT!
DON'T CUT!
DON'T CUT!
DON'T CUT ME!!
PHEW... WHAT THE HELL WAS THAT!?

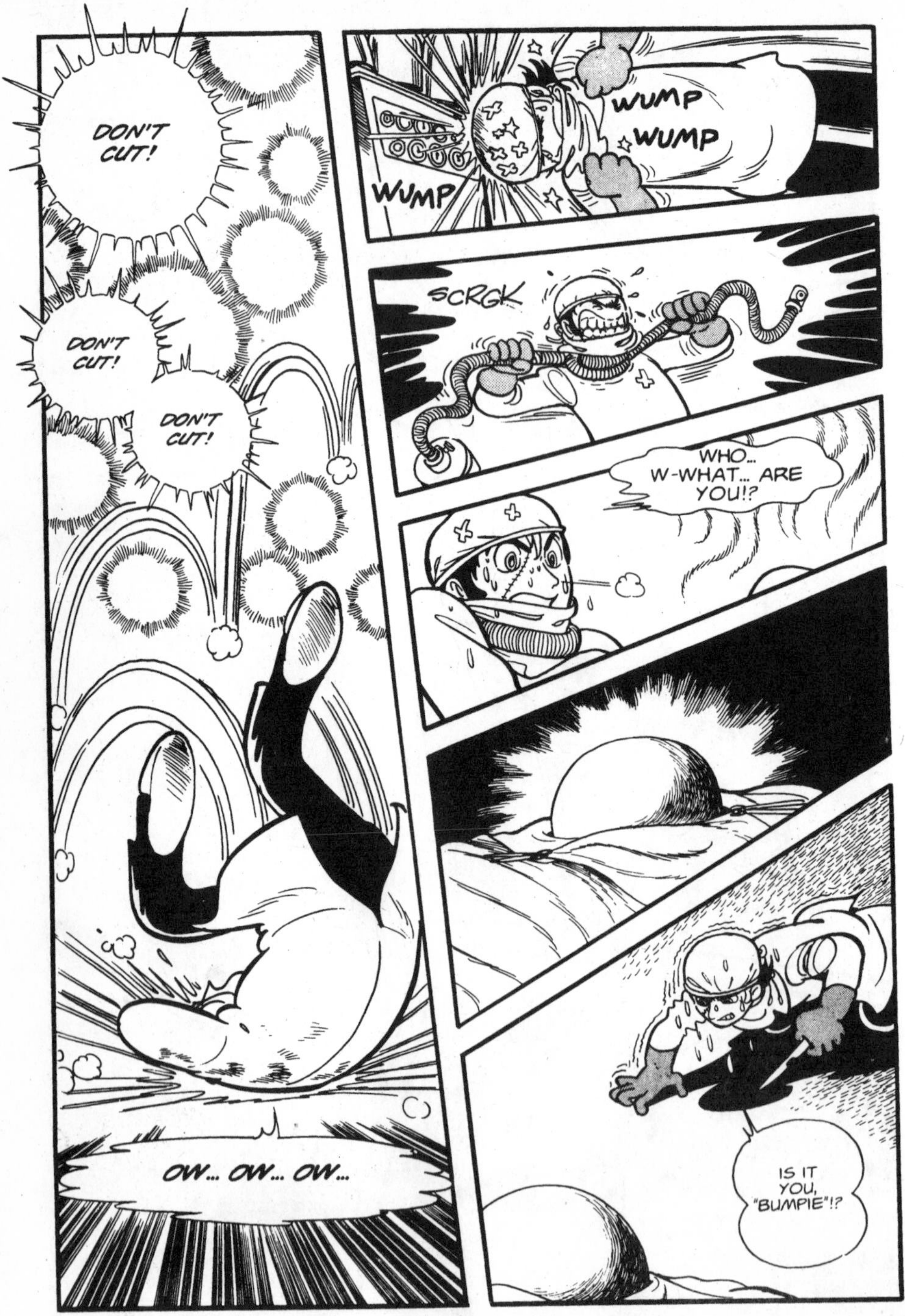
DON'T CUT!
DON'T CUT!
DON'T CUT!
OW... OW... OW...
WUMP
WUMP
WUMP
SCRGK
WHO... W-WHAT... ARE YOU!?
IS IT YOU, "BUMPIE"!?

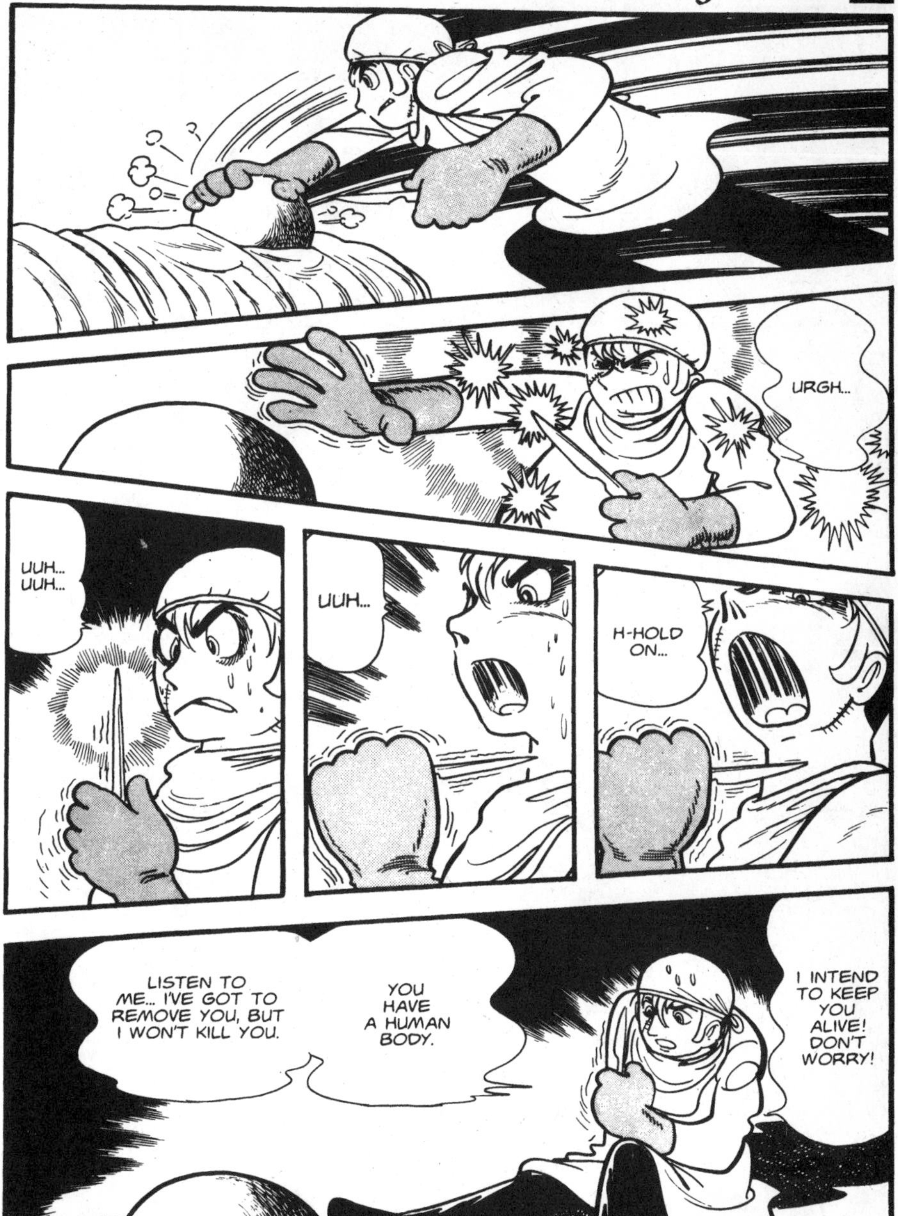
URGH...
UUH... UUH...
UUH...
H-HOLD ON...
LISTEN TO ME... I'VE GOT TO REMOVE YOU, BUT I WON'T KILL YOU.
YOU HAVE A HUMAN BODY.
I INTEND TO KEEP YOU ALIVE! DON'T WORRY!

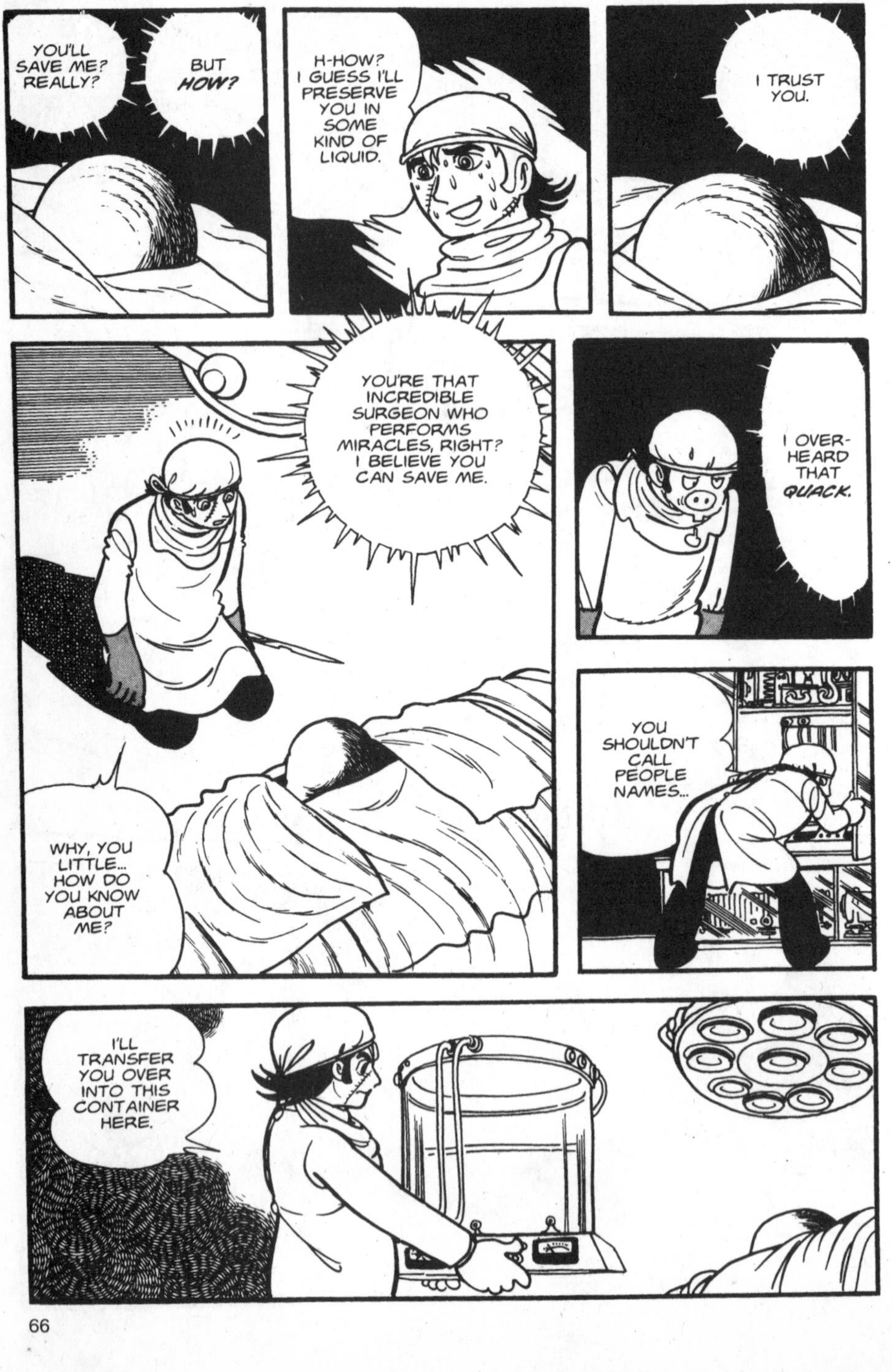
YOU'LL SAVE ME? REALLY?
BUT *HOW?*
H-HOW? I GUESS I'LL PRESERVE YOU IN SOME KIND OF LIQUID.
I TRUST YOU.
YOU'RE THAT INCREDIBLE SURGEON WHO PERFORMS MIRACLES, RIGHT? I BELIEVE YOU CAN SAVE ME.
WHY, YOU LITTLE... HOW DO YOU KNOW ABOUT ME?
I OVER-HEARD THAT *QUACK.*
YOU SHOULDN'T CALL PEOPLE NAMES...
I'LL TRANSFER YOU OVER INTO THIS CONTAINER HERE.

I CAN KEEP YOU ALIVE BY PRESERVING YOU IN THIS FLUID.
ALL RIGHT THEN.
NOW DON'T INTERFERE.
ZING
STOP THAT.
HERE'S SOME ANESTHETIC.
...
TAKE A NAP.

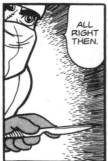

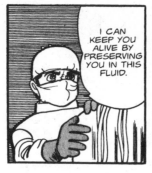

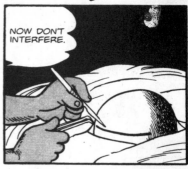

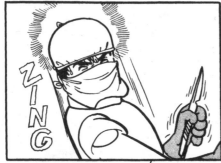

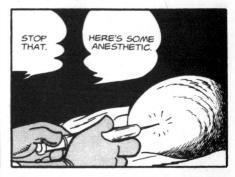

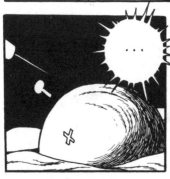

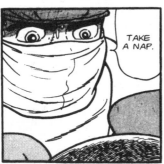

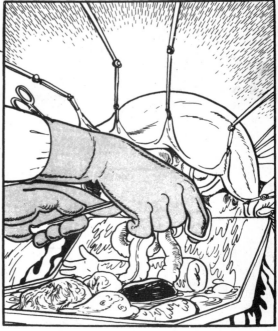

DONE.

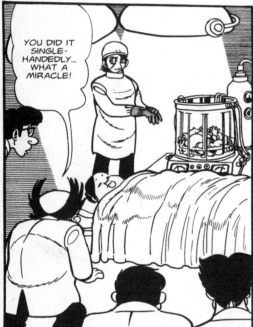

YOU DID IT SINGLE-HANDEDLY... WHAT A MIRACLE!

THE GROWTH IS PRESERVED IN THIS LIQUID. I'M GOING TO KEEP IT ALIVE.

WHAT-EVER FOR!?

NO POINT IN LETTING IT DIE.

GET RID OF THAT THING!

IT'S GROTESQUE!

YOU'LL BE CURSED, I TELL YOU.

IT'S UP TO ME WHETHER I DECIDE TO...

...TOSS IT OUT... OR INCINERATE IT... OR...

UNLESS YOU'D PREFER TO FORK OVER A MILLION YEN FOR IT! HA, HA, HA...

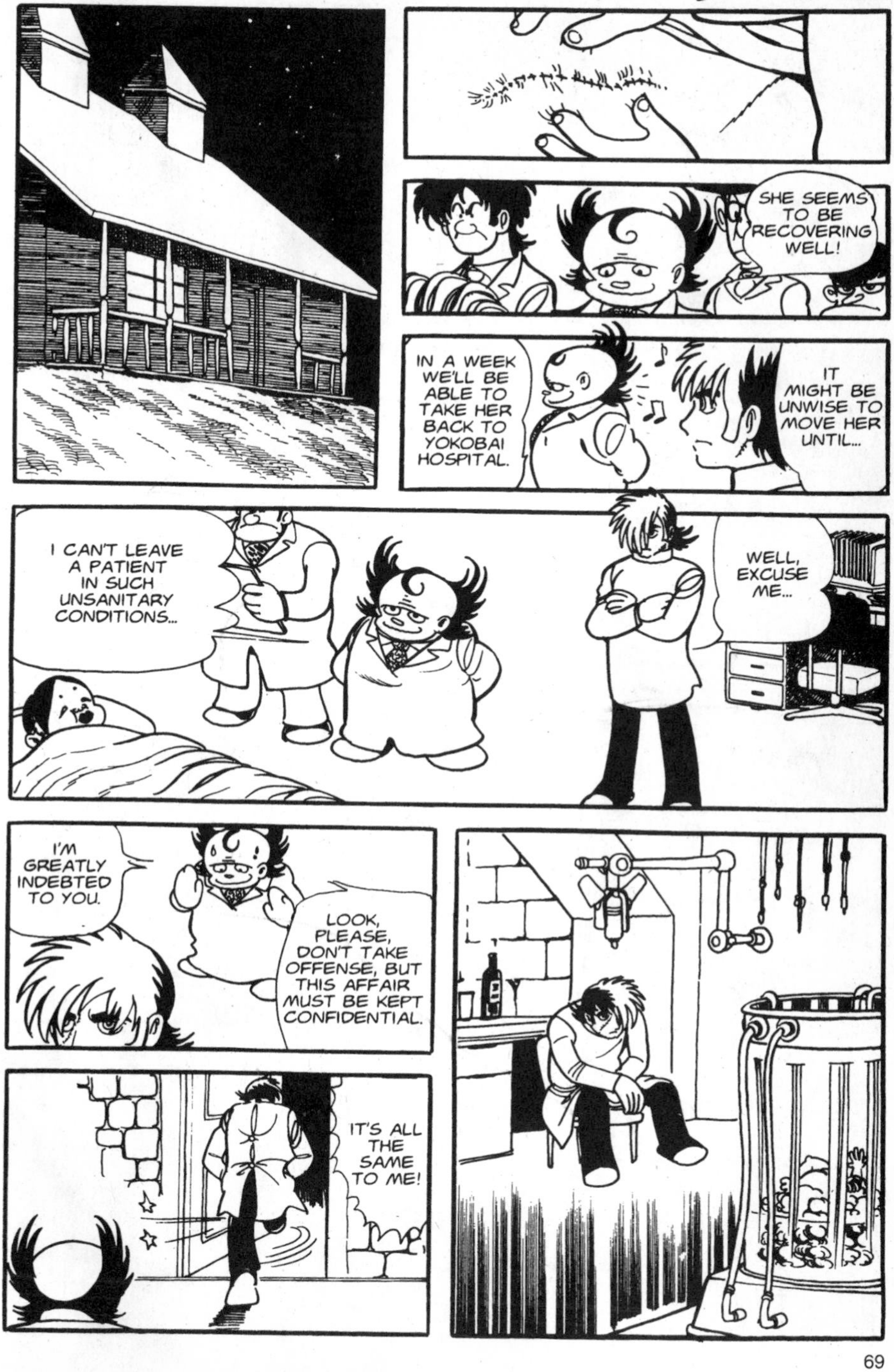
SHE SEEMS TO BE RECOVERING WELL!
IN A WEEK WE'LL BE ABLE TO TAKE HER BACK TO YOKOBAI HOSPITAL.
IT MIGHT BE UNWISE TO MOVE HER UNTIL...
I CAN'T LEAVE A PATIENT IN SUCH UNSANITARY CONDITIONS...
WELL, EXCUSE ME...
I'M GREATLY INDEBTED TO YOU.
LOOK, PLEASE, DON'T TAKE OFFENSE, BUT THIS AFFAIR MUST BE KEPT CONFIDENTIAL.
IT'S ALL THE SAME TO ME!

SHAA

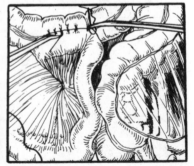

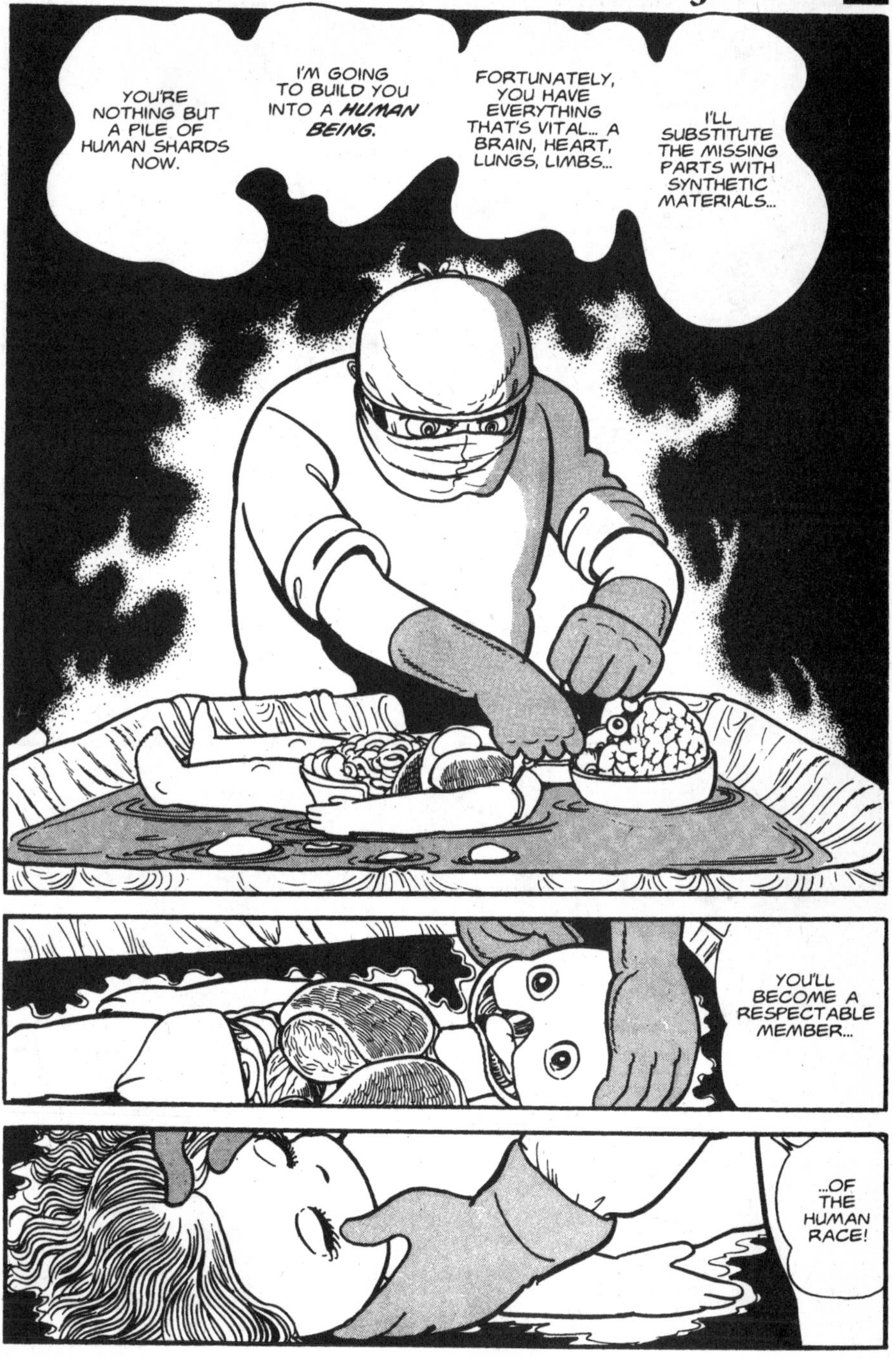
YOU'RE NOTHING BUT A PILE OF HUMAN SHARDS NOW.
I'M GOING TO BUILD YOU INTO A ***HUMAN BEING.***
FORTUNATELY, YOU HAVE EVERYTHING THAT'S VITAL... A BRAIN, HEART, LUNGS, LIMBS...
I'LL SUBSTITUTE THE MISSING PARTS WITH SYNTHETIC MATERIALS...
YOU'LL BECOME A RESPECTABLE MEMBER...
...OF THE HUMAN RACE!

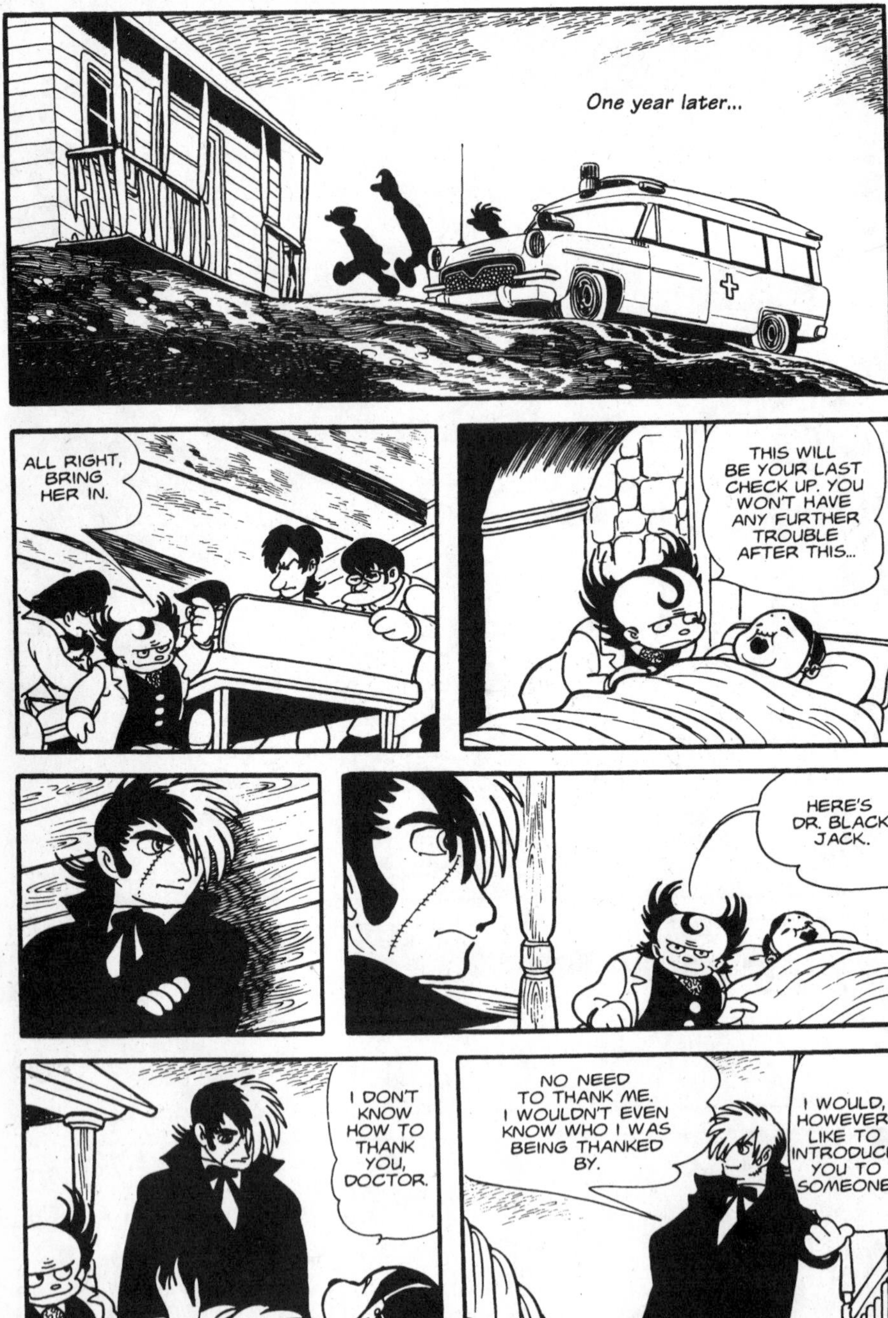
One year later...
ALL RIGHT, BRING HER IN.
THIS WILL BE YOUR LAST CHECK UP. YOU WON'T HAVE ANY FURTHER TROUBLE AFTER THIS...
HERE'S DR. BLACK JACK.
I DON'T KNOW HOW TO THANK YOU, DOCTOR.
NO NEED TO THANK ME. I WOULDN'T EVEN KNOW WHO I WAS BEING THANKED BY.
I WOULD, HOWEVER, LIKE TO INTRODUCE YOU TO SOMEONE.

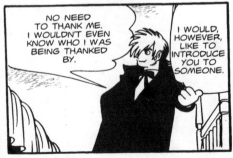

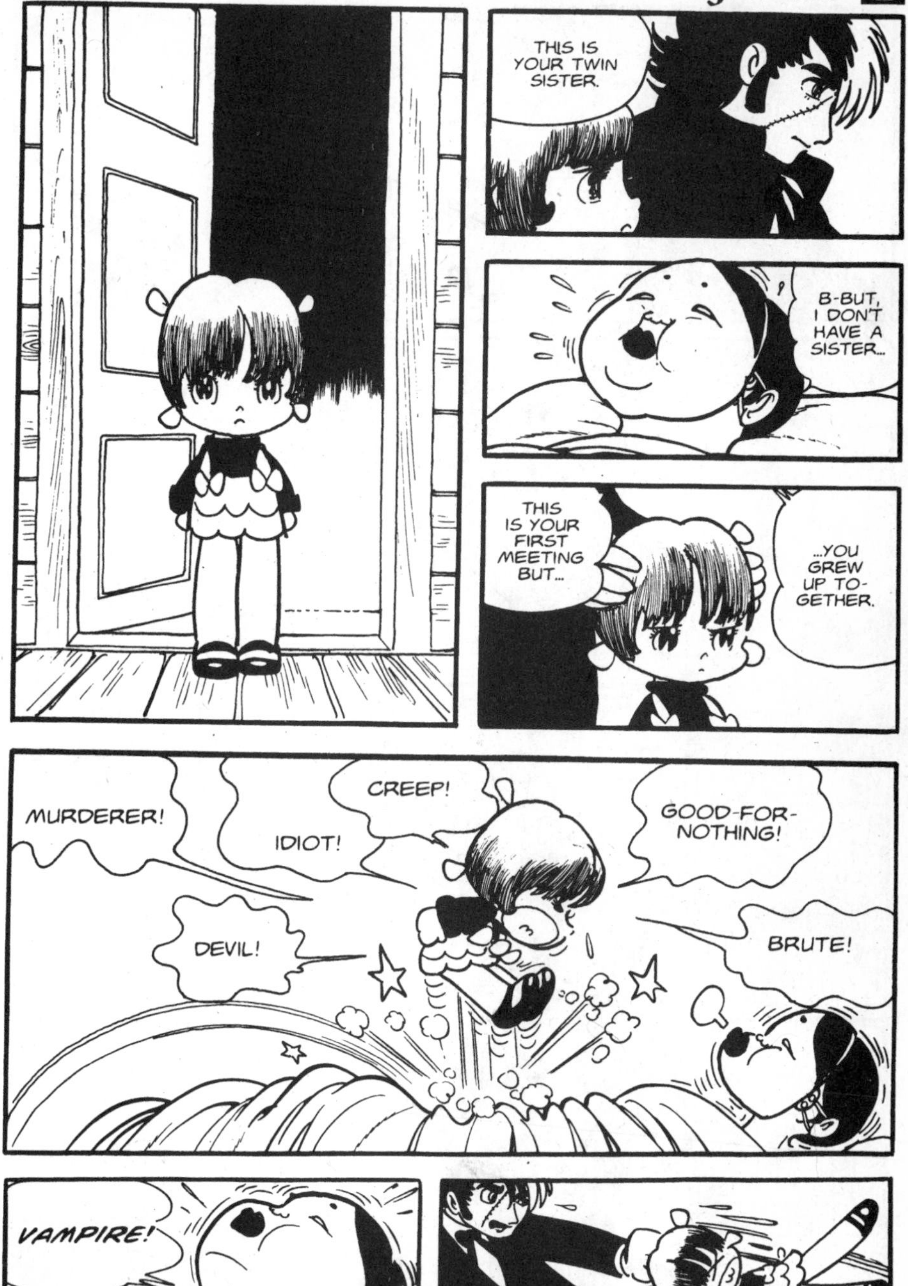
THIS IS YOUR TWIN SISTER.
B-BUT, I DON'T HAVE A SISTER...
THIS IS YOUR FIRST MEETING BUT...
...YOU GREW UP TO-GETHER.
MURDERER!
IDIOT!
CREEP!
GOOD-FOR-NOTHING!
DEVIL!
BRUTE!
VAMPIRE!

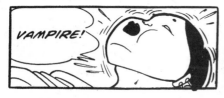

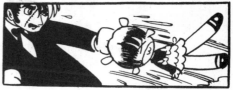

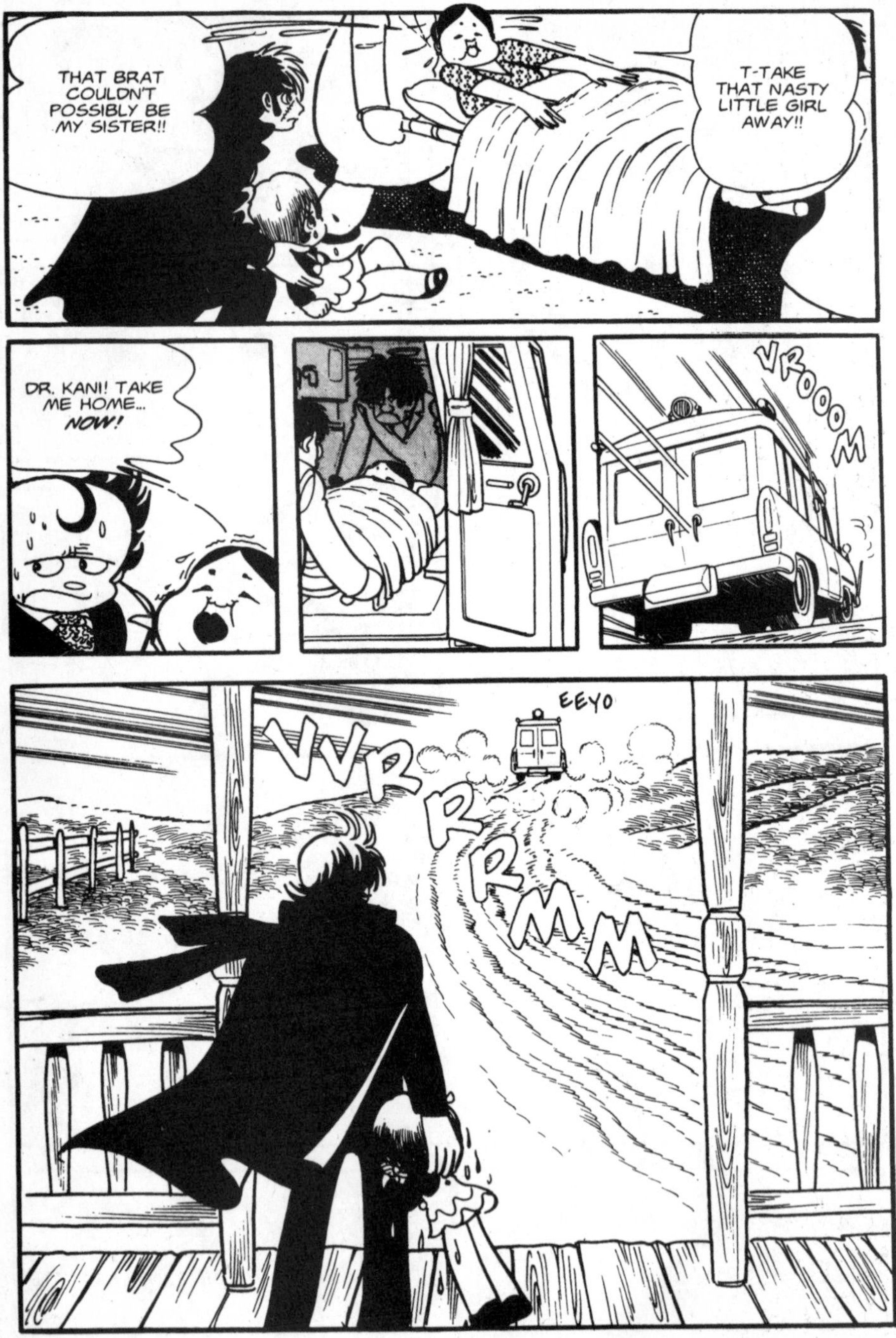
THAT BRAT COULDN'T POSSIBLY BE MY SISTER!!
T-TAKE THAT NASTY LITTLE GIRL AWAY!!
DR. KANI! TAKE ME HOME... *NOW!*
VROOOM
EEYO
VVRRRMMM

OPERATION FOUR

THE
ENCOUNTER

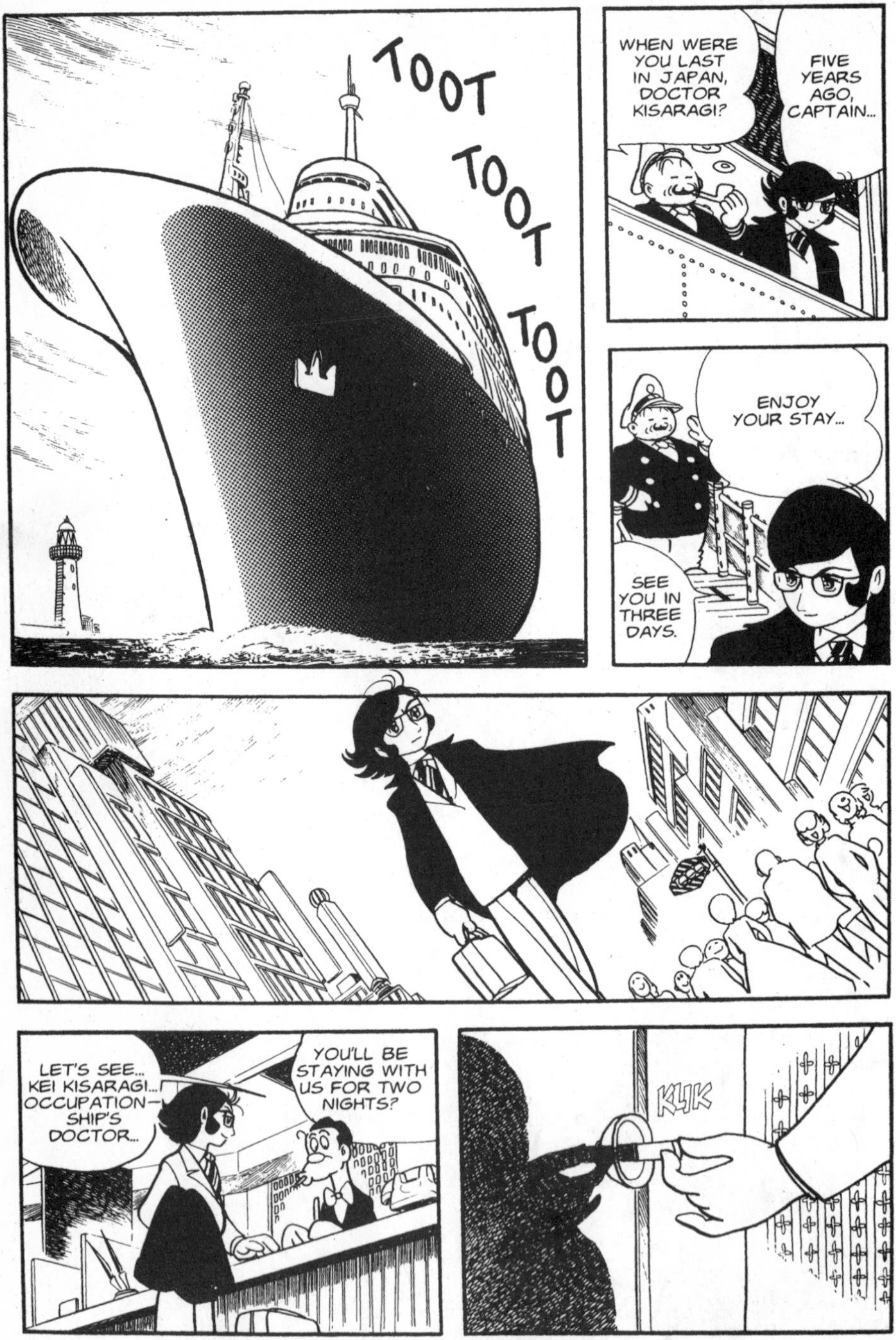
TOOT TOOT TOOT TOOT
WHEN WERE YOU LAST IN JAPAN, DOCTOR KISARAGI?
FIVE YEARS AGO, CAPTAIN...
ENJOY YOUR STAY...
SEE YOU IN THREE DAYS.
LET'S SEE... KEI KISARAGI... OCCUPATION— SHIP'S DOCTOR...
YOU'LL BE STAYING WITH US FOR TWO NIGHTS?
KLIK

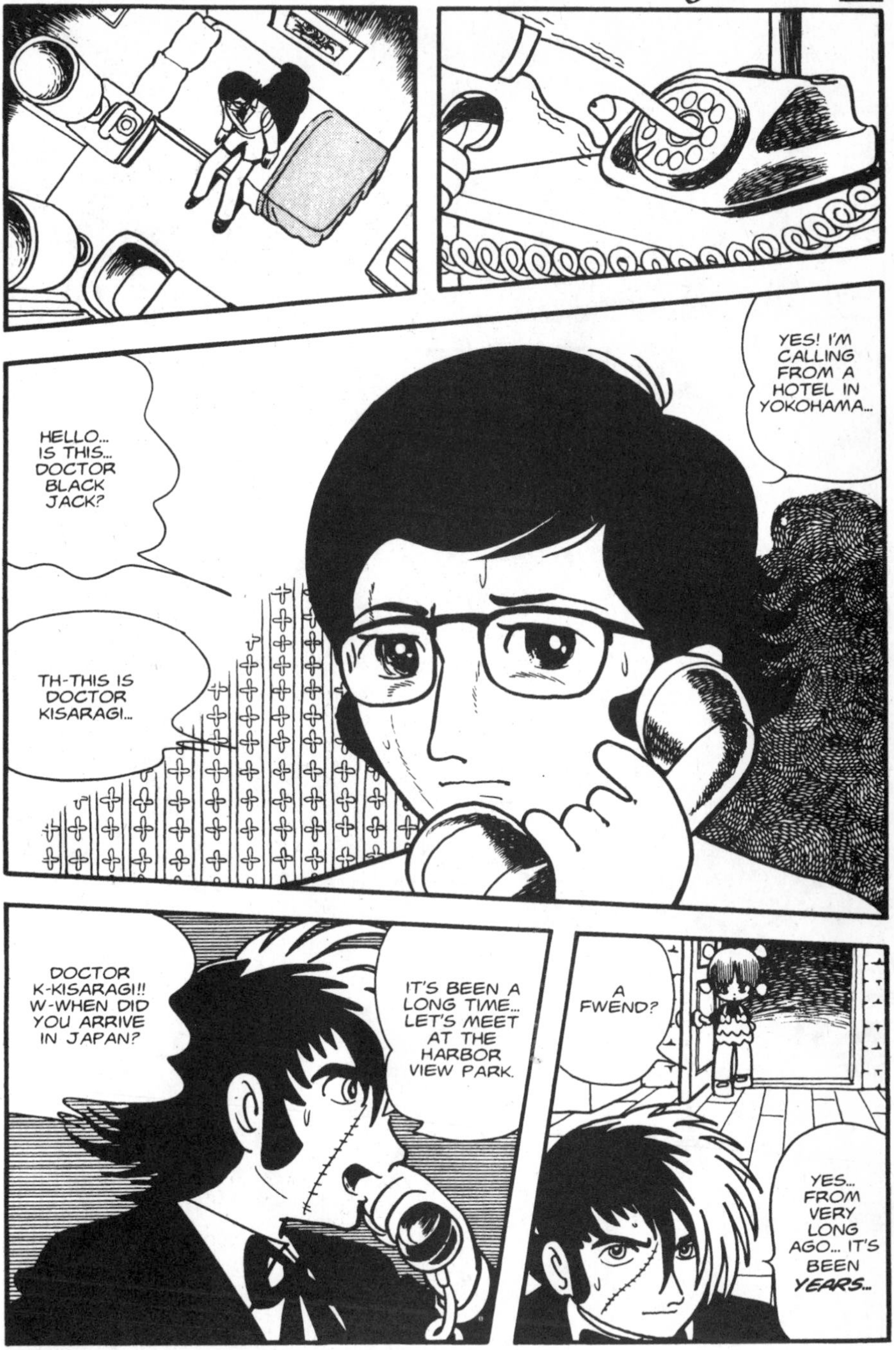
HELLO... IS THIS... DOCTOR BLACK JACK?
TH-THIS IS DOCTOR KISARAGI...
YES! I'M CALLING FROM A HOTEL IN YOKOHAMA...
DOCTOR K-KISARAGI!! W-WHEN DID YOU ARRIVE IN JAPAN?
IT'S BEEN A LONG TIME... LET'S MEET AT THE HARBOR VIEW PARK.
A FWEND?
YES... FROM VERY LONG AGO... IT'S BEEN *YEARS*...

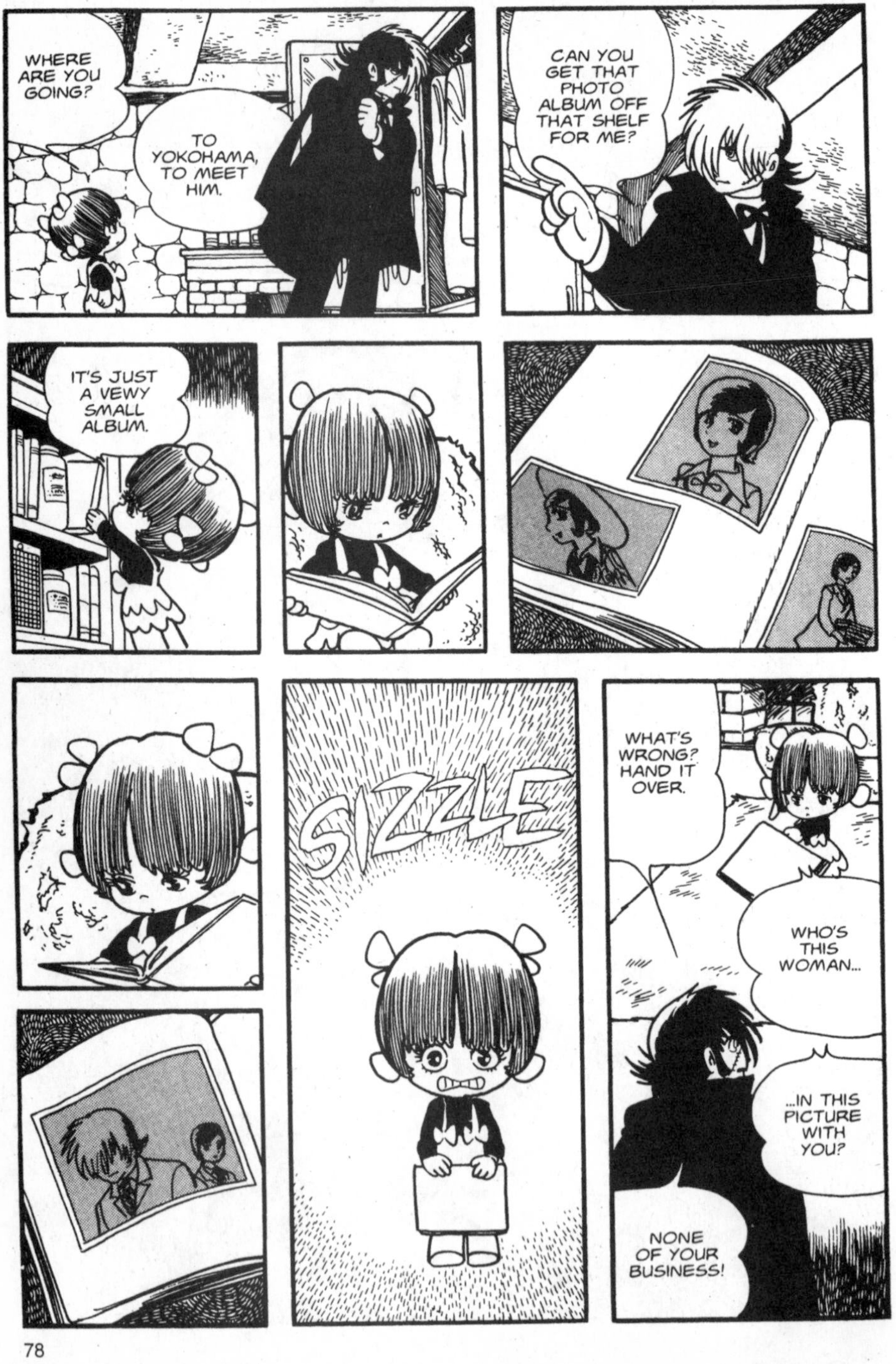
WHERE ARE YOU GOING?
TO YOKOHAMA, TO MEET HIM.
CAN YOU GET THAT PHOTO ALBUM OFF THAT SHELF FOR ME?
IT'S JUST A VEWY SMALL ALBUM.
SIZZLE
WHAT'S WRONG? HAND IT OVER.
WHO'S THIS WOMAN...
...IN THIS PICTURE WITH YOU?
NONE OF YOUR BUSINESS!

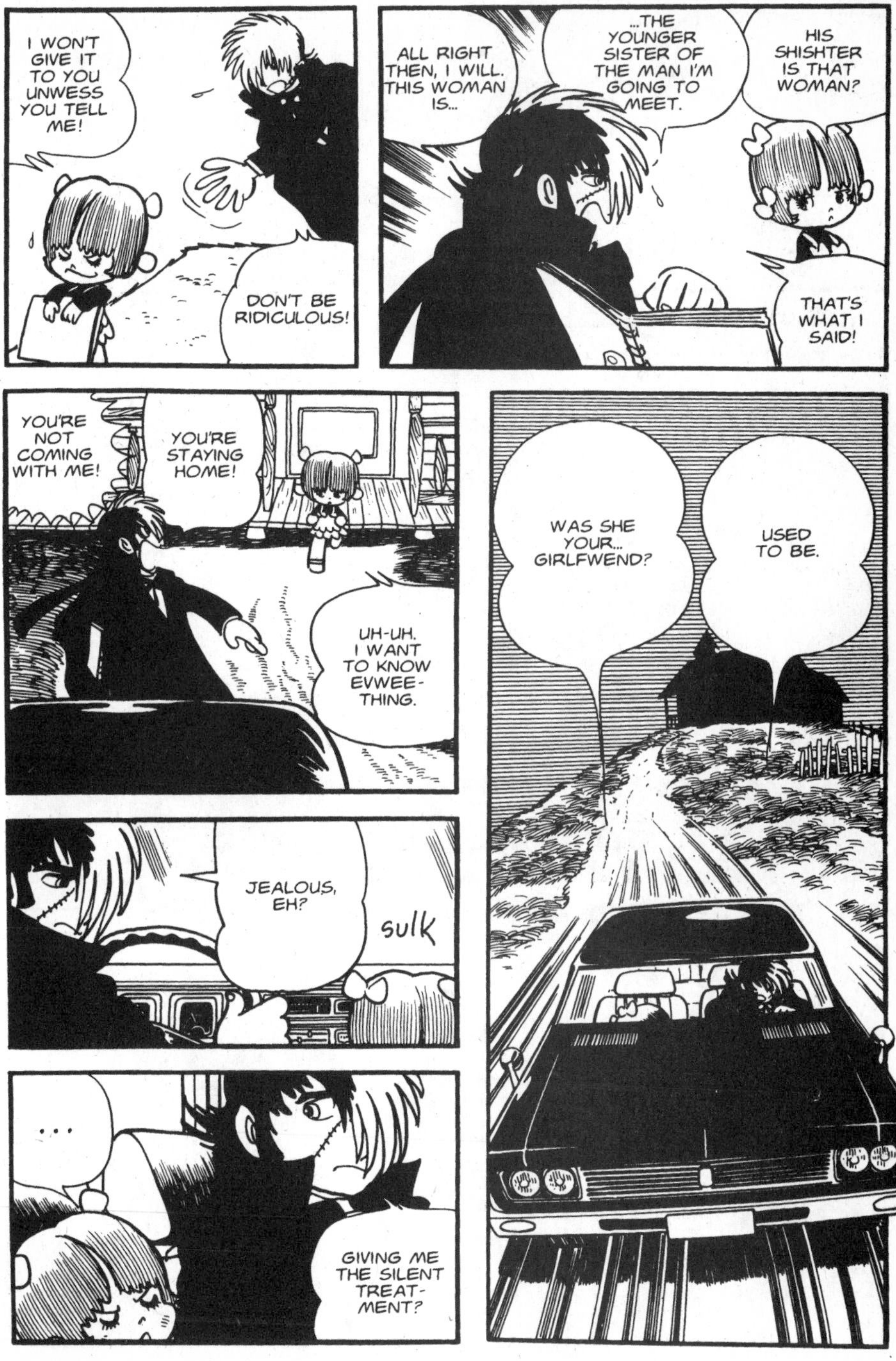
I WON'T GIVE IT TO YOU UNWESS YOU TELL ME!
DON'T BE RIDICULOUS!
ALL RIGHT THEN, I WILL. THIS WOMAN IS...
...THE YOUNGER SISTER OF THE MAN I'M GOING TO MEET.
HIS SHISHTER IS THAT WOMAN?
THAT'S WHAT I SAID!
YOU'RE NOT COMING WITH ME!
YOU'RE STAYING HOME!
UH-UH. I WANT TO KNOW EVWEE-THING.
JEALOUS, EH?
sulk
...
GIVING ME THE SILENT TREAT-MENT?
WAS SHE YOUR... GIRLFWEND?
USED TO BE.

DON'T WORRY. SHE'S GONE NOW... FOREVER.

SHE DIED?

SOME-THING LIKE THAT.

THAT'S WHY YOU'RE GIVING THAT ALBUM TO HER BWOTHER?

I HAVE TO COME TO TERMS WITH MY MEMORIES... UNDER-STAND?

TEE HEE...

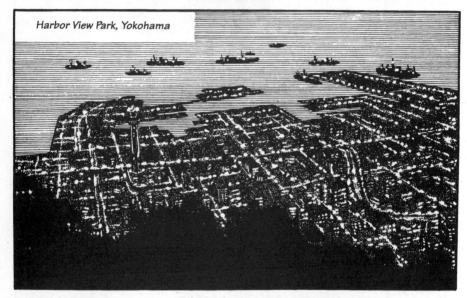

Harbor View Park, Yokohama

I'VE NEVER BEEN TO YOKOHAMA BEFORE!

WOW! IT'S SO *PWETTY*.

DOCTOR BLACK JACK...

80

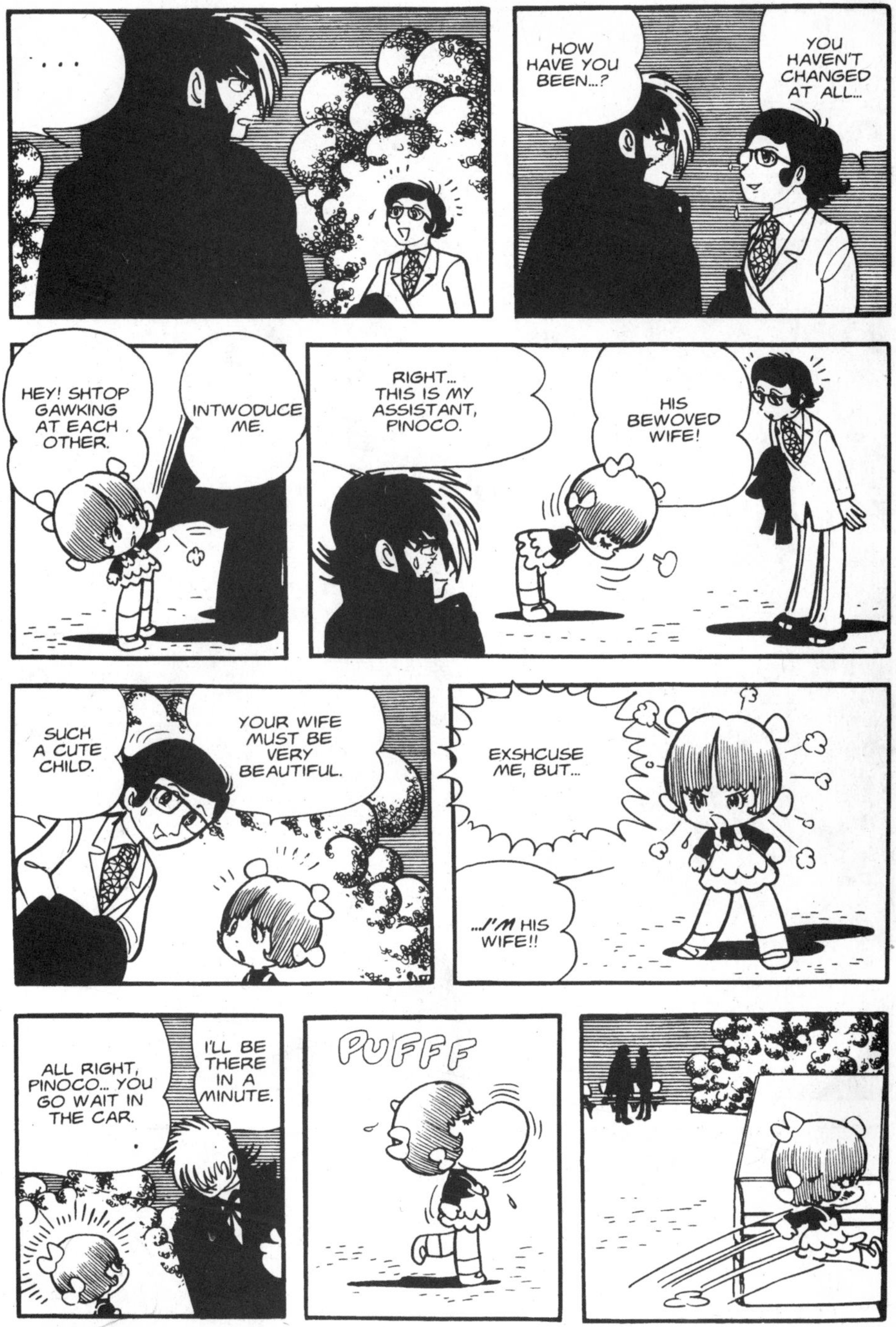
....
HOW HAVE YOU BEEN...?
YOU HAVEN'T CHANGED AT ALL...
HEY! SHTOP GAWKING AT EACH OTHER.
INTWODUCE ME.
RIGHT... THIS IS MY ASSISTANT, PINOCO.
HIS BEWOVED WIFE!
SUCH A CUTE CHILD.
YOUR WIFE MUST BE VERY BEAUTIFUL.
EXSHCUSE ME, BUT...
...I'M HIS WIFE!!
ALL RIGHT, PINOCO... YOU GO WAIT IN THE CAR.
I'LL BE THERE IN A MINUTE.
PUFFF

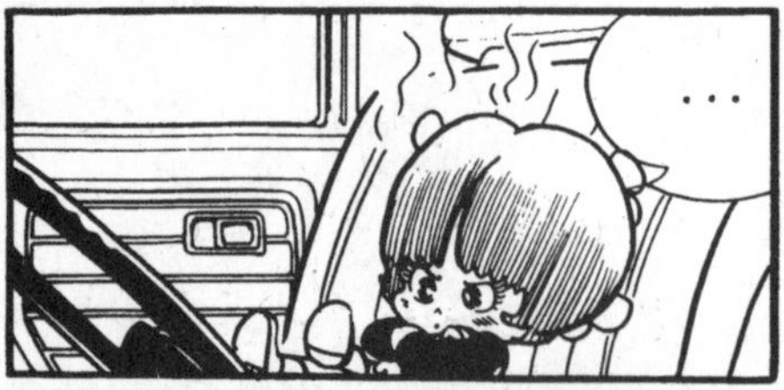
. . .
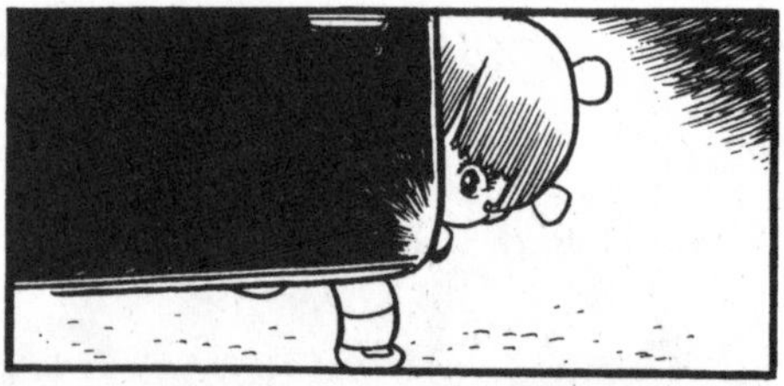
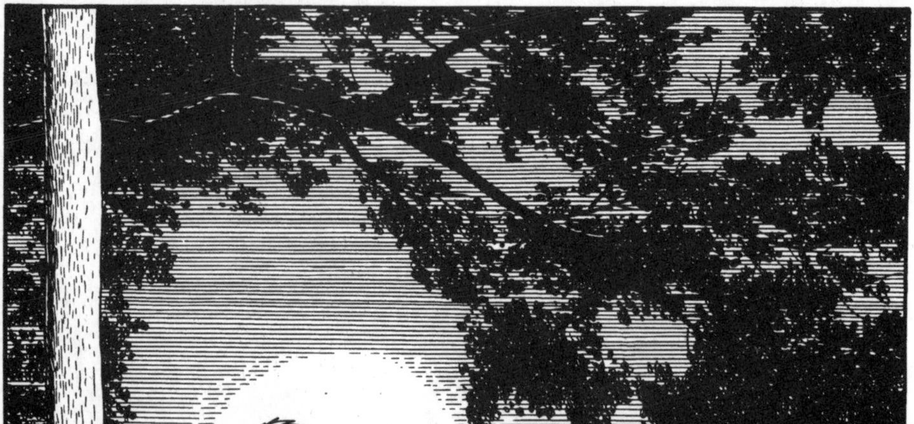
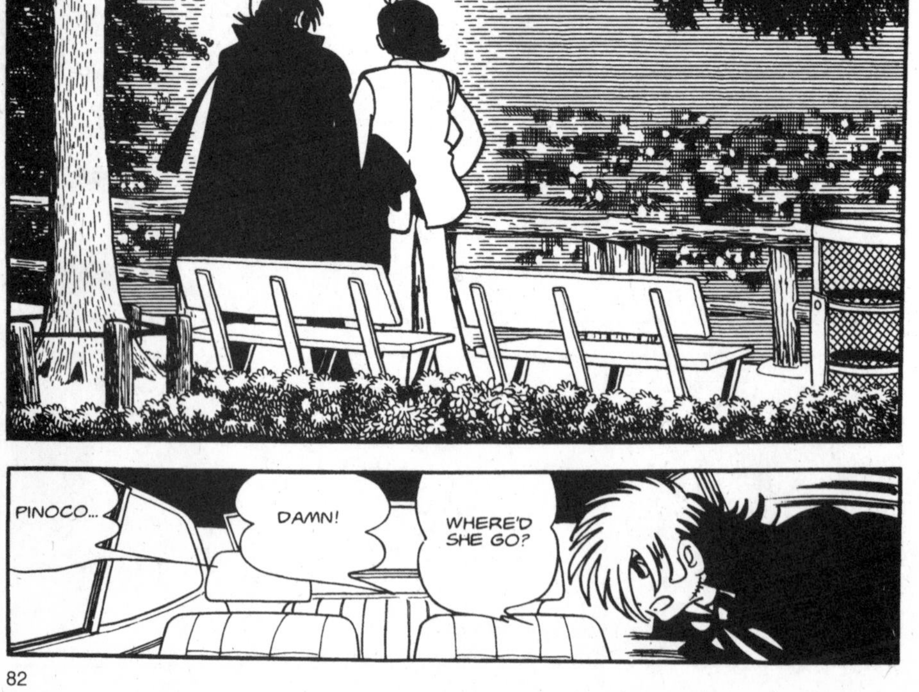
PINOCO...
DAMN!
WHERE'D SHE GO?

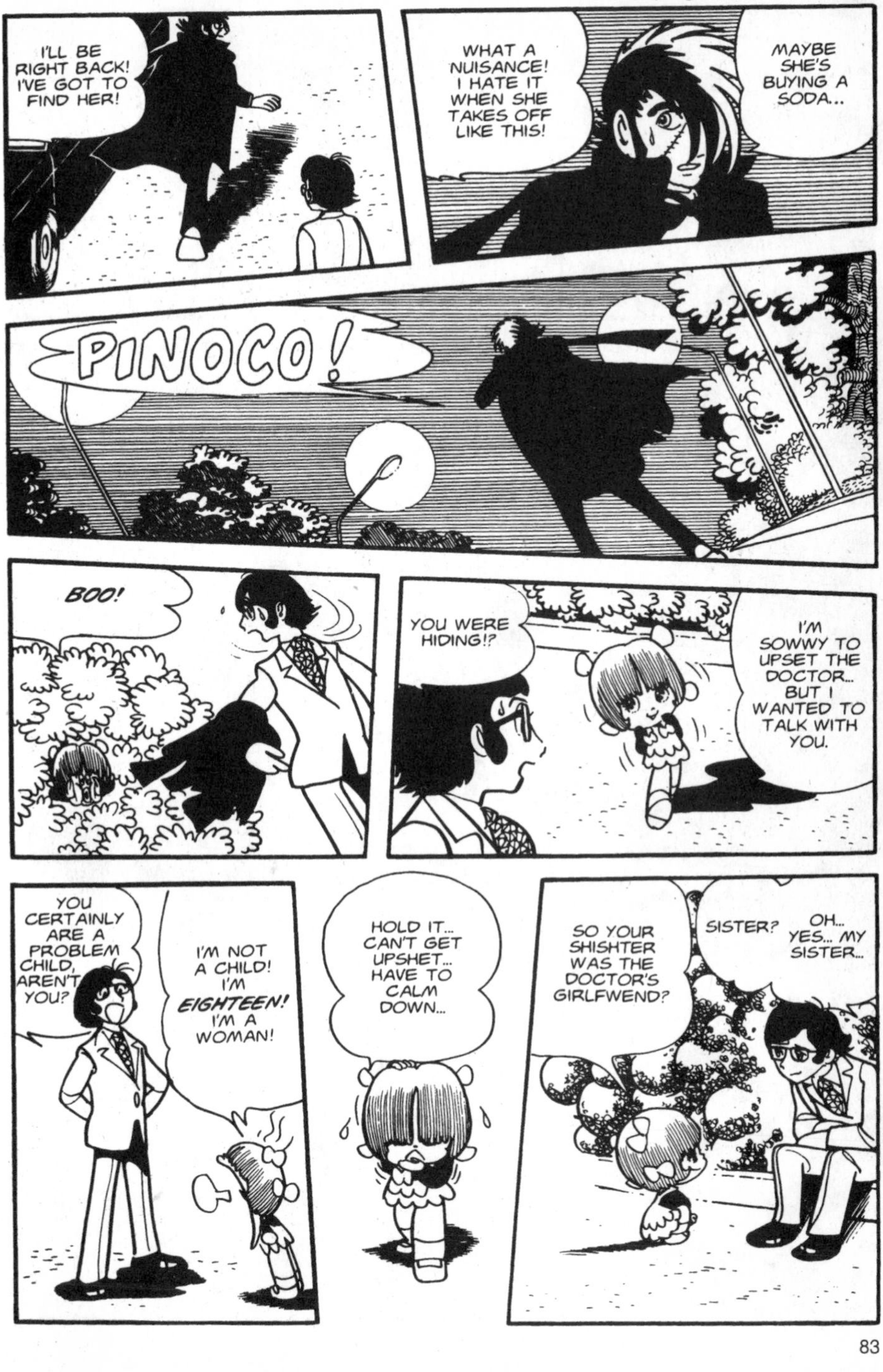
I'LL BE RIGHT BACK! I'VE GOT TO FIND HER!
WHAT A NUISANCE! I HATE IT WHEN SHE TAKES OFF LIKE THIS!
MAYBE SHE'S BUYING A SODA...
PINOCO!
BOO!
YOU WERE HIDING!?
I'M SOWWY TO UPSET THE DOCTOR... BUT I WANTED TO TALK WITH YOU.
YOU CERTAINLY ARE A PROBLEM CHILD, AREN'T YOU?
I'M NOT A CHILD! I'M EIGHTEEN! I'M A WOMAN!
HOLD IT... CAN'T GET UPSHET... HAVE TO CALM DOWN...
SO YOUR SHISHTER WAS THE DOCTOR'S GIRLFWEND?
SISTER?
OH... YES... MY SISTER...

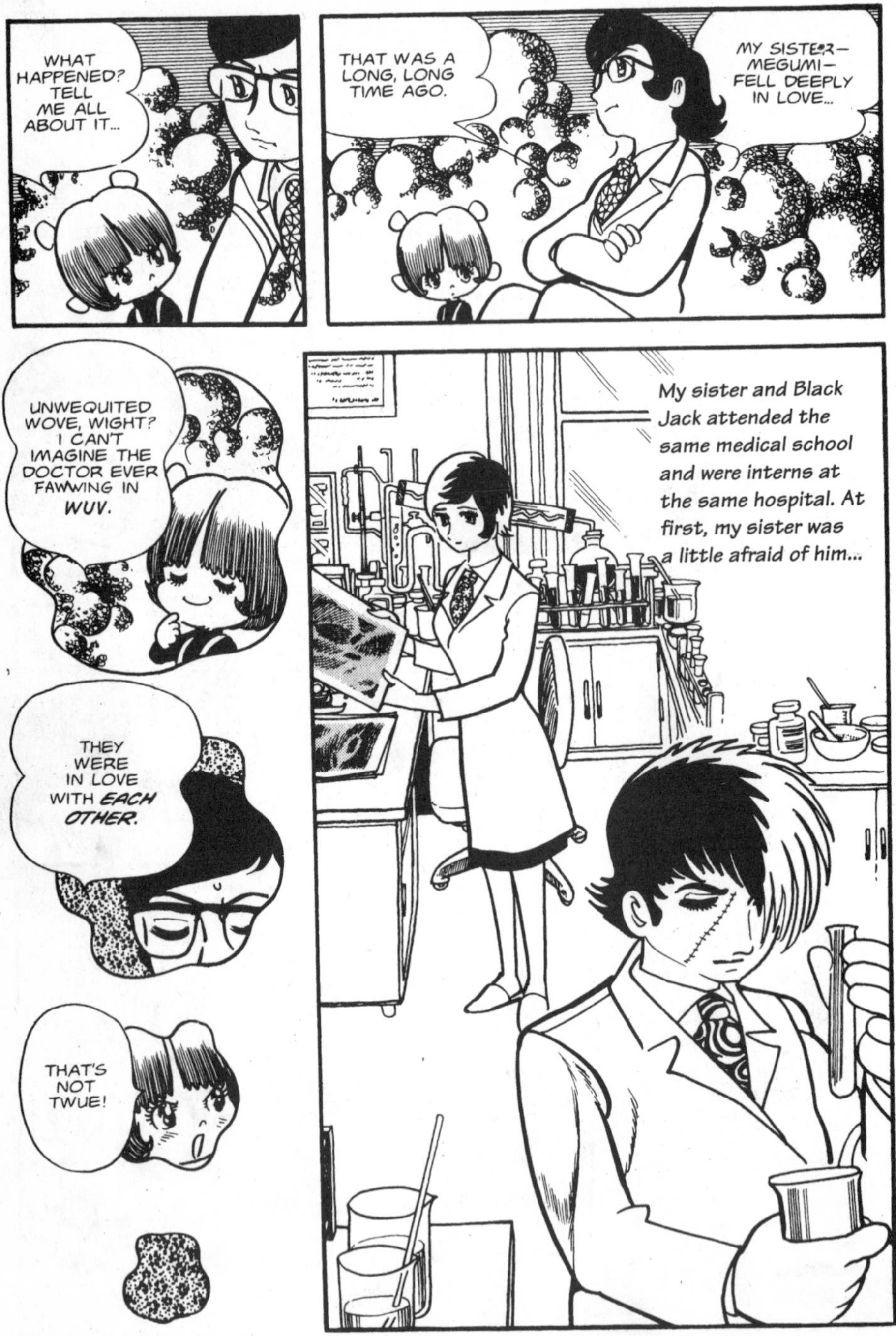
WHAT HAPPENED? TELL ME ALL ABOUT IT...
THAT WAS A LONG, LONG TIME AGO.
MY SISTER— MEGUMI— FELL DEEPLY IN LOVE...
UNWEQUITED WOVE, WIGHT? I CAN'T IMAGINE THE DOCTOR EVER FAWWING IN *WUV*.
THEY WERE IN LOVE WITH *EACH OTHER*.
THAT'S NOT TWUE!
My sister and Black Jack attended the same medical school and were interns at the same hospital. At first, my sister was a little afraid of him...

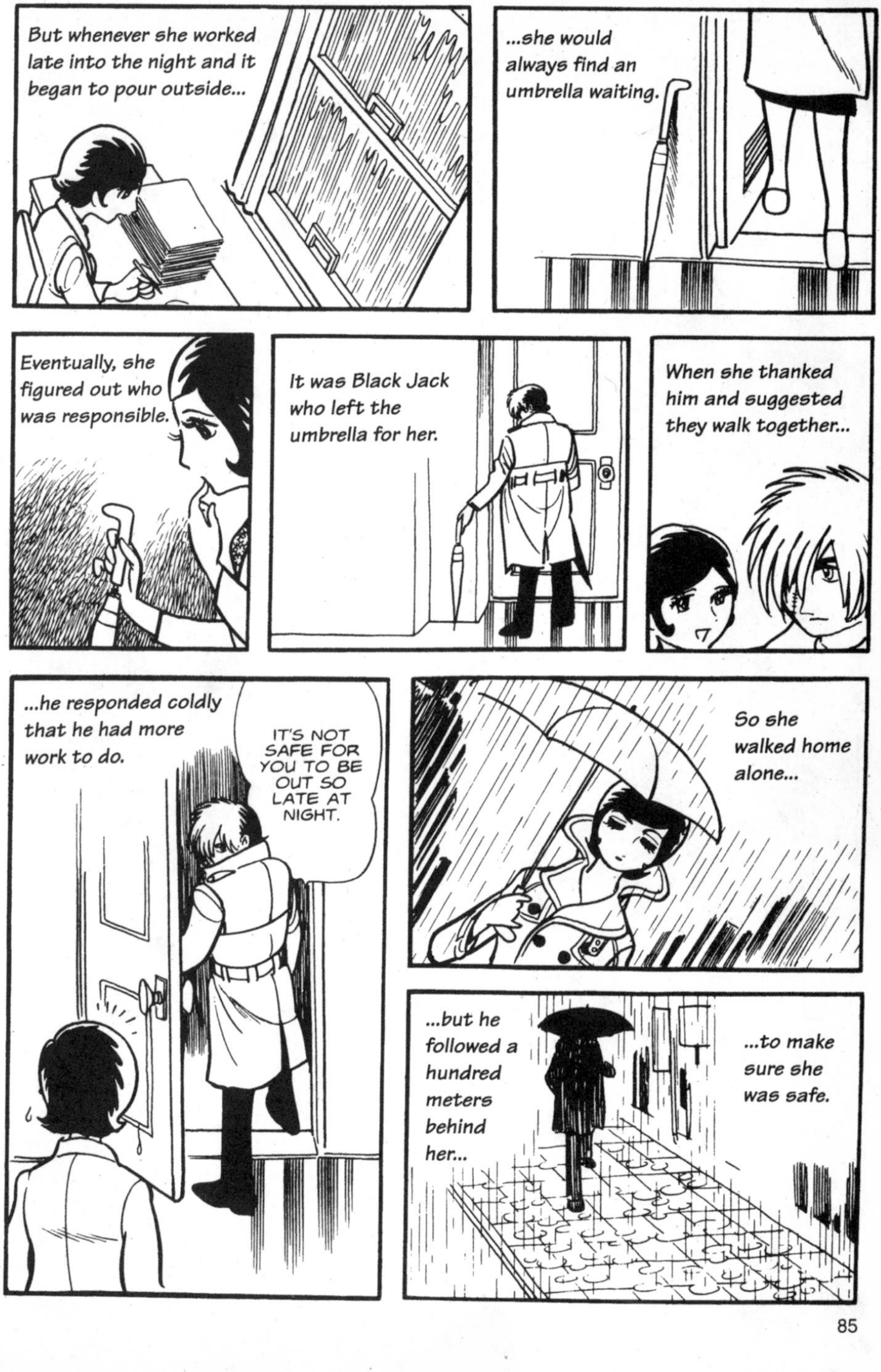
But whenever she worked late into the night and it began to pour outside...
...she would always find an umbrella waiting.
Eventually, she figured out who was responsible.
It was Black Jack who left the umbrella for her.
When she thanked him and suggested they walk together...
...he responded coldly that he had more work to do.
IT'S NOT SAFE FOR YOU TO BE OUT SO LATE AT NIGHT.
So she walked home alone...
...but he followed a hundred meters behind her...
...to make sure she was safe.

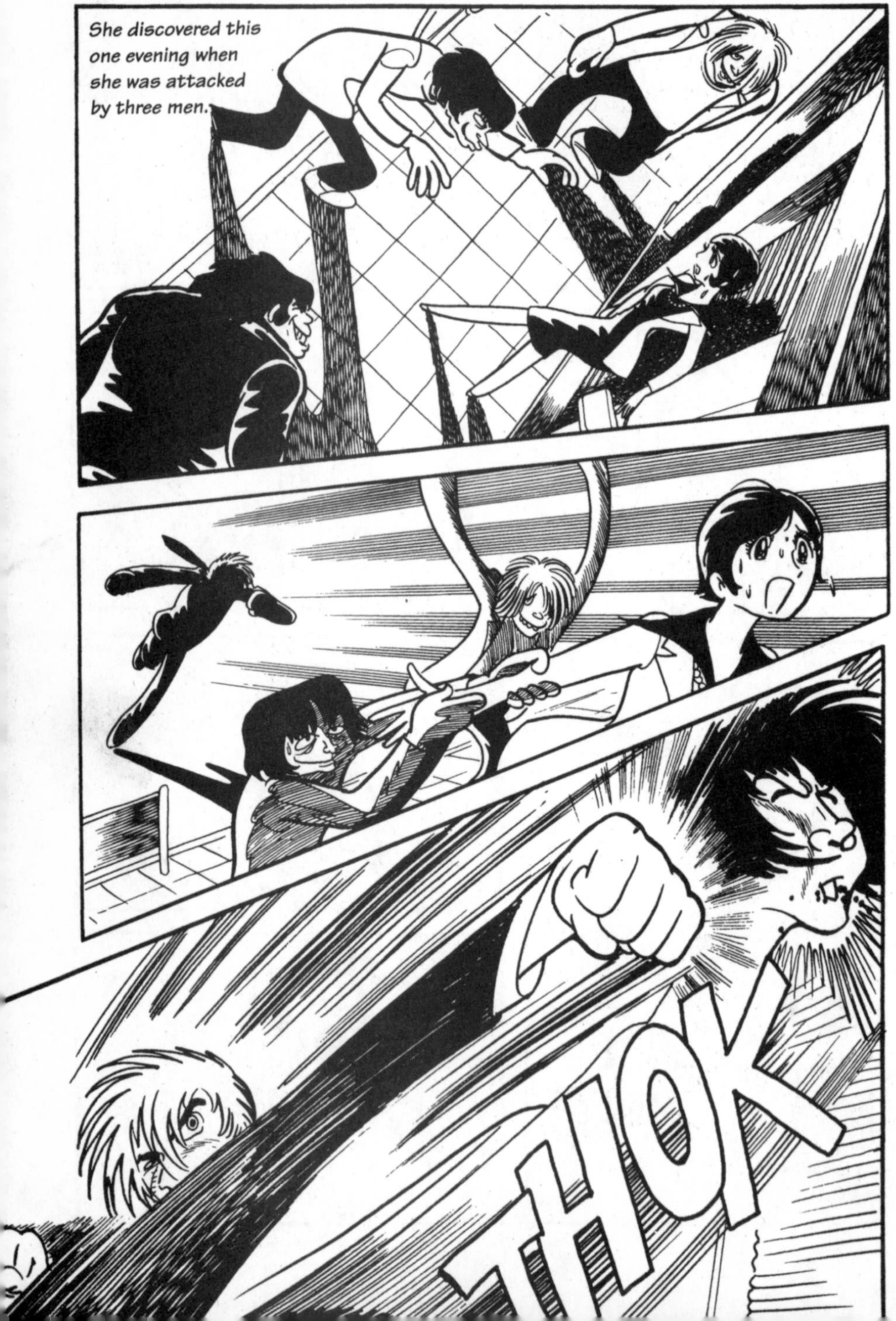
She discovered this one evening when she was attacked by three men.
THOK

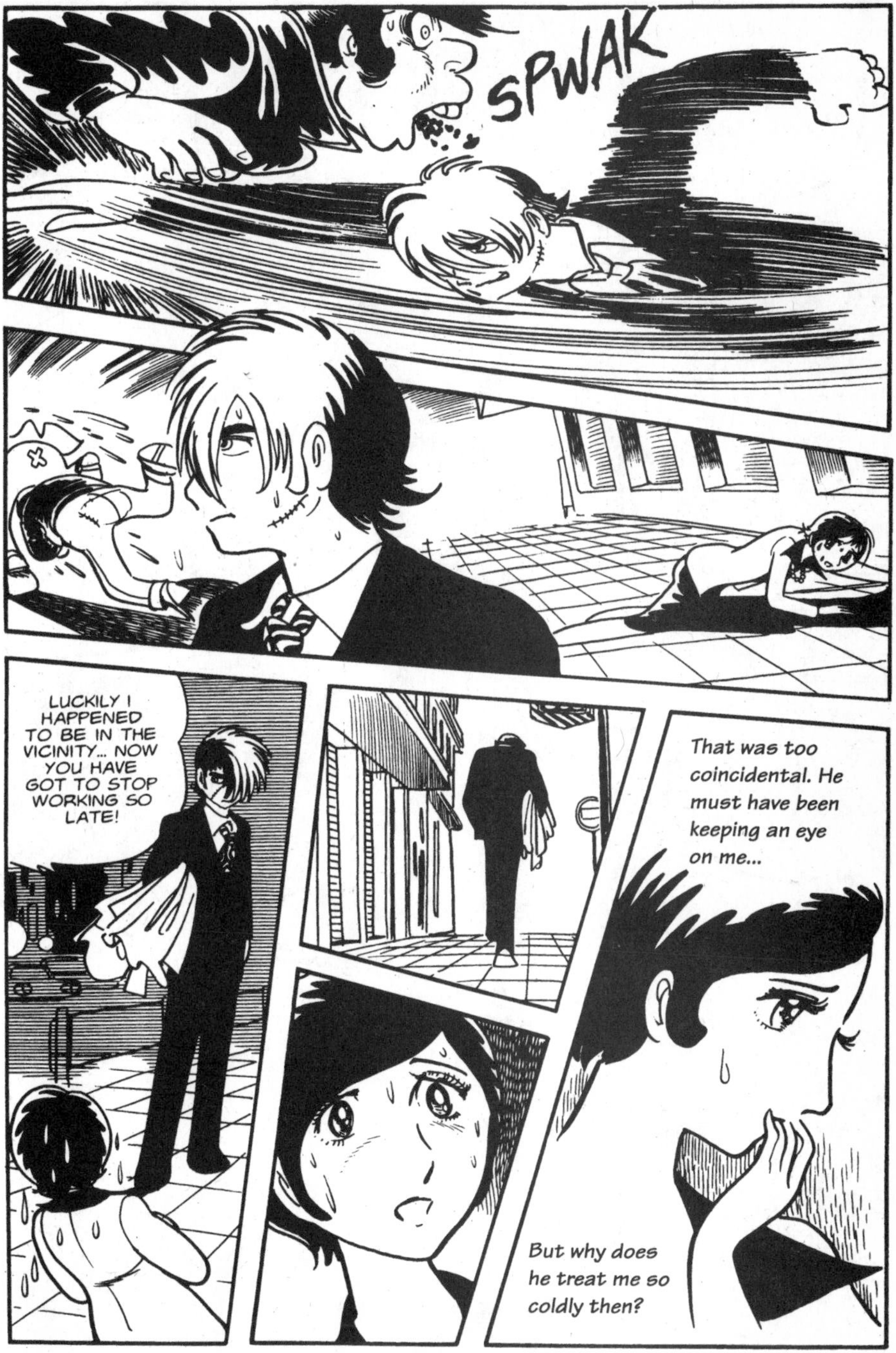
SPWAK
LUCKILY I HAPPENED TO BE IN THE VICINITY... NOW YOU HAVE GOT TO STOP WORKING SO LATE!
That was too coincidental. He must have been keeping an eye on me...
But why does he treat me so coldly then?

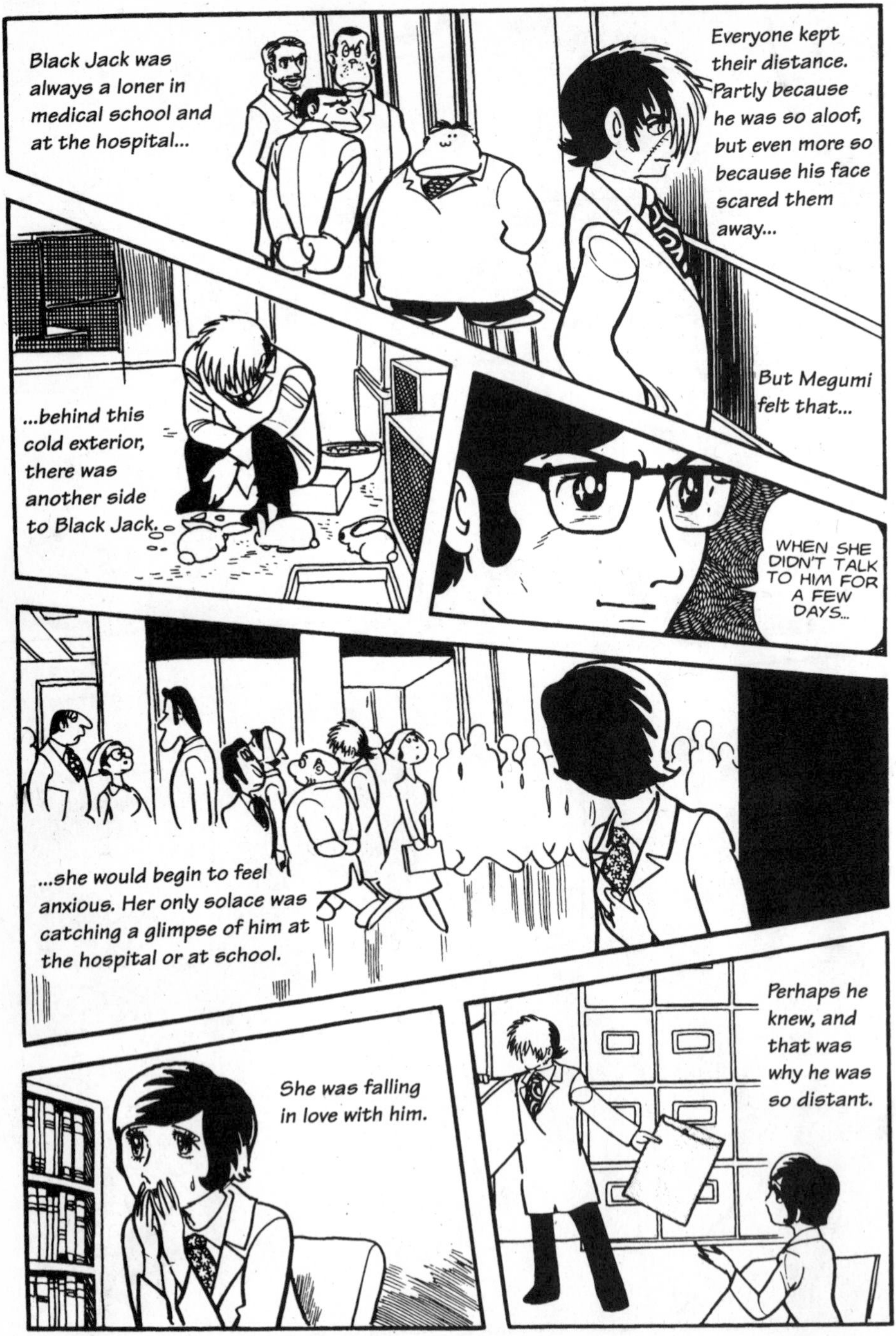
Black Jack was always a loner in medical school and at the hospital...
Everyone kept their distance. Partly because he was so aloof, but even more so because his face scared them away...
But Megumi felt that...
...behind this cold exterior, there was another side to Black Jack.
WHEN SHE DIDN'T TALK TO HIM FOR A FEW DAYS...
...she would begin to feel anxious. Her only solace was catching a glimpse of him at the hospital or at school.
She was falling in love with him.
Perhaps he knew, and that was why he was so distant.

THE MORE INVOLVED YOU GET, THE HARDER IT IS TO CONTROL YOUR FEELINGS.

YOU'RE TOO YOUNG TO UNDERSTAND...

NO I'M NOT.

WHY DIDN'T YOUR SHISHTER TELL HIM SHE WAS IN WUV WITH HIM?

SHE DIDN'T HAVE A CHANCE TO... YOU SEE...

...SOMETHING TERRIBLE HAPPENED TO HER.

Cancer. She was diagnosed with ovarian cancer!

Ovarian cancer is one of the rarest and most fatal forms of cancer in a woman.

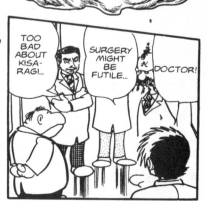

TOO BAD ABOUT KISARAGI...

SURGERY MIGHT BE FUTILE...

DOCTOR!

PLEASE LET ME OPERATE ON HER!!

YOU'RE STILL AN INTERN, BLACK JACK!

KISARAGI'S CANCER IS IN THE ADVANCED STAGES, SO THE OPERATION WILL BE EXTREMELY DIFFICULT. YOU CAN'T POSSIBLY HANDLE IT.

YOU'LL *KILL* HER!

I KNOW I CAN DO IT!

PLEASE LET ME TRY!!

ALL RIGHT, BUT PROFESSOR MURAKAMI WILL OVERSEE YOUR SURGERY.

NO THANK YOU. I CAN DO IT ALONE.

YOU'RE PRETTY FULL OF YOURSELF!

From that day on, he cared for my sister as if even the thought of anyone else touching her was unbearable.

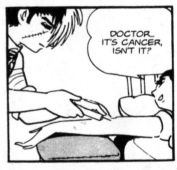

DOCTOR... IT'S CANCER, ISN'T IT?

THAT'S RIGHT.

IT'S PRETTY BAD...

YES. I'LL OPERATE TOMORROW.

IT'S NO EASY TASK TELLING A PATIENT SHE HAS CANCER.

IT'S LIKE GIVING A DEATH SENTENCE. BUT BLACK JACK WAS HONEST WITH HER, AND THIS MADE HER TRUST HIM ALL THE MORE...

...

I'LL HAVE TO REMOVE YOUR OVARIES AND YOUR UTERUS.

IN OTHER WORDS, ALL YOUR FEMALE ORGANS.

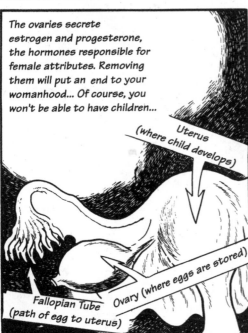

The ovaries secrete estrogen and progesterone, the hormones responsible for female attributes. Removing them will put an end to your womanhood... Of course, you won't be able to have children...

Uterus
(where child develops)

Ovary (where eggs are stored)

Fallopian Tube
(path of egg to uterus)

YOU UNDER-STAND, MEGUMI?

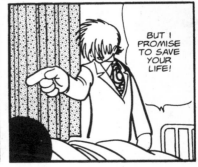

BUT I PROMISE TO SAVE YOUR LIFE!

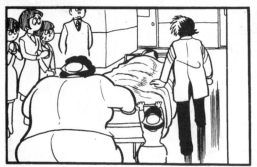

THIS IS A MATTER OF LIFE AND DEATH. HOW DARE YOU INSIST ON DOING IT ALL BY YOURSELF!?

I CAN DO IT ALONE. IF ANYTHING HAPPENS, I'LL ASSUME FULL RESPONSIBILITY.

BUT THIS JUST WON'T DO!

HOW DID HE GET SO CONFIDENT? HE'S STILL WET BEHIND THE EARS!

HOW CAN HE CONDUCT SURGERY ON A CANCER PATIENT SINGLE-HANDEDLY!?

DO YOU HAVE FAITH IN ME?

I DO.

THANK YOU.

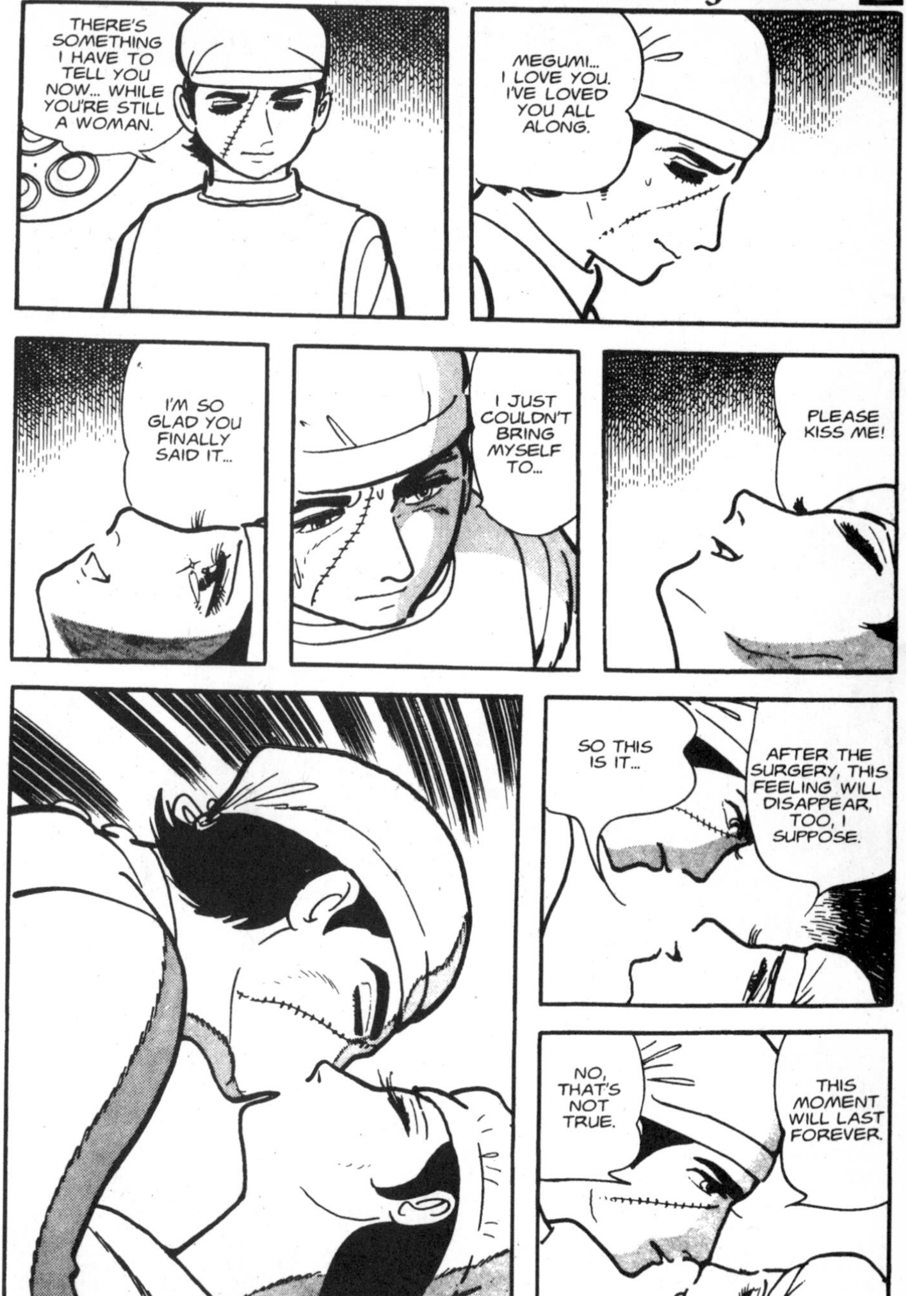
THERE'S SOMETHING I HAVE TO TELL YOU NOW... WHILE YOU'RE STILL A WOMAN.
MEGUMI... I LOVE YOU. I'VE LOVED YOU ALL ALONG.
I'M SO GLAD YOU FINALLY SAID IT...
I JUST COULDN'T BRING MYSELF TO...
PLEASE KISS ME!
SO THIS IS IT...
AFTER THE SURGERY, THIS FEELING WILL DISAPPEAR, TOO, I SUPPOSE.
NO, THAT'S NOT TRUE.
THIS MOMENT WILL LAST FOREVER.

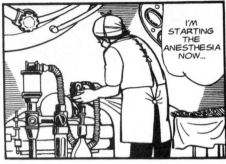

...

I'M STARTING THE ANESTHESIA NOW...

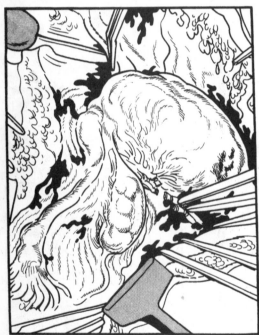

Megumi fell into a quiet, deep sleep. Black Jack removed her uterus and ovaries. The operation was completed in an hour.

The surgery was a success, but...

...MEGUMI WAS NO LONGER A WOMAN.

AND THEN?

PINOCO!

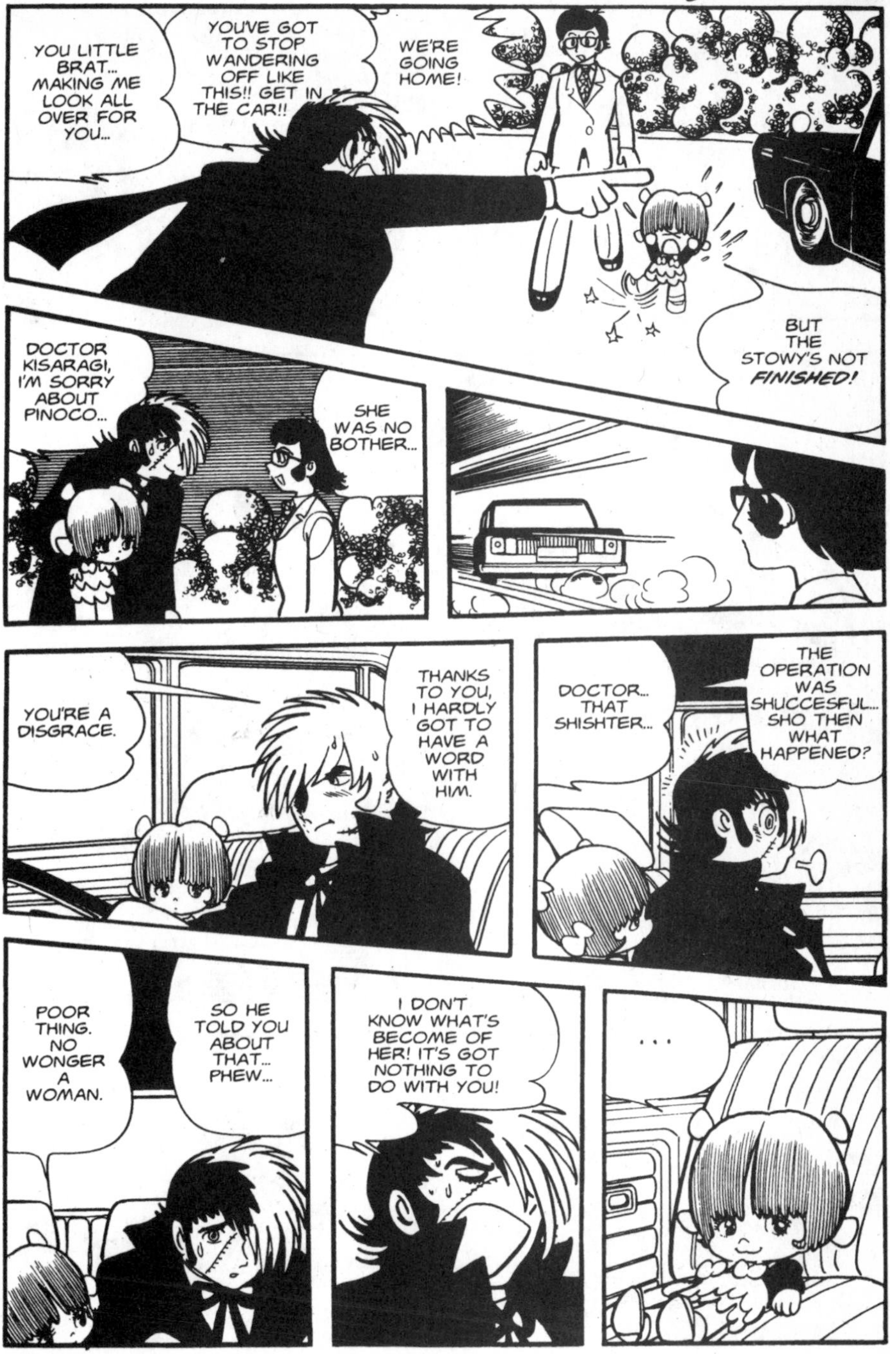
YOU LITTLE BRAT... MAKING ME LOOK ALL OVER FOR YOU...
YOU'VE GOT TO STOP WANDERING OFF LIKE THIS!! GET IN THE CAR!!
WE'RE GOING HOME!
BUT THE STOWY'S NOT *FINISHED!*
DOCTOR KISARAGI, I'M SORRY ABOUT PINOCO...
SHE WAS NO BOTHER...
YOU'RE A DISGRACE.
THANKS TO YOU, I HARDLY GOT TO HAVE A WORD WITH HIM.
DOCTOR... THAT SHISHTER...
THE OPERATION WAS SHUCCESFUL... SHO THEN WHAT HAPPENED?
POOR THING. NO WONGER A WOMAN.
SO HE TOLD YOU ABOUT THAT... PHEW...
I DON'T KNOW WHAT'S BECOME OF HER! IT'S GOT NOTHING TO DO WITH YOU!
. . .

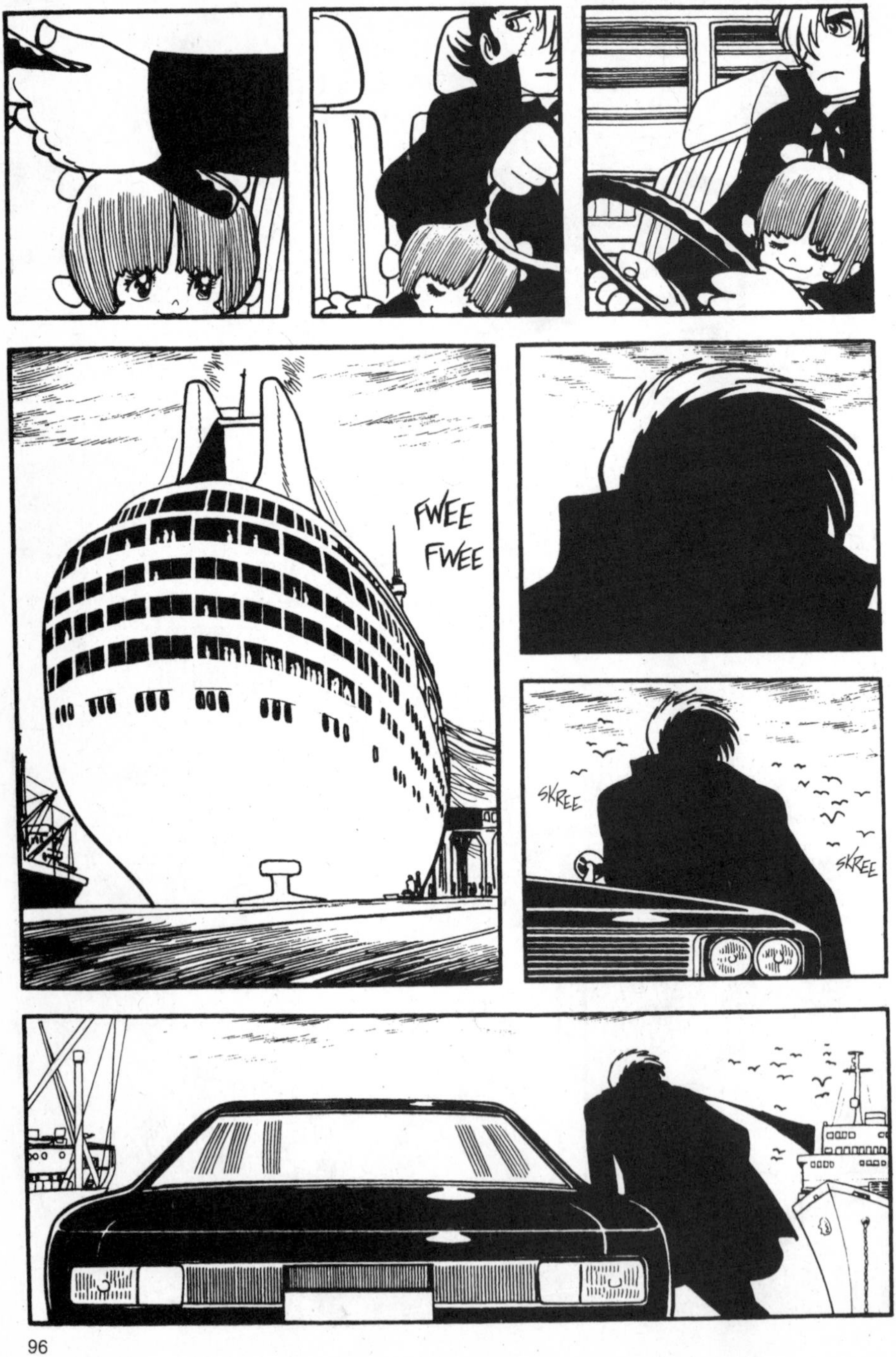
SKREE
SKREE
FWEE
FWEE

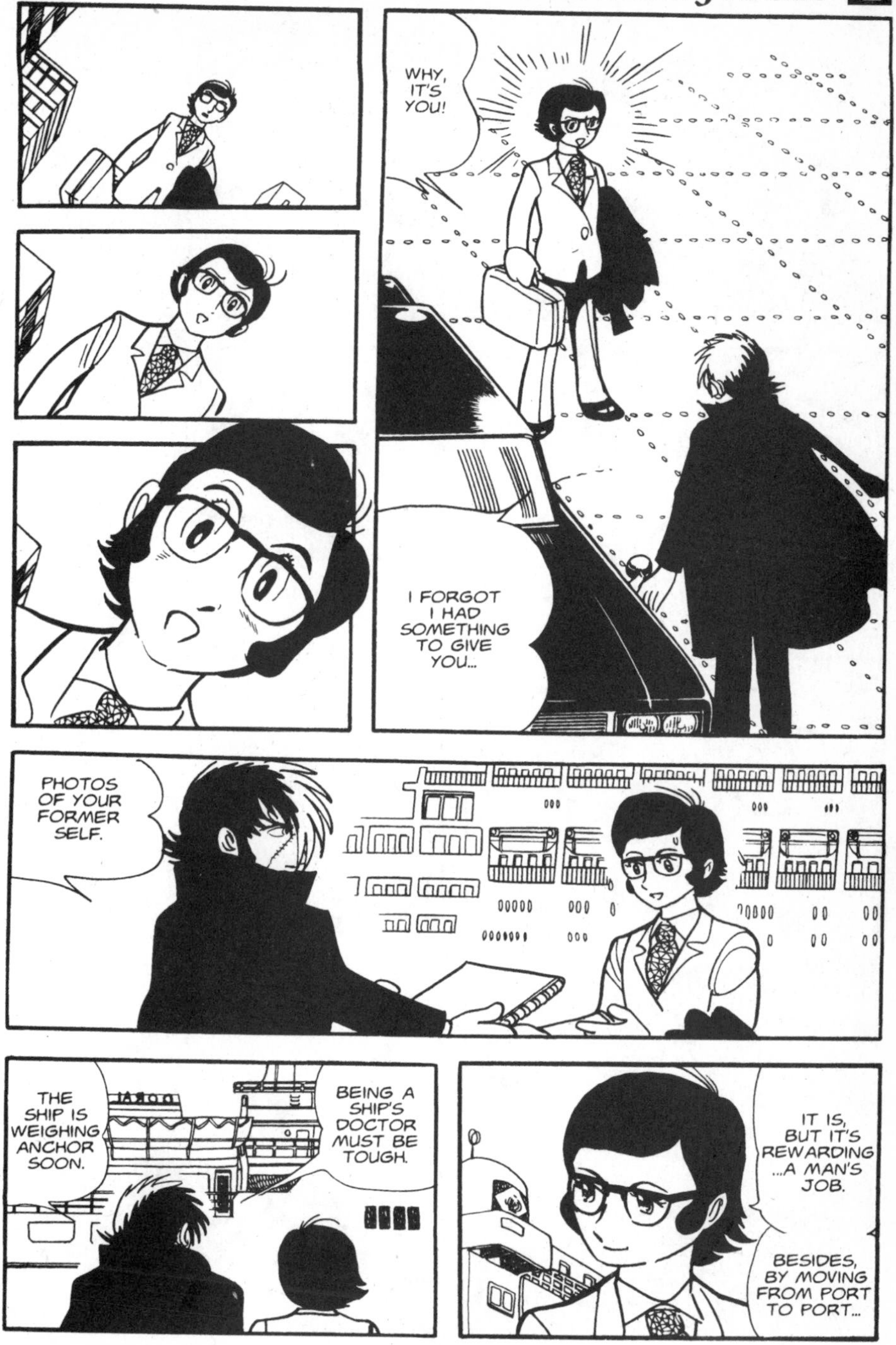
WHY, IT'S YOU!
I FORGOT I HAD SOMETHING TO GIVE YOU...
PHOTOS OF YOUR FORMER SELF.
THE SHIP IS WEIGHING ANCHOR SOON.
BEING A SHIP'S DOCTOR MUST BE TOUGH.
IT IS, BUT IT'S REWARDING ...A MAN'S JOB.
BESIDES, BY MOVING FROM PORT TO PORT...

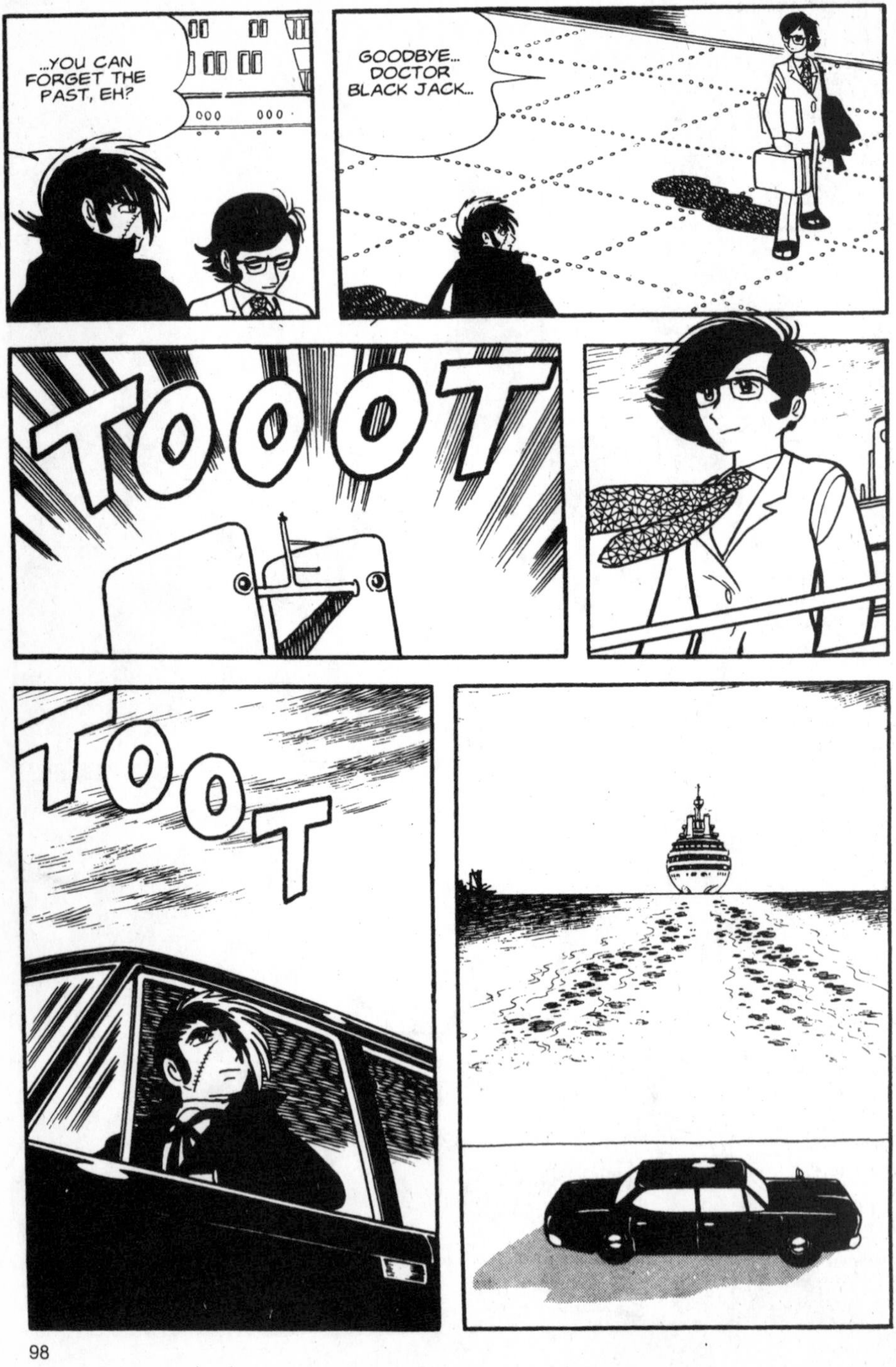
...YOU CAN FORGET THE PAST, EH?
GOODBYE... DOCTOR BLACK JACK...
TOOOT
TOOOT

OPERATION FIVE

TWO
LOVES

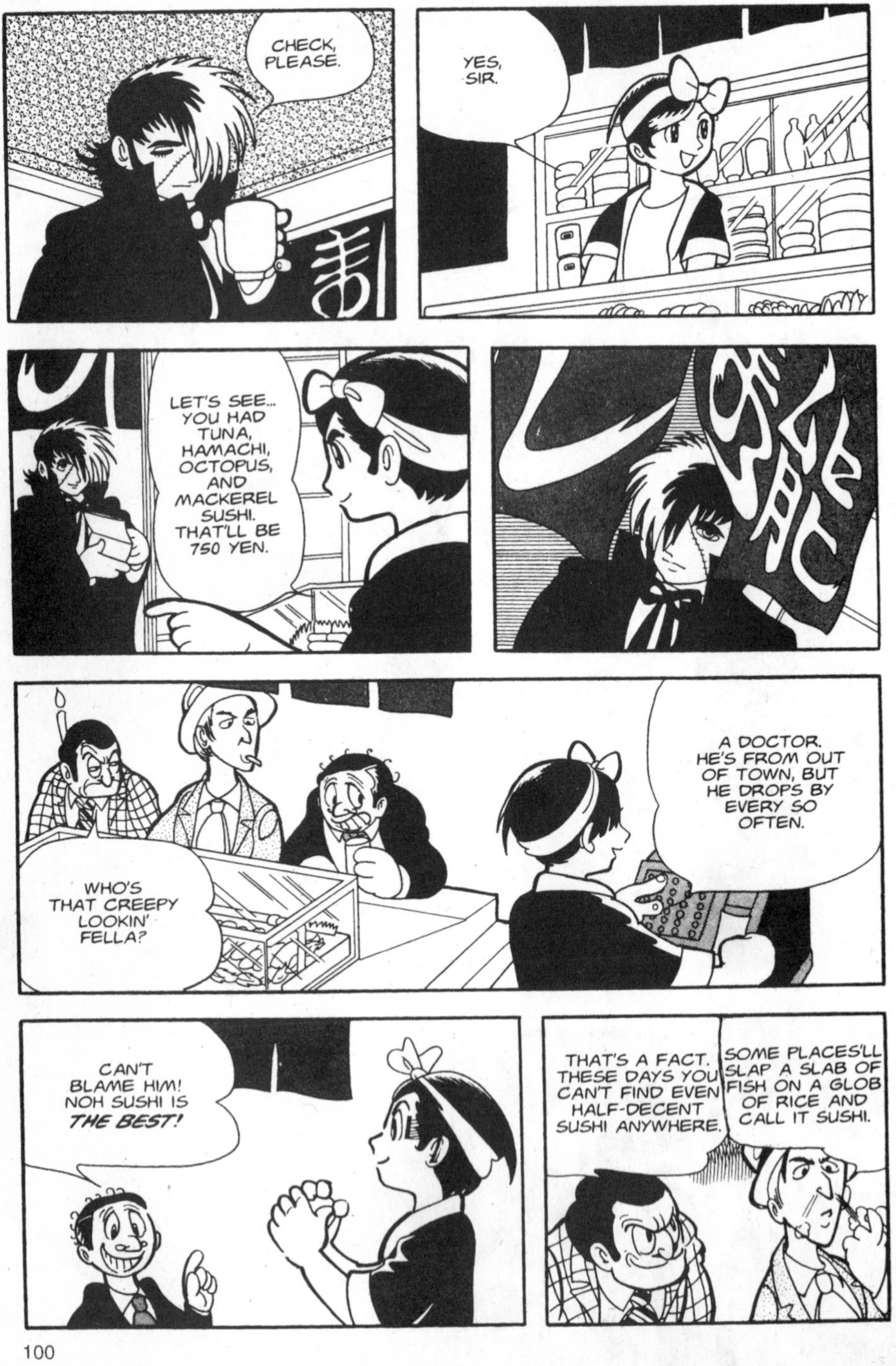
CHECK, PLEASE.
YES, SIR.
LET'S SEE... YOU HAD TUNA, HAMACHI, OCTOPUS, AND MACKEREL SUSHI. THAT'LL BE 750 YEN.
WHO'S THAT CREEPY LOOKIN' FELLA?
A DOCTOR. HE'S FROM OUT OF TOWN, BUT HE DROPS BY EVERY SO OFTEN.
CAN'T BLAME HIM! NOH SUSHI IS *THE BEST!*
THAT'S A FACT. THESE DAYS YOU CAN'T FIND EVEN HALF-DECENT SUSHI ANYWHERE.
SOME PLACES'LL SLAP A SLAB OF FISH ON A GLOB OF RICE AND CALL IT SUSHI.

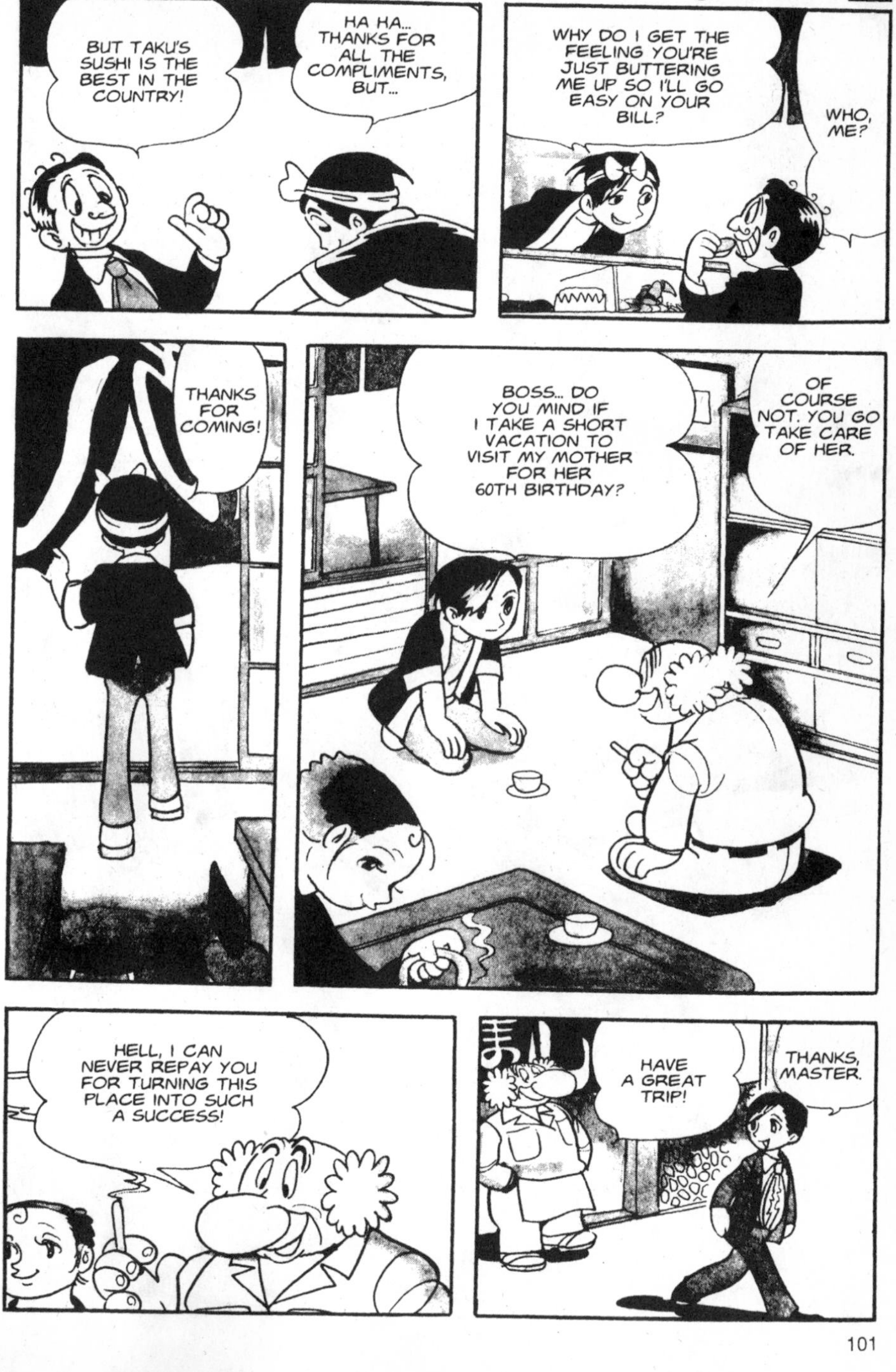
BUT TAKU'S SUSHI IS THE BEST IN THE COUNTRY!
HA HA... THANKS FOR ALL THE COMPLIMENTS, BUT...
WHY DO I GET THE FEELING YOU'RE JUST BUTTERING ME UP SO I'LL GO EASY ON YOUR BILL?
WHO, ME?
THANKS FOR COMING!
BOSS... DO YOU MIND IF I TAKE A SHORT VACATION TO VISIT MY MOTHER FOR HER 60TH BIRTHDAY?
OF COURSE NOT. YOU GO TAKE CARE OF HER.
HELL, I CAN NEVER REPAY YOU FOR TURNING THIS PLACE INTO SUCH A SUCCESS!
HAVE A GREAT TRIP!
THANKS, MASTER.

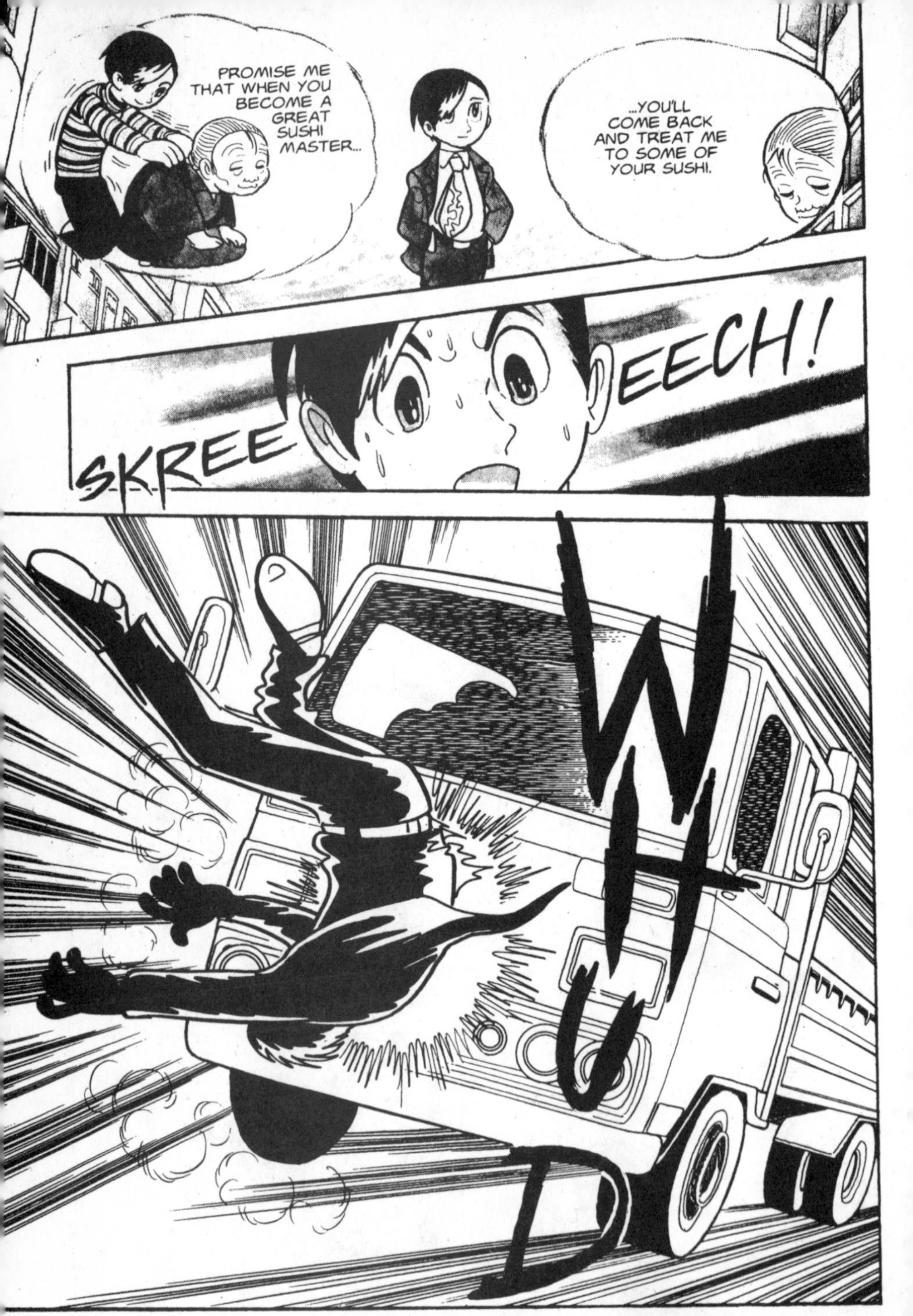
PROMISE ME THAT WHEN YOU BECOME A GREAT SUSHI MASTER...
...YOU'LL COME BACK AND TREAT ME TO SOME OF YOUR SUSHI.
SKREE
EECH!
WHUD

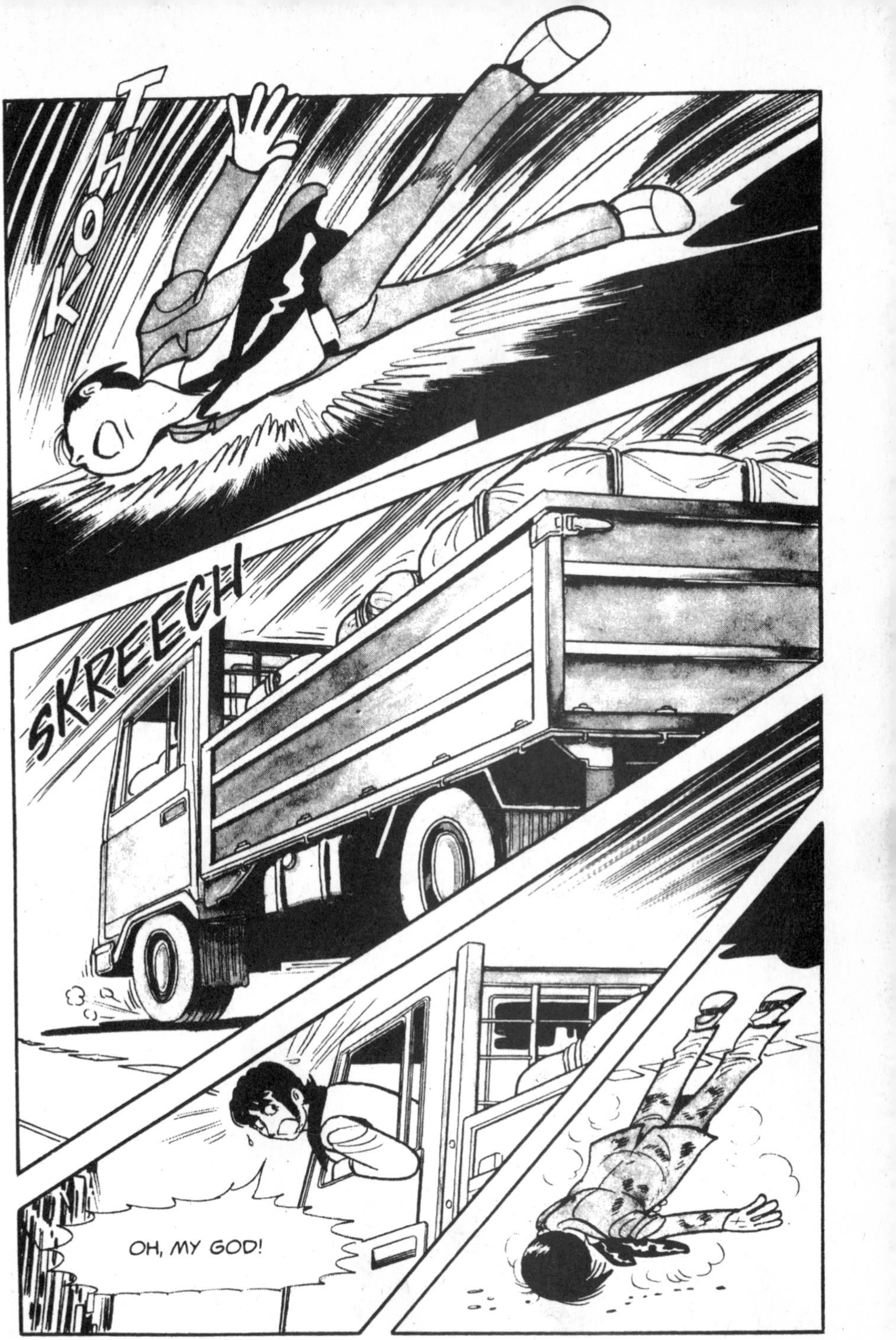
THOK
SKREECH
OH, MY GOD!

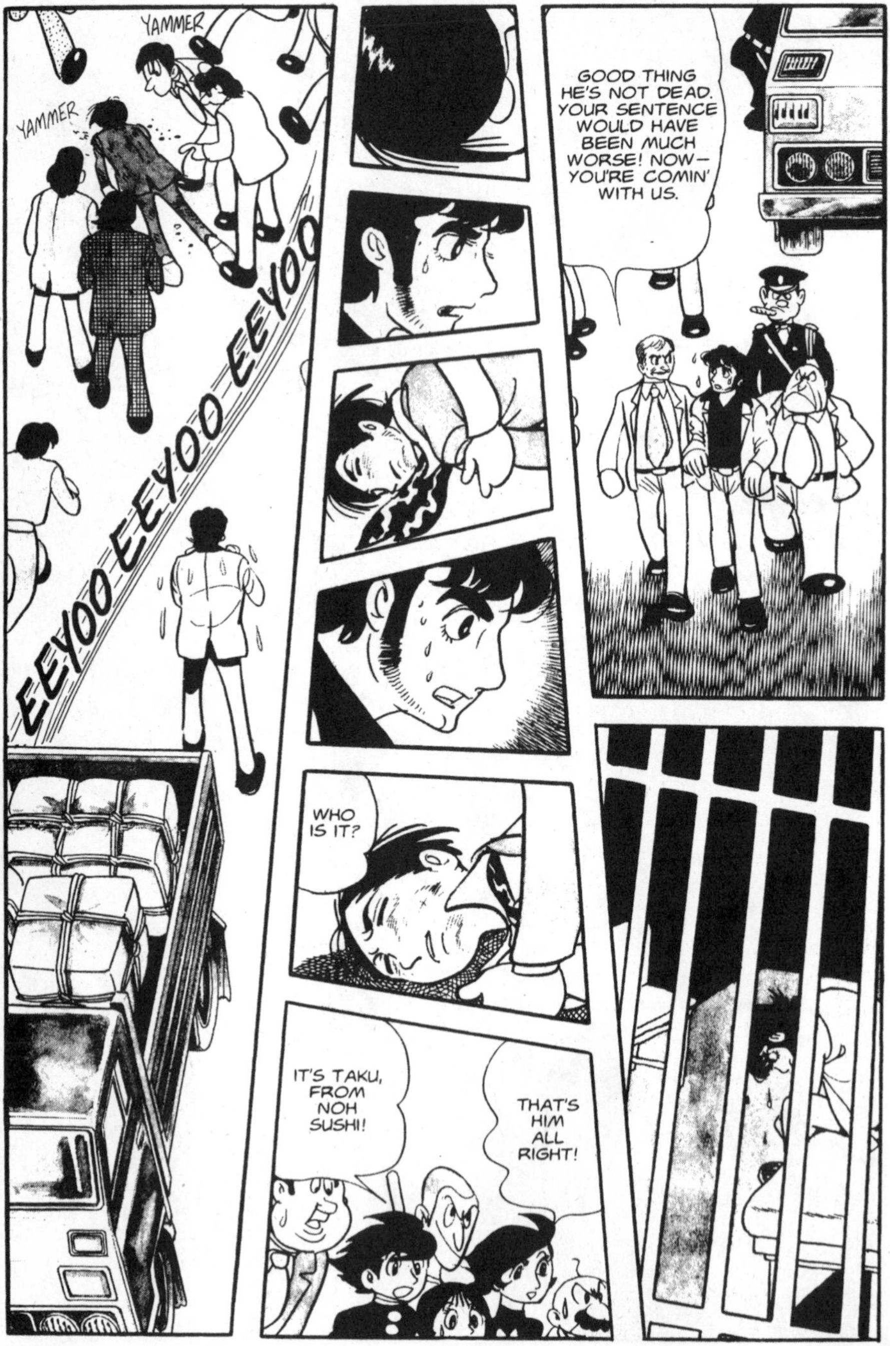
GOOD THING HE'S NOT DEAD. YOUR SENTENCE WOULD HAVE BEEN MUCH WORSE! NOW— YOU'RE COMIN' WITH US.
WHO IS IT?
IT'S TAKU, FROM NOH SUSHI!
THAT'S HIM ALL RIGHT!
YAMMER
YAMMER
EEYOO EEYOO EEYOO EEYOO

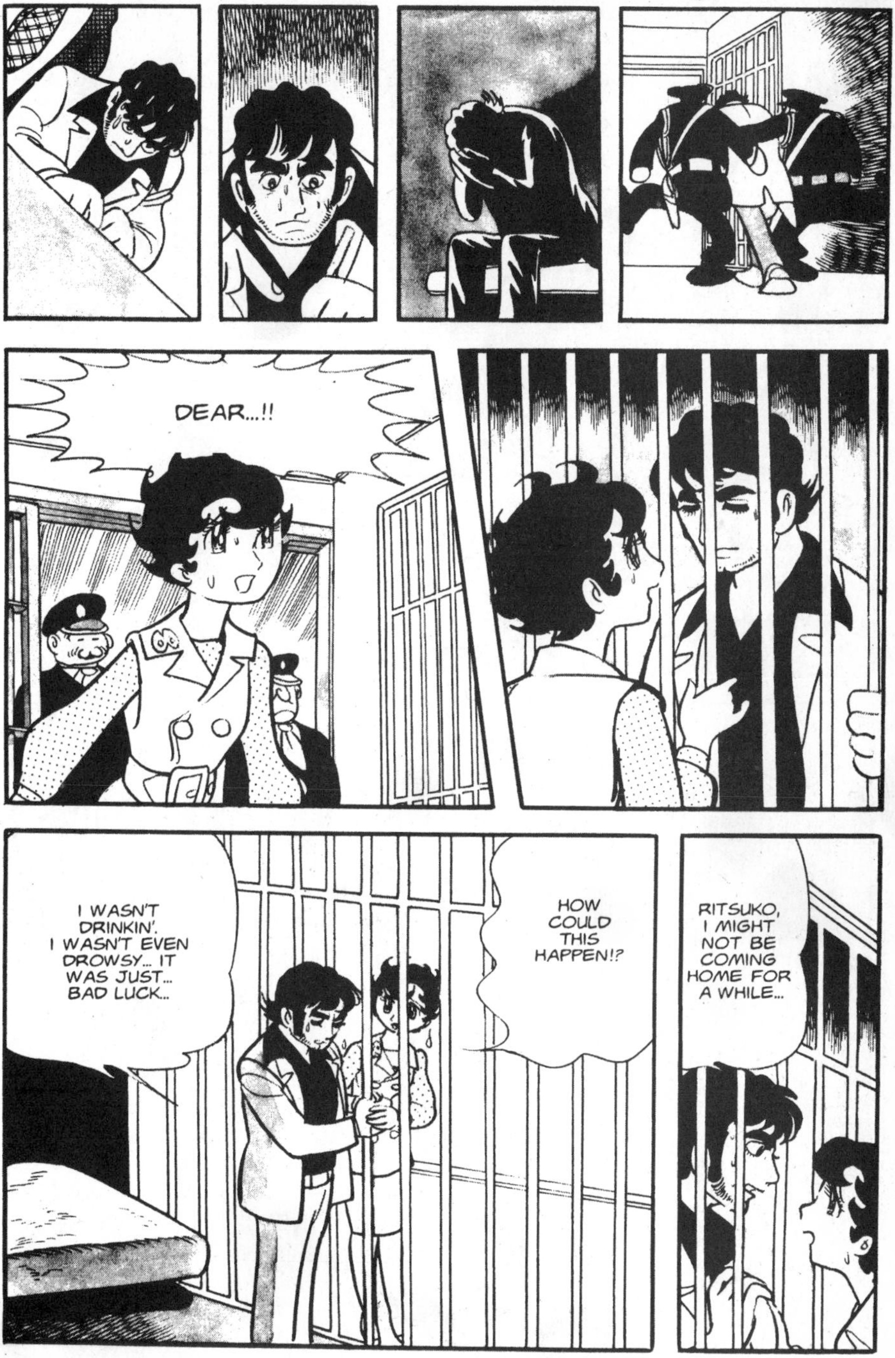
DEAR...!!
RITSUKO, I MIGHT NOT BE COMING HOME FOR A WHILE...
HOW COULD THIS HAPPEN!?
I WASN'T DRINKIN'. I WASN'T EVEN DROWSY... IT WAS JUST... BAD LUCK...

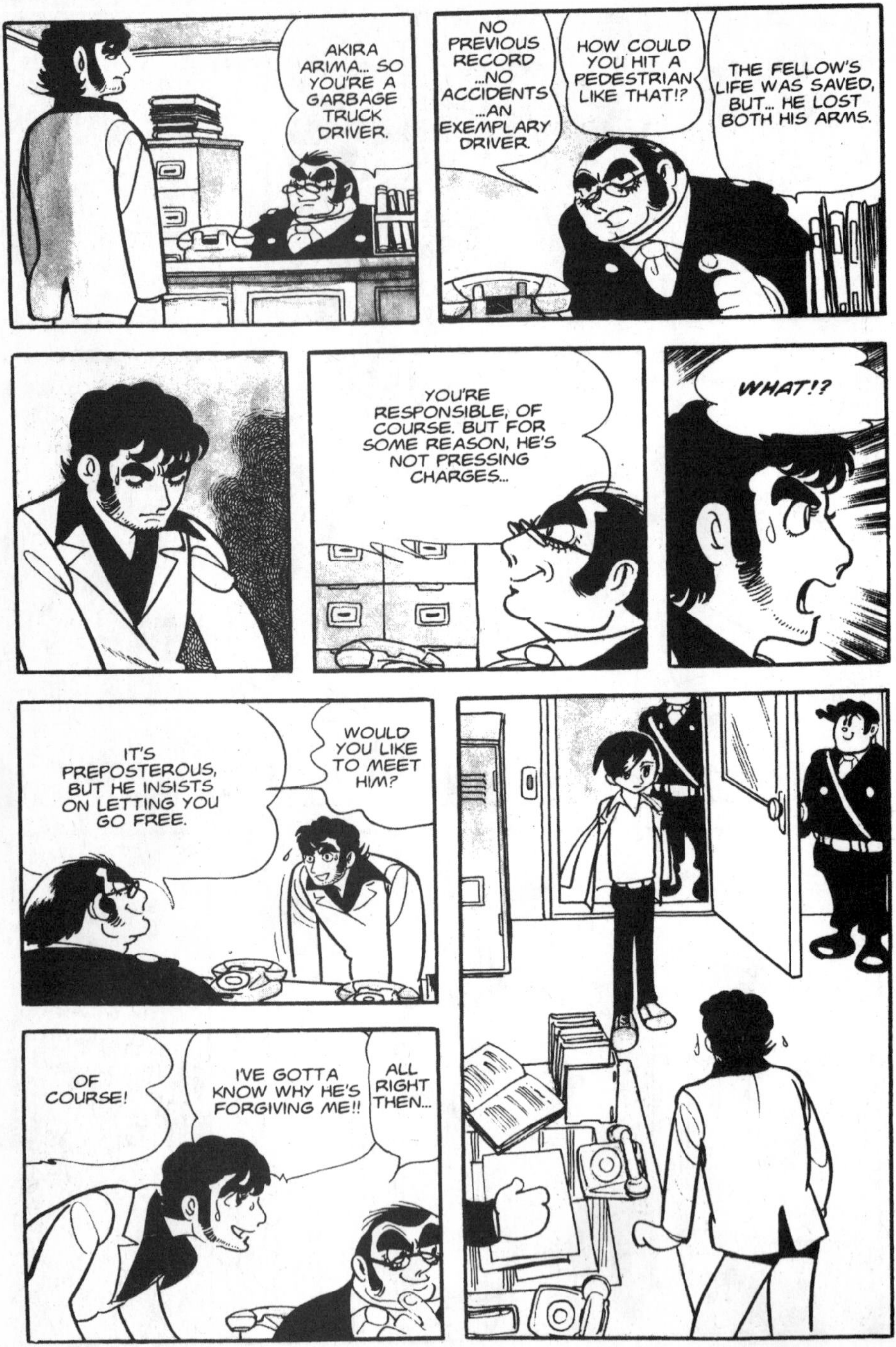
AKIRA ARIMA... SO YOU'RE A GARBAGE TRUCK DRIVER.
NO PREVIOUS RECORD ...NO ACCIDENTS ...AN EXEMPLARY DRIVER.
HOW COULD YOU HIT A PEDESTRIAN LIKE THAT!?
THE FELLOW'S LIFE WAS SAVED, BUT... HE LOST BOTH HIS ARMS.
YOU'RE RESPONSIBLE, OF COURSE. BUT FOR SOME REASON, HE'S NOT PRESSING CHARGES...
WHAT!?
IT'S PREPOSTEROUS, BUT HE INSISTS ON LETTING YOU GO FREE.
WOULD YOU LIKE TO MEET HIM?
OF COURSE!
I'VE GOTTA KNOW WHY HE'S FORGIVING ME!!
ALL RIGHT THEN...

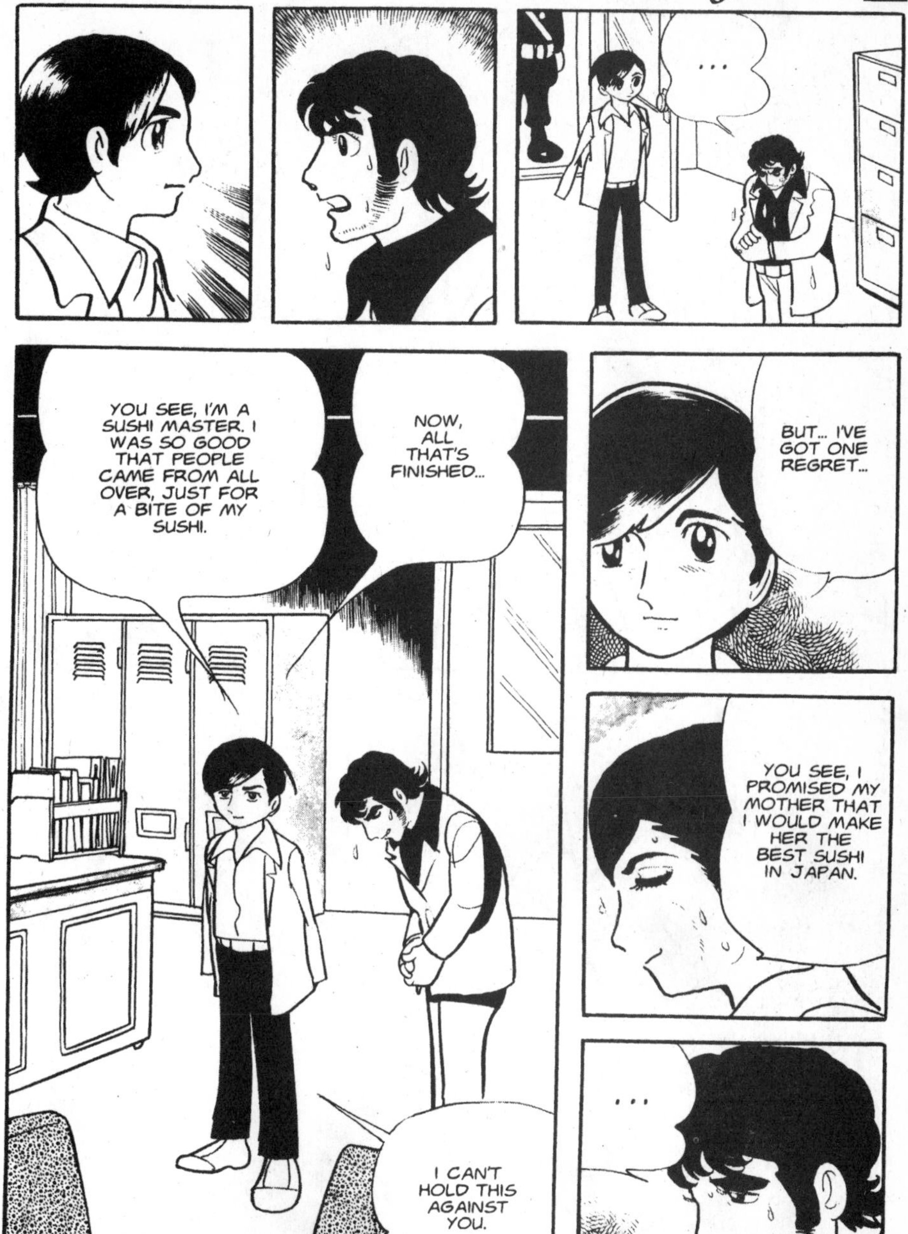
...
I CAN'T HOLD THIS AGAINST YOU.
YOU SEE, I'M A SUSHI MASTER. I WAS SO GOOD THAT PEOPLE CAME FROM ALL OVER, JUST FOR A BITE OF MY SUSHI.
NOW, ALL THAT'S FINISHED...
BUT... I'VE GOT ONE REGRET...
YOU SEE, I PROMISED MY MOTHER THAT I WOULD MAKE HER THE BEST SUSHI IN JAPAN.
...

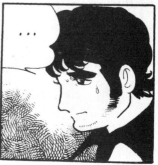

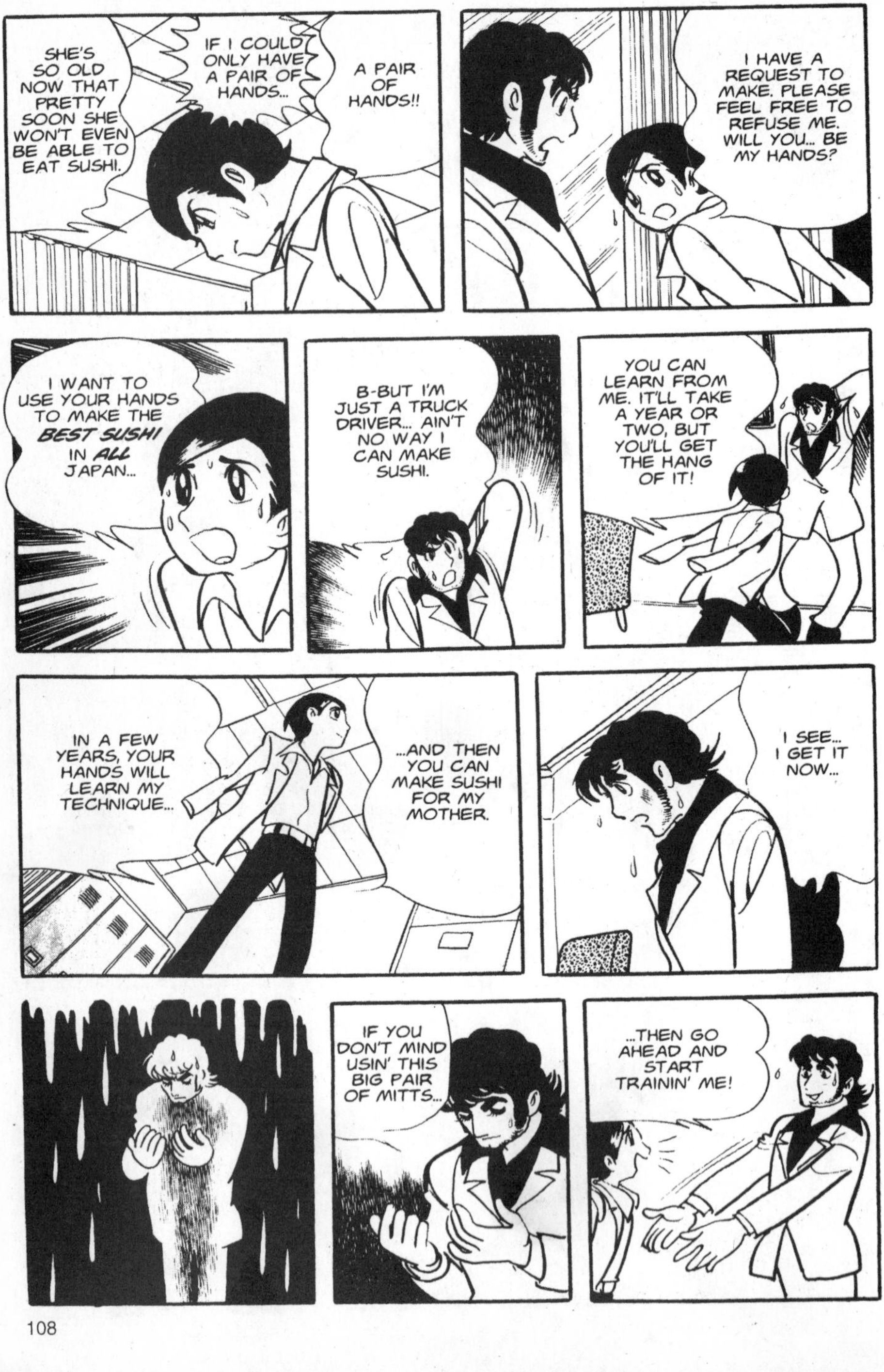
SHE'S SO OLD NOW THAT PRETTY SOON SHE WON'T EVEN BE ABLE TO EAT SUSHI.
IF I COULD ONLY HAVE A PAIR OF HANDS...
A PAIR OF HANDS!!
I HAVE A REQUEST TO MAKE. PLEASE FEEL FREE TO REFUSE ME. WILL YOU... BE MY HANDS?
I WANT TO USE YOUR HANDS TO MAKE THE *BEST SUSHI* IN *ALL* JAPAN...
B-BUT I'M JUST A TRUCK DRIVER... AIN'T NO WAY I CAN MAKE SUSHI.
YOU CAN LEARN FROM ME. IT'LL TAKE A YEAR OR TWO, BUT YOU'LL GET THE HANG OF IT!
IN A FEW YEARS, YOUR HANDS WILL LEARN MY TECHNIQUE...
...AND THEN YOU CAN MAKE SUSHI FOR MY MOTHER.
I SEE... I GET IT NOW...
IF YOU DON'T MIND USIN' THIS BIG PAIR OF MITTS...
...THEN GO AHEAD AND START TRAININ' ME!

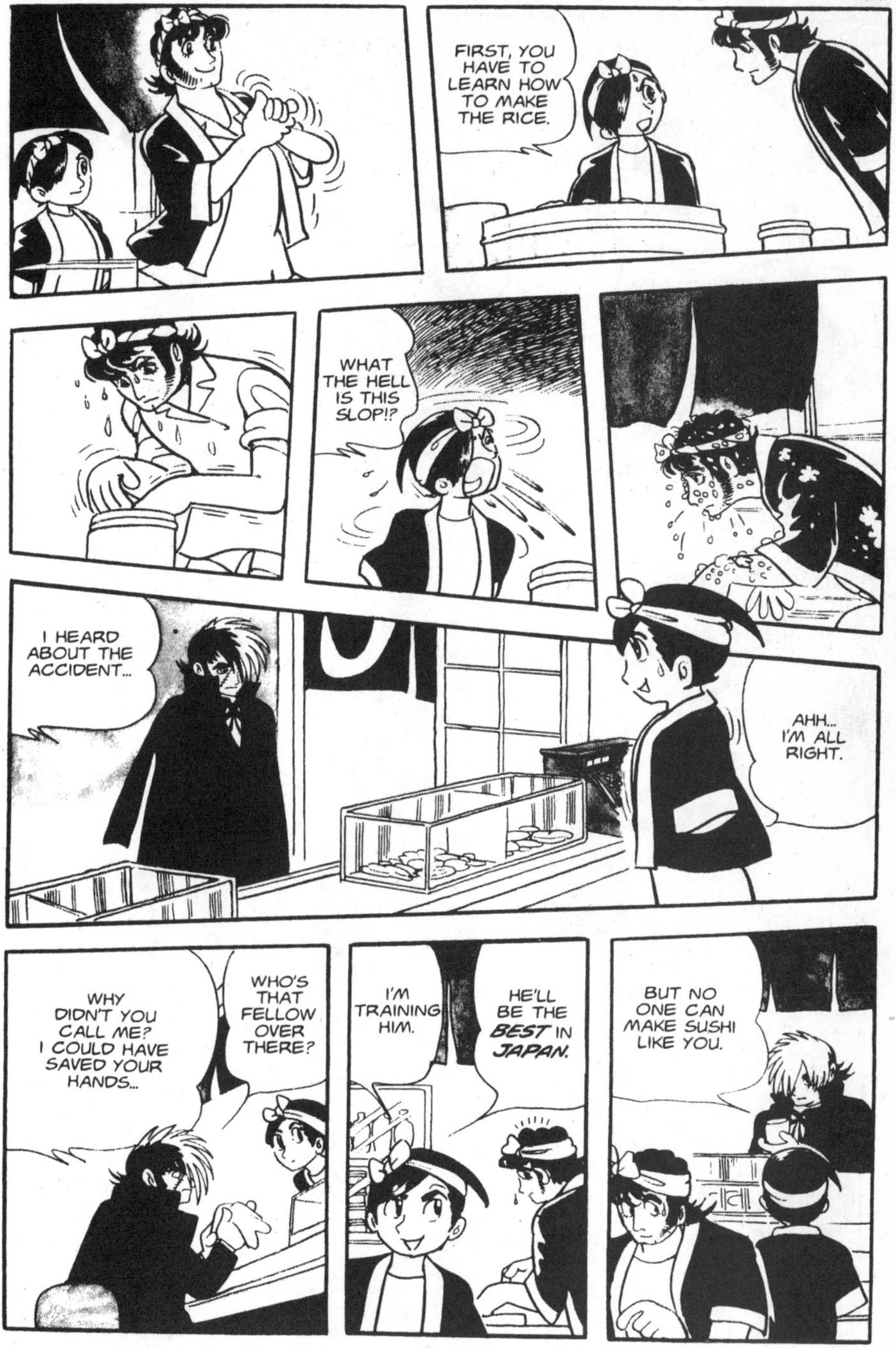
FIRST, YOU HAVE TO LEARN HOW TO MAKE THE RICE.
WHAT THE HELL IS THIS SLOP!?
I HEARD ABOUT THE ACCIDENT...
AHH... I'M ALL RIGHT.
WHY DIDN'T YOU CALL ME? I COULD HAVE SAVED YOUR HANDS...
WHO'S THAT FELLOW OVER THERE?
I'M TRAINING HIM.
HE'LL BE THE BEST IN JAPAN.
BUT NO ONE CAN MAKE SUSHI LIKE YOU.

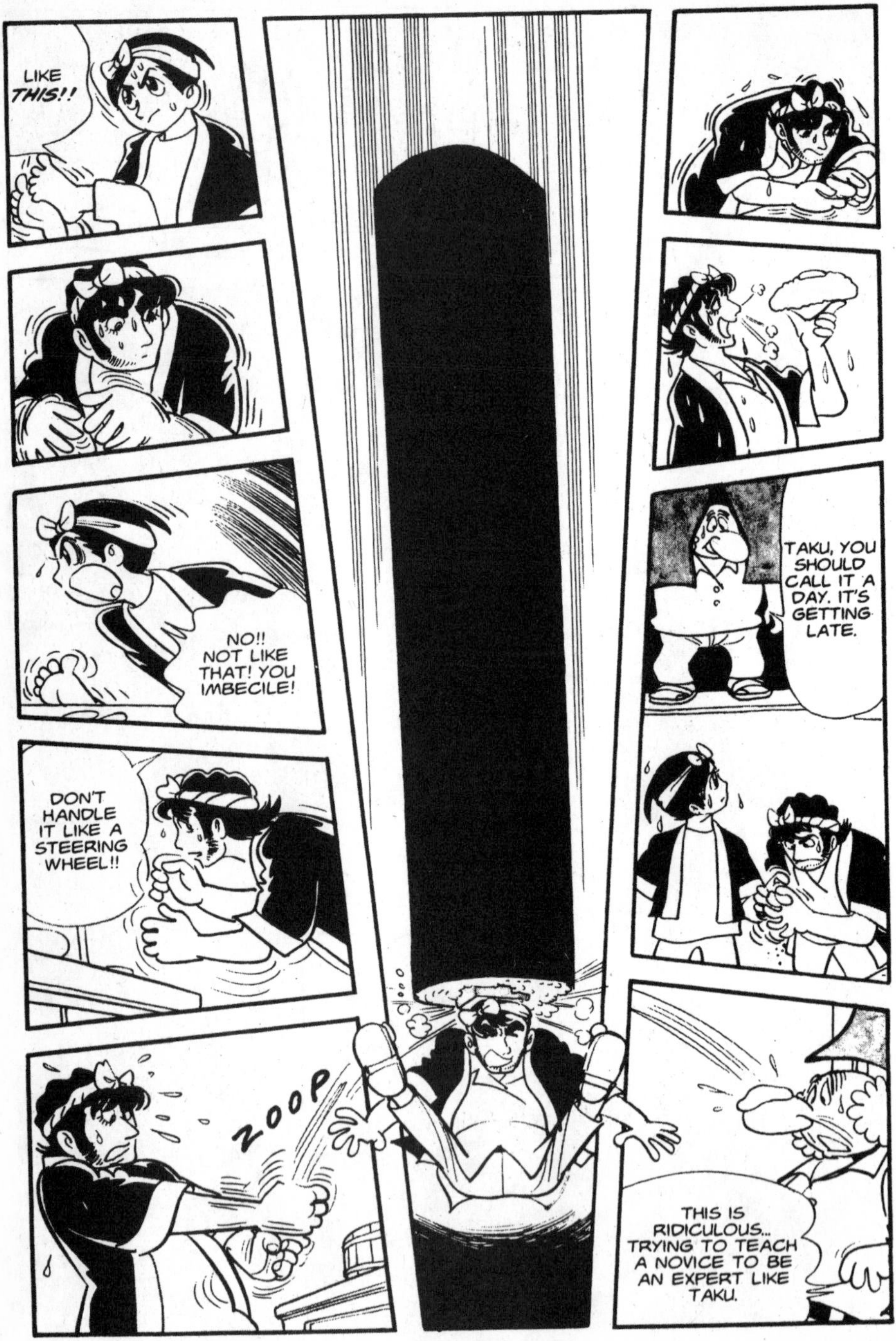
LIKE THIS!!
NO!! NOT LIKE THAT! YOU IMBECILE!
DON'T HANDLE IT LIKE A STEERING WHEEL!!
ZOOP
TAKU, YOU SHOULD CALL IT A DAY. IT'S GETTING LATE.
THIS IS RIDICULOUS... TRYING TO TEACH A NOVICE TO BE AN EXPERT LIKE TAKU.

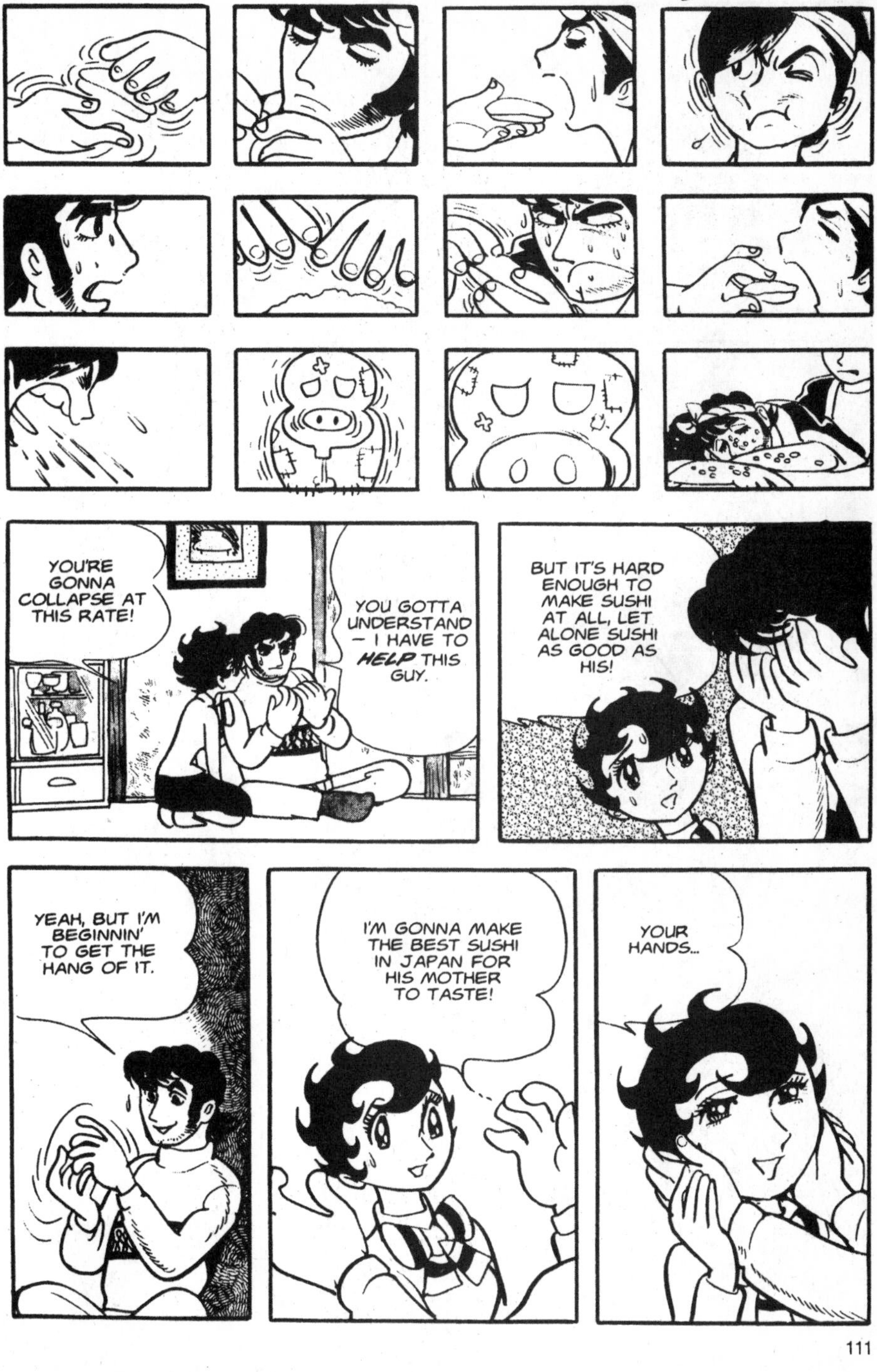
YOU'RE GONNA COLLAPSE AT THIS RATE!
YOU GOTTA UNDERSTAND – I HAVE TO HELP THIS GUY.
BUT IT'S HARD ENOUGH TO MAKE SUSHI AT ALL, LET ALONE SUSHI AS GOOD AS HIS!
YEAH, BUT I'M BEGINNIN' TO GET THE HANG OF IT.
I'M GONNA MAKE THE BEST SUSHI IN JAPAN FOR HIS MOTHER TO TASTE!
YOUR HANDS...

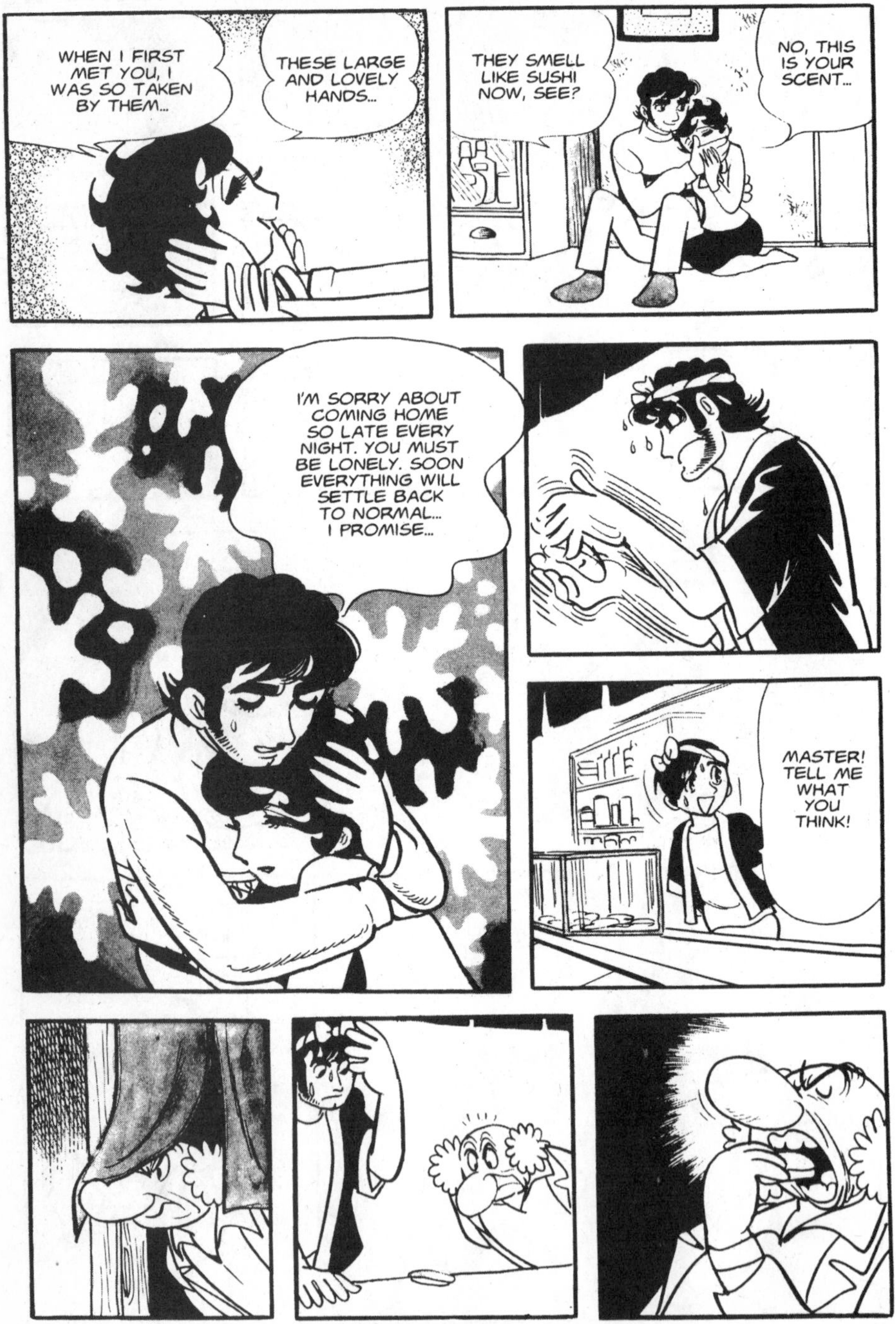
WHEN I FIRST MET YOU, I WAS SO TAKEN BY THEM...
THESE LARGE AND LOVELY HANDS...
THEY SMELL LIKE SUSHI NOW, SEE?
NO, THIS IS YOUR SCENT...
I'M SORRY ABOUT COMING HOME SO LATE EVERY NIGHT. YOU MUST BE LONELY. SOON EVERYTHING WILL SETTLE BACK TO NORMAL... I PROMISE...
MASTER! TELL ME WHAT YOU THINK!

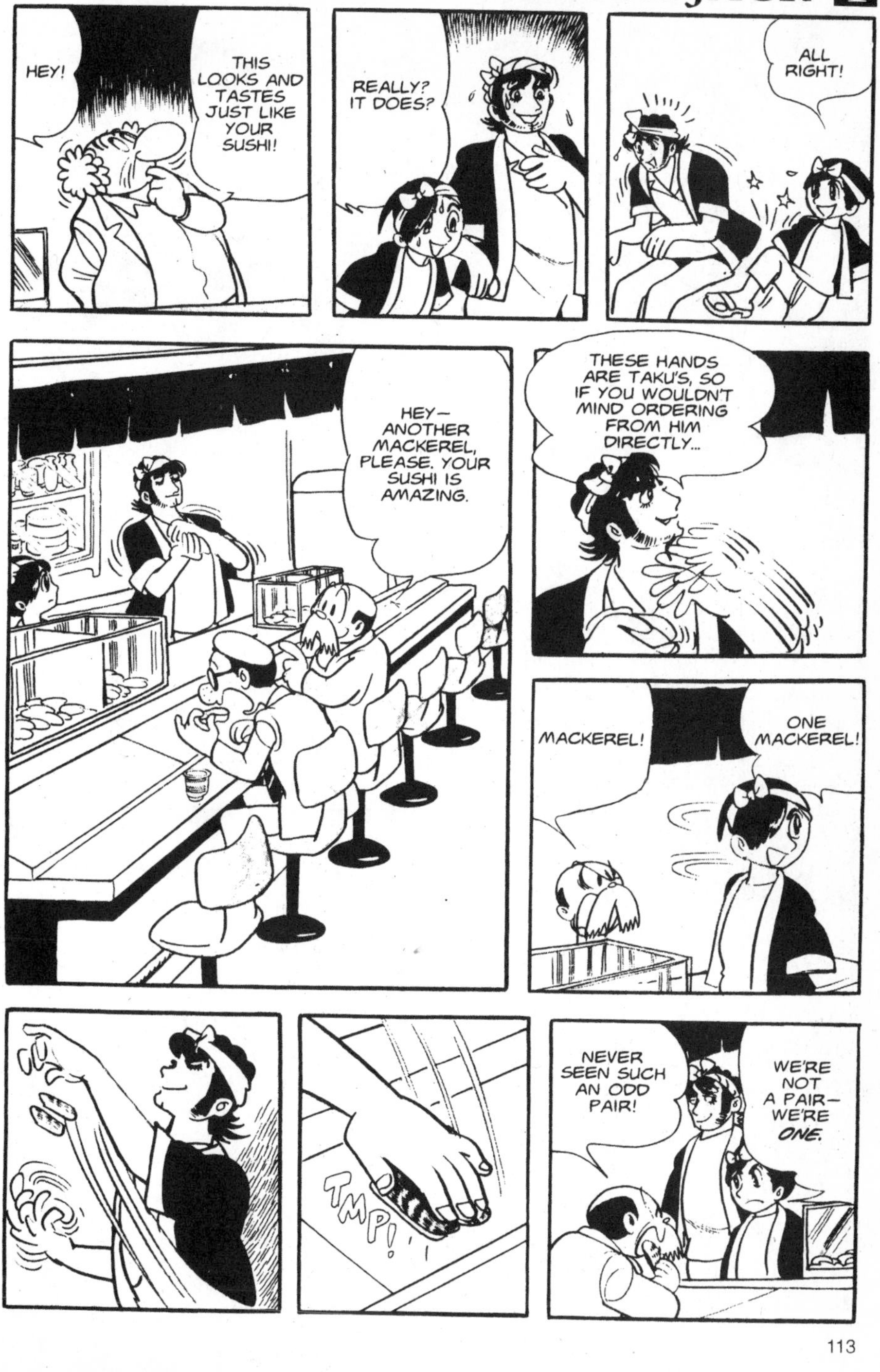
HEY!
THIS LOOKS AND TASTES JUST LIKE YOUR SUSHI!
REALLY? IT DOES?
ALL RIGHT!
HEY— ANOTHER MACKEREL, PLEASE. YOUR SUSHI IS AMAZING.
THESE HANDS ARE TAKU'S, SO IF YOU WOULDN'T MIND ORDERING FROM HIM DIRECTLY...
MACKEREL!
ONE MACKEREL!
TMP!
NEVER SEEN SUCH AN ODD PAIR!
WE'RE NOT A PAIR— WE'RE *ONE*.

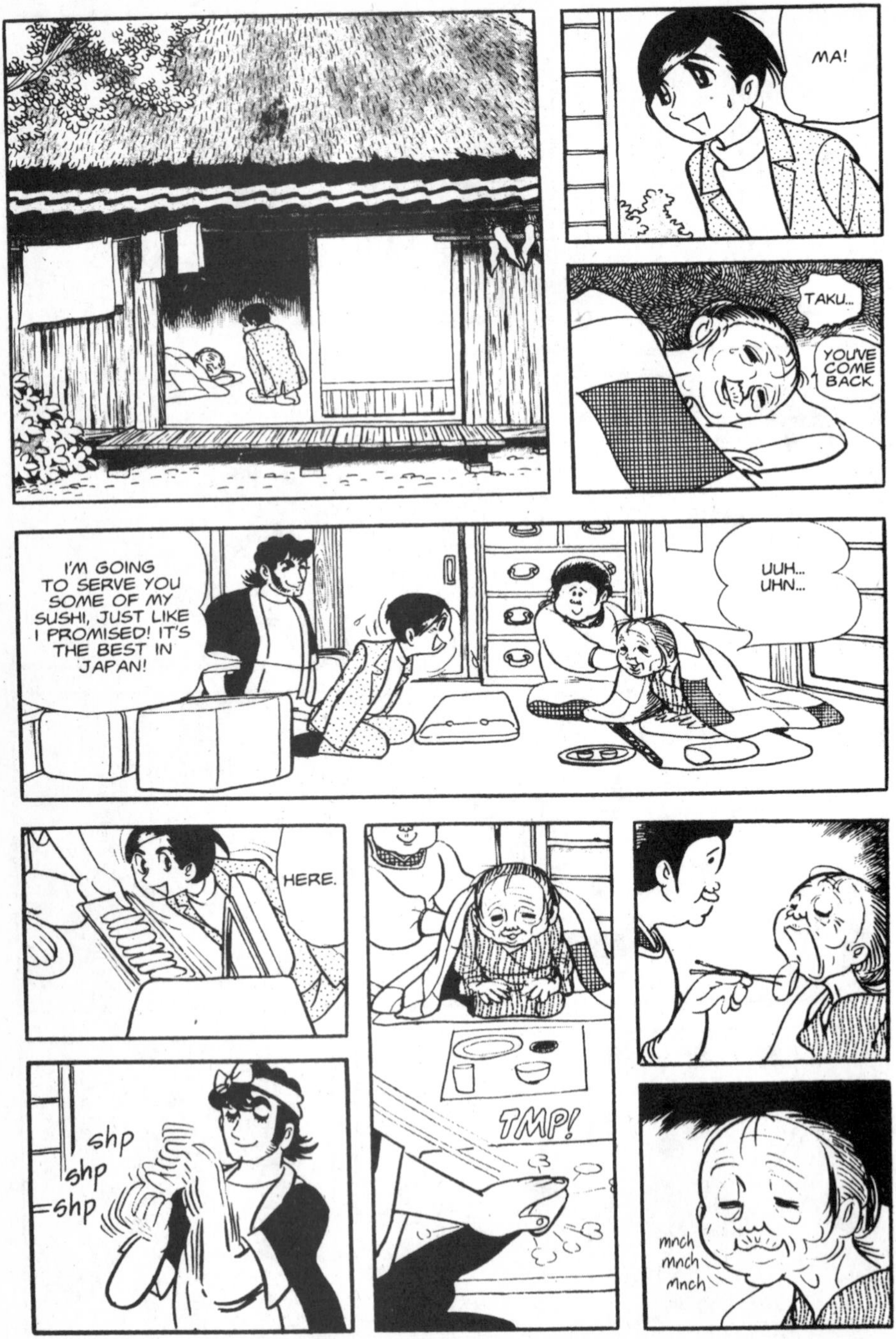

MA!
TAKU...
YOU'VE COME BACK.
I'M GOING TO SERVE YOU SOME OF MY SUSHI, JUST LIKE I PROMISED! IT'S THE BEST IN JAPAN!
UUH... UHN...
HERE.
shp shp shp
TMP!
mnch mnch mnch

aah...

HOW IS IT, MA? I KNOW YOU CAN'T SEE VERY WELL, BUT I'M SURE THE TASTE COMES THROUGH...

D-DELI...

TAKU... IT'S DE-*LI*-CIOUS...

THE MASTER SAID HE'S GOING TO LET ME HAVE THE RESTAURANT.

MA, I'M GONNA HAVE THE BEST SUSHI RESTAURANT IN THE COUNTRY!

TAKU... I'M SO PROUD...

I FEEL LIKE WE PULLED ONE OVER ON YOUR MOTHER...

BUT WE *DIDN'T*. WE USED *MY* HANDS.

I-I DON'T KNOW HOW TO THANK YOU, AKIRA...

115

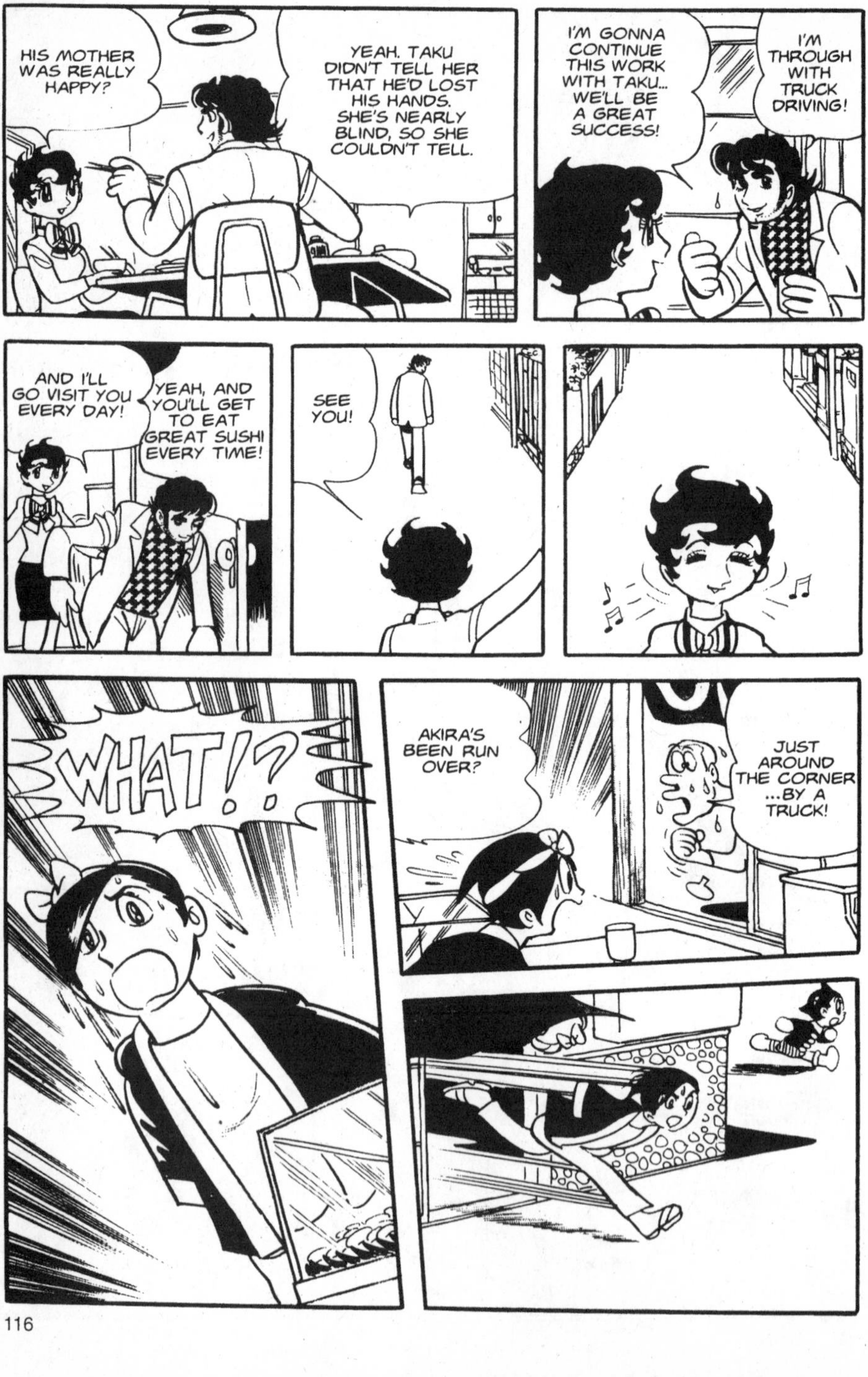
HIS MOTHER WAS REALLY HAPPY?
YEAH. TAKU DIDN'T TELL HER THAT HE'D LOST HIS HANDS. SHE'S NEARLY BLIND, SO SHE COULDN'T TELL.
I'M GONNA CONTINUE THIS WORK WITH TAKU... WE'LL BE A GREAT SUCCESS!
I'M THROUGH WITH TRUCK DRIVING!
AND I'LL GO VISIT YOU EVERY DAY!
YEAH, AND YOU'LL GET TO EAT GREAT SUSHI EVERY TIME!
SEE YOU!
WHAT!?
AKIRA'S BEEN RUN OVER?
JUST AROUND THE CORNER ...BY A TRUCK!

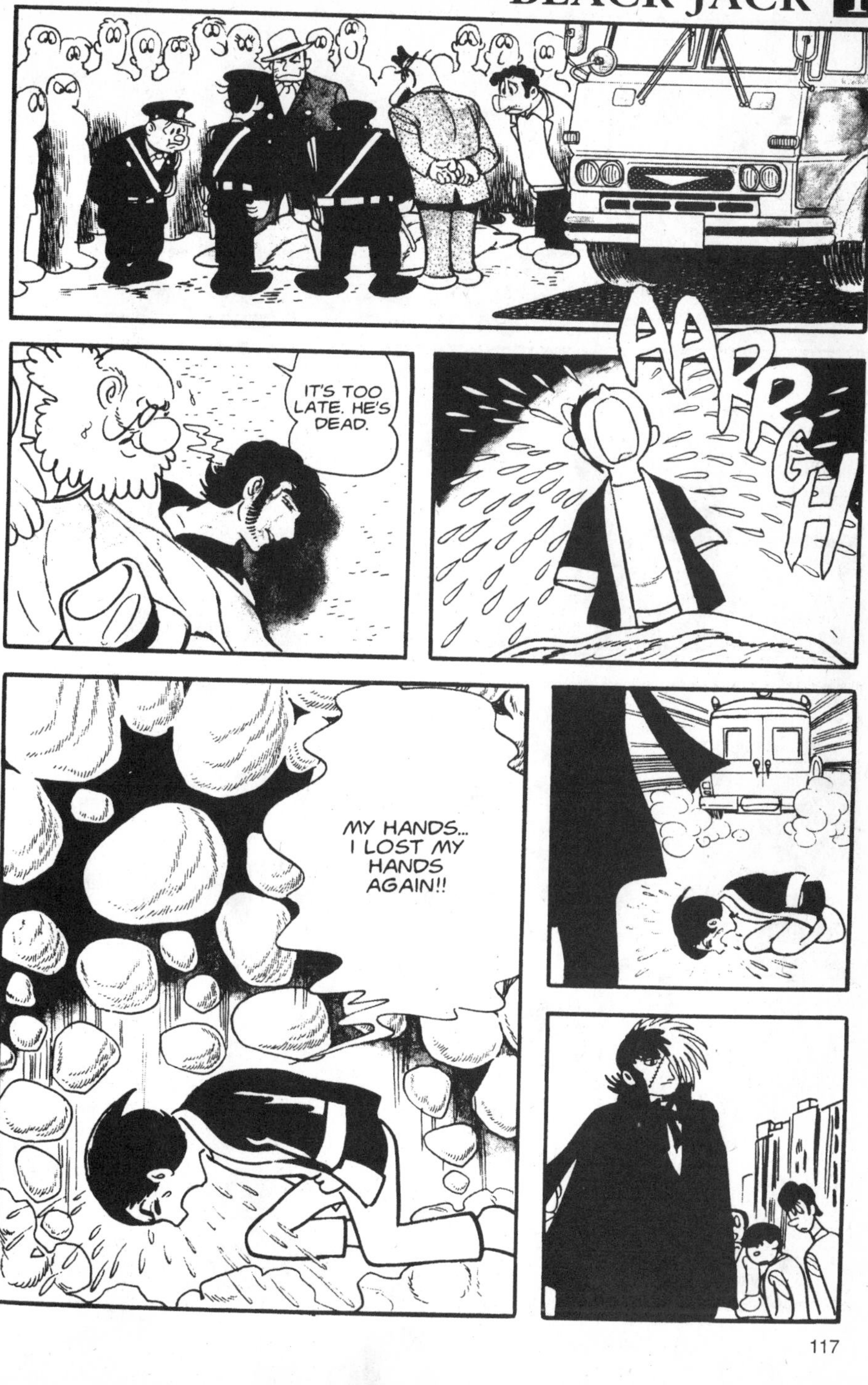
IT'S TOO LATE. HE'S DEAD.
AARRGH
MY HANDS... I LOST MY HANDS AGAIN!!

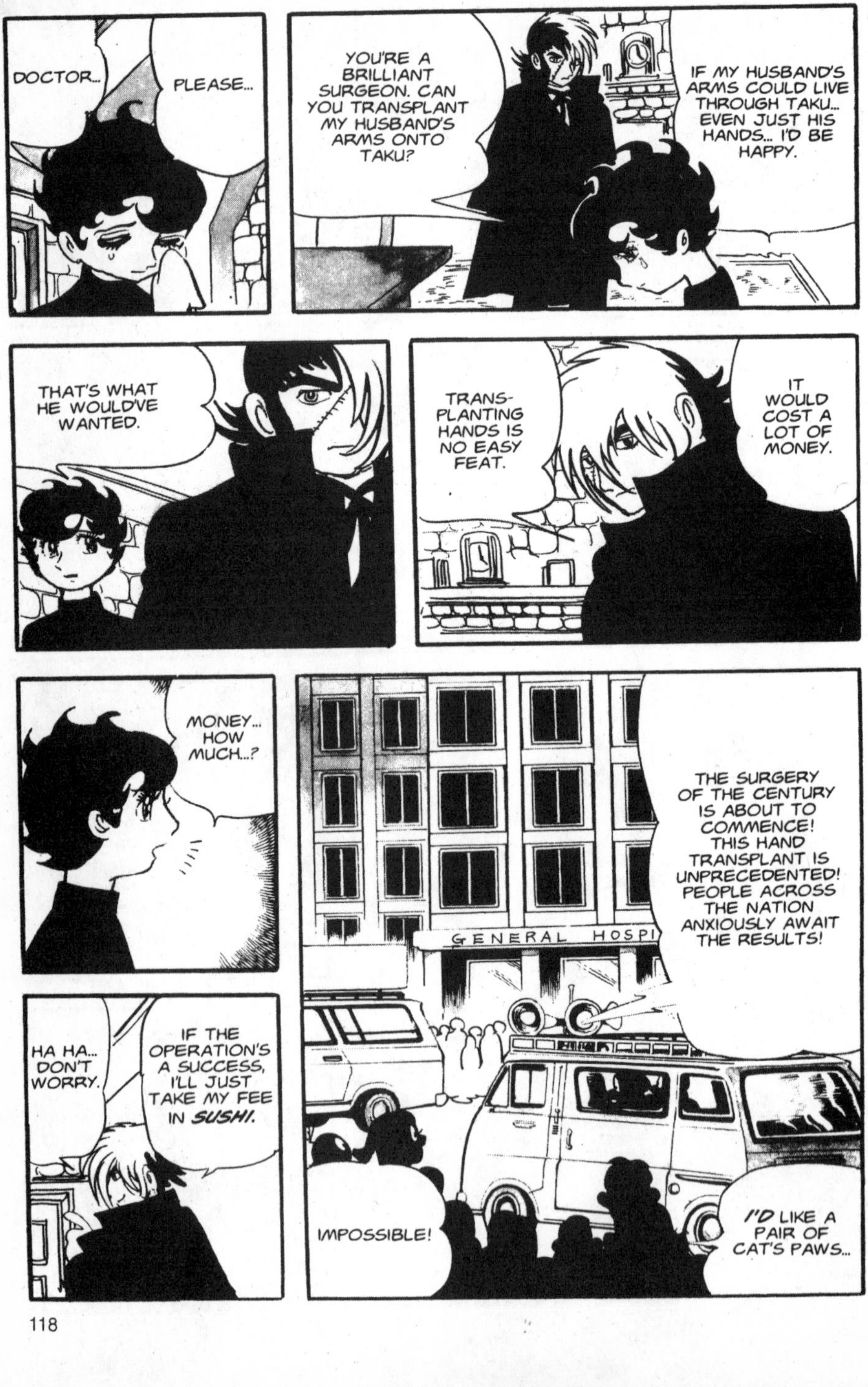

DOCTOR...
PLEASE...
YOU'RE A BRILLIANT SURGEON. CAN YOU TRANSPLANT MY HUSBAND'S ARMS ONTO TAKU?
IF MY HUSBAND'S ARMS COULD LIVE THROUGH TAKU... EVEN JUST HIS HANDS... I'D BE HAPPY.
THAT'S WHAT HE WOULD'VE WANTED.
TRANS-PLANTING HANDS IS NO EASY FEAT.
IT WOULD COST A LOT OF MONEY.
MONEY... HOW MUCH...?
HA HA... DON'T WORRY.
IF THE OPERATION'S A SUCCESS, I'LL JUST TAKE MY FEE IN *SUSHI*.
GENERAL HOSPI
THE SURGERY OF THE CENTURY IS ABOUT TO COMMENCE! THIS HAND TRANSPLANT IS UNPRECEDENTED! PEOPLE ACROSS THE NATION ANXIOUSLY AWAIT THE RESULTS!
IMPOSSIBLE!
I'D LIKE A PAIR OF CAT'S PAWS...

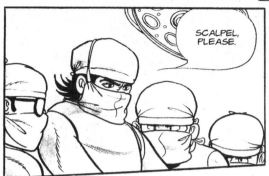

SCALPEL, PLEASE.
DOUBLE LIGATURE FOLLOWED BY SEVERING OF THE VEINS.
SLK SLK SLK SLK SLK SLK
GIVE ME AKIRA'S ARM.
NERVE AND VASCULAR SUTURES.
I'LL TAKE IT FROM HERE.

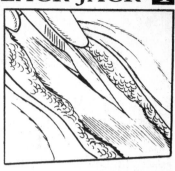

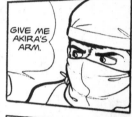

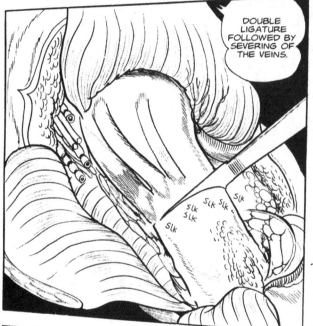

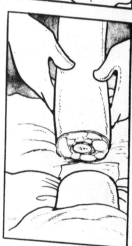

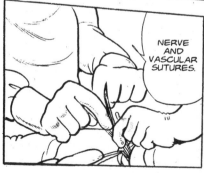

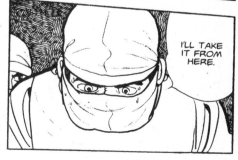

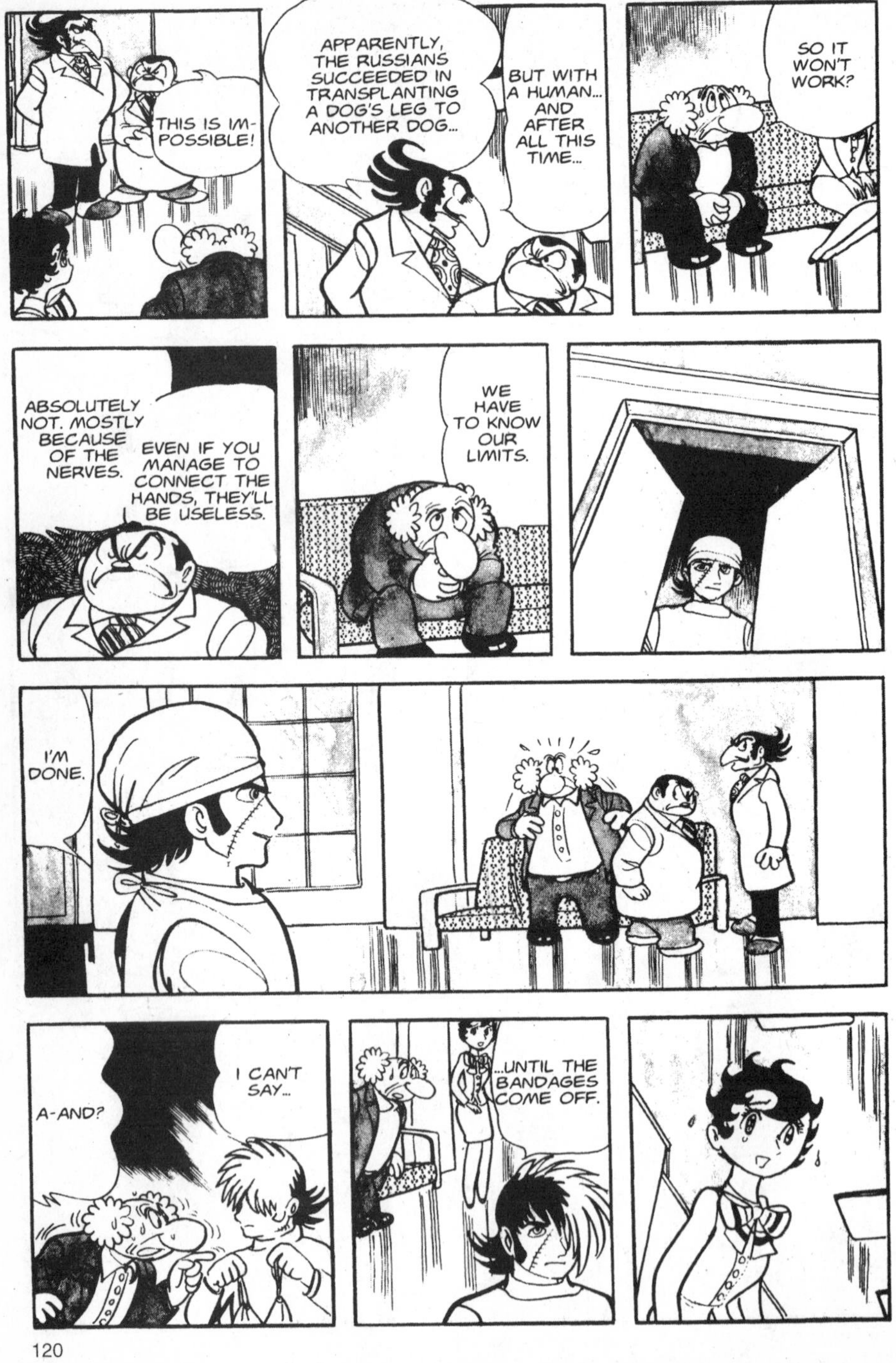
THIS IS IMPOSSIBLE!
APPARENTLY, THE RUSSIANS SUCCEEDED IN TRANSPLANTING A DOG'S LEG TO ANOTHER DOG...
BUT WITH A HUMAN... AND AFTER ALL THIS TIME...
SO IT WON'T WORK?
ABSOLUTELY NOT. MOSTLY BECAUSE OF THE NERVES.
EVEN IF YOU MANAGE TO CONNECT THE HANDS, THEY'LL BE USELESS.
WE HAVE TO KNOW OUR LIMITS.
I'M DONE.
A-AND?
I CAN'T SAY...
...UNTIL THE BANDAGES COME OFF.

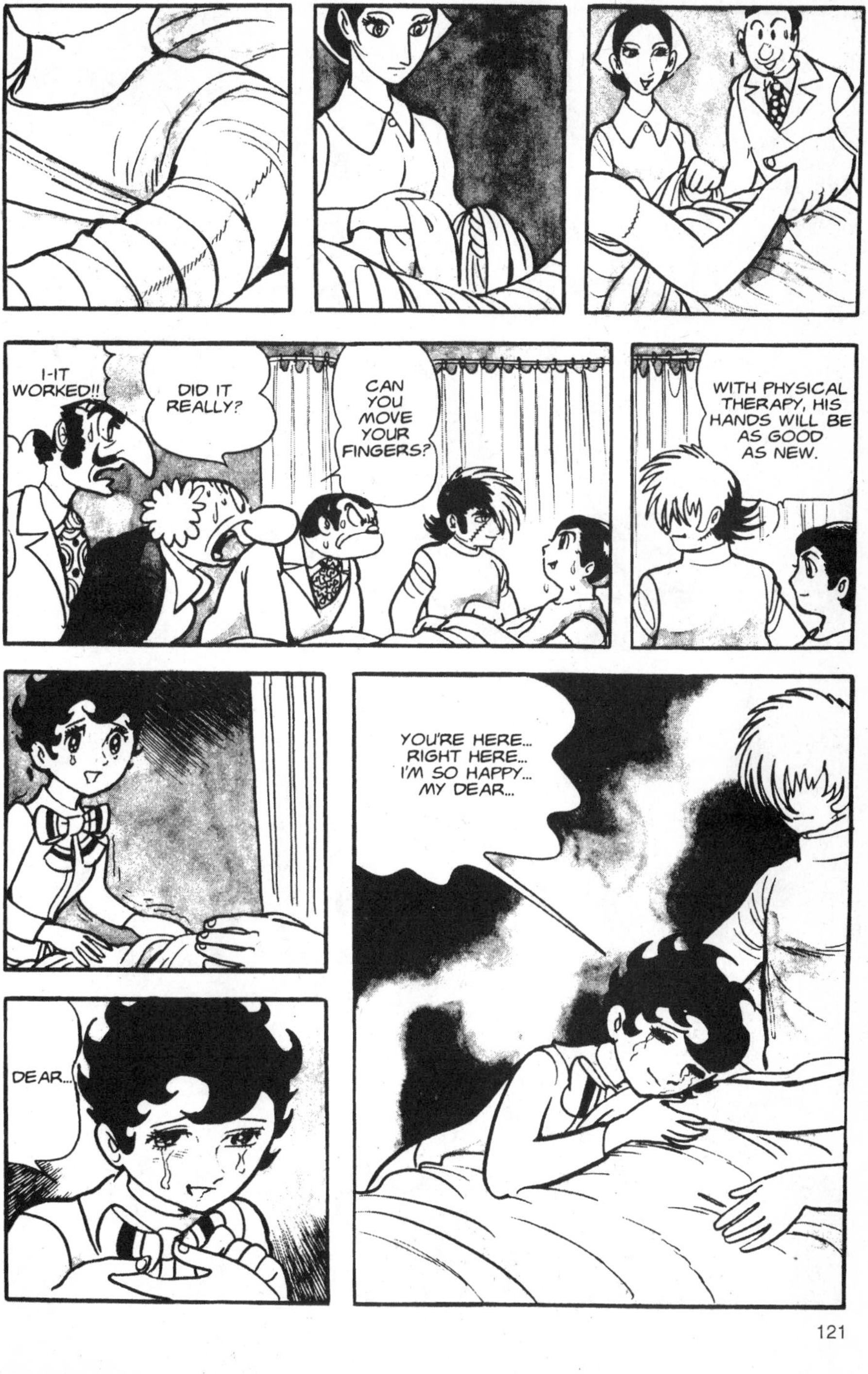
I-IT WORKED!!
DID IT REALLY?
CAN YOU MOVE YOUR FINGERS?
WITH PHYSICAL THERAPY, HIS HANDS WILL BE AS GOOD AS NEW.
YOU'RE HERE... RIGHT HERE... I'M SO HAPPY... MY DEAR...
DEAR...

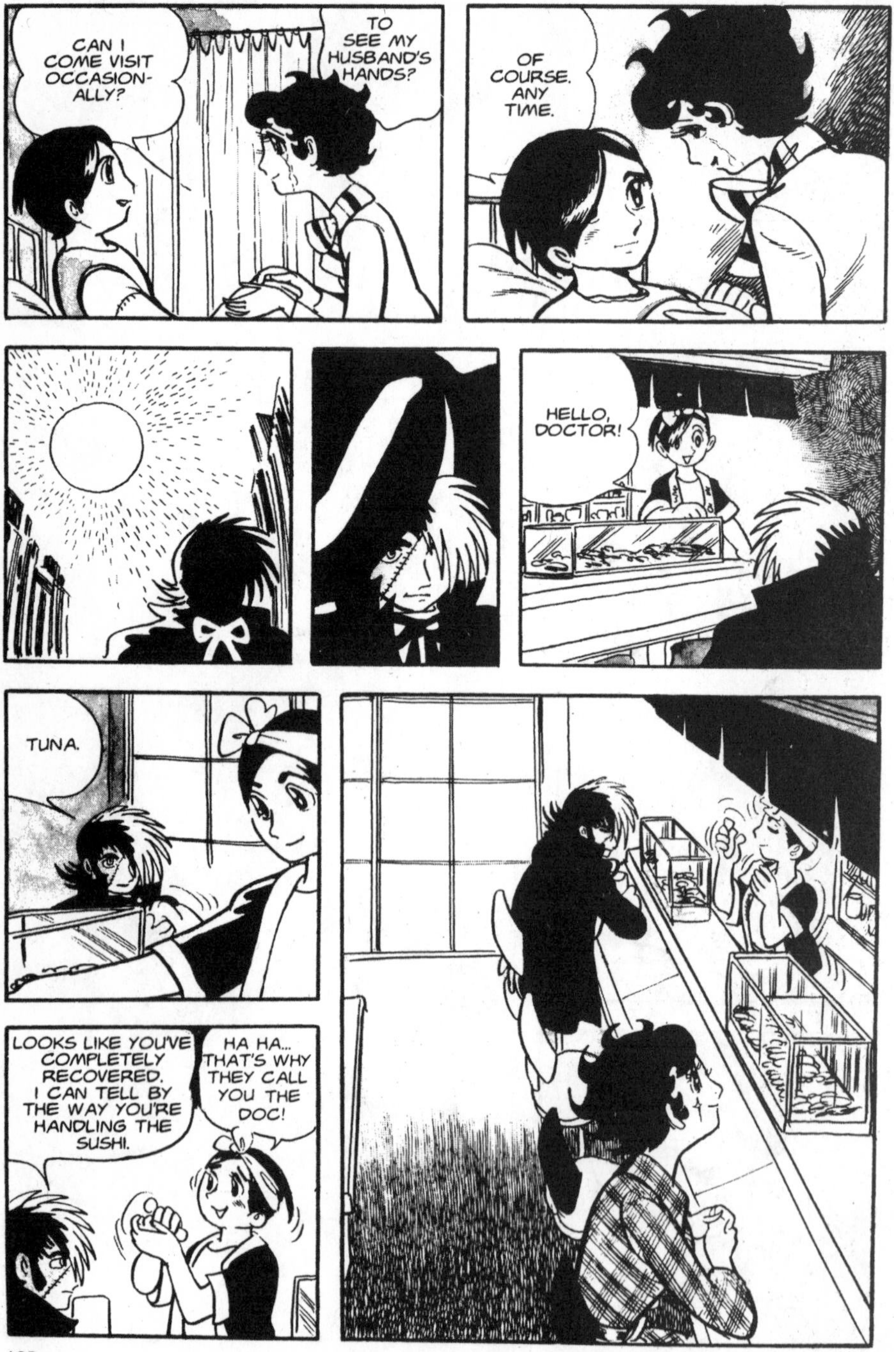
CAN I COME VISIT OCCASION-ALLY?
TO SEE MY HUSBAND'S HANDS?
OF COURSE. ANY TIME.
HELLO, DOCTOR!
TUNA.
LOOKS LIKE YOU'VE COMPLETELY RECOVERED. I CAN TELL BY THE WAY YOU'RE HANDLING THE SUSHI.
HA HA... THAT'S WHY THEY CALL YOU THE DOC!

OPERATION SIX

SOMETIMES
LIKE PEARLS

A PACKAGE FOR THE DOCTOR?

CAN I OPEN IT? IF IT'S CANDY, CAN I HAVE SOME?

WOOK! IT KEEPS GETTING SHMALLER.

IT'S SOME KIND OF KNIFE.

IT'S KINDA CRUDDY.

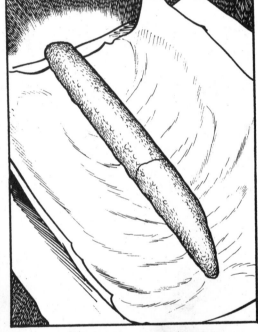

A KNIFE?

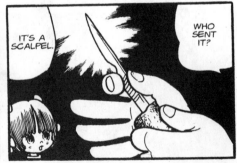

IT'S A SCALPEL.

WHO SENT IT?

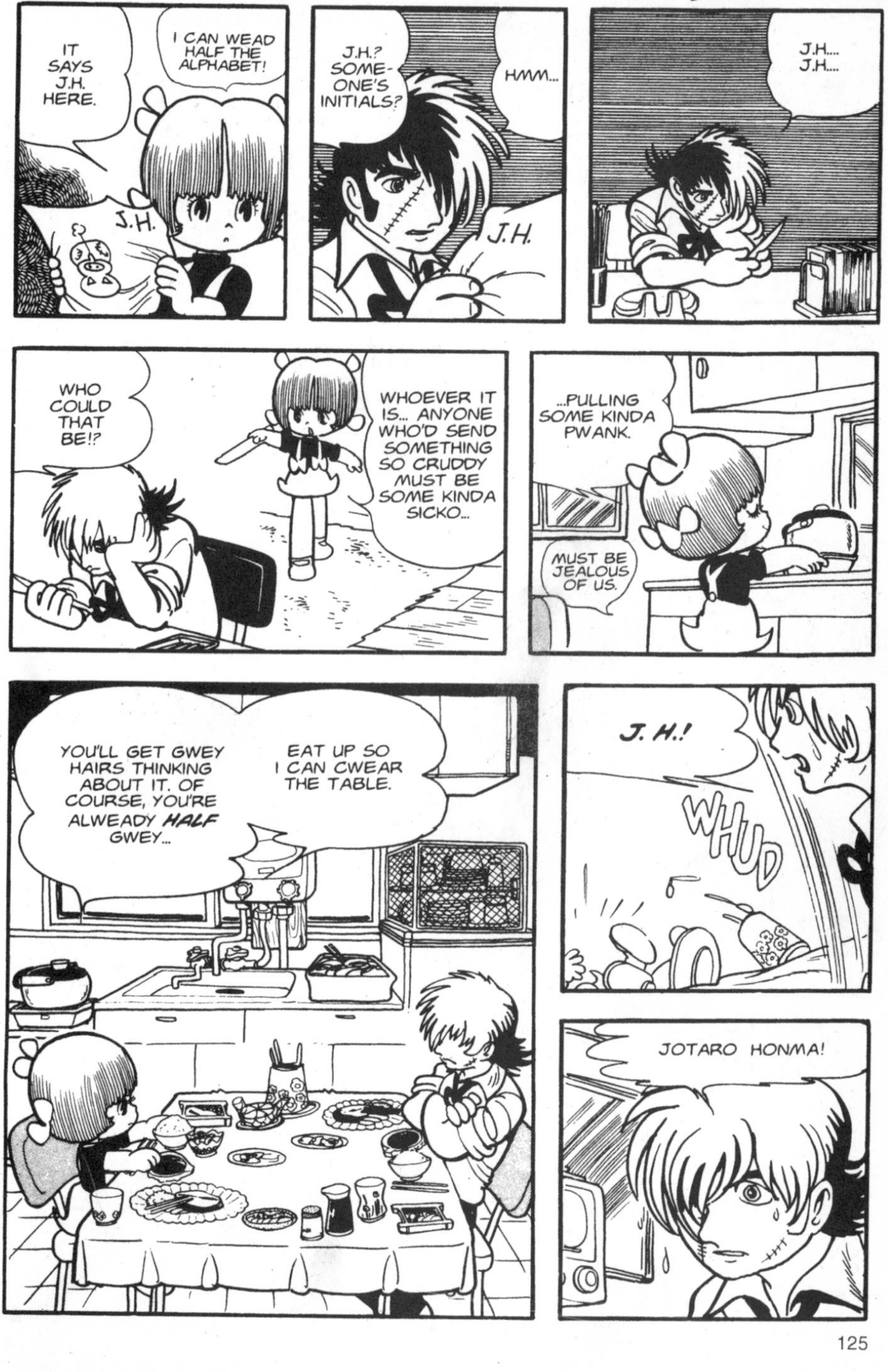
IT SAYS J.H. HERE.
I CAN WEAD HALF THE ALPHABET!
J.H.
J.H.? SOME-ONE'S INITIALS?
HMM...
J.H.
J.H.... J.H....
WHO COULD THAT BE!?
WHOEVER IT IS... ANYONE WHO'D SEND SOMETHING SO CRUDDY MUST BE SOME KINDA SICKO...
...PULLING SOME KINDA PWANK.
MUST BE JEALOUS OF US.
YOU'LL GET GWEY HAIRS THINKING ABOUT IT. OF COURSE, YOU'RE ALWEADY *HALF* GWEY...
EAT UP SO I CAN CWEAR THE TABLE.
J. H.!
WHUD
JOTARO HONMA!

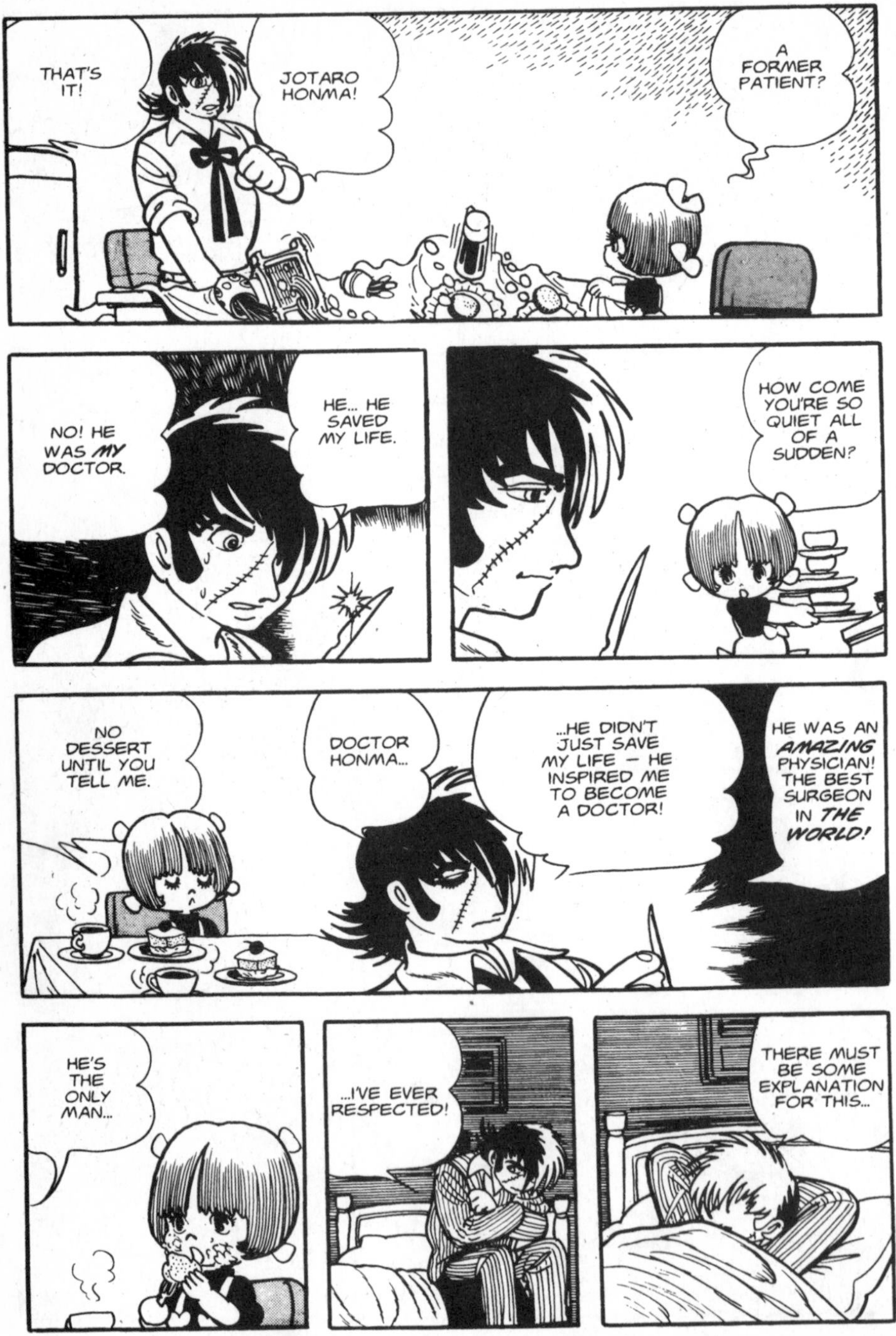
THAT'S IT!
JOTARO HONMA!
A FORMER PATIENT?
NO! HE WAS MY DOCTOR.
HE... HE SAVED MY LIFE.
HOW COME YOU'RE SO QUIET ALL OF A SUDDEN?
NO DESSERT UNTIL YOU TELL ME.
DOCTOR HONMA...
...HE DIDN'T JUST SAVE MY LIFE — HE INSPIRED ME TO BECOME A DOCTOR!
HE WAS AN AMAZING PHYSICIAN! THE BEST SURGEON IN THE WORLD!
HE'S THE ONLY MAN...
...I'VE EVER RESPECTED!
THERE MUST BE SOME EXPLANATION FOR THIS...

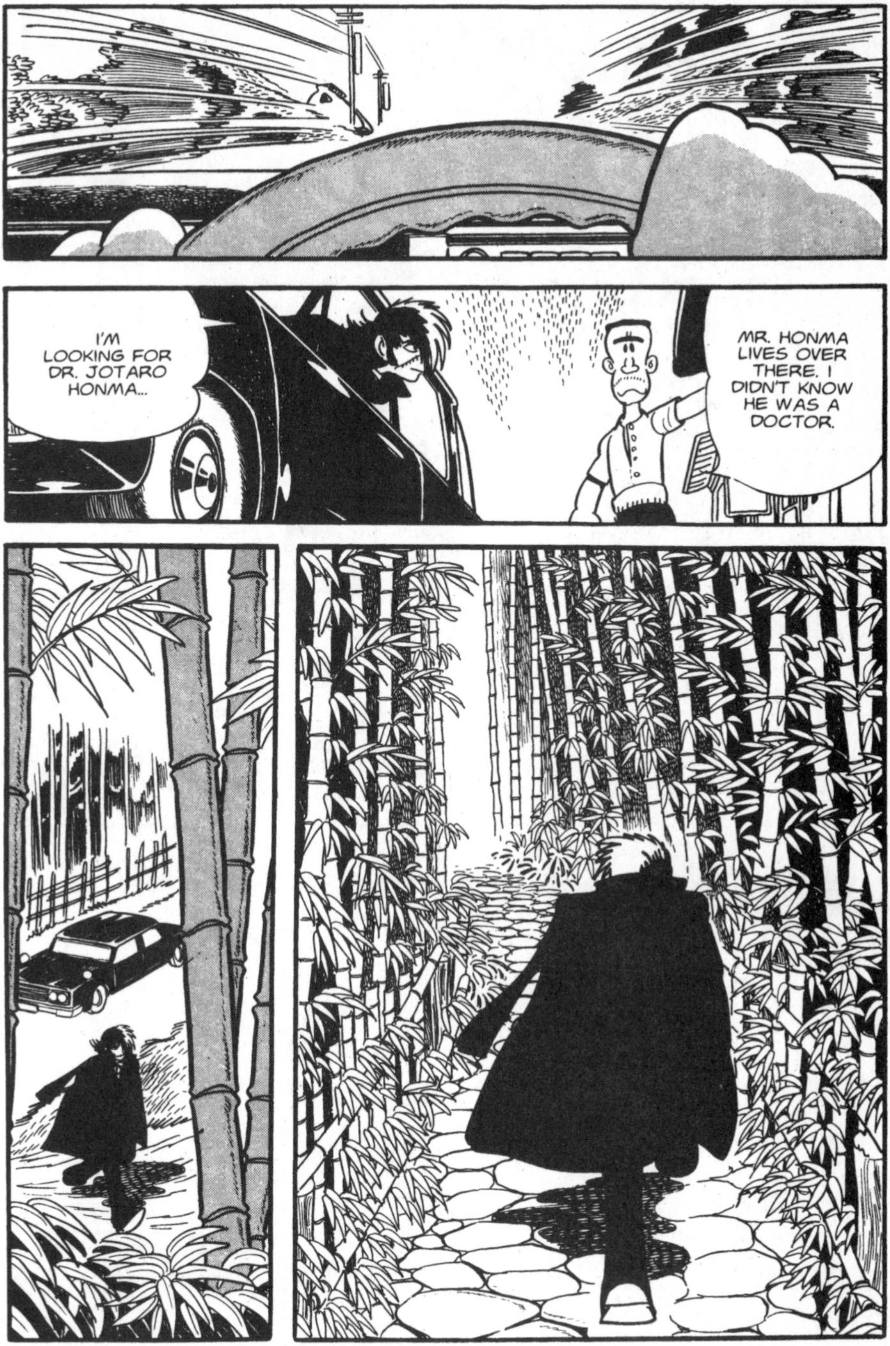
I'M LOOKING FOR DR. JOTARO HONMA...
MR. HONMA LIVES OVER THERE. I DIDN'T KNOW HE WAS A DOCTOR.

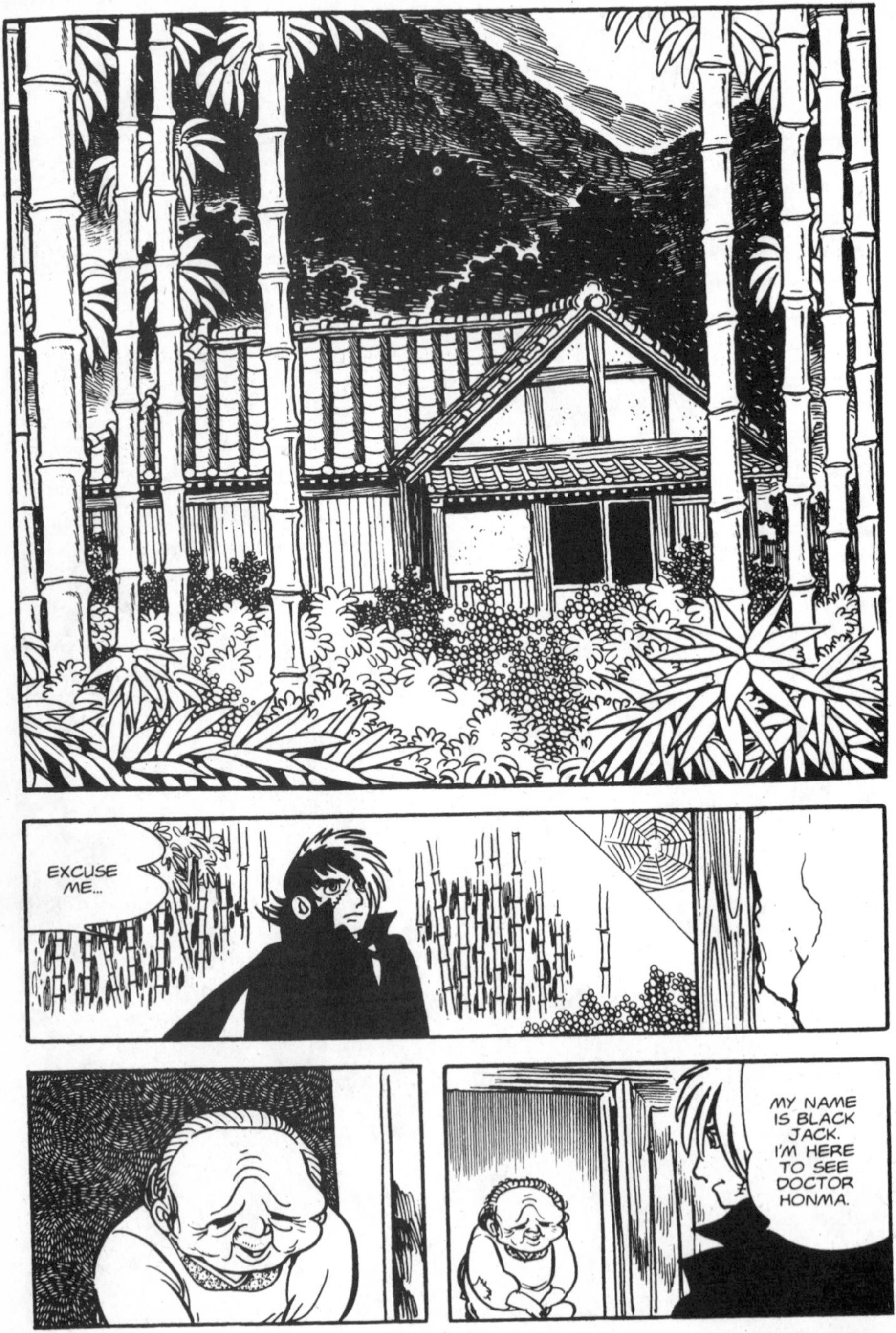
EXCUSE ME...
MY NAME IS BLACK JACK. I'M HERE TO SEE DOCTOR HONMA.

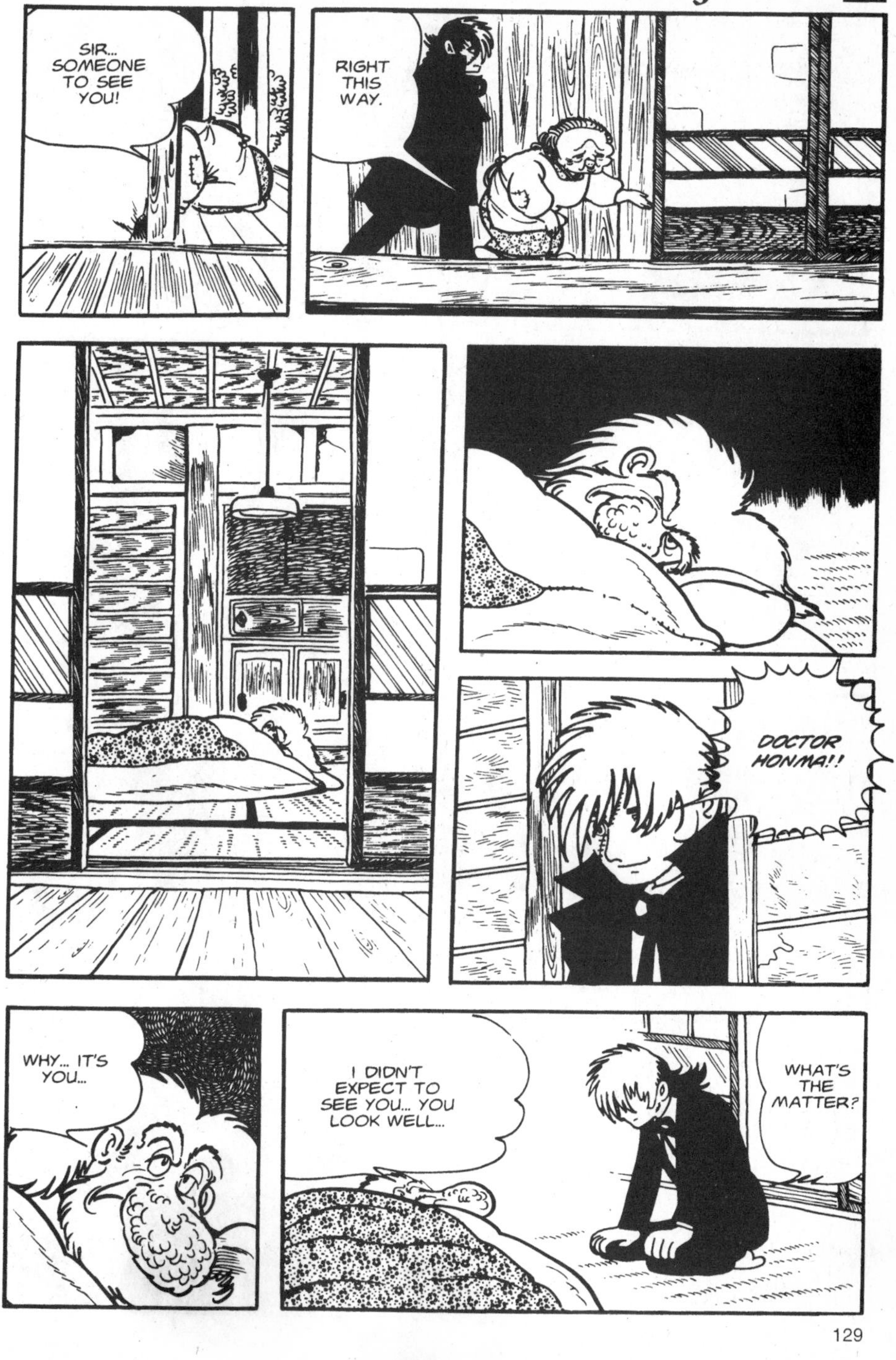
SIR... SOMEONE TO SEE YOU!
RIGHT THIS WAY.
DOCTOR HONMA!!
WHY... IT'S YOU...
I DIDN'T EXPECT TO SEE YOU... YOU LOOK WELL...
WHAT'S THE MATTER?

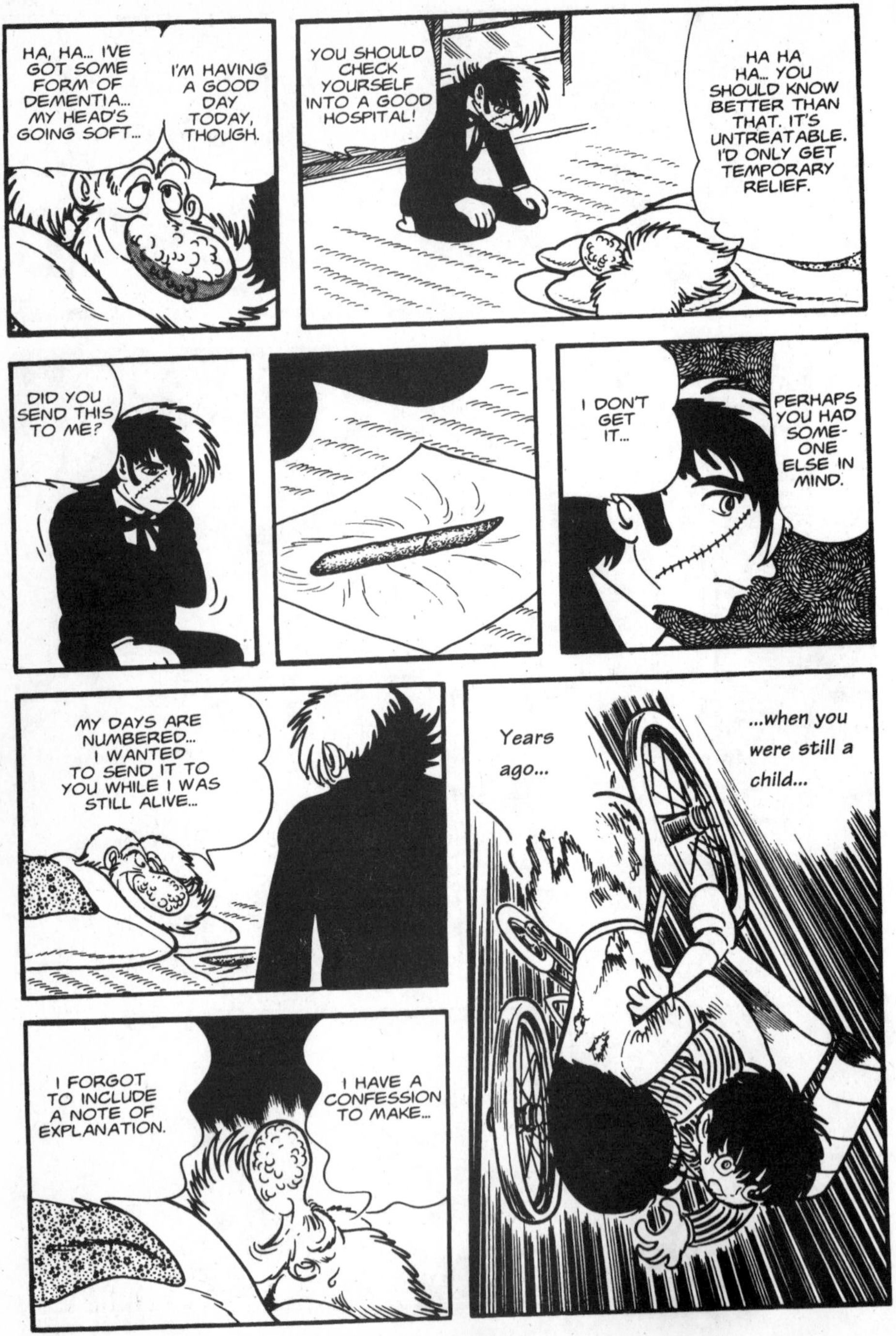
HA, HA... I'VE GOT SOME FORM OF DEMENTIA... MY HEAD'S GOING SOFT...
I'M HAVING A GOOD DAY TODAY, THOUGH.
YOU SHOULD CHECK YOURSELF INTO A GOOD HOSPITAL!
HA HA HA... YOU SHOULD KNOW BETTER THAN THAT. IT'S UNTREATABLE. I'D ONLY GET TEMPORARY RELIEF.
DID YOU SEND THIS TO ME?
I DON'T GET IT...
PERHAPS YOU HAD SOME-ONE ELSE IN MIND.
MY DAYS ARE NUMBERED... I WANTED TO SEND IT TO YOU WHILE I WAS STILL ALIVE...
I FORGOT TO INCLUDE A NOTE OF EXPLANATION.
I HAVE A CONFESSION TO MAKE...
Years ago...
...when you were still a child...

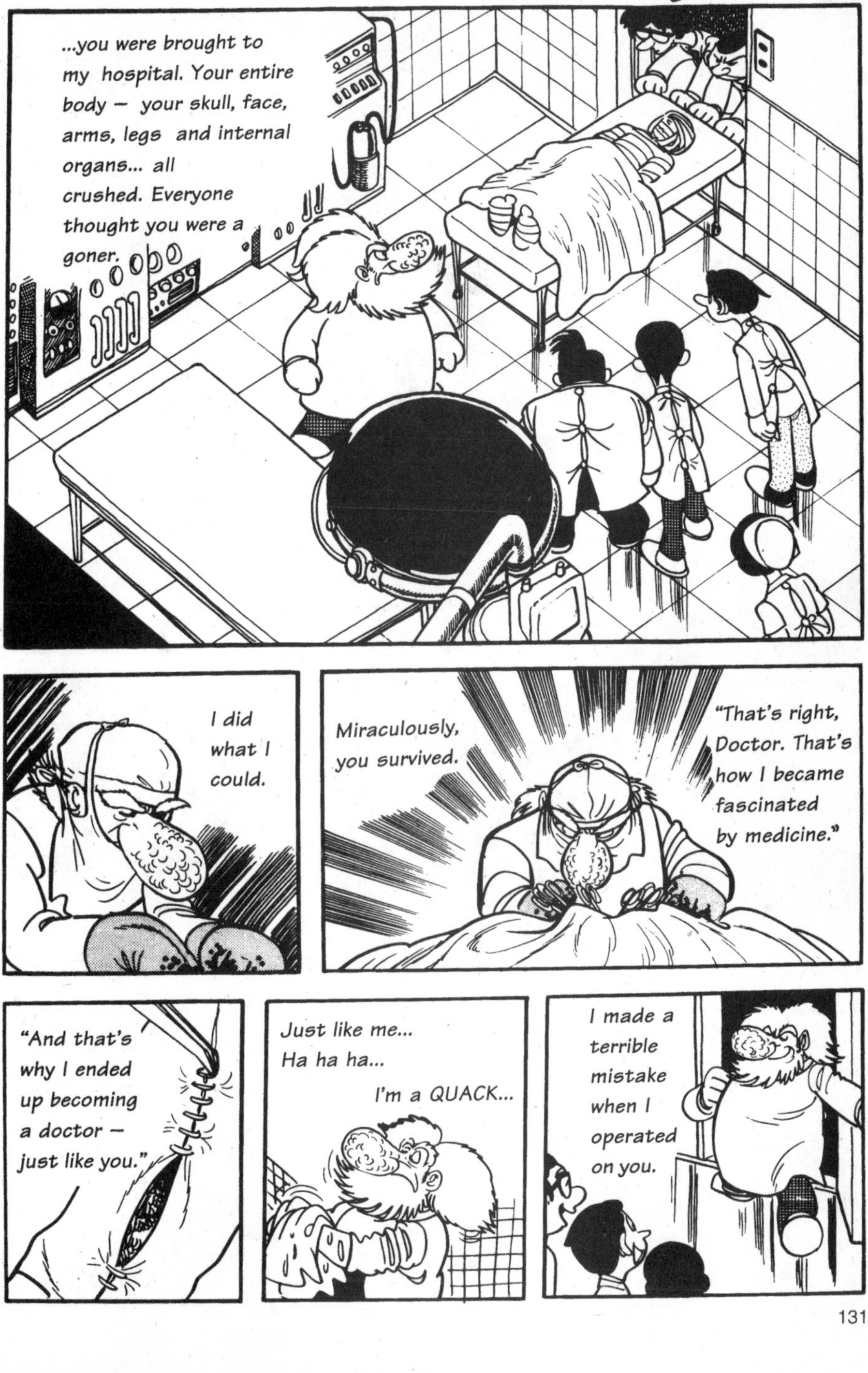
...you were brought to my hospital. Your entire body — your skull, face, arms, legs and internal organs... all crushed. Everyone thought you were a goner.
I did what I could.
Miraculously, you survived.
"That's right, Doctor. That's how I became fascinated by medicine."
"And that's why I ended up becoming a doctor — just like you."
Just like me... Ha ha ha...
I'm a QUACK...
I made a terrible mistake when I operated on you.

NOW I CAN FINALLY TELL YOU...

IT WAS NEARLY FATAL.

IF YOU HAD DIED, I WOULD HAVE BEEN BANISHED FROM THE MEDICAL WORLD FOREVER...

...DESPISED BY EVERY- ONE AROUND ME.

I CAN'T BELIEVE *YOU* COULD HAVE MADE A MISTAKE!

HUMAN BEINGS AREN'T GODS. BESIDES, I WAS NO GENIUS TO BEGIN WITH.

YOU RECALL THAT SEVEN YEARS LATER I OPERATED ON YOU AGAIN?

YES. YOU SAID YOU HAD TO CHECK UP ON ME.

THE TRUTH IS... DURING THE FIRST OPERATION...

DOCTOR, WE'RE MISSING A SCALPEL!

WHAT!?

A *SCALPEL* ?

OH NO! I MUST HAVE LEFT IT INSIDE HIM BEFORE I STITCHED HIM UP.

IT MUST BE IN HIS STOMACH — OR RIGHT BELOW HIS LIVER.

WHAT IF THIS BLOWS UP INTO A SCANDAL?

SHOULD I RESUME THE OPERATION NOW?

NO, THAT WON'T DO!!

I'D BECOME A LAUGHING-STOCK!

I WAS A FOOL!! I LET YOU LEAVE THE HOSPITAL WITHOUT REMOVING THE SCALPEL!!

BUT I'M EN-DANGERING THE LIFE OF THAT CHILD!

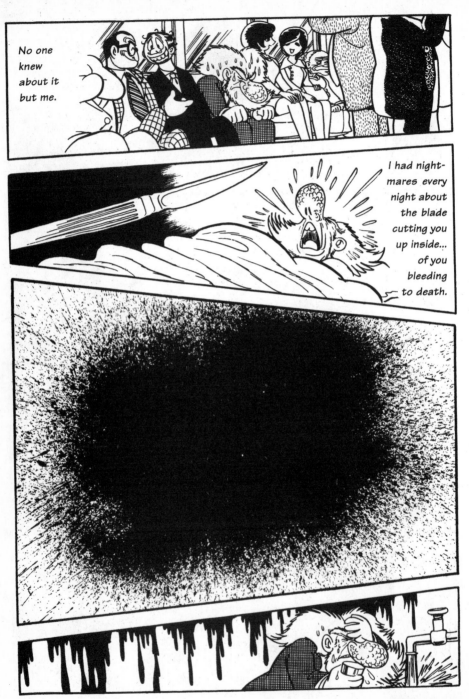

No one knew about it but me.

I had night-mares every night about the blade cutting you up inside... of you bleeding to death.

134

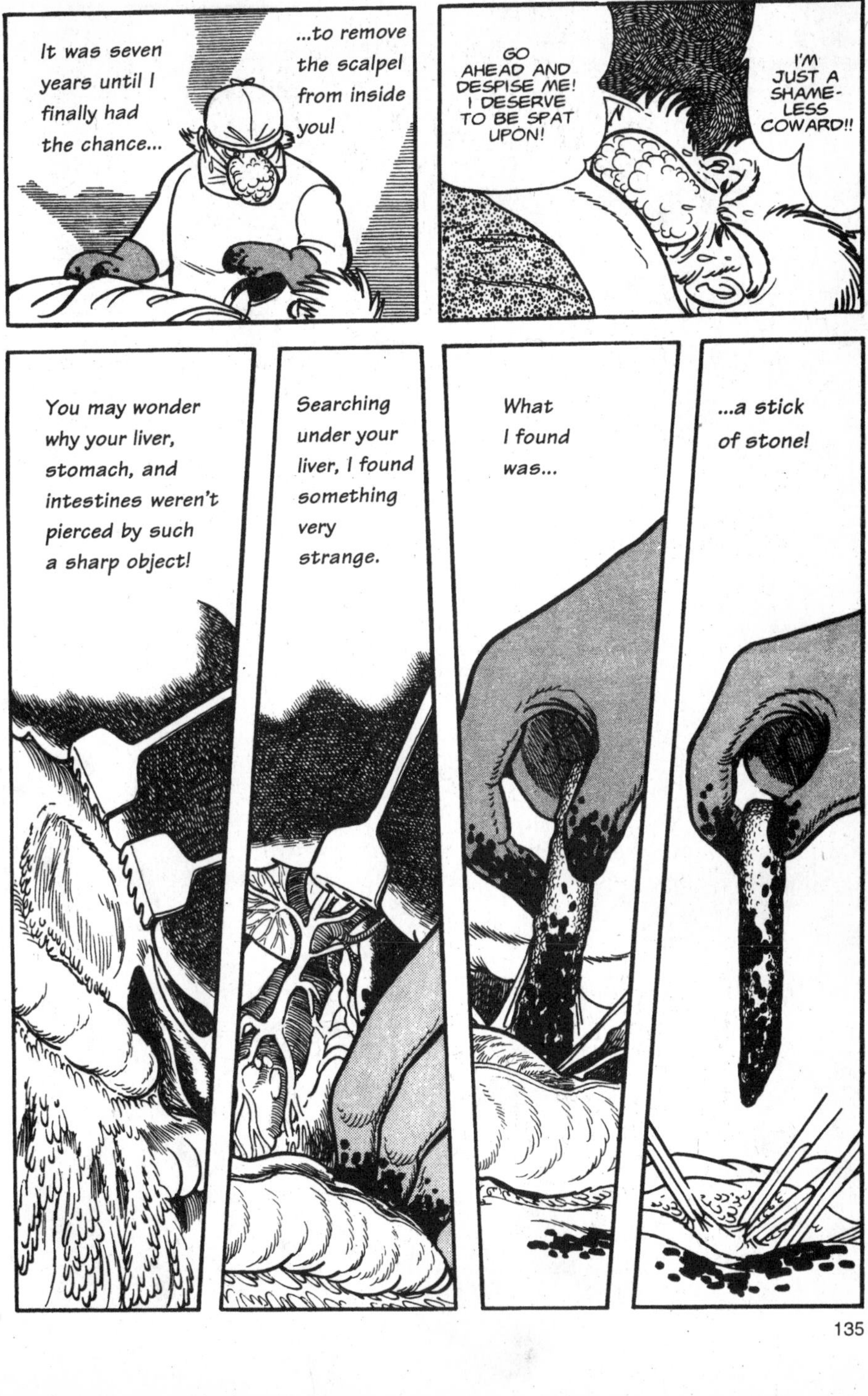
It was seven years until I finally had the chance...
...to remove the scalpel from inside you!
GO AHEAD AND DESPISE ME! I DESERVE TO BE SPAT UPON!
I'M JUST A SHAME-LESS COWARD!!
You may wonder why your liver, stomach, and intestines weren't pierced by such a sharp object!
Searching under your liver, I found something very strange.
What I found was...
...a stick of stone!

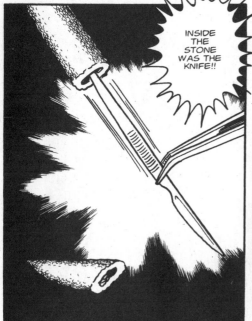

INSIDE THE STONE WAS THE KNIFE!!

It was unbelievable. The knife was SEALED inside a SHEATH of CALCIUM.

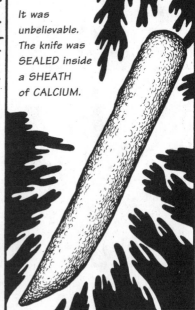

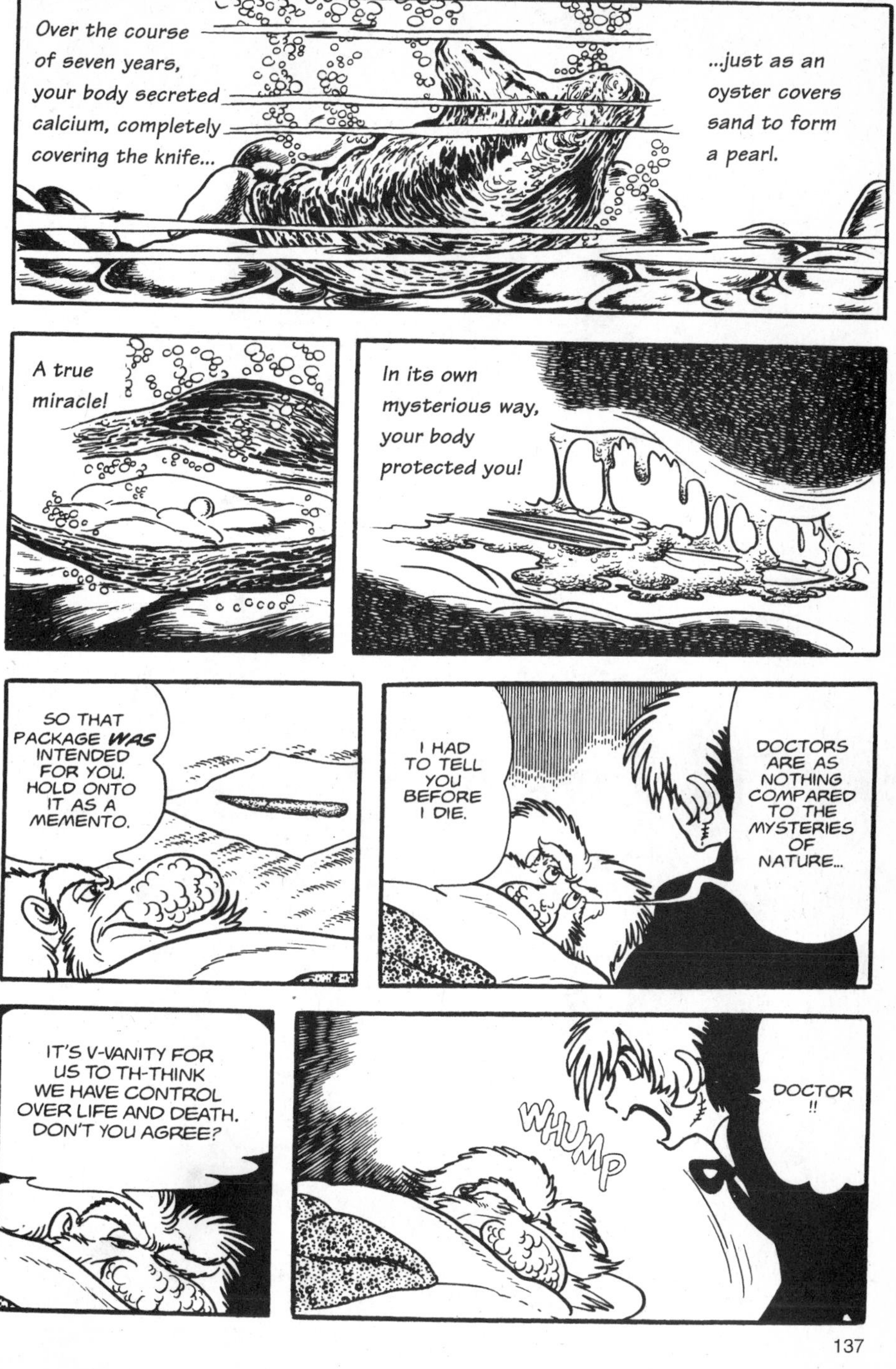
Over the course of seven years, your body secreted calcium, completely covering the knife...
...just as an oyster covers sand to form a pearl.
A true miracle!
In its own mysterious way, your body protected you!
SO THAT PACKAGE WAS INTENDED FOR YOU. HOLD ONTO IT AS A MEMENTO.
I HAD TO TELL YOU BEFORE I DIE.
DOCTORS ARE AS NOTHING COMPARED TO THE MYSTERIES OF NATURE...
IT'S V-VANITY FOR US TO TH-THINK WE HAVE CONTROL OVER LIFE AND DEATH. DON'T YOU AGREE?
WHUMP
DOCTOR !!

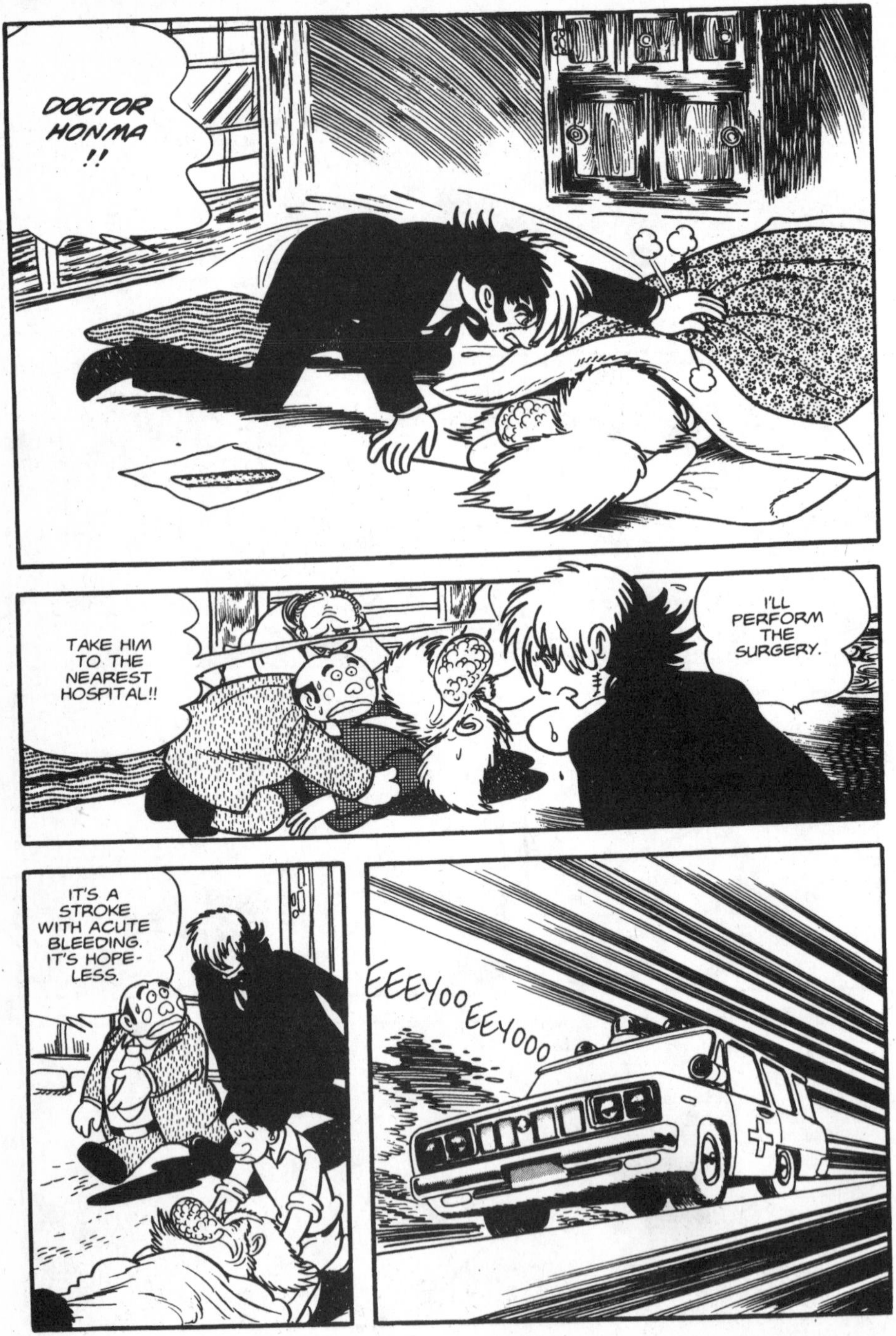
DOCTOR HONMA !!
TAKE HIM TO THE NEAREST HOSPITAL!!
I'LL PERFORM THE SURGERY.
IT'S A STROKE WITH ACUTE BLEEDING. IT'S HOPE-LESS.
EEEYOO EEYOOO

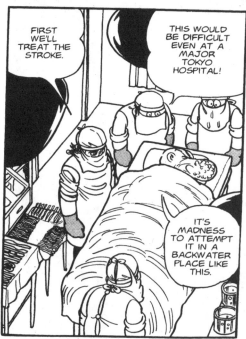

INTERNAL MEDICINE
EXTERNAL MEDICINE
OTHER
FIRST WE'LL TREAT THE STROKE.
THIS WOULD BE DIFFICULT EVEN AT A MAJOR TOKYO HOSPITAL!
IT'S MADNESS TO ATTEMPT IT IN A BACKWATER PLACE LIKE THIS.
WE'LL NEED BURR HOLES...
KRK
KRK
WHAT'S THE EKG READING?
NORMAL, SIR.

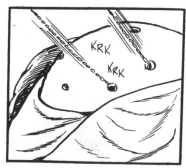

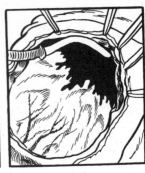

THAT MAN DOESN'T EVEN HAVE A LICENSE TO PRACTICE!

BUT HE'S REPUTED TO BE AN INCREDIBLE SURGEON!

WOW...

...

CLAMP!

HIS EKG IS IRREGULAR.

IT'S WEAKENING.

DOCTOR! HIS PULSE HAS STOPPED!

STOP THE OPERATION... WE HAVE TO START CPR, *NOW!*

EPINEPHRINE!

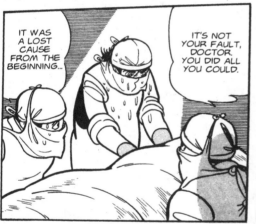

IT WAS A LOST CAUSE FROM THE BEGINNING...

IT'S NOT YOUR FAULT, DOCTOR. YOU DID ALL YOU COULD.

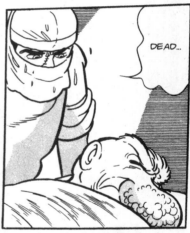

DEAD...

THAT'S *IMPOSSIBLE!* I DIDN'T MAKE A SINGLE MISTAKE!

HE'S REALLY DEAD...

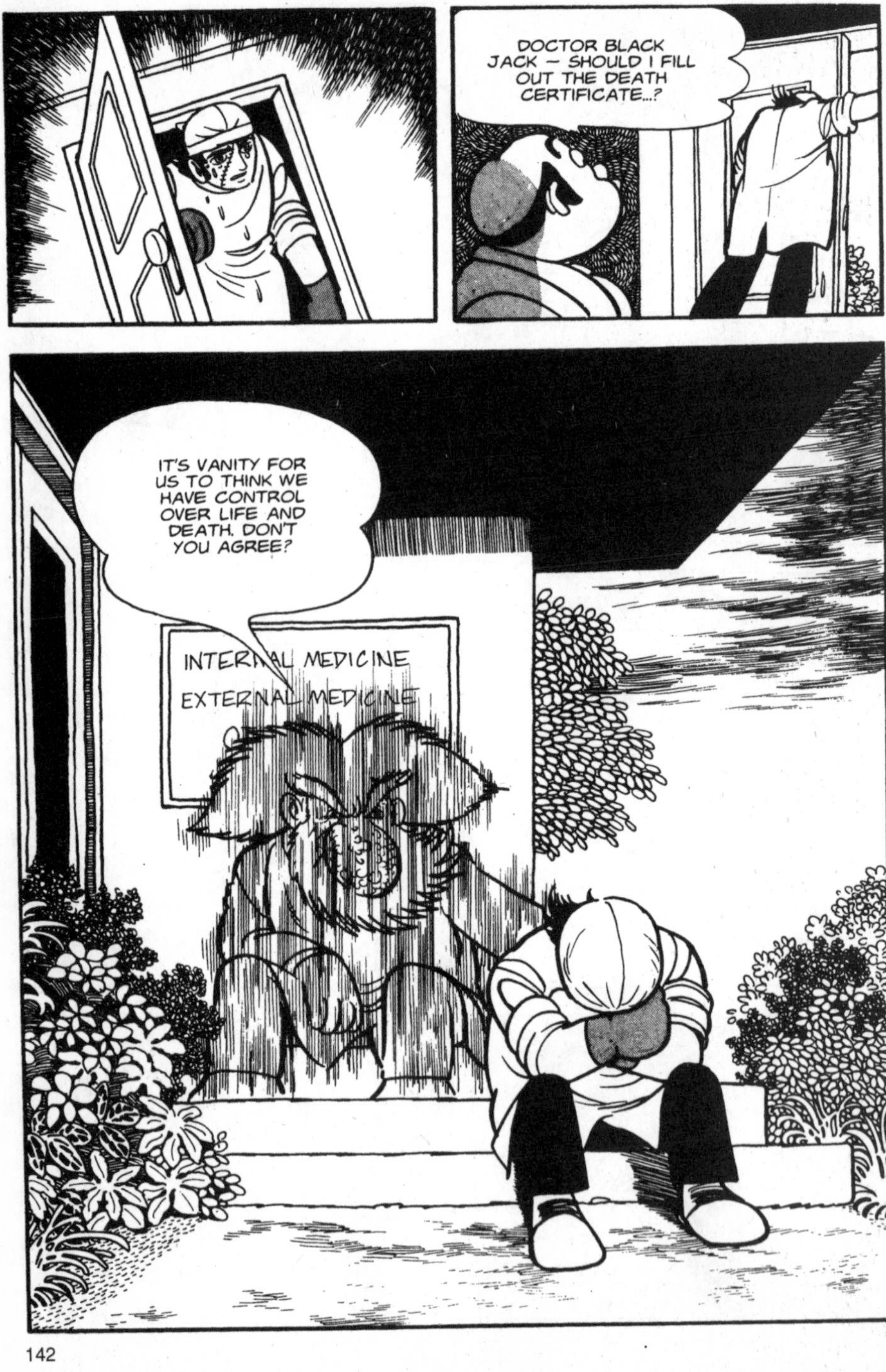
DOCTOR BLACK JACK — SHOULD I FILL OUT THE DEATH CERTIFICATE...?
IT'S VANITY FOR US TO THINK WE HAVE CONTROL OVER LIFE AND DEATH. DON'T YOU AGREE?
INTERNAL MEDICINE
EXTERNAL MEDICINE

OPERATION SEVEN

TO EACH
HIS OWN

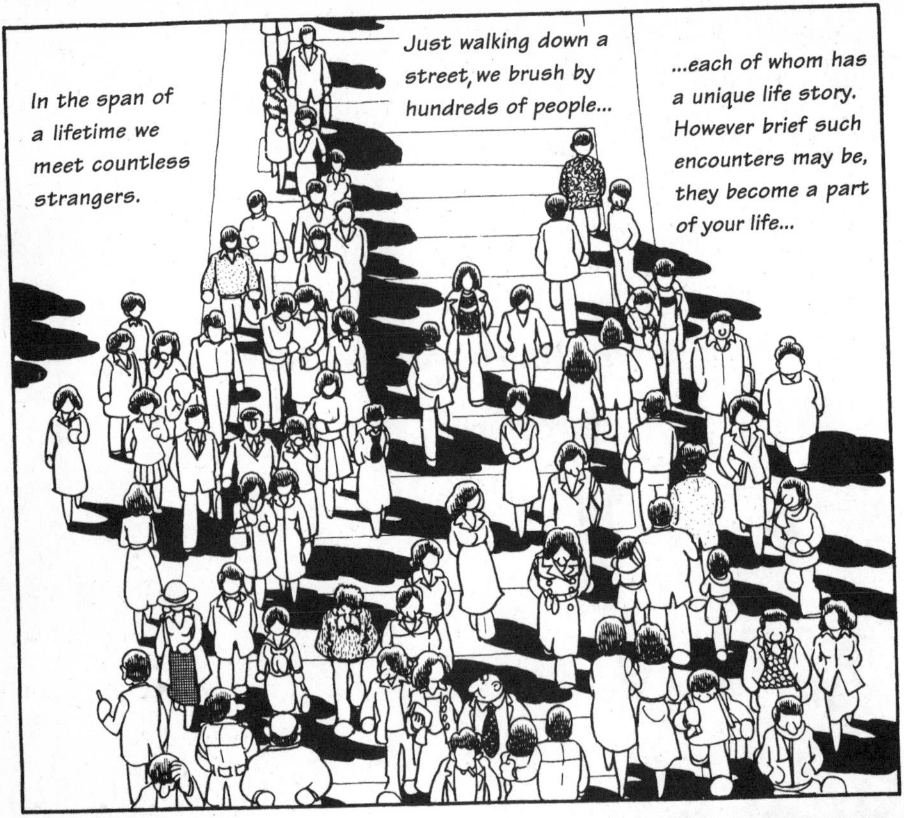
In the span of a lifetime we meet countless strangers.
Just walking down a street, we brush by hundreds of people...
...each of whom has a unique life story. However brief such encounters may be, they become a part of your life...

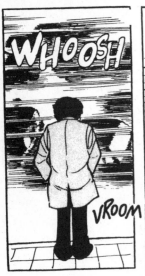

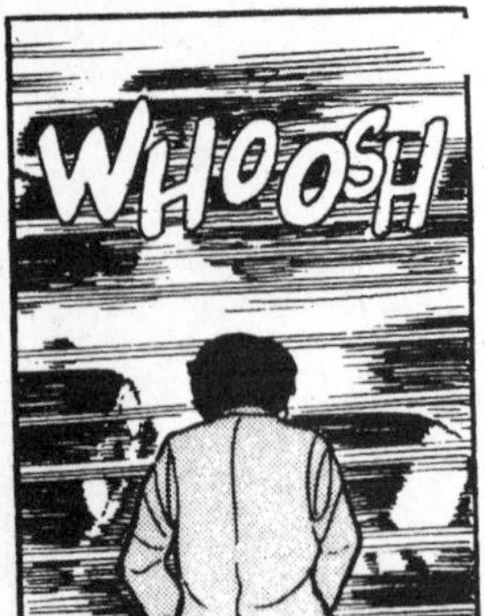
WHOOSH
VROOM

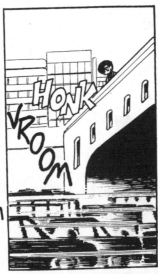

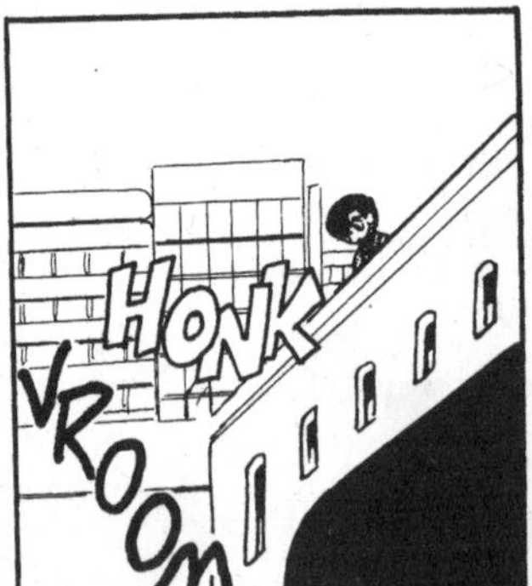
HONK
VROOM

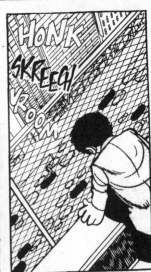

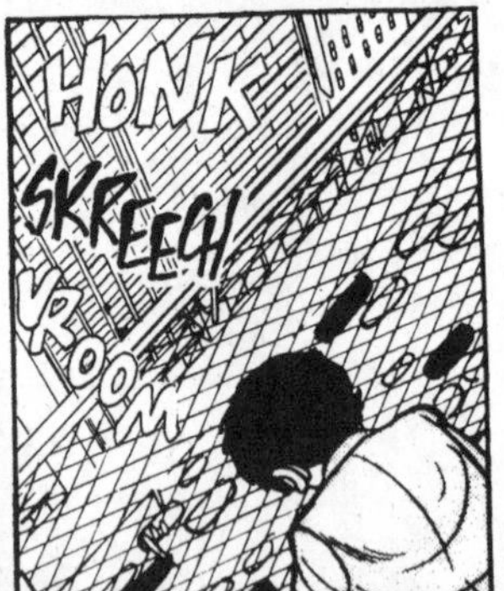
HONK
SKREECH
VROOM

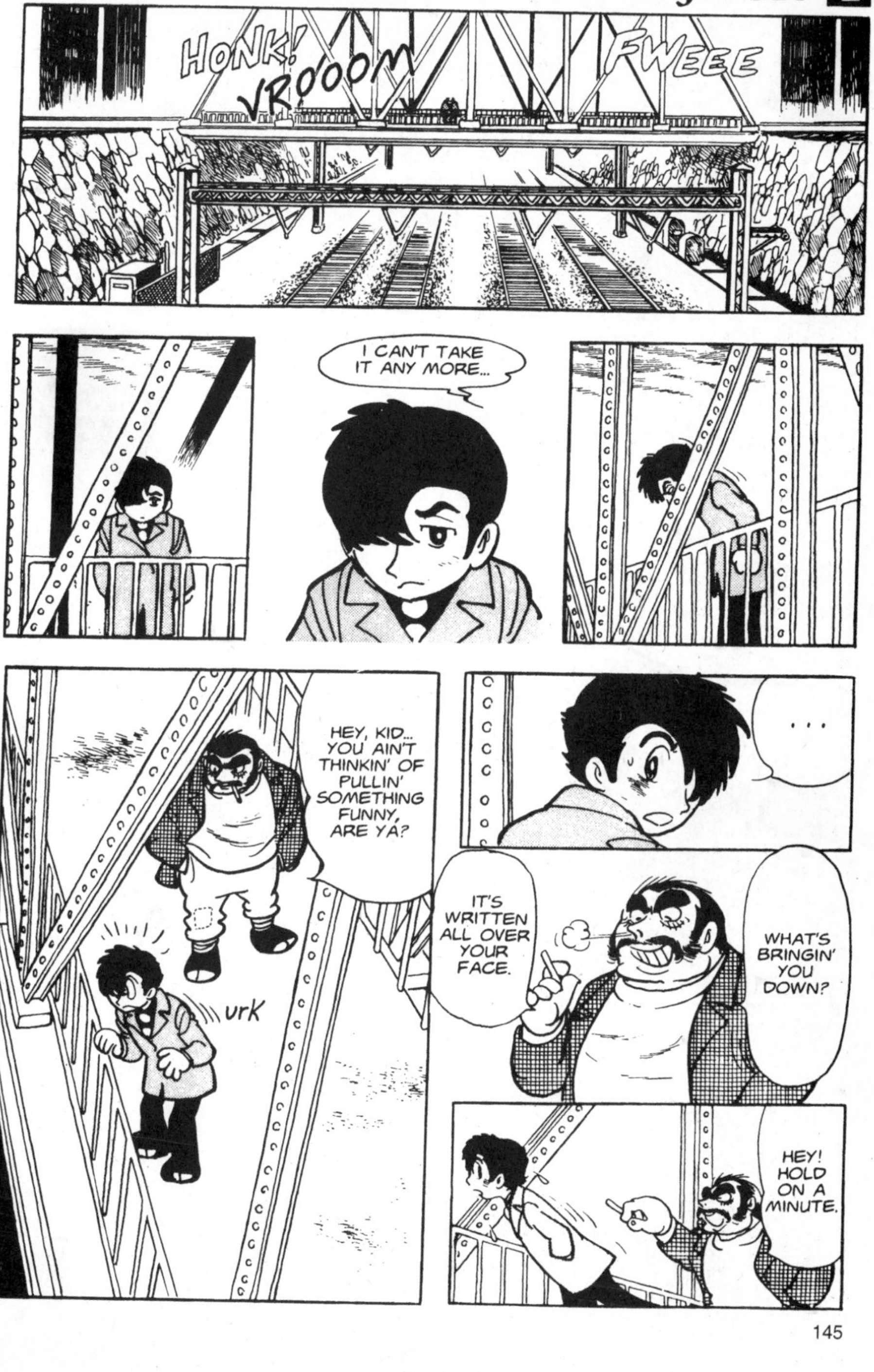
HONK!
VROOOM
FWEEE
I CAN'T TAKE IT ANY MORE...
HEY, KID... YOU AIN'T THINKIN' OF PULLIN' SOMETHING FUNNY, ARE YA?
urK
...
IT'S WRITTEN ALL OVER YOUR FACE.
WHAT'S BRINGIN' YOU DOWN?
HEY! HOLD ON A MINUTE.

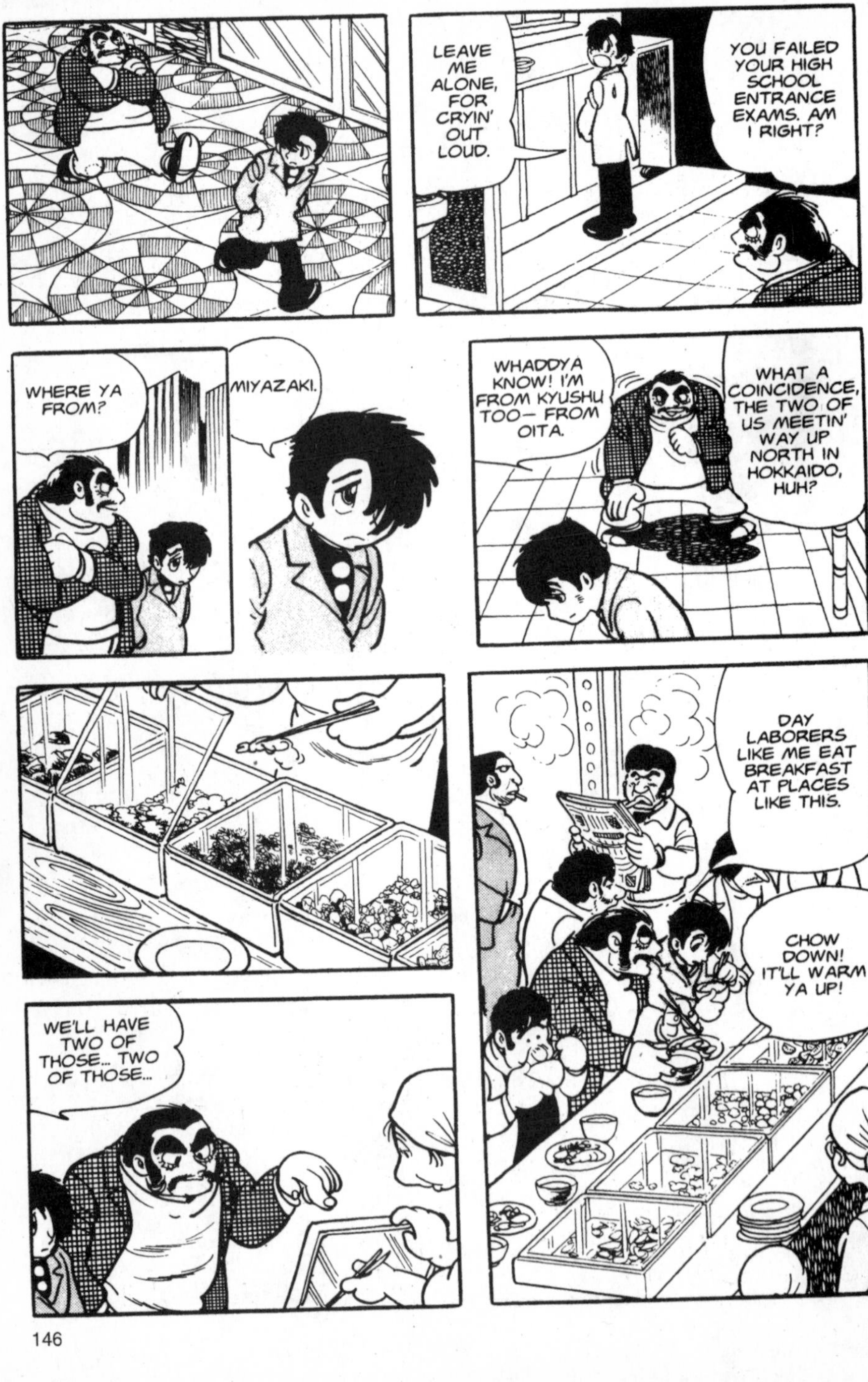
YOU FAILED YOUR HIGH SCHOOL ENTRANCE EXAMS. AM I RIGHT?
LEAVE ME ALONE, FOR CRYIN' OUT LOUD.
WHERE YA FROM?
MIYAZAKI.
WHADDYA KNOW! I'M FROM KYUSHU TOO— FROM OITA.
WHAT A COINCIDENCE, THE TWO OF US MEETIN' WAY UP NORTH IN HOKKAIDO, HUH?
WE'LL HAVE TWO OF THOSE... TWO OF THOSE...
DAY LABORERS LIKE ME EAT BREAKFAST AT PLACES LIKE THIS.
CHOW DOWN! IT'LL WARM YA UP!

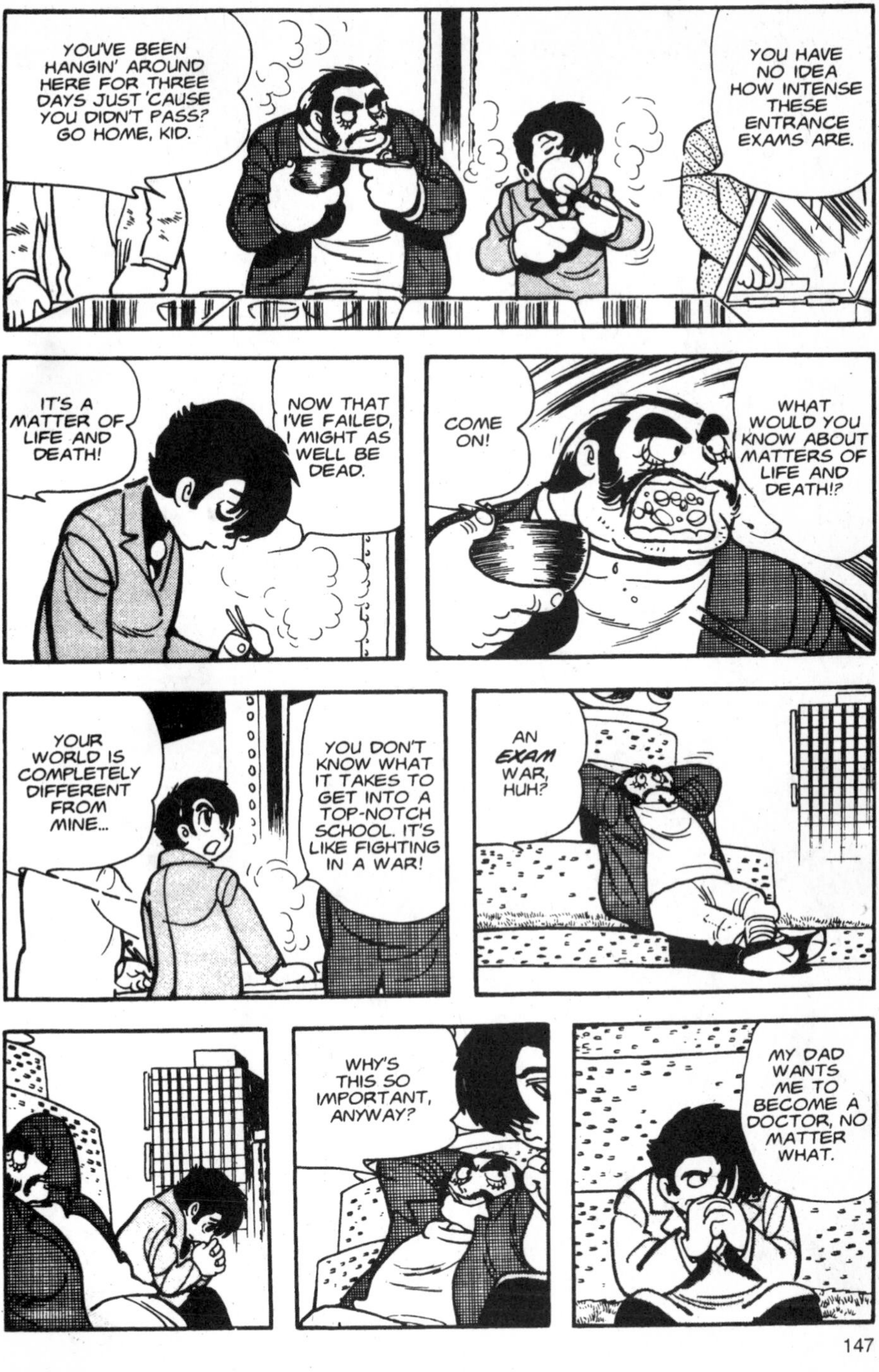
YOU'VE BEEN HANGIN' AROUND HERE FOR THREE DAYS JUST 'CAUSE YOU DIDN'T PASS? GO HOME, KID.
YOU HAVE NO IDEA HOW INTENSE THESE ENTRANCE EXAMS ARE.
IT'S A MATTER OF LIFE AND DEATH!
NOW THAT I'VE FAILED, I MIGHT AS WELL BE DEAD.
COME ON!
WHAT WOULD YOU KNOW ABOUT MATTERS OF LIFE AND DEATH!?
YOUR WORLD IS COMPLETELY DIFFERENT FROM MINE...
YOU DON'T KNOW WHAT IT TAKES TO GET INTO A TOP-NOTCH SCHOOL. IT'S LIKE FIGHTING IN A WAR!
AN EXAM WAR, HUH?
WHY'S THIS SO IMPORTANT, ANYWAY?
MY DAD WANTS ME TO BECOME A DOCTOR, NO MATTER WHAT.

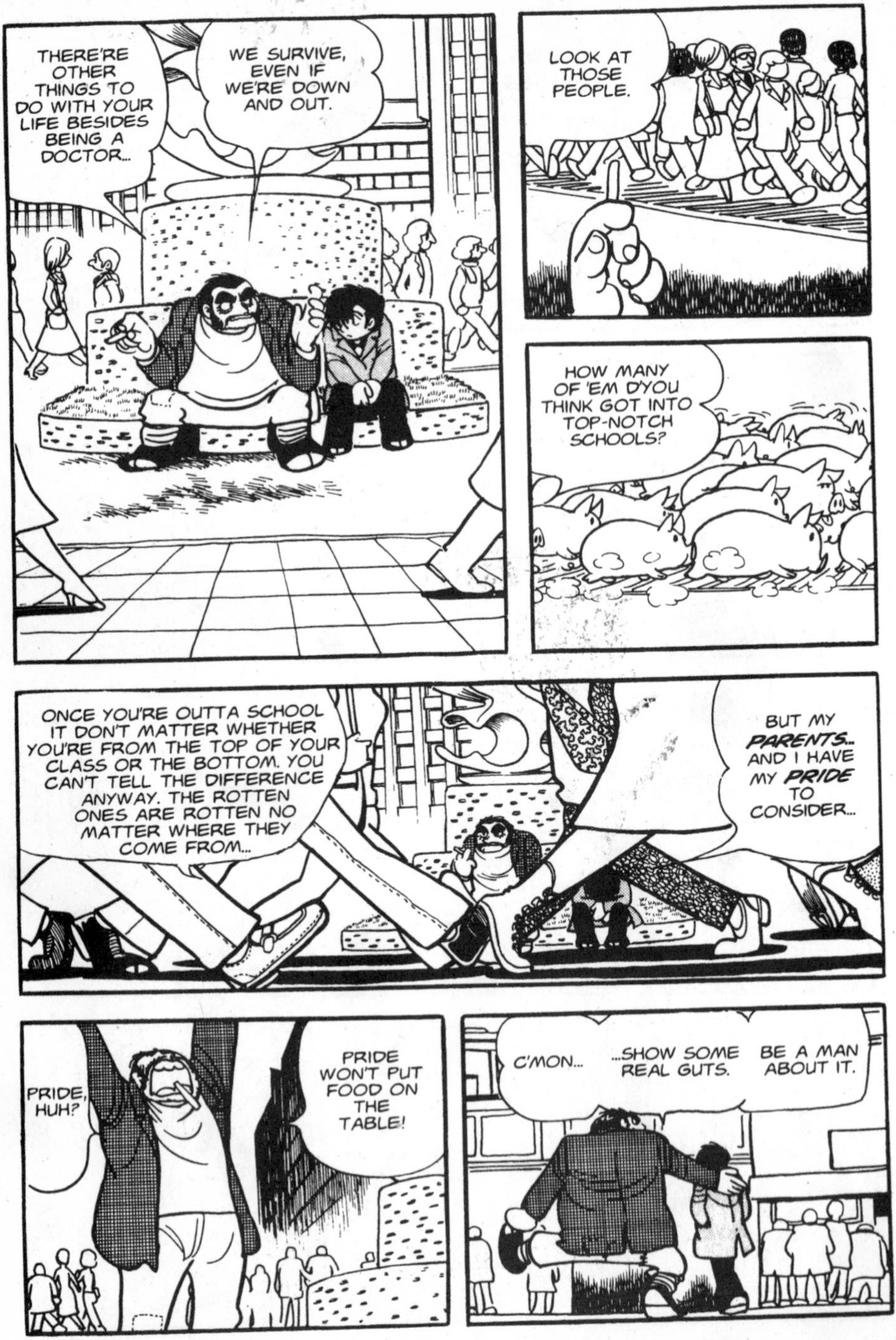
THERE'RE OTHER THINGS TO DO WITH YOUR LIFE BESIDES BEING A DOCTOR...
WE SURVIVE, EVEN IF WE'RE DOWN AND OUT.
LOOK AT THOSE PEOPLE.
HOW MANY OF 'EM D'YOU THINK GOT INTO TOP-NOTCH SCHOOLS?
ONCE YOU'RE OUTTA SCHOOL IT DON'T MATTER WHETHER YOU'RE FROM THE TOP OF YOUR CLASS OR THE BOTTOM. YOU CAN'T TELL THE DIFFERENCE ANYWAY. THE ROTTEN ONES ARE ROTTEN NO MATTER WHERE THEY COME FROM...
BUT MY PARENTS... AND I HAVE MY PRIDE TO CONSIDER...
PRIDE, HUH?
PRIDE WON'T PUT FOOD ON THE TABLE!
C'MON...
...SHOW SOME REAL GUTS.
BE A MAN ABOUT IT.

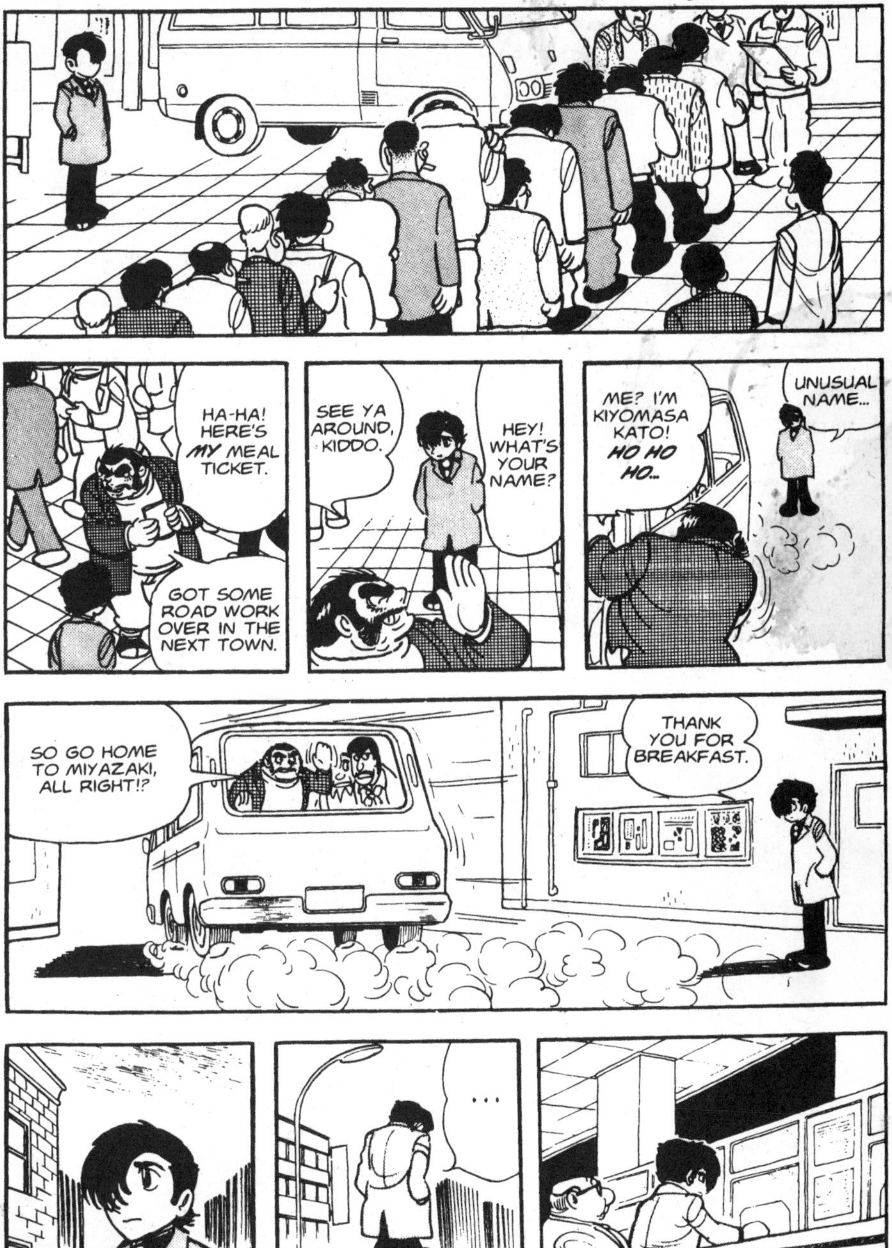
HA-HA! HERE'S MY MEAL TICKET.
GOT SOME ROAD WORK OVER IN THE NEXT TOWN.
SEE YA AROUND, KIDDO.
HEY! WHAT'S YOUR NAME?
ME? I'M KIYOMASA KATO! HO HO HO...
UNUSUAL NAME...
SO GO HOME TO MIYAZAKI, ALL RIGHT!?
THANK YOU FOR BREAKFAST.
...

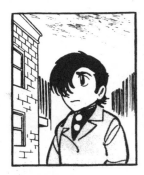

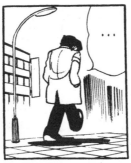

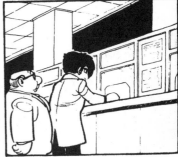

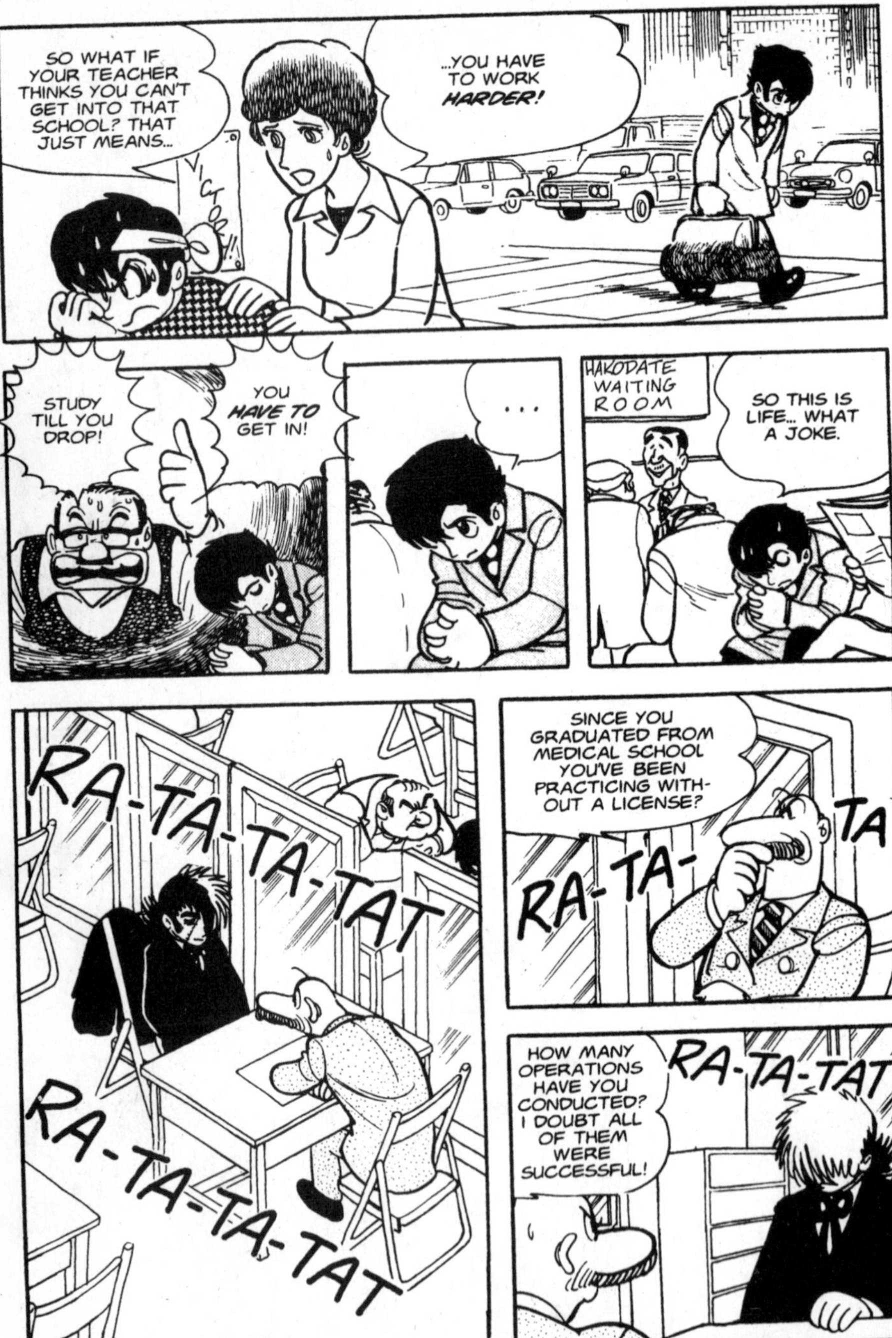
SO WHAT IF YOUR TEACHER THINKS YOU CAN'T GET INTO THAT SCHOOL? THAT JUST MEANS...
VICTORY!!
...YOU HAVE TO WORK *HARDER!*
STUDY TILL YOU DROP!
YOU *HAVE TO* GET IN!
. . .
HAKODATE WAITING ROOM
SO THIS IS LIFE... WHAT A JOKE.
RA-TA-TA-TAT
RA-TA-TA-TA-TAT
SINCE YOU GRADUATED FROM MEDICAL SCHOOL YOU'VE BEEN PRACTICING WITH-OUT A LICENSE?
RA-TA-TA
HOW MANY OPERATIONS HAVE YOU CONDUCTED? I DOUBT ALL OF THEM WERE SUCCESSFUL!
RA-TA-TAT

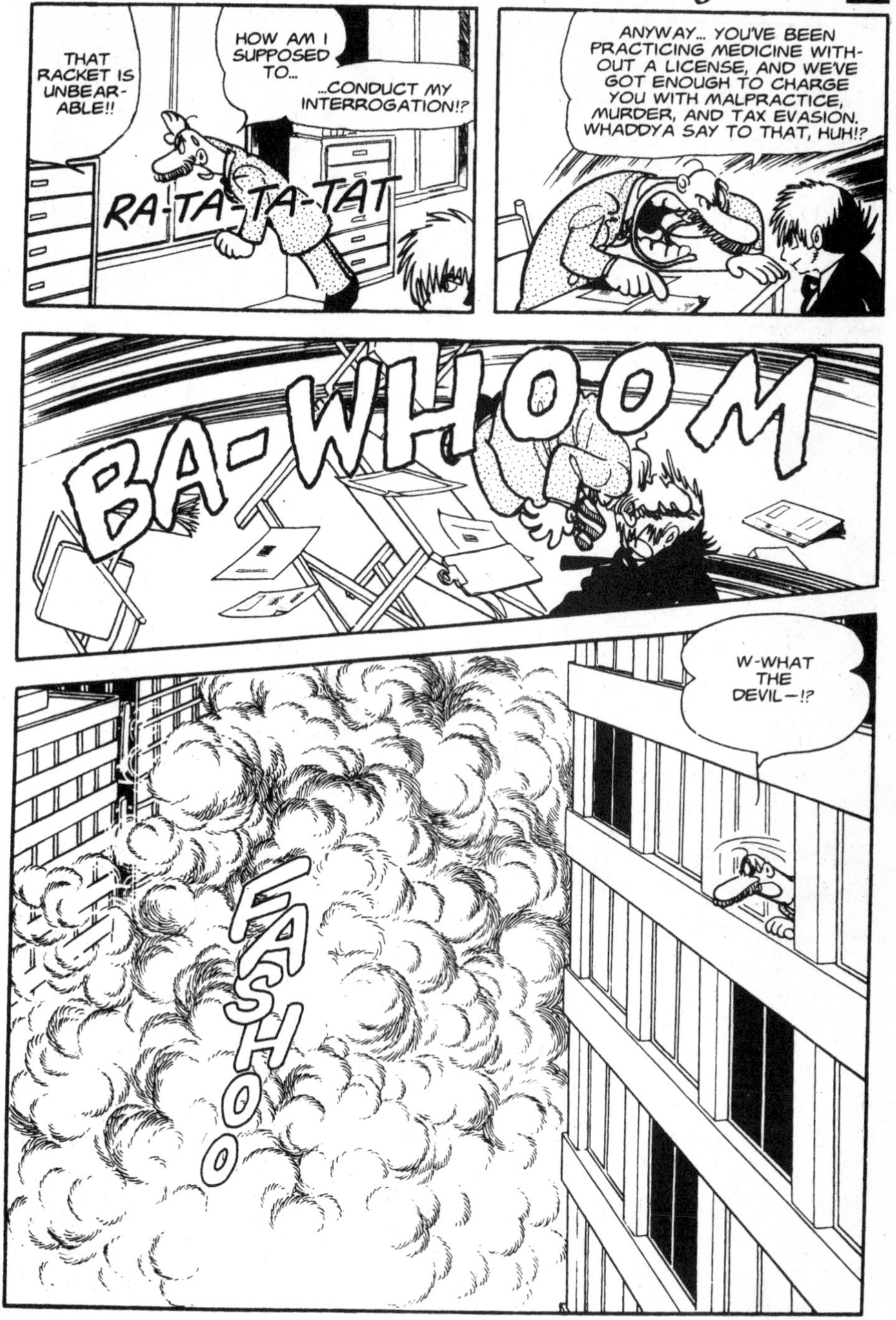
THAT RACKET IS UNBEARABLE!!
HOW AM I SUPPOSED TO...
...CONDUCT MY INTERROGATION!?
RA-TA-TA-TAT
ANYWAY... YOU'VE BEEN PRACTICING MEDICINE WITHOUT A LICENSE, AND WE'VE GOT ENOUGH TO CHARGE YOU WITH MALPRACTICE, MURDER, AND TAX EVASION. WHADDYA SAY TO THAT, HUH!?
BA-WHOOM
W-WHAT THE DEVIL—!?
FASHOO

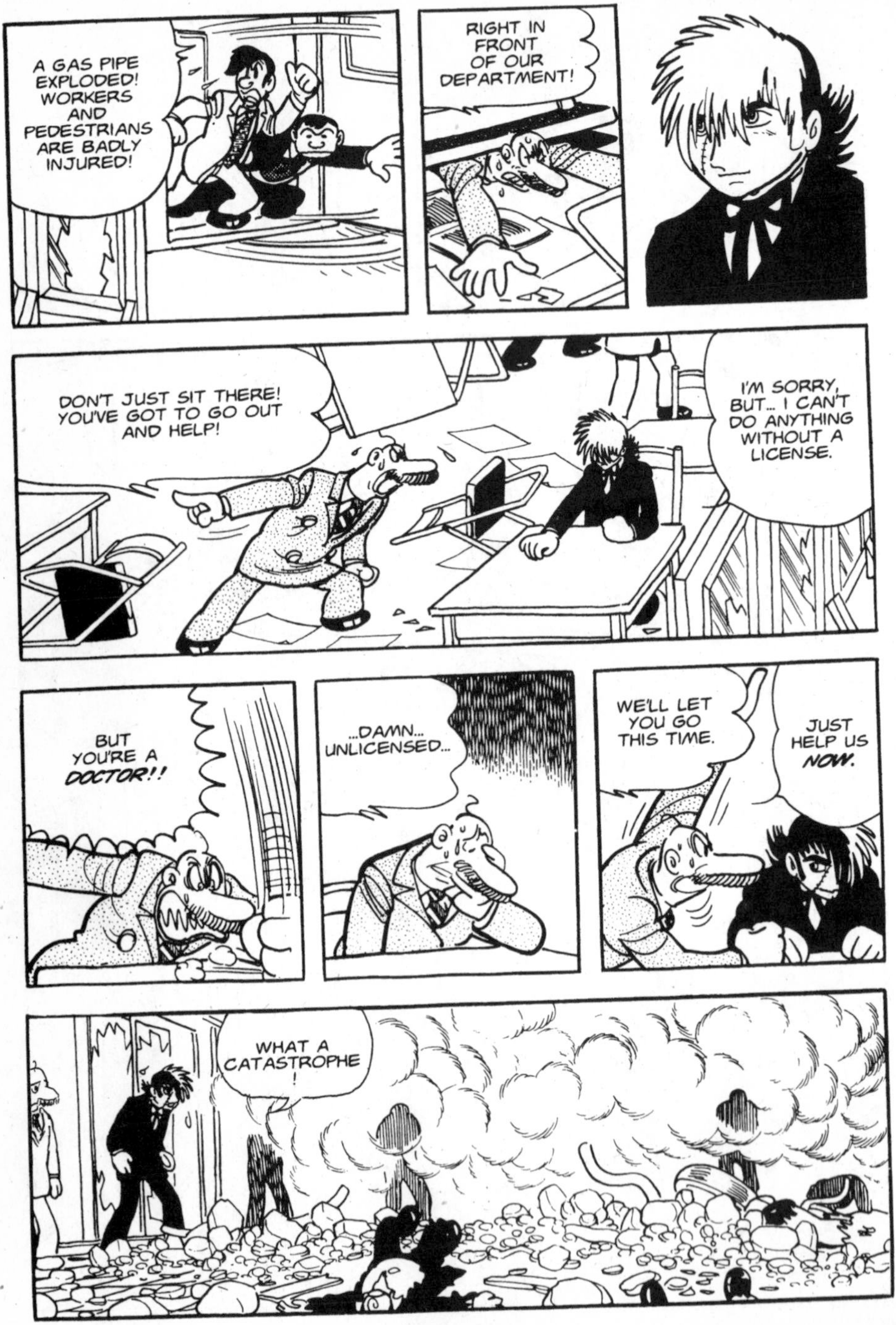
A GAS PIPE EXPLODED! WORKERS AND PEDESTRIANS ARE BADLY INJURED!
RIGHT IN FRONT OF OUR DEPARTMENT!
DON'T JUST SIT THERE! YOU'VE GOT TO GO OUT AND HELP!
I'M SORRY, BUT... I CAN'T DO ANYTHING WITHOUT A LICENSE.
BUT YOU'RE A *DOCTOR*!!
...DAMN... UNLICENSED...
WE'LL LET YOU GO THIS TIME.
JUST HELP US *NOW*.
WHAT A CATASTROPHE !

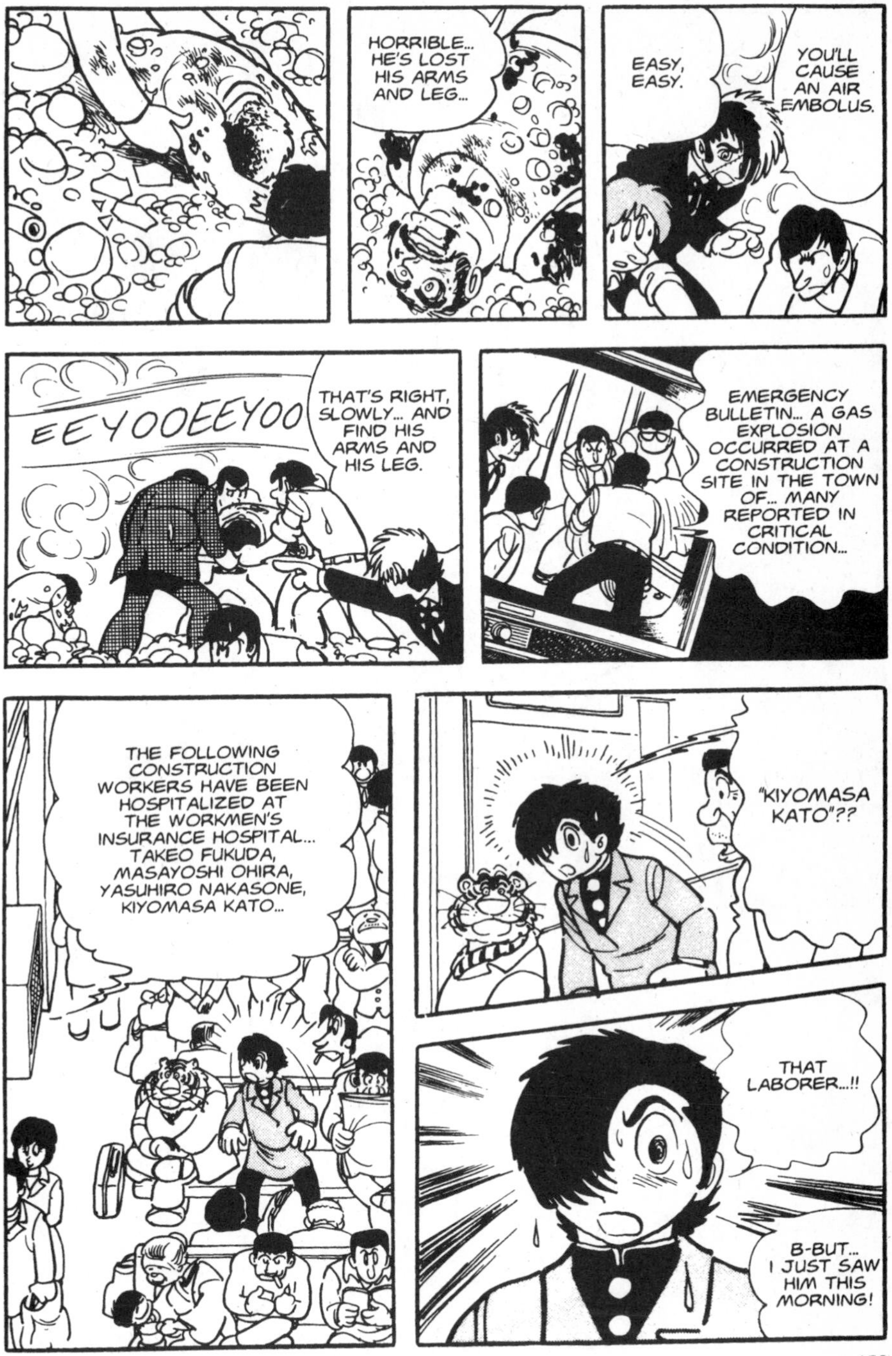
HORRIBLE... HE'S LOST HIS ARMS AND LEG...
EASY, EASY.
YOU'LL CAUSE AN AIR EMBOLUS.
EEYOOEEYOO
THAT'S RIGHT, SLOWLY... AND FIND HIS ARMS AND HIS LEG.
EMERGENCY BULLETIN... A GAS EXPLOSION OCCURRED AT A CONSTRUCTION SITE IN THE TOWN OF... MANY REPORTED IN CRITICAL CONDITION...
THE FOLLOWING CONSTRUCTION WORKERS HAVE BEEN HOSPITALIZED AT THE WORKMEN'S INSURANCE HOSPITAL... TAKEO FUKUDA, MASAYOSHI OHIRA, YASUHIRO NAKASONE, KIYOMASA KATO...
"KIYOMASA KATO"??
THAT LABORER...!!
B-BUT... I JUST SAW HIM THIS MORNING!

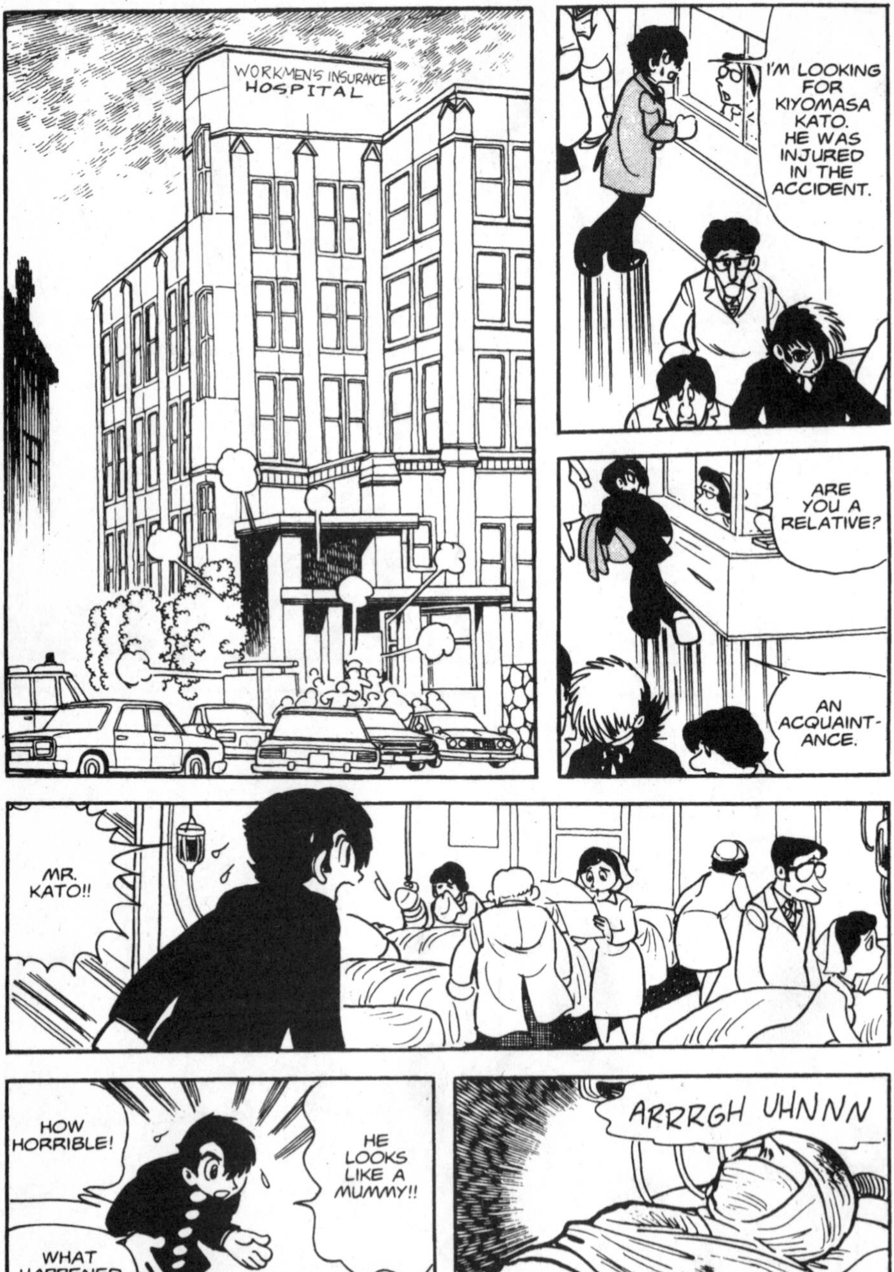
WORKMEN'S INSURANCE HOSPITAL
I'M LOOKING FOR KIYOMASA KATO. HE WAS INJURED IN THE ACCIDENT.
ARE YOU A RELATIVE?
AN ACQUAINT-ANCE.
MR. KATO!!
HOW HORRIBLE!
HE LOOKS LIKE A MUMMY!!
WHAT HAPPENED TO HIS ARMS AND LEG?
ARRRGH UHNNN

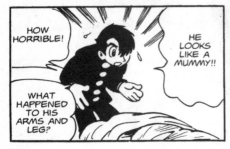

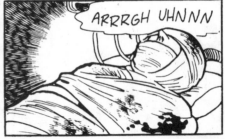

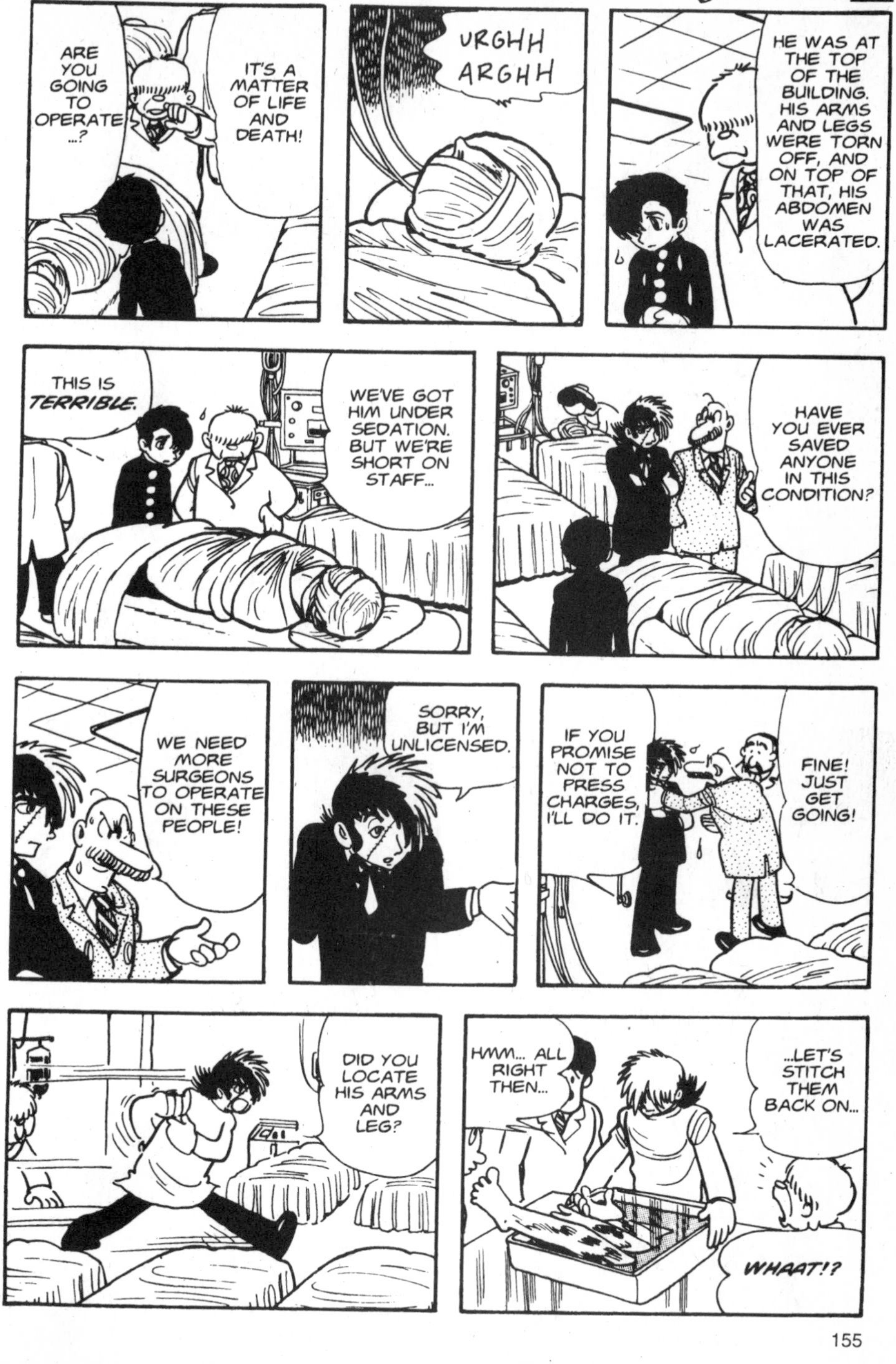
ARE YOU GOING TO OPERATE ...?
IT'S A MATTER OF LIFE AND DEATH!
URGHH ARGHH
HE WAS AT THE TOP OF THE BUILDING. HIS ARMS AND LEGS WERE TORN OFF, AND ON TOP OF THAT, HIS ABDOMEN WAS LACERATED.
THIS IS *TERRIBLE*.
WE'VE GOT HIM UNDER SEDATION. BUT WE'RE SHORT ON STAFF...
HAVE YOU EVER SAVED ANYONE IN THIS CONDITION?
WE NEED MORE SURGEONS TO OPERATE ON THESE PEOPLE!
SORRY, BUT I'M UNLICENSED.
IF YOU PROMISE NOT TO PRESS CHARGES, I'LL DO IT.
FINE! JUST GET GOING!
DID YOU LOCATE HIS ARMS AND LEG?
HMM... ALL RIGHT THEN...
...LET'S STITCH THEM BACK ON...
WHAAT!?

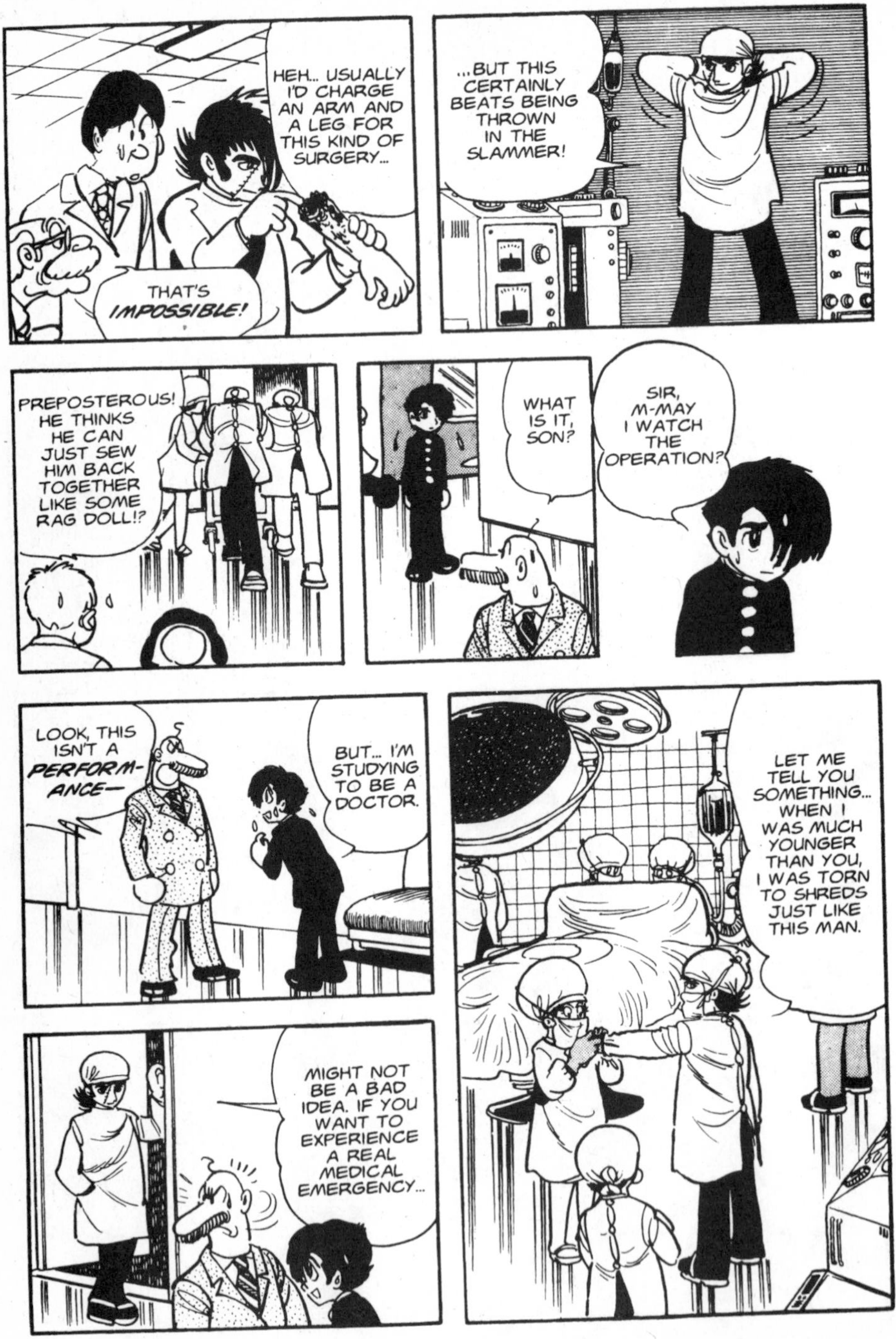
HEH... USUALLY I'D CHARGE AN ARM AND A LEG FOR THIS KIND OF SURGERY...
THAT'S *IMPOSSIBLE!*
...BUT THIS CERTAINLY BEATS BEING THROWN IN THE SLAMMER!
PREPOSTEROUS! HE THINKS HE CAN JUST SEW HIM BACK TOGETHER LIKE SOME RAG DOLL!?
WHAT IS IT, SON?
SIR, M-MAY I WATCH THE OPERATION?
LOOK, THIS ISN'T A *PERFORM-ANCE—*
BUT... I'M STUDYING TO BE A DOCTOR.
MIGHT NOT BE A BAD IDEA. IF YOU WANT TO EXPERIENCE A REAL MEDICAL EMERGENCY...
LET ME TELL YOU SOMETHING... WHEN I WAS MUCH YOUNGER THAN YOU, I WAS TORN TO SHREDS JUST LIKE THIS MAN.

 I WAS SUPPOSED TO DIE.

 BUT I WAS SAVED. THAT'S WHY I BECAME A DOCTOR.

 WE'LL START WITH REPOSITION AND ANASTOMOSIS OF THE ABDOMINAL ORGANS, AND THEN WE'LL REATTACH THE LEFT AND RIGHT ARMS, FOLLOWED BY THE RIGHT LEG.

APPROXIMATE TIME WILL BE... THREE HOURS.

 THE ILEUM DAMAGE IS PRETTY SEVERE.

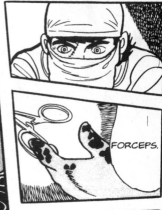 FORCEPS.

SLTSSH

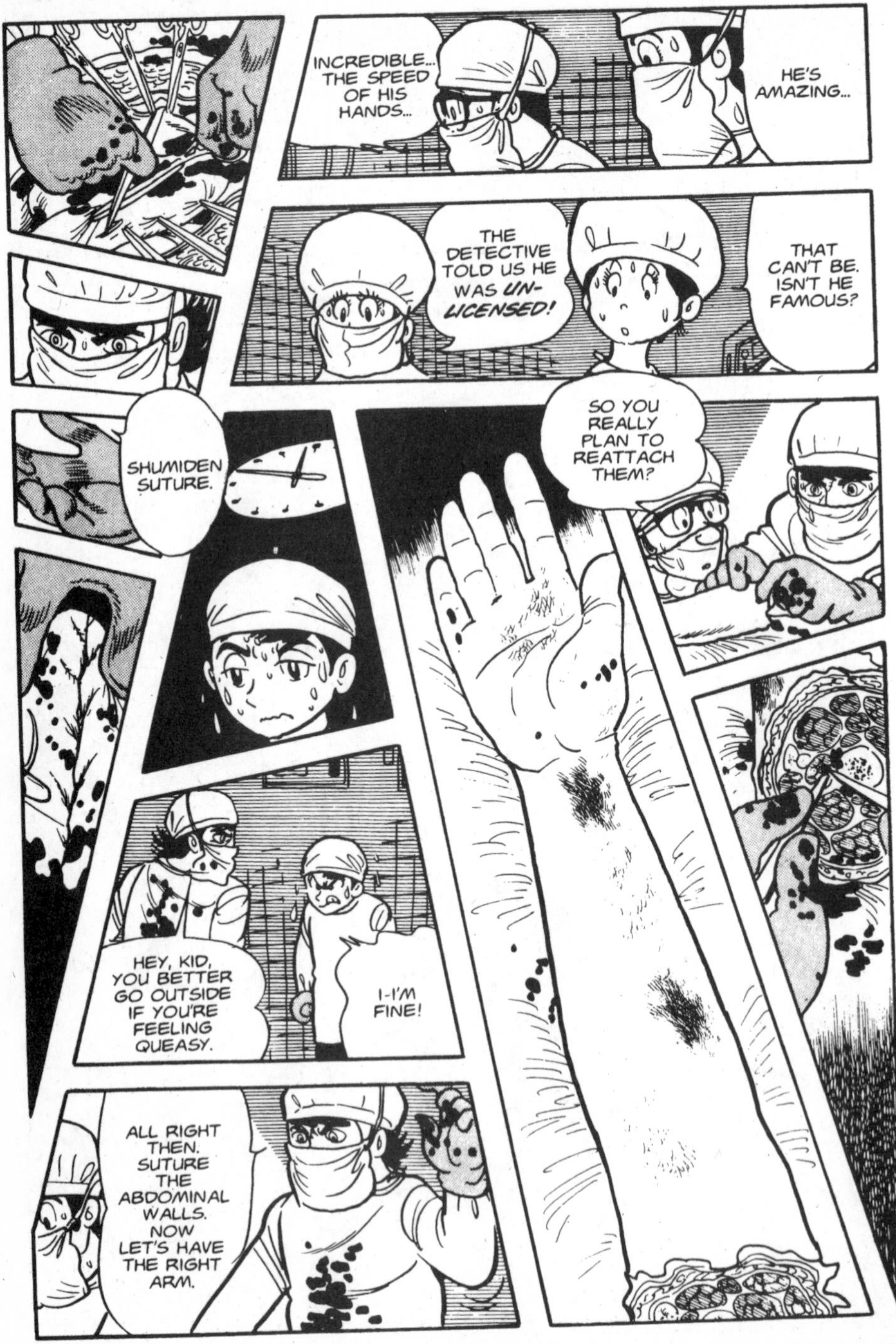
INCREDIBLE... THE SPEED OF HIS HANDS...
HE'S AMAZING...
THE DETECTIVE TOLD US HE WAS *UN-LICENSED!*
THAT CAN'T BE. ISN'T HE FAMOUS?
SHUMIDEN SUTURE.
SO YOU REALLY PLAN TO REATTACH THEM?
HEY, KID, YOU BETTER GO OUTSIDE IF YOU'RE FEELING QUEASY.
I-I'M FINE!
ALL RIGHT THEN. SUTURE THE ABDOMINAL WALLS. NOW LET'S HAVE THE RIGHT ARM.

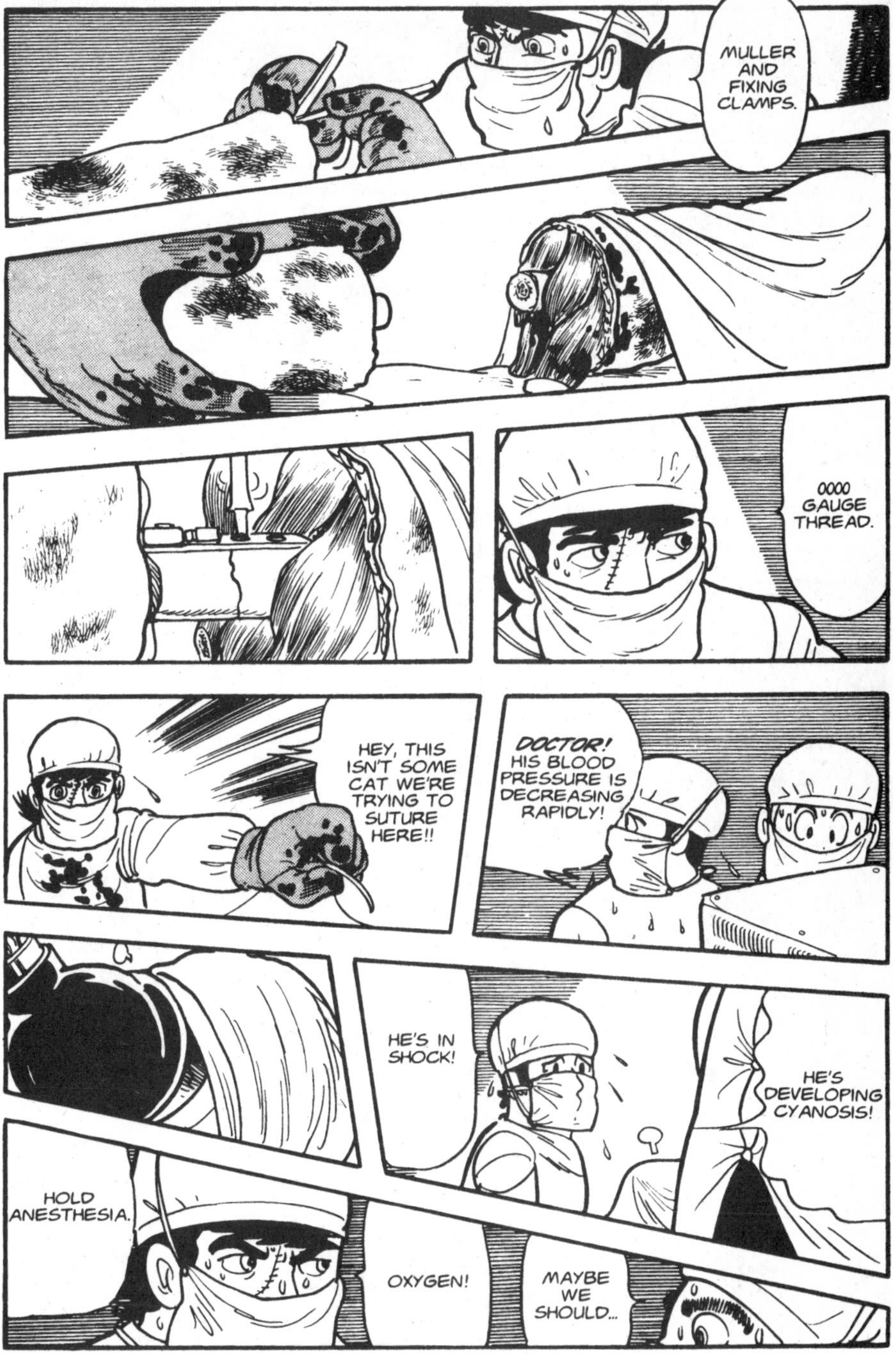
MULLER AND FIXING CLAMPS.
0000 GAUGE THREAD.
DOCTOR! HIS BLOOD PRESSURE IS DECREASING RAPIDLY!
HEY, THIS ISN'T SOME CAT WE'RE TRYING TO SUTURE HERE!!
HE'S DEVELOPING CYANOSIS!
HE'S IN SHOCK!
HOLD ANESTHESIA.
OXYGEN!
MAYBE WE SHOULD...

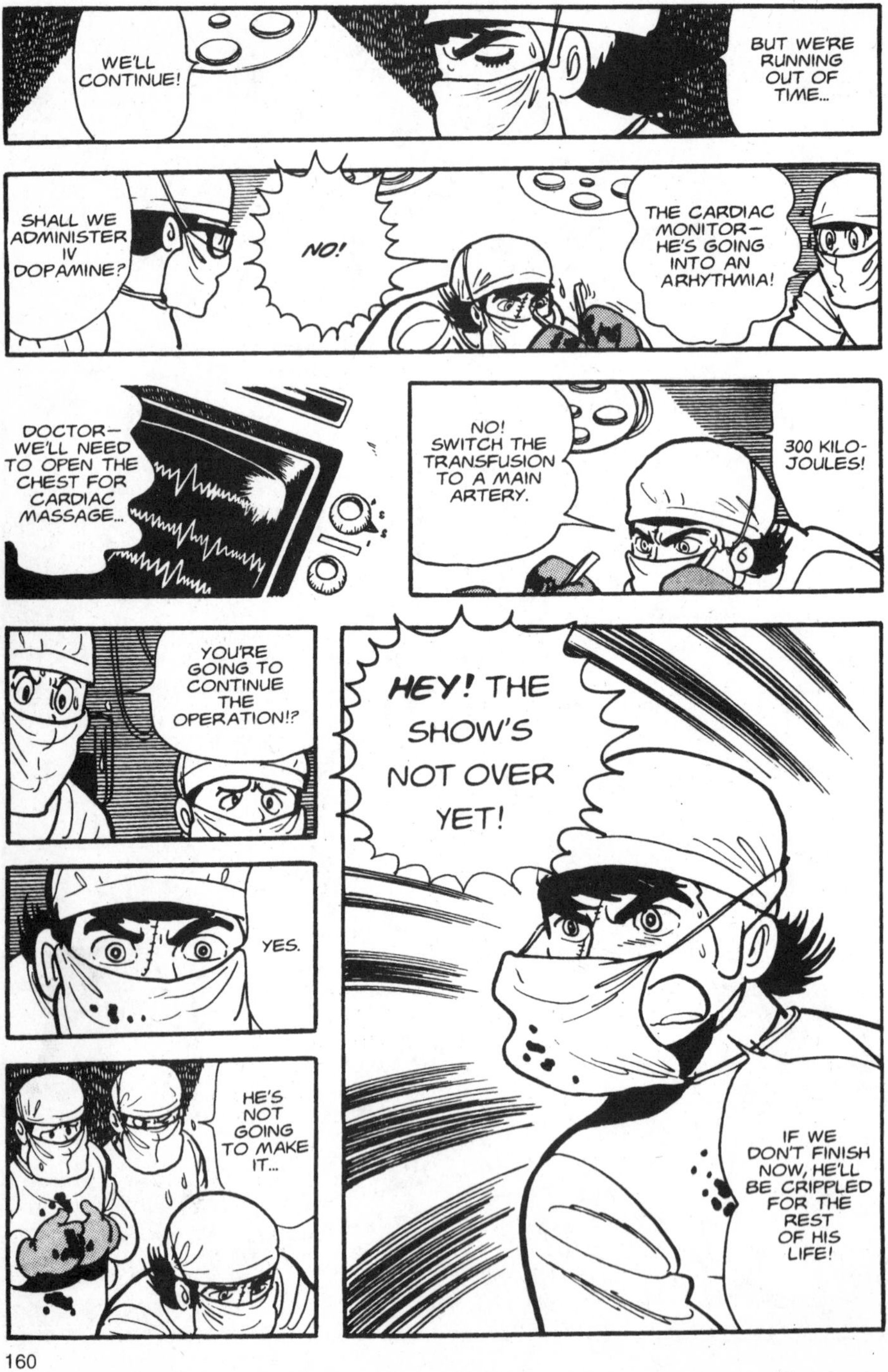

WE'LL CONTINUE!
BUT WE'RE RUNNING OUT OF TIME...
SHALL WE ADMINISTER IV DOPAMINE?
NO!
THE CARDIAC MONITOR— HE'S GOING INTO AN ARHYTHMIA!
DOCTOR— WE'LL NEED TO OPEN THE CHEST FOR CARDIAC MASSAGE...
NO! SWITCH THE TRANSFUSION TO A MAIN ARTERY.
300 KILO-JOULES!
YOU'RE GOING TO CONTINUE THE OPERATION!?
YES.
HE'S NOT GOING TO MAKE IT...
HEY! THE SHOW'S NOT OVER YET!
IF WE DON'T FINISH NOW, HE'LL BE CRIPPLED FOR THE REST OF HIS LIFE!

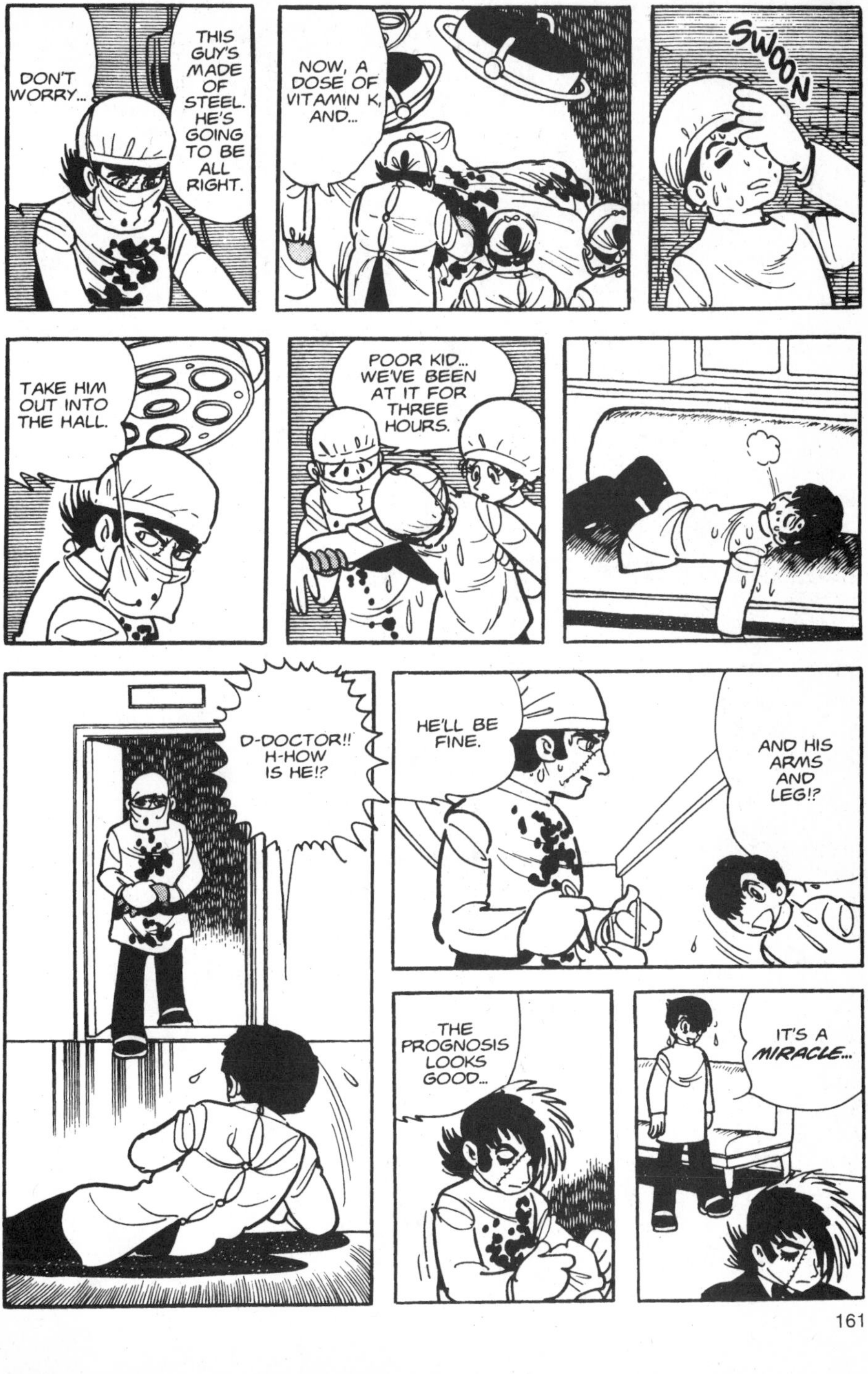
DON'T WORRY...
THIS GUY'S MADE OF STEEL. HE'S GOING TO BE ALL RIGHT.
NOW, A DOSE OF VITAMIN K, AND...
SWOON
TAKE HIM OUT INTO THE HALL.
POOR KID... WE'VE BEEN AT IT FOR THREE HOURS.
D-DOCTOR!! H-HOW IS HE!?
HE'LL BE FINE.
AND HIS ARMS AND LEG!?
THE PROGNOSIS LOOKS GOOD...
IT'S A *MIRACLE*...

SO I'M FREE TO GO NOW, RIGHT?

SEE YOU...

DOCTOR!

DOCTOR...

I WAS PLANNING TO KILL MYSELF THIS MORNING.

WHY?

I FAILED MY ENTRANCE EXAMS.

BUT NOW I KNOW WHAT A REAL MATTER OF LIFE AND DEATH IS!

WHAT ARE YOU SMILING ABOUT?

OH... NOTHING... IT'S JUST THAT I'VE BEEN A FOOL.

This boy, Black Jack, and Kato will most likely never meet again.

But from this brief encounter, this boy learned a valuable life lesson.

OPERATION EIGHT

EMERGENCY
SHELTER

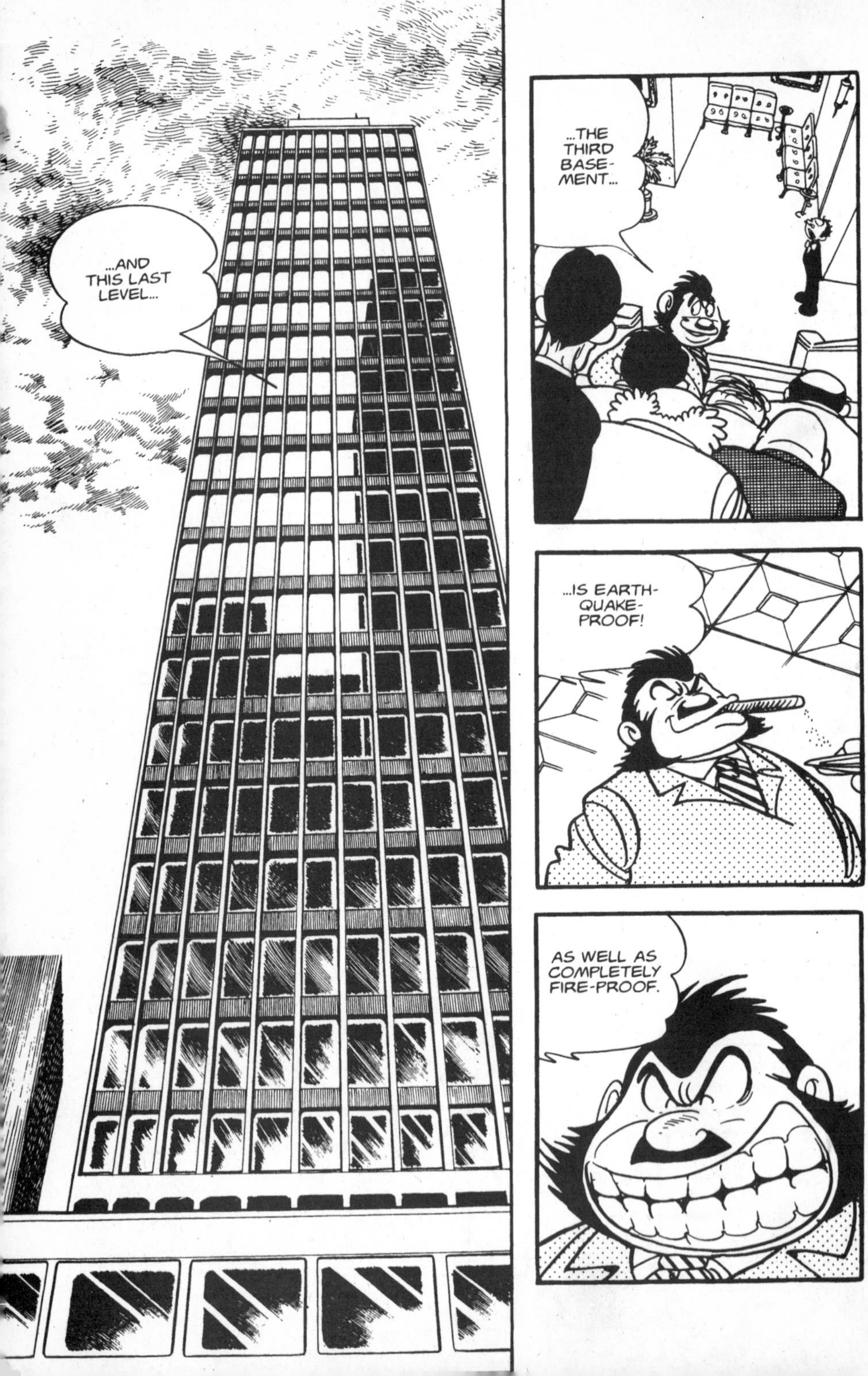
...AND THIS LAST LEVEL...
...THE THIRD BASE-MENT...
...IS EARTH-QUAKE-PROOF!
AS WELL AS COMPLETELY FIRE-PROOF.

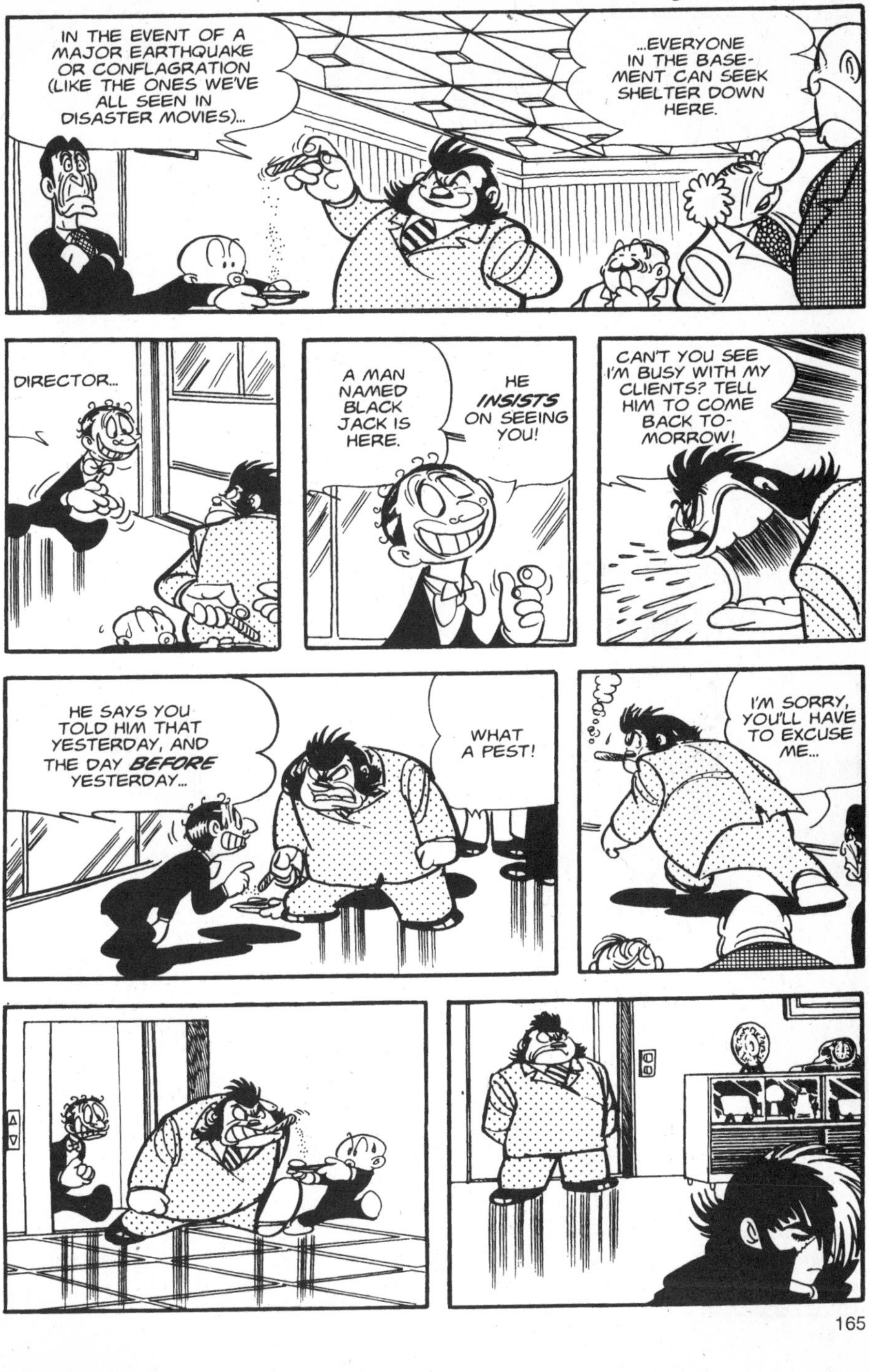
IN THE EVENT OF A MAJOR EARTHQUAKE OR CONFLAGRATION (LIKE THE ONES WE'VE ALL SEEN IN DISASTER MOVIES)...
...EVERYONE IN THE BASE-MENT CAN SEEK SHELTER DOWN HERE.
DIRECTOR...
A MAN NAMED BLACK JACK IS HERE.
HE *INSISTS* ON SEEING YOU!
CAN'T YOU SEE I'M BUSY WITH MY CLIENTS? TELL HIM TO COME BACK TO-MORROW!
HE SAYS YOU TOLD HIM THAT YESTERDAY, AND THE DAY *BEFORE* YESTERDAY...
WHAT A PEST!
I'M SORRY, YOU'LL HAVE TO EXCUSE ME...

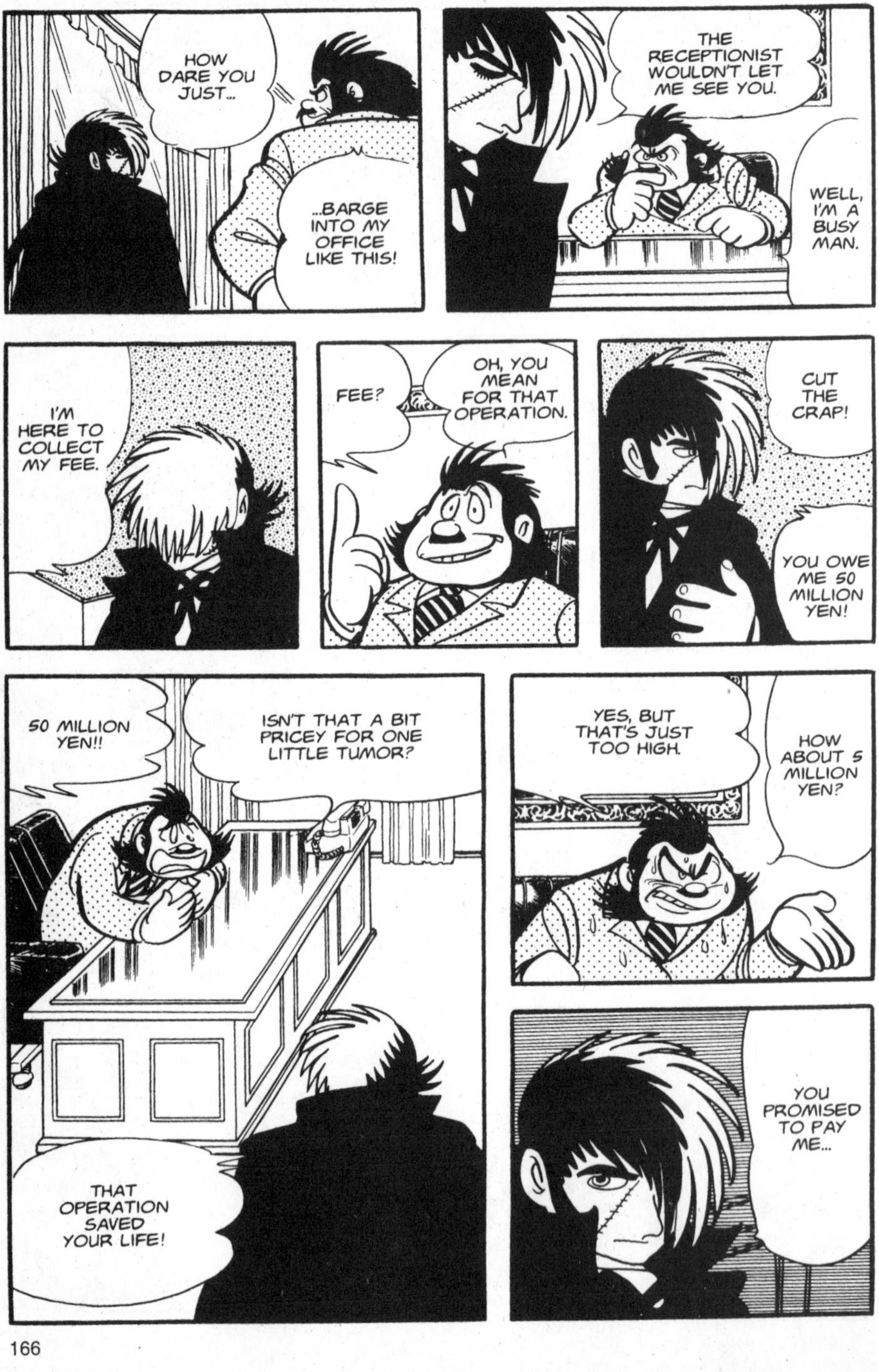
HOW DARE YOU JUST...
...BARGE INTO MY OFFICE LIKE THIS!
THE RECEPTIONIST WOULDN'T LET ME SEE YOU.
WELL, I'M A BUSY MAN.
I'M HERE TO COLLECT MY FEE.
FEE?
OH, YOU MEAN FOR THAT OPERATION.
CUT THE CRAP!
YOU OWE ME 50 MILLION YEN!
50 MILLION YEN!!
ISN'T THAT A BIT PRICEY FOR ONE LITTLE TUMOR?
THAT OPERATION SAVED YOUR LIFE!
YES, BUT THAT'S JUST TOO HIGH.
HOW ABOUT 5 MILLION YEN?
YOU PROMISED TO PAY ME...

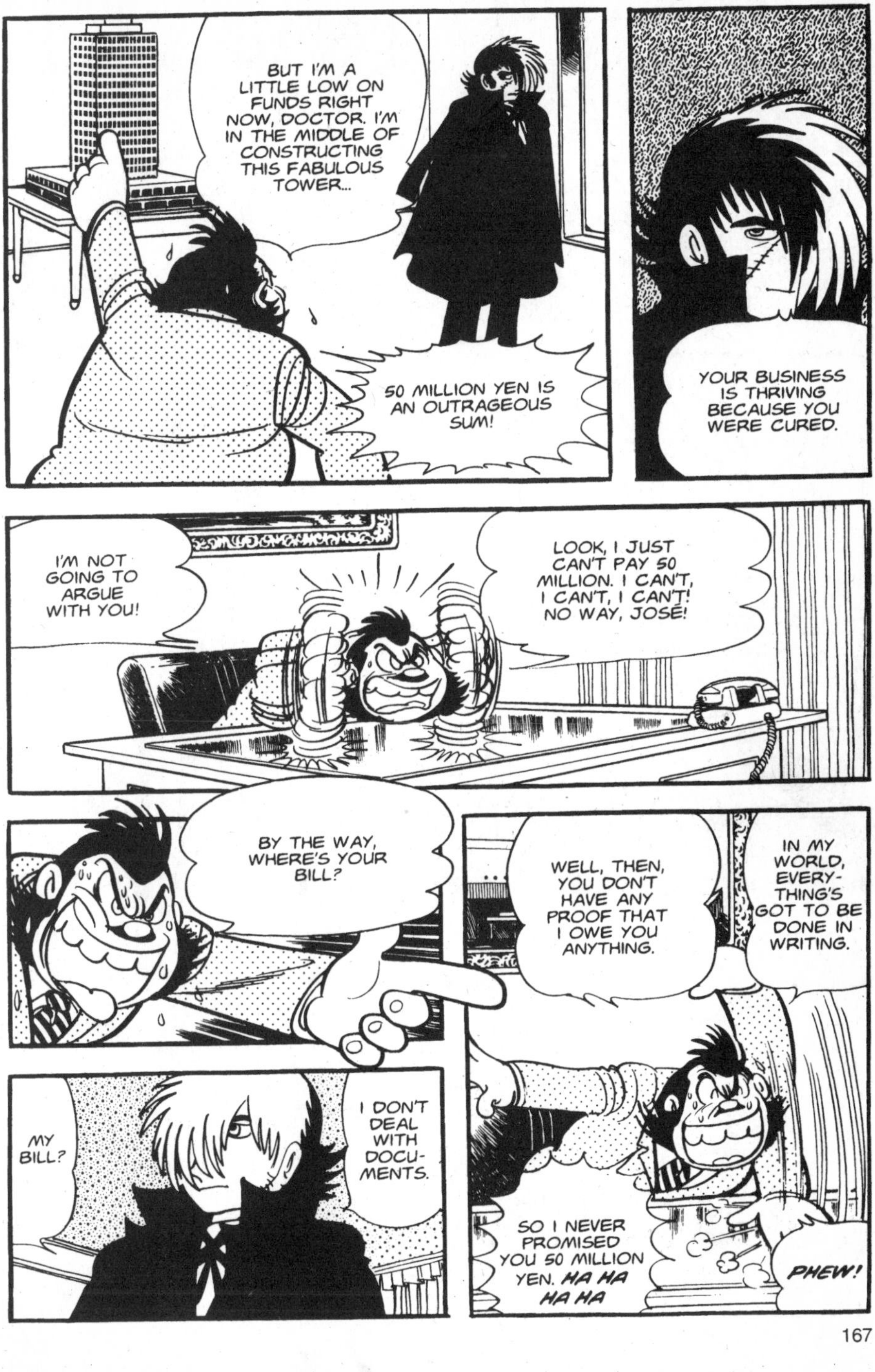
BUT I'M A LITTLE LOW ON FUNDS RIGHT NOW, DOCTOR. I'M IN THE MIDDLE OF CONSTRUCTING THIS FABULOUS TOWER...
50 MILLION YEN IS AN OUTRAGEOUS SUM!
YOUR BUSINESS IS THRIVING BECAUSE YOU WERE CURED.
I'M NOT GOING TO ARGUE WITH YOU!
LOOK, I JUST CAN'T PAY 50 MILLION. I CAN'T, I CAN'T, I CAN'T! NO WAY, JOSÉ!
BY THE WAY, WHERE'S YOUR BILL?
MY BILL?
I DON'T DEAL WITH DOCU- MENTS.
WELL, THEN, YOU DON'T HAVE ANY PROOF THAT I OWE YOU ANYTHING.
IN MY WORLD, EVERY- THING'S GOT TO BE DONE IN WRITING.
SO I NEVER PROMISED YOU 50 MILLION YEN. HA HA HA HA
PHEW!

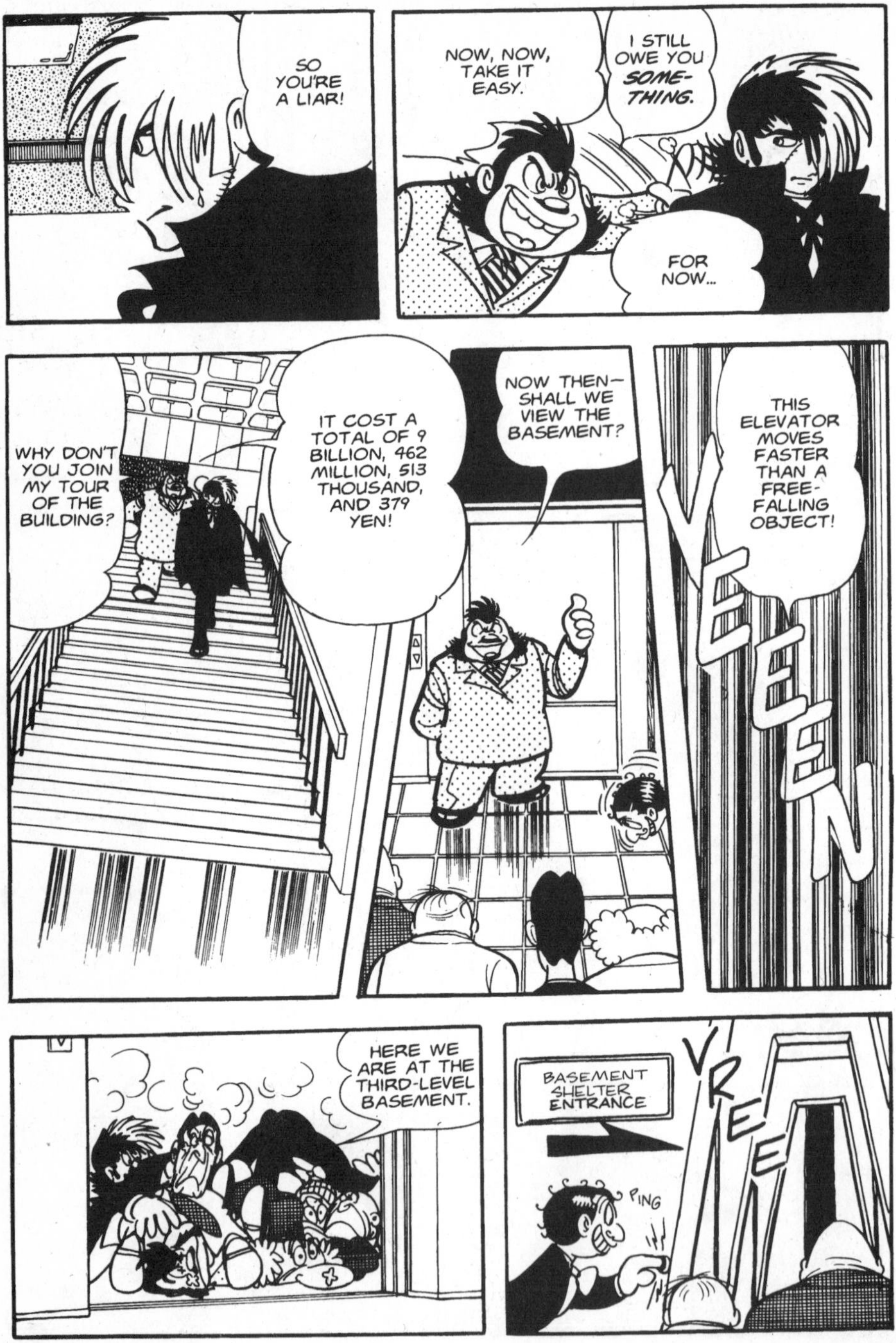
SO YOU'RE A LIAR!
NOW, NOW, TAKE IT EASY.
I STILL OWE YOU *SOMETHING.*
FOR NOW...
WHY DON'T YOU JOIN MY TOUR OF THE BUILDING?
IT COST A TOTAL OF 9 BILLION, 462 MILLION, 513 THOUSAND, AND 379 YEN!
NOW THEN— SHALL WE VIEW THE BASEMENT?
THIS ELEVATOR MOVES FASTER THAN A FREE-FALLING OBJECT!
VEEEEN
HERE WE ARE AT THE THIRD-LEVEL BASEMENT.
BASEMENT SHELTER ENTRANCE
VREEE
PING

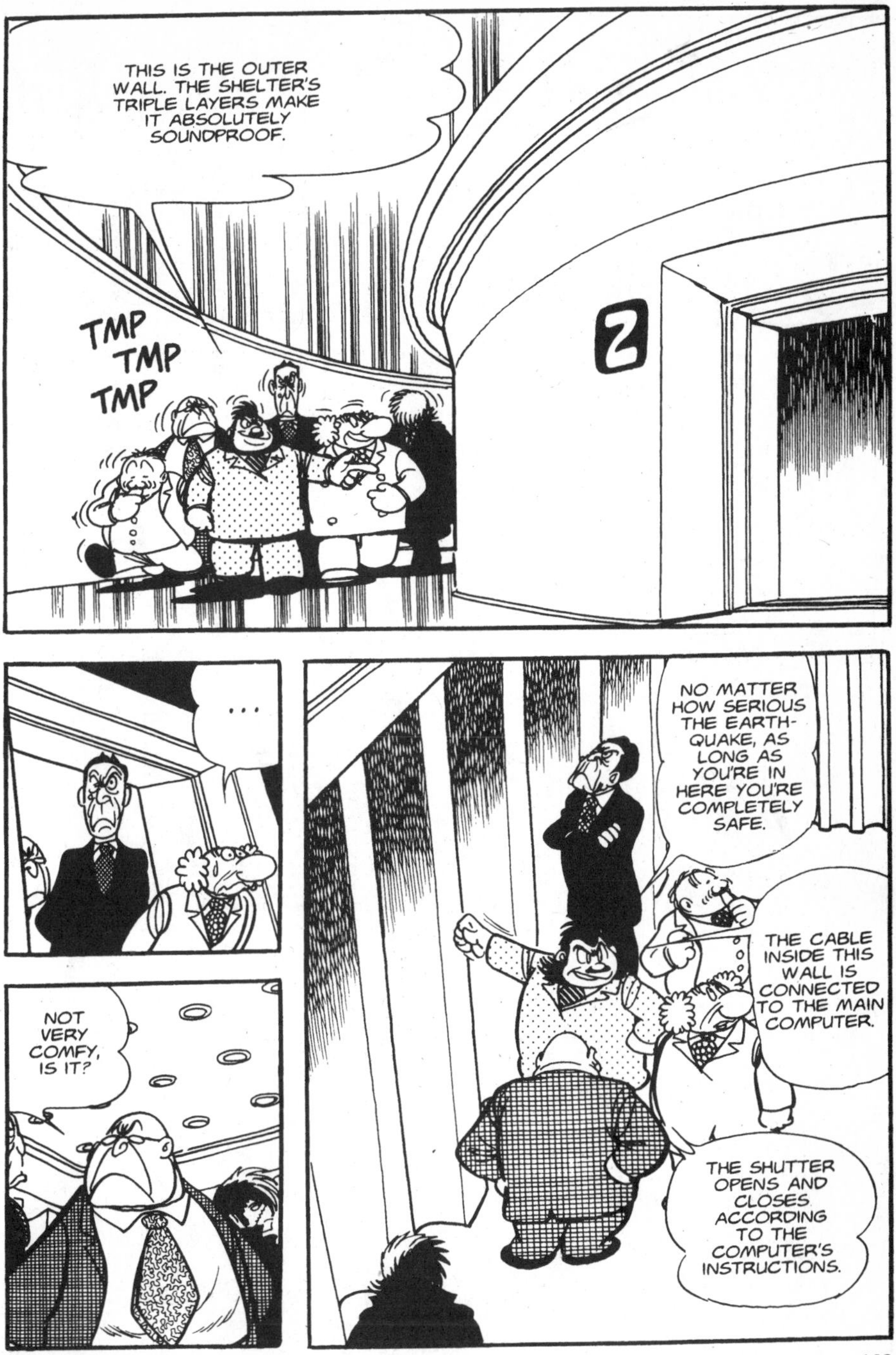
THIS IS THE OUTER WALL. THE SHELTER'S TRIPLE LAYERS MAKE IT ABSOLUTELY SOUNDPROOF.
TMP TMP TMP
2
...
NOT VERY COMFY, IS IT?
NO MATTER HOW SERIOUS THE EARTH-QUAKE, AS LONG AS YOU'RE IN HERE YOU'RE COMPLETELY SAFE.
THE CABLE INSIDE THIS WALL IS CONNECTED TO THE MAIN COMPUTER.
THE SHUTTER OPENS AND CLOSES ACCORDING TO THE COMPUTER'S INSTRUCTIONS.

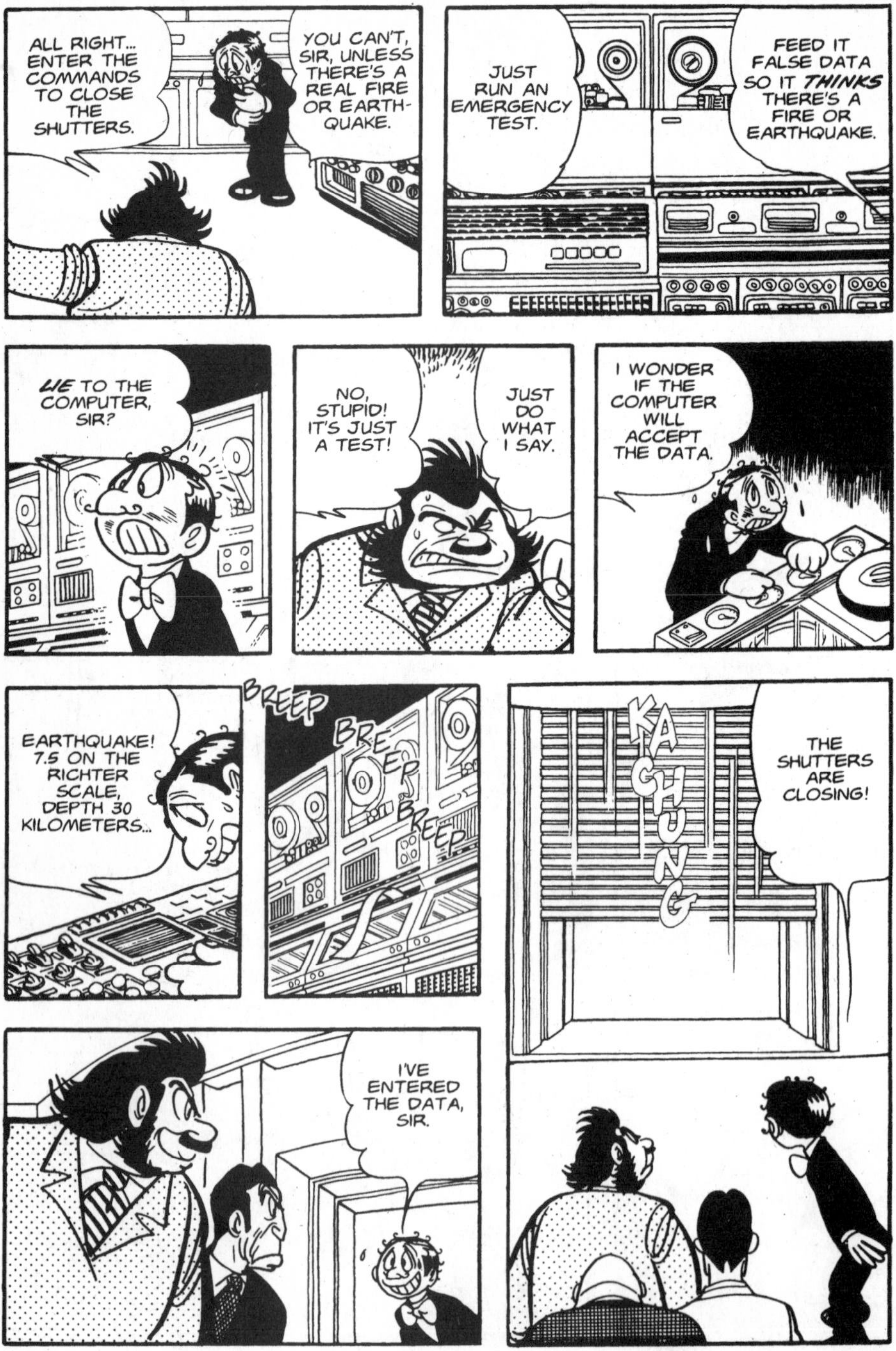
ALL RIGHT... ENTER THE COMMANDS TO CLOSE THE SHUTTERS.
YOU CAN'T, SIR, UNLESS THERE'S A REAL FIRE OR EARTH-QUAKE.
JUST RUN AN EMERGENCY TEST.
FEED IT FALSE DATA SO IT THINKS THERE'S A FIRE OR EARTHQUAKE.
LIE TO THE COMPUTER, SIR?
NO, STUPID! IT'S JUST A TEST!
JUST DO WHAT I SAY.
I WONDER IF THE COMPUTER WILL ACCEPT THE DATA.
EARTHQUAKE! 7.5 ON THE RICHTER SCALE, DEPTH 30 KILOMETERS...
BREEP
BREEP
BREEP
I'VE ENTERED THE DATA, SIR.
KACHUNG
THE SHUTTERS ARE CLOSING!

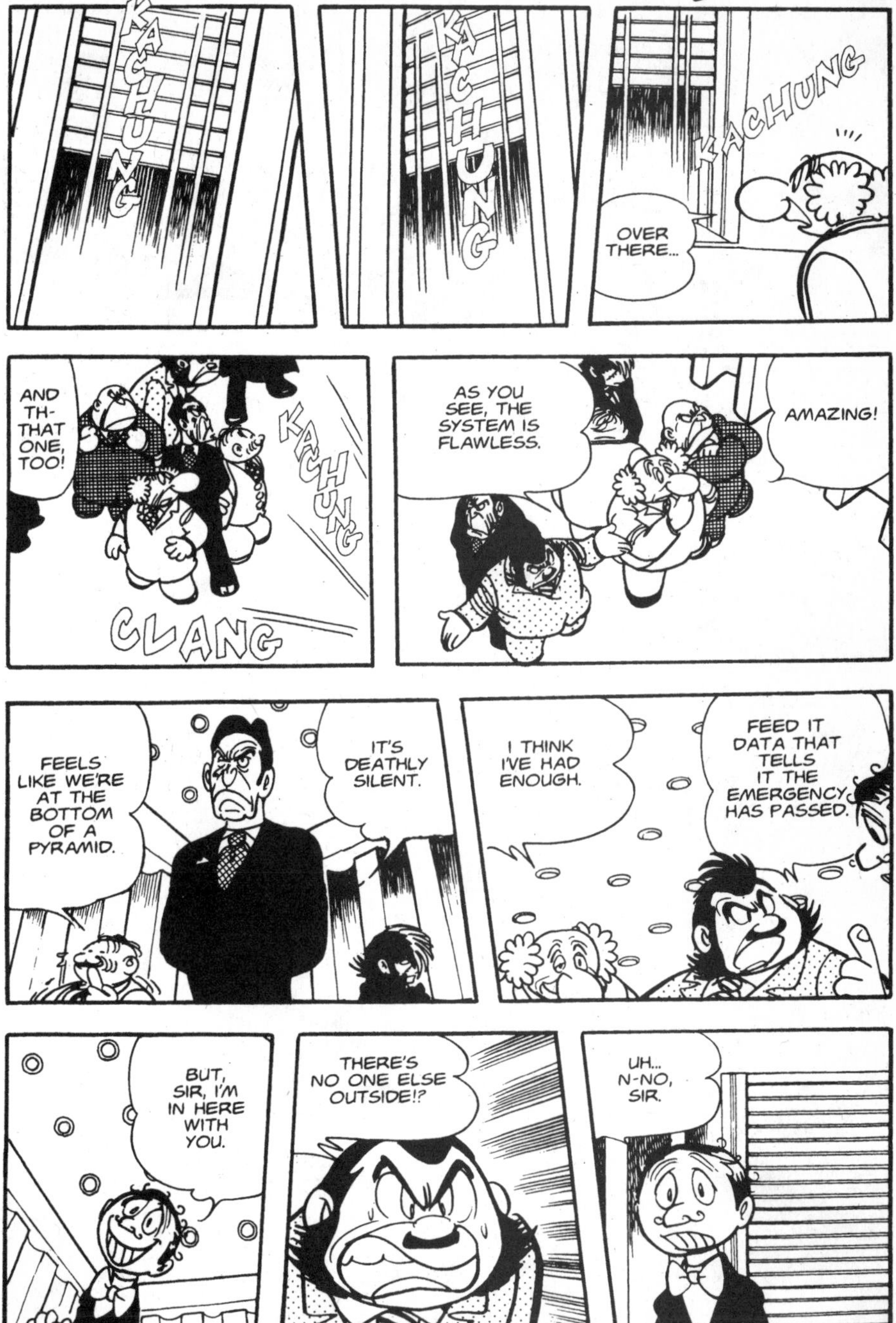
KACHUNG
KACHUNG
KACHUNG
OVER THERE...
AND TH-THAT ONE, TOO!
KACHUNG
CLANG
AS YOU SEE, THE SYSTEM IS FLAWLESS.
AMAZING!
FEELS LIKE WE'RE AT THE BOTTOM OF A PYRAMID.
IT'S DEATHLY SILENT.
I THINK I'VE HAD ENOUGH.
FEED IT DATA THAT TELLS IT THE EMERGENCY HAS PASSED.
BUT, SIR, I'M IN HERE WITH YOU.
THERE'S NO ONE ELSE OUTSIDE!?
UH... N-NO, SIR.

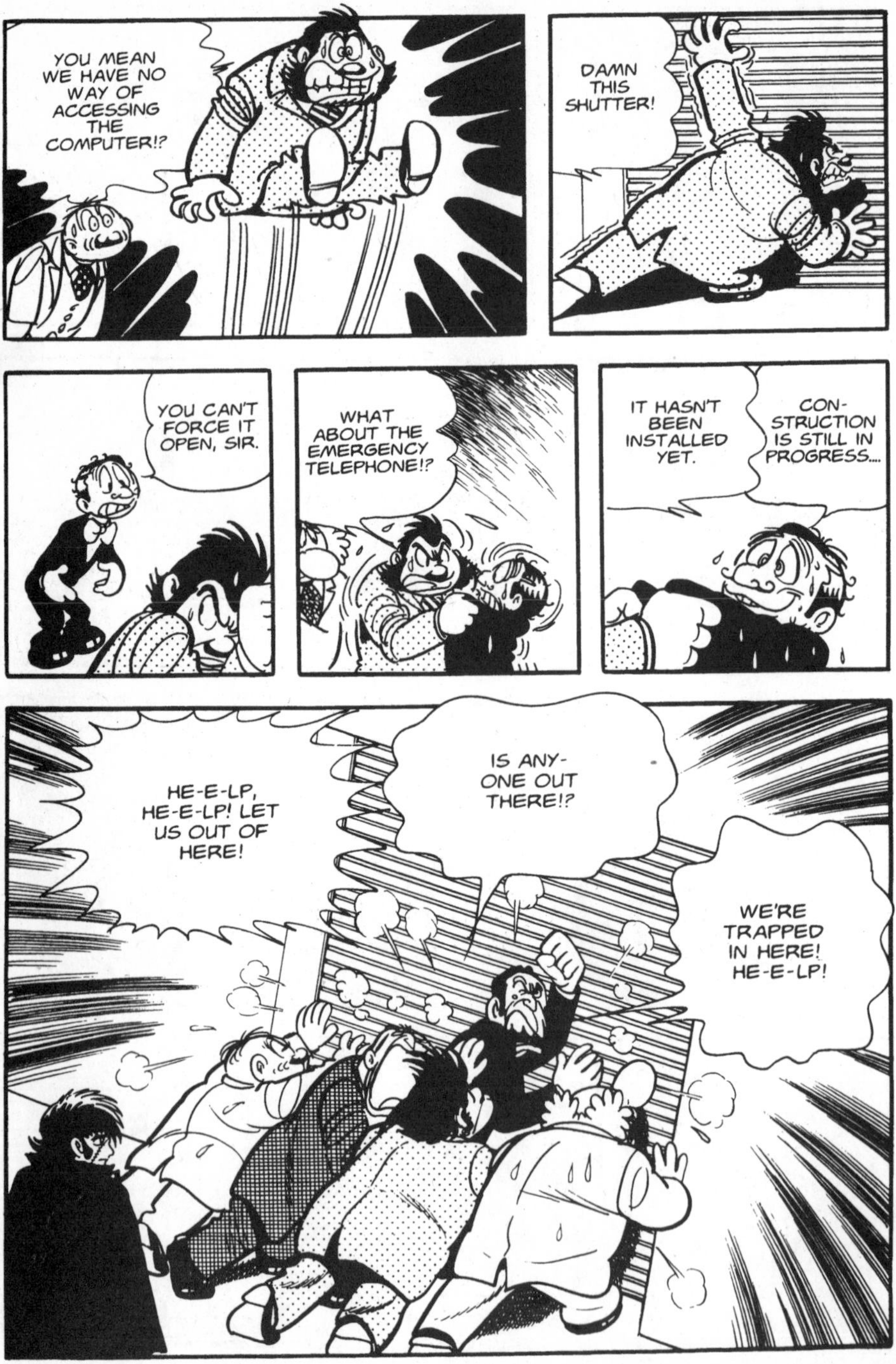
YOU MEAN WE HAVE NO WAY OF ACCESSING THE COMPUTER!?
DAMN THIS SHUTTER!
YOU CAN'T FORCE IT OPEN, SIR.
WHAT ABOUT THE EMERGENCY TELEPHONE!?
IT HASN'T BEEN INSTALLED YET.
CON-STRUCTION IS STILL IN PROGRESS....
HE-E-LP, HE-E-LP! LET US OUT OF HERE!
IS ANY-ONE OUT THERE!?
WE'RE TRAPPED IN HERE! HE-E-LP!

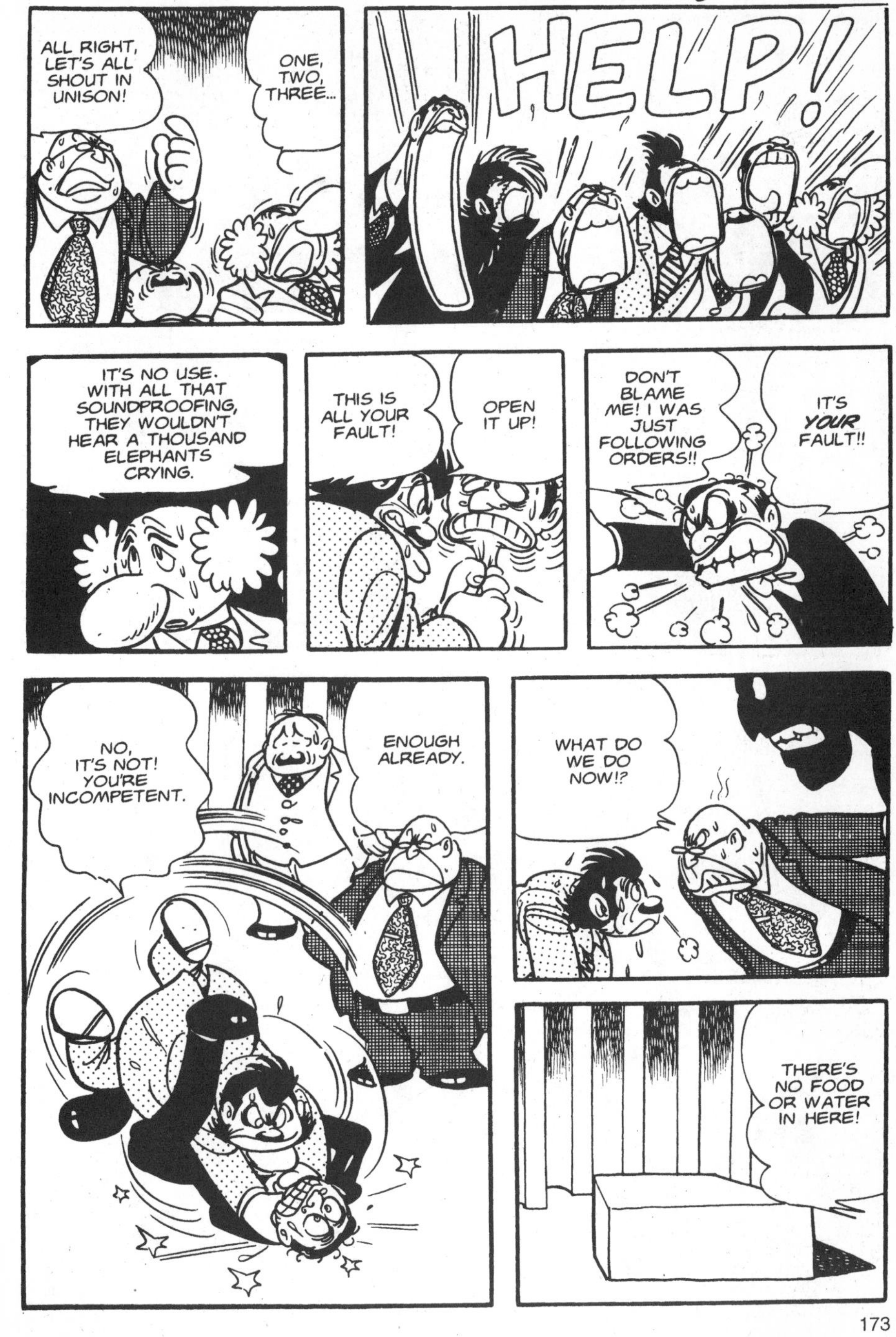
ALL RIGHT, LET'S ALL SHOUT IN UNISON!
ONE, TWO, THREE...
HELP!
IT'S NO USE. WITH ALL THAT SOUNDPROOFING, THEY WOULDN'T HEAR A THOUSAND ELEPHANTS CRYING.
THIS IS ALL YOUR FAULT!
OPEN IT UP!
DON'T BLAME ME! I WAS JUST FOLLOWING ORDERS!!
IT'S *YOUR* FAULT!!
NO, IT'S NOT! YOU'RE INCOMPETENT.
ENOUGH ALREADY.
WHAT DO WE DO NOW!?
THERE'S NO FOOD OR WATER IN HERE!

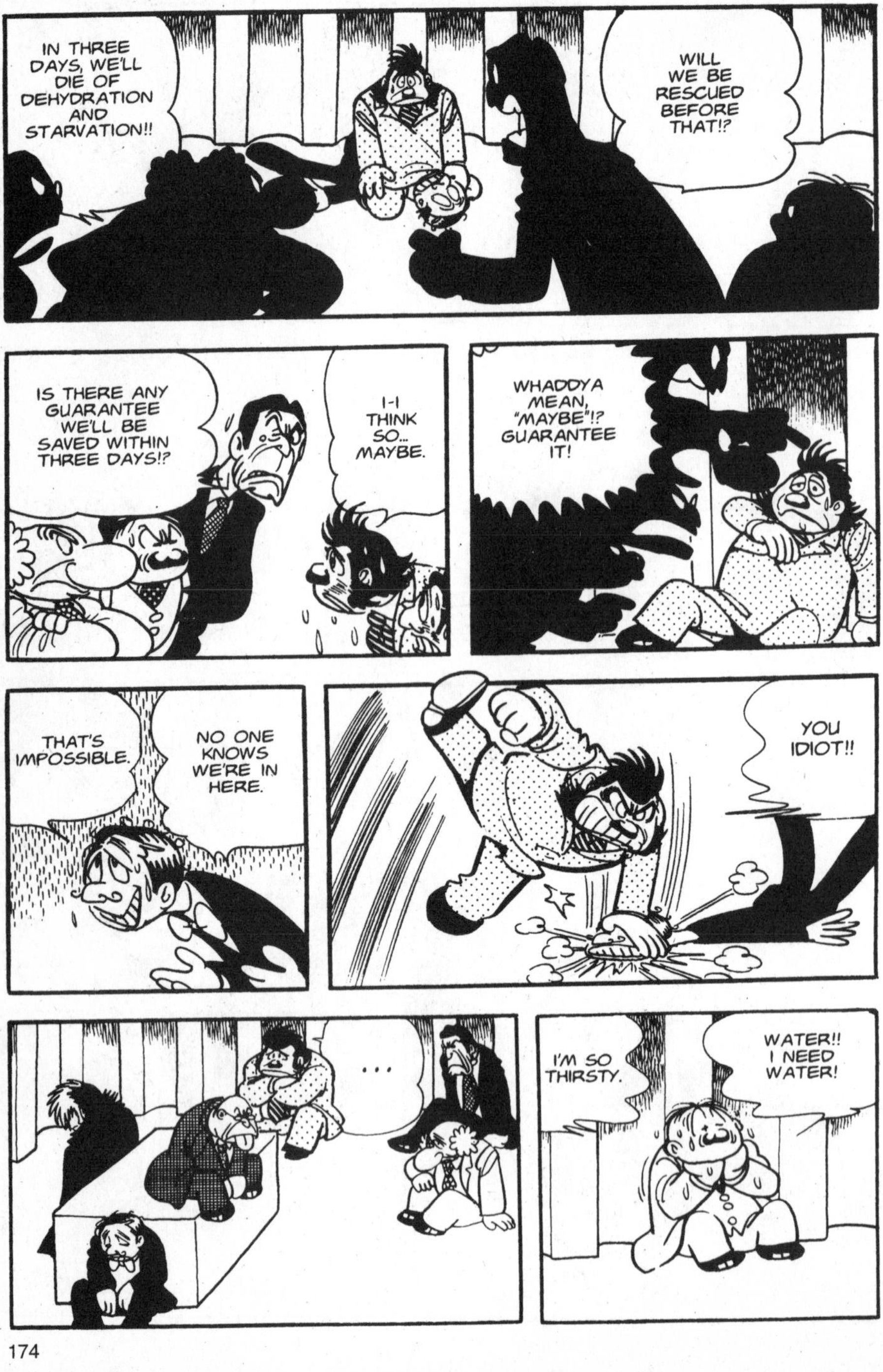
IN THREE DAYS, WE'LL DIE OF DEHYDRATION AND STARVATION!!
WILL WE BE RESCUED BEFORE THAT!?
IS THERE ANY GUARANTEE WE'LL BE SAVED WITHIN THREE DAYS!?
I-I THINK SO... MAYBE.
WHADDYA MEAN, "MAYBE"!? GUARANTEE IT!
THAT'S IMPOSSIBLE.
NO ONE KNOWS WE'RE IN HERE.
YOU IDIOT!!
...
I'M SO THIRSTY.
WATER!! I NEED WATER!

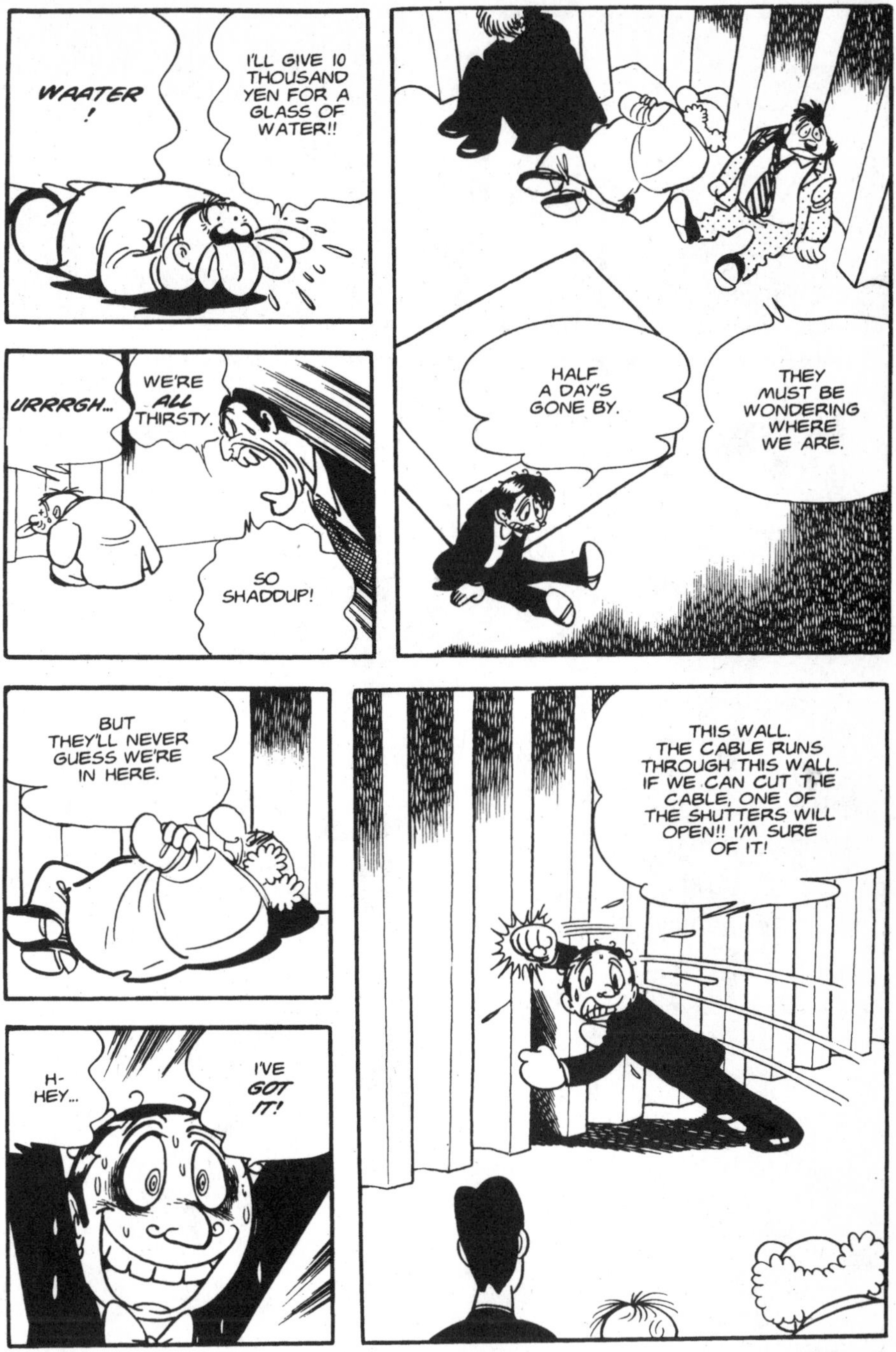
WAATER!
I'LL GIVE 10 THOUSAND YEN FOR A GLASS OF WATER!!
URRRGH...
WE'RE ALL THIRSTY.
SO SHADDUP!
HALF A DAY'S GONE BY.
THEY MUST BE WONDERING WHERE WE ARE.
BUT THEY'LL NEVER GUESS WE'RE IN HERE.
H-HEY...
I'VE GOT IT!
THIS WALL. THE CABLE RUNS THROUGH THIS WALL. IF WE CAN CUT THE CABLE, ONE OF THE SHUTTERS WILL OPEN!! I'M SURE OF IT!

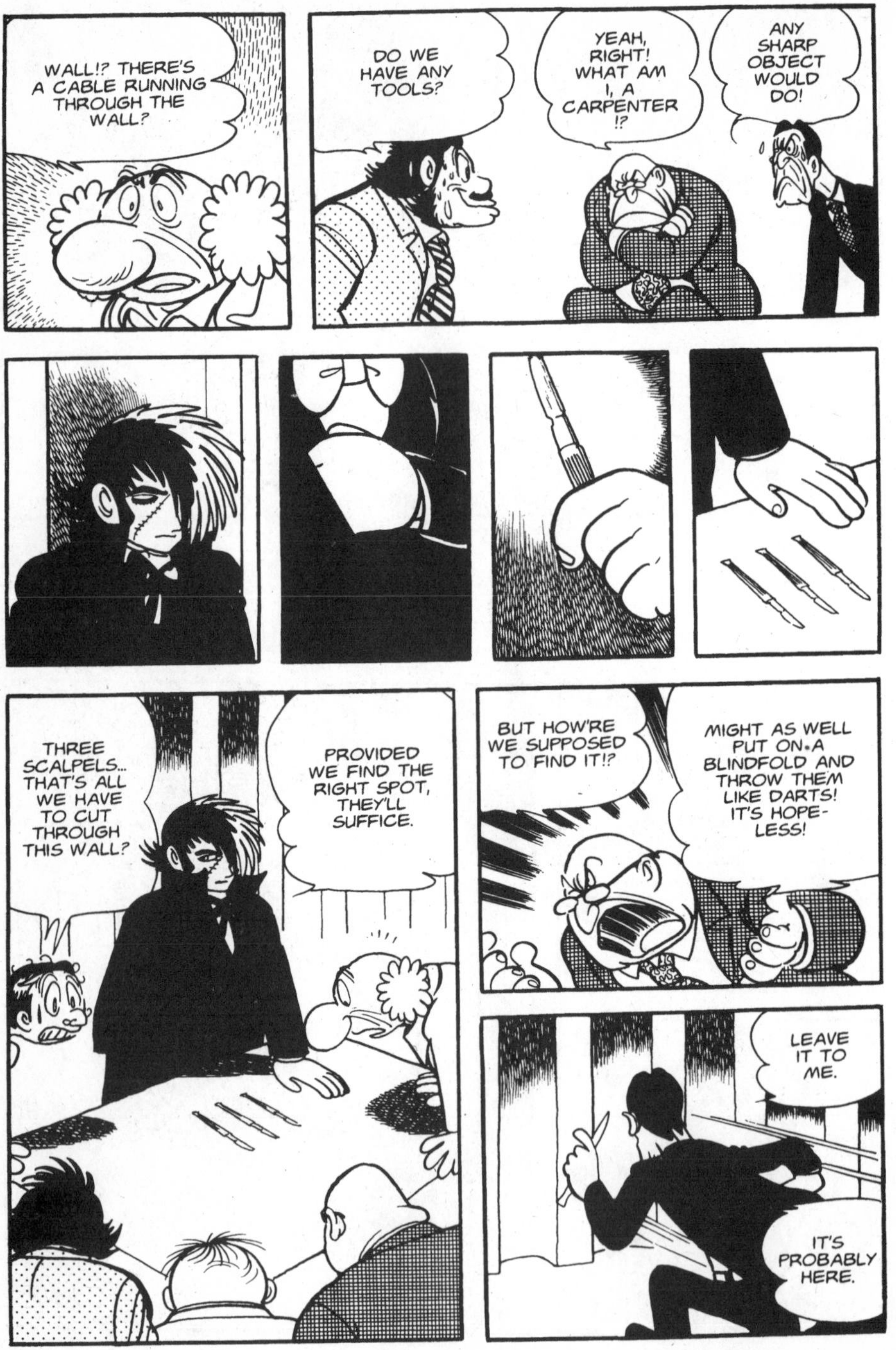
WALL!? THERE'S A CABLE RUNNING THROUGH THE WALL?
DO WE HAVE ANY TOOLS?
YEAH, RIGHT! WHAT AM I, A CARPENTER !?
ANY SHARP OBJECT WOULD DO!
THREE SCALPELS... THAT'S ALL WE HAVE TO CUT THROUGH THIS WALL?
PROVIDED WE FIND THE RIGHT SPOT, THEY'LL SUFFICE.
BUT HOW'RE WE SUPPOSED TO FIND IT!?
MIGHT AS WELL PUT ON A BLINDFOLD AND THROW THEM LIKE DARTS! IT'S HOPELESS!
LEAVE IT TO ME.
IT'S PROBABLY HERE.

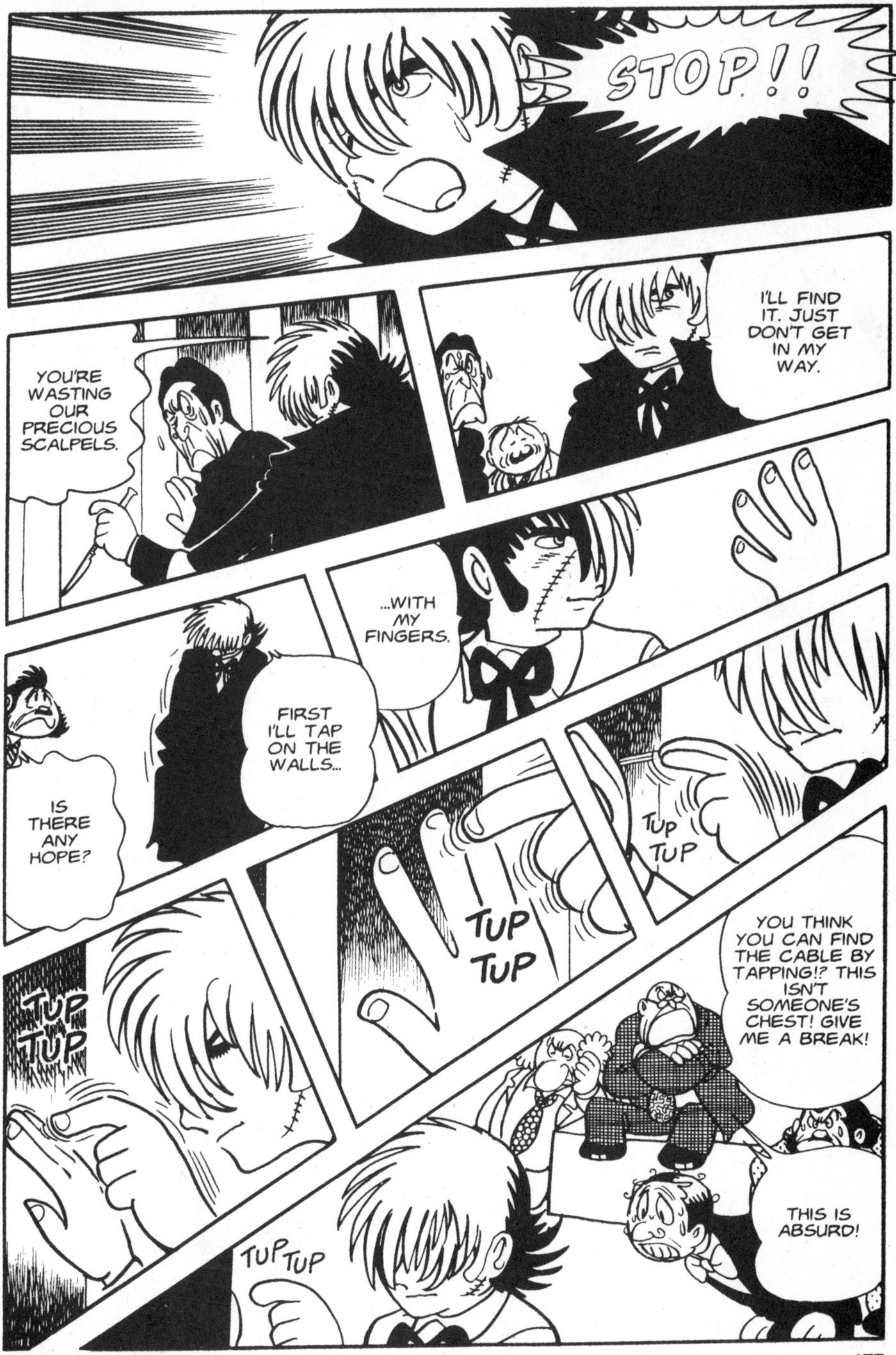
STOP!!
YOU'RE WASTING OUR PRECIOUS SCALPELS.
I'LL FIND IT. JUST DON'T GET IN MY WAY.
...WITH MY FINGERS.
FIRST I'LL TAP ON THE WALLS...
IS THERE ANY HOPE?
TUP TUP
TUP TUP
TUP TUP
TUP TUP
YOU THINK YOU CAN FIND THE CABLE BY TAPPING!? THIS ISN'T SOMEONE'S CHEST! GIVE ME A BREAK!
THIS IS ABSURD!

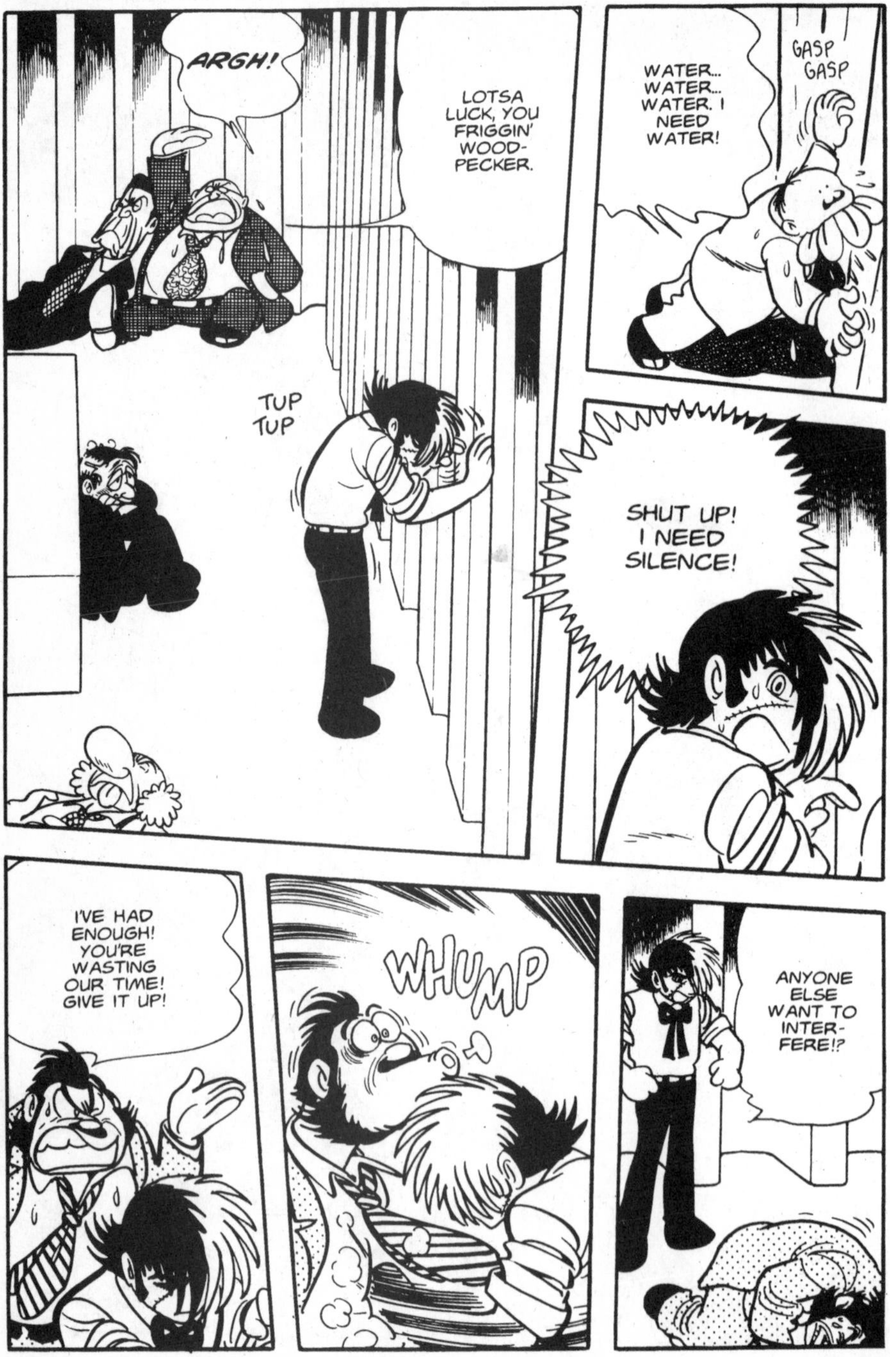
ARGH!
LOTSA LUCK, YOU FRIGGIN' WOOD-PECKER.
TUP TUP
WATER... WATER... WATER. I NEED WATER!
GASP GASP
SHUT UP! I NEED SILENCE!
I'VE HAD ENOUGH! YOU'RE WASTING OUR TIME! GIVE IT UP!
WHUMP
ANYONE ELSE WANT TO INTER-FERE!?

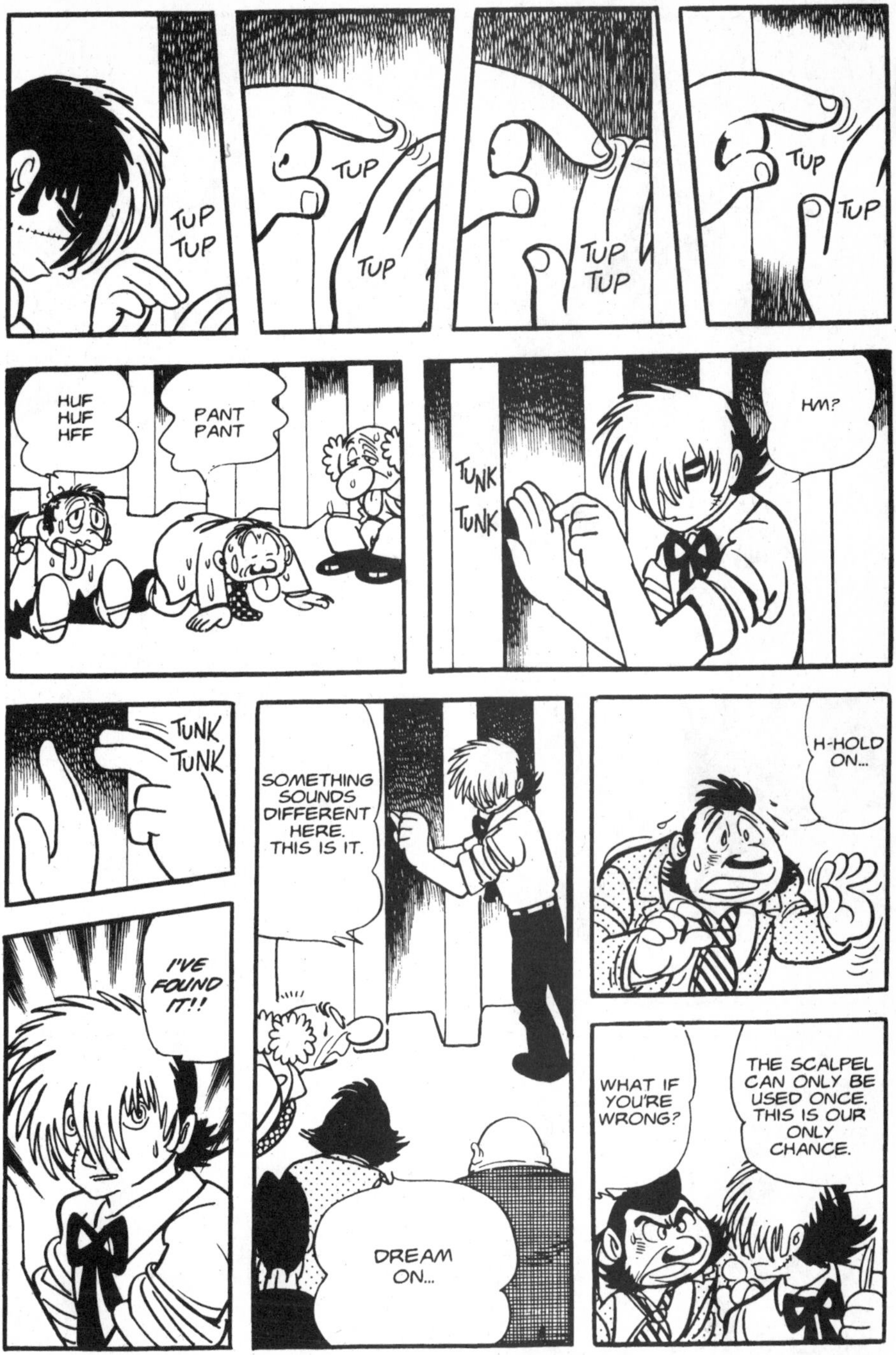
TUP
TUP
TUP
TUP
TUP
TUP
TUP
TUP
TUP
HUF HUF HFF
PANT PANT
TUNK
TUNK
HM?
TUNK
TUNK
I'VE FOUND IT!!
SOMETHING SOUNDS DIFFERENT HERE. THIS IS IT.
DREAM ON...
H-HOLD ON...
WHAT IF YOU'RE WRONG?
THE SCALPEL CAN ONLY BE USED ONCE. THIS IS OUR ONLY CHANCE.

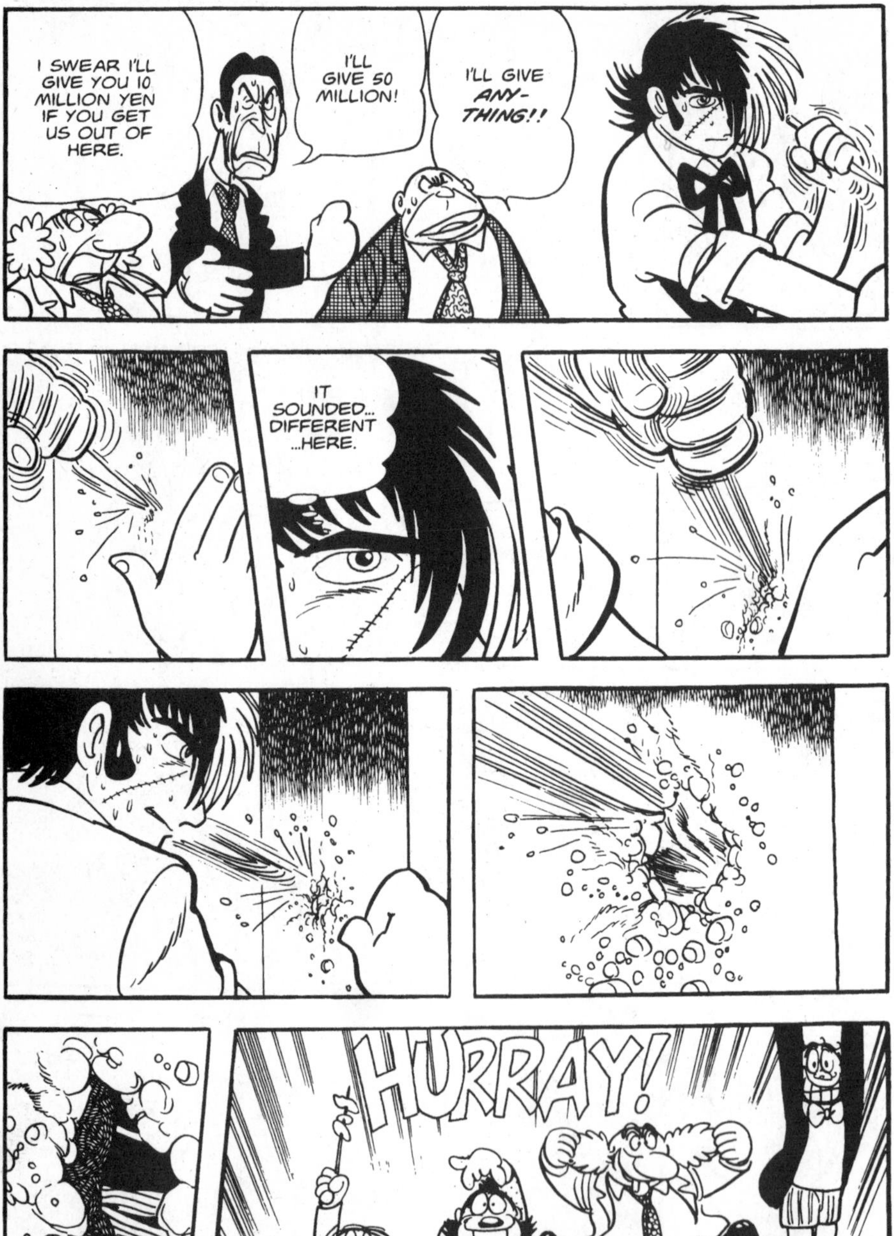
I SWEAR I'LL GIVE YOU 10 MILLION YEN IF YOU GET US OUT OF HERE.
I'LL GIVE 50 MILLION!
I'LL GIVE ANY-THING!!
IT SOUNDED... DIFFERENT ...HERE.
HURRAY!

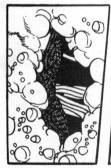

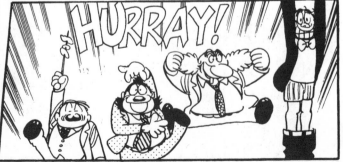

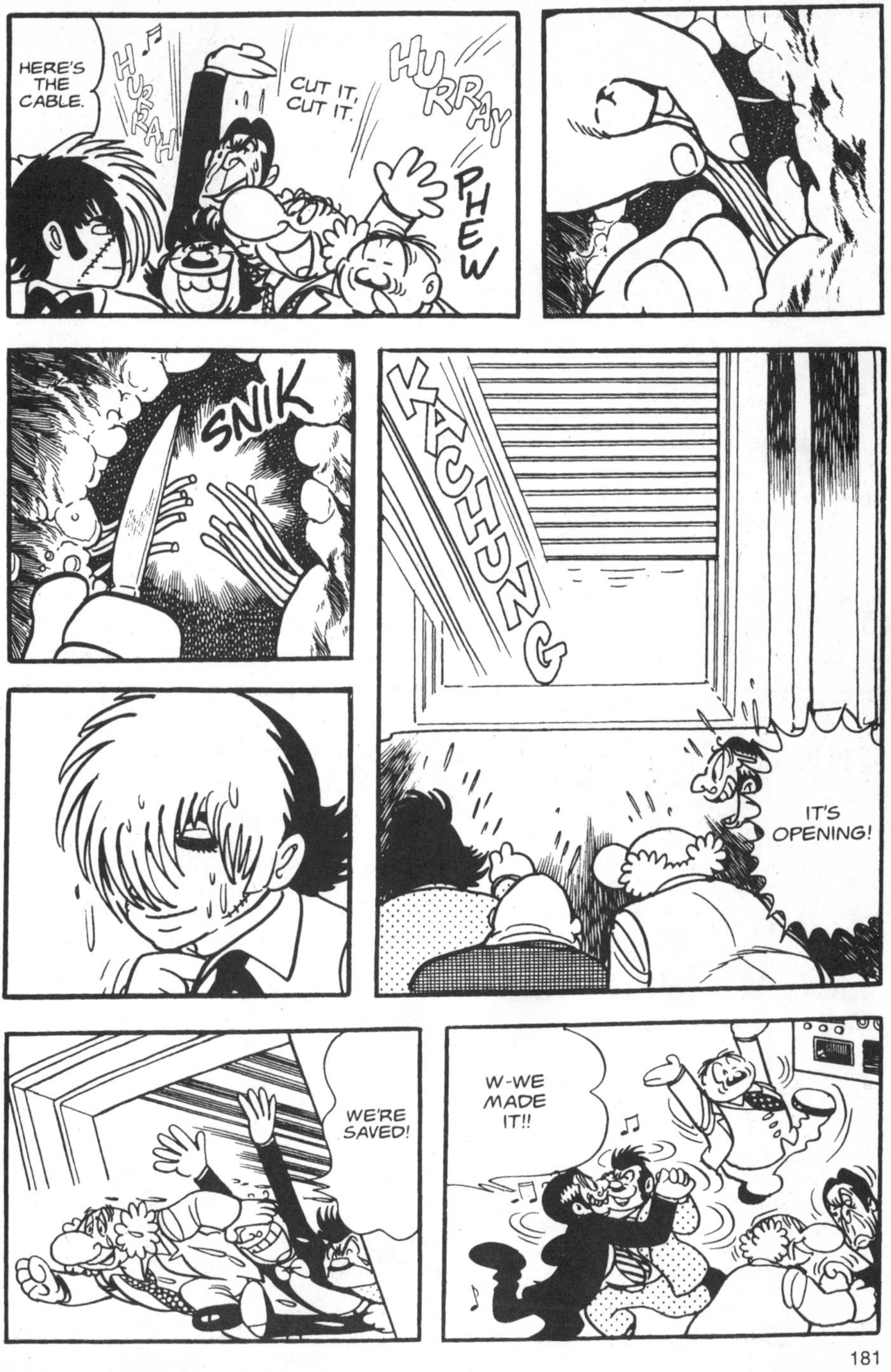
HERE'S THE CABLE.
HURRAH
CUT IT, CUT IT.
HURRAY
PHEW
SNIK
KACHUNG
IT'S OPENING!
WE'RE SAVED!
W-WE MADE IT!!

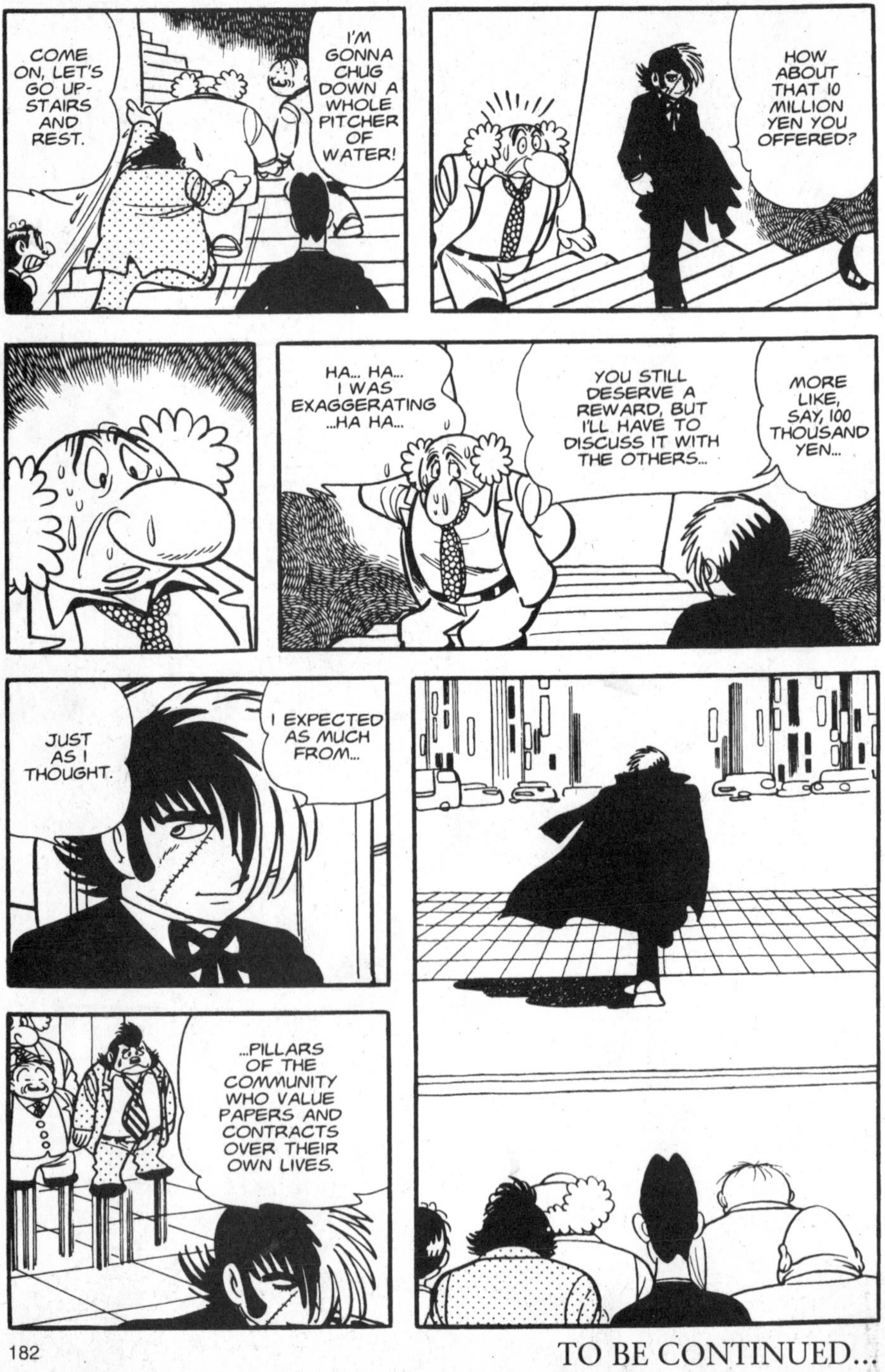
COME ON, LET'S GO UP-STAIRS AND REST.
I'M GONNA CHUG DOWN A WHOLE PITCHER OF WATER!
HOW ABOUT THAT 10 MILLION YEN YOU OFFERED?
HA... HA... I WAS EXAGGERATING ...HA HA...
YOU STILL DESERVE A REWARD, BUT I'LL HAVE TO DISCUSS IT WITH THE OTHERS...
MORE LIKE, SAY, 100 THOUSAND YEN...
JUST AS I THOUGHT.
I EXPECTED AS MUCH FROM...
...PILLARS OF THE COMMUNITY WHO VALUE PAPERS AND CONTRACTS OVER THEIR OWN LIVES.

TO BE CONTINUED...

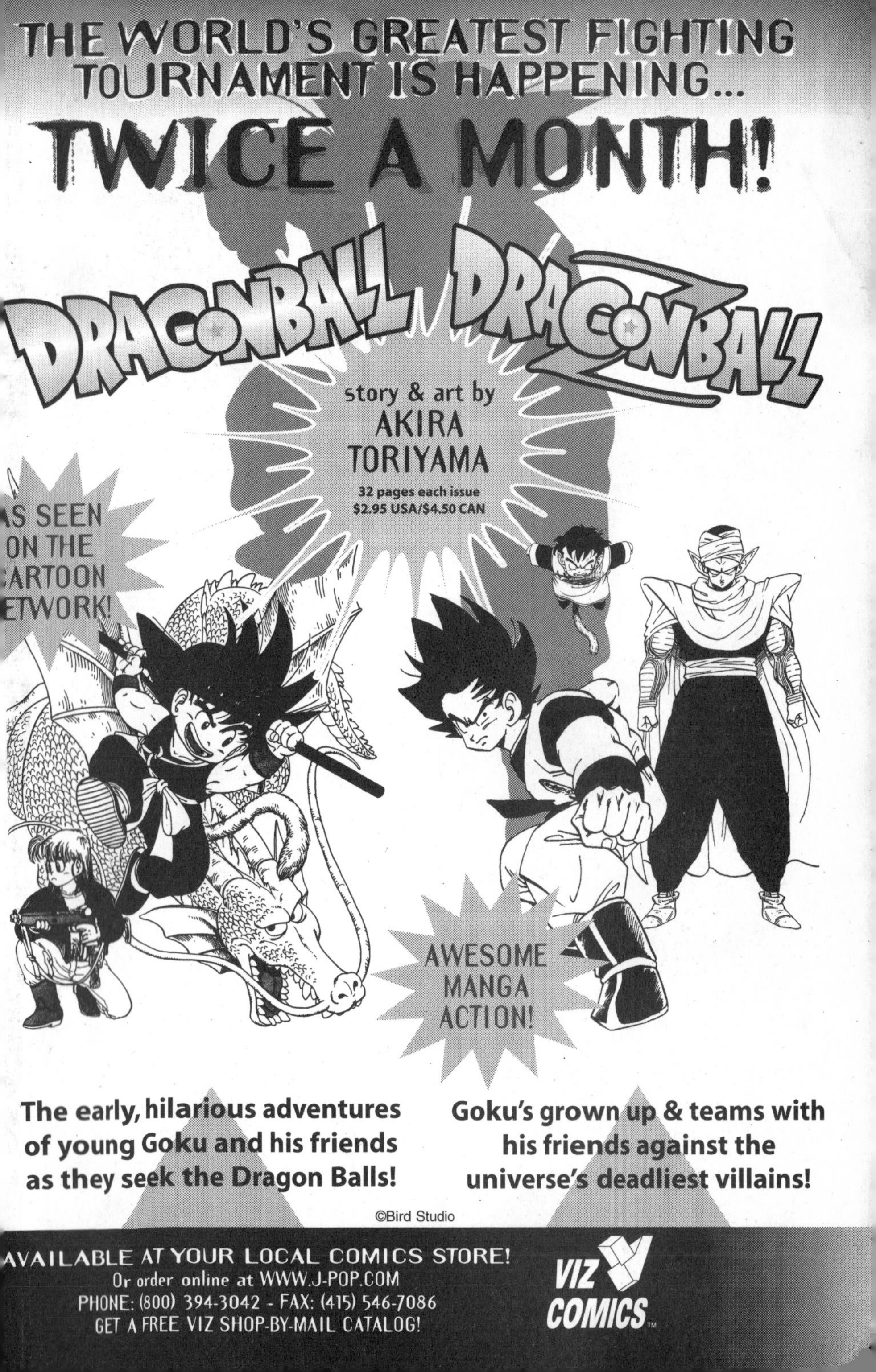
THE WORLD'S GREATEST FIGHTING TOURNAMENT IS HAPPENING...
TWICE A MONTH!
DRAGONBALL
DRAGONBALL Z
story & art by AKIRA TORIYAMA
32 pages each issue
$2.95 USA/$4.50 CAN
S SEEN ON THE ARTOON ETWORK!
AWESOME MANGA ACTION!
The early, hilarious adventures of young Goku and his friends as they seek the Dragon Balls!
Goku's grown up & teams with his friends against the universe's deadliest villains!
©Bird Studio
AVAILABLE AT YOUR LOCAL COMICS STORE!
Or order online at WWW.J-POP.COM
PHONE: (800) 394-3042 - FAX: (415) 546-7086
GET A FREE VIZ SHOP-BY-MAIL CATALOG!
VIZ COMICS™